D1230766

THE
SHADOW
OF
GOD

A
NOVEL
OF WAR
AND
FAITH

ANTHONY A. GOODMAN

SOURCEBOOKS LANDMARK™
AN IMPRINT OF SOURCEBOOKS, INC.®
NAPERVILLE, ILLINOIS

Published by Sourcebooks, Inc.
P.O. Box 4410, Naperville, Illinois 60567-4410
(630) 961-3900
FAX: (630) 961-2168
www.sourcebooks.com

ISBN 1-4022-0150-8

Library of Congress Cataloging-in-Publication Data

Goodman, Anthony A.
  The shadow of God: a novel of war and faith / by Anthony A. Goodman.
    p. cm.
  ISBN 1-57071-904-7
  1. Rhodes (Greece: Island)—History—Siege, 1522—Fiction. 2. Sieges—Fiction.
I. Title.
  PS3607.O564 S53 2002
  813'.6—dc21

                                                                    2002003854

Printed and bound in the United States of America

LB 10 9 8 7 6 5 4 3 2 1

This book could not have been written without the love and support of my wife, Maribeth, and my children, Katie and Cameron.

Men never do evil so completely and cheerfully as when they do it from religious conviction.

—Blaise Pascal

⊰ TABLE OF CONTENTS ⊱

⊰FOREWORD⊱

In the fifty years surrounding the turn of the sixteenth century, the world witnessed changes that surpassed almost any previous era in human history. East and West collided on a scale that spanned thousands of geographic miles, at a cost of hundreds of thousands of human lives.

In the Middle East, five centuries of Christian Crusades were coming to an end. The waves of European armies sent forth to protect Christians traveling to Jerusalem and to slaughter the Muslim Infidels were in retreat. The uses of gunpowder were expanded and refined. New cannons were forged with huge cannonballs, and remarkable accuracy. Muskets and rifles were used alongside the crossbow and lance. Fortifications were massively strengthened to meet the increase in firepower.

In the Holy Lands, the fortresses of Jerusalem, St. Jean d'Acre, and Krak de Chevaliers successively fell before the Muslim armies, driving the Christian Crusaders to still another far-off fortress and still another confrontation with Islam in *Outremer*. Ottoman Sultans of Turkey, who had conquered the lands of the Arabian Peninsula, embraced the fast-growing religion of Islam. At the dawn of the sixteenth century, Muslim and Christian, East and West, were about to meet in the final battles for dominion.

This is the story of those final days.

Though this book is a work of fiction, almost all of the characters in it are based on historical figures. Today, we are fortunate to have access to the writings of many contemporary observers who were on the scene at the time. There were ambassadors and envoys who spent decades at the inner court of the sultans. And there were soldier-writers who participated in the battles, who kept voluminous diaries and wrote detailed letters home, many of which have survived to this day. Though each observer may have been biased by his or her particular position in society, we can still get a well balanced and detailed picture of the period.

I believe that historical fiction can serve the dual, and not contradictory, purposes of entertaining as well as educating. History has too often been left to the writers of textbooks, and has been overburdened with dates and minutiae. The peoples of the era are often placed in a position secondary to the events. I hope that the story of *The Shadow of God* will allow an understanding of the hearts of the people as well as the events in which they participated.

Nearly five hundred years after the era of this story, much has changed in our world, and much has remained the same. Unfortunately, many followers and true believers of the great religions of the world have little tolerance for those who do not share their own specific beliefs. This intolerance seems to have intensified over the centuries. On many fronts, religion has severed its ties to spirituality; compassion is losing the battle against prejudice. There have been moments in time when some of the believers made room in their hearts for those with different beliefs. We can only hope that such a time might yet come again.

—Anthony A. Goodman, 2002

❧CAST OF CHARACTERS❧

The Ottoman Turks

Suleiman. The Magnificent. Kanuni. The Lawgiver. Son of Selim, the Grim.

Piri Pasha. Grand Vizier of Selim and of Suleiman. Descendent of Abu Bakr, Companion to the Prophet, Mohammed.

Mustapha Pasha. Brother-in-law of Suleiman, *Seraskier,* Commander-in-Chief. Second Vizier under Piri Pasha.

Ibrahim. Greek slave and boyhood companion of Suleiman.

Ali Bey. Agha of the Azabs.

Bali Agha. Agha of the Janissaries. "The Raging Lion."

Achmed Agha. Third Vizier. Albanian, promoted to *Beylerbey* of Rumelia after the capture of Belgrade.

Ayas Agha. Albanian. One-time Agha of the Janissaries.

Qasim Pasha. Son of a slave of Bayazid II. First in the ranks of heroes of Anatolia. Commands forces opposite Post of England.

Pilaq Mustapha Pasha. *Kapudan* (Admiral) of the Navy.

Cortoglu. A Corsair, Naval Chief-of-Staff under Pilaq. But, in reality, in charge of the entire naval fighting force at Rhodes.

Ferhad Pasha. Sent to Siwas to put down revolt by Shiite, Shah-Suwar Oghli Bey.

Hafiza. Suleiman's mother, widow of Selim; called the *Sultan Valideh.*

Gülbehar. "Flower of Spring." Suleiman's First Woman of the harem, and mother of his first child, Mustapha.

Khürrem. Suleiman's Second Woman of the harem. "The Laughing One." Later to be named La Ruselanna, (the Russian) and finally known to history as Roxelanna.

Dr. Moshe Hamon. Physician to the Sultan. Son of Joseph Hamon, first of the dynasty of Sephardic Jewish doctors who were physicians to the Ottoman Sultans.

Knights of Rhodes

Grand Master
Philippe Villiers de L'Isle Adam. France.

Knights and Their Langues
Andrea d'Amaral. Chancellor. Portugal.

Antonio Bosio. Italy. Servant-at-arms. Skilled negotiator.

John Buck. England. Lieutenant to the Grand Master. Turcopilier (Commander of the Cavalry).

Henry Mansell. England. Standard bearer for the Grand Master.

Prejan de Bidoux. Provence. Prior of St. Giles. Bailiff of Kos.

Pierre de Cluys. France. Grand Prior.

Michel d'Argillemont. France. Captain of the galleys.

Jacques de Bourbon. Knight of Provence.

Antoine de Grollée. France. Truce envoy.

Nicholas Hussey. Provence.

Juan de Barabon. Commander of Post of Aragon.

Juan d'Homedes y Cascón. Aragon. Future Grand Master, Knights of St. John.

Gregoire de Morgut. Prior of Navarre.

Fra Jean de Beauluoys. "The Wolf." Captures a Turkish brig en route to Rhodes.

Gabriel de Pommerols. Another Lieutenant of the Grand Master.

Fra Emeric Depreaulx. Sent to Naples to enlist help.

Fra Lopes de Pas. Aragon. Emissary to Suleiman.

Fra Didier de Tholon. France. Command of artillery.

Blasco Diaz. Portugal. Servant-at-arms to Chancellor d'Amaral

Thomas Docwra. England.
Nicholas Fairfax. England.
Jean Bin de Malincorne. France.
Henry Mansell. England. Standard bearer of the Grand Master.
Fra Raimondo Marquet. Emissary to Suleiman.
Nicholas Roberts. England.
Thomas Scheffield. England. Seneschal of the Grand Master. Commander of the Palace of the Grand Master.
Gabriele Tadini da Martinengo. Italy. Expert military engineer. In charge of countermining.

Residents of Rhodes
Leonardo Balestrieri. Latin bishop of Rhodes.
Bishop Clement. Greek bishop of Rhodes.
Apella Renato. Doctor in the Hospital of the Knights.
Bonaldi. Ship's master, volunteers services and goods for siege.
Basilios Carpazio. Greek fisherman, offers to spy for the knights.
Domenico Fornari. Conscripted with his ships to help knights.

Command by Sector: All Knights Grand Crosse
D'Amaral. Auvergne and Germany.
Buck. Aragon and England.
De Cluys. France and Castile.
De Morgut. Provence and Italy.

Key Commands
Commanders of Posts
Guidot de Castellac. Provence. Tower of St. Nicholas.
Raimond Rogier. Auvergne.
Jean de St. Simon. France.
Fra Raimond Ricard. Provence.
Giorgio Aimari. Italy.
William Weston. England.
Juan de Barabon. Aragon.
Christopher Waldners. Germany.

Fernando de Sollier. Castile and Portugal.
Thomas Scheffield. Palace of the Grand Master (Part of the Post of France).

Bastions
  Jean de Mesnyl. Auvergne.
  Tomas Escarierros. Spain.
  Nicholas Hussey. England.
  Jean de Brinquier de Lioncel. Provence.
  Andretto Gentile. Italy.

Commissioners in Charge of Supplies
  Andrea d'Amaral. Chancellor.
  Gabriel de Pommerols.
  John Buck.

Legendary Characters

Jean de Morelle. Knight, *langue* of France.
Melina. Rhodian Greek, wife of Jean de Morelle.
Ekaterina and Marie. Twin girls, children of Jean and Melina.

Fictional Characters

Hélène.

Fishermen
  Nicolo Ciocchi.
  Petros Rivallo.
  Marcantonio Rivallo.

Oh, East is East, and West is West,
and never the twain shall meet,

Till Earth and Sky stand presently
at God's great Judgment Seat;

But, there is neither East nor West,
Border, nor Breed, nor Birth,

When two strong men stand face to face,
tho' they come from the ends of the earth!

—Rudyard Kipling, *Ballad of East and West*

⊰PROLOGUE⊱
THE TRAITOR

Rhodes, The Fortress of the Knights of St. John
October 27, 1522

Even the rabbit knows to remain perfectly still, yet is discovered by the mere opening of an eye. So the man risked betraying himself when he moved to reach inside his black cape and retrieve his crossbow.

Absolute darkness had reduced the visibility to little more than a few yards; and even then, it was only his movement that could reveal his presence on the ramparts. The guards on duty along the high walls of the fortress walked their tour with little concern about being seen. There had been no sniper fire for several days. No stray arrows. The enemy had, no doubt, realized its ineffectiveness at such a long range, for the walls of the fortress were high, and the surrounding ditches dug wide and deep. With the light fog for cover, and the cloudy winter sky louring upon them, the guards felt invisible. But invisibility works both ways, and the knights guarding the walls were well aware of that.

The Captain of the guard had been by within the past hour. He reminded everyone to be fully alert. Their losses had been heavy, and the bodies of three more knights had been buried that morning. They could ill afford to lose extra lives to carelessness, inattention, or neglect.

With great care, the man moved in from the cover of the Tower of Italy, at the east side of the Post of Provence. He made his way along the battlement, crouching low. His black cape trailed almost to the ground. The hood was pulled over his head. He held his crossbow tightly to his side as he made his way in the darkness. He stopped frequently, crouching down with his back to the massive stone wall. The surfaces were slick with moisture that had condensed from the cool night fog. He waited. Motionless. Each time he saw the passing guard move out of sight, he resumed his stealthful walk in the shadows. The night was very still, and for that he was glad. The absence of any breeze would make his shot easier, more accurate.

Though, for this shot, accuracy was hardly an issue.

Suddenly, and quite unexpectedly, he came across a gathering of three knights talking quietly on the battlement near the wall overlooking the Post of England. They should have been asleep, for it was well past midnight. They would surely question him if they found him out so late. He was momentarily seized with panic, and several drops of sweat trickled down the middle of his back beneath his robes. The drops coalesced and puddled for a moment above his hips, then were absorbed by the fabric of his shirt. There, the sweat made a cold and uncomfortable wet spot that held his attention. He tried to regain his focus, but fear held him immobile.

Finally, as the knights moved off, he stepped quietly from the darkness, and made his way quickly down a wooden ladder, off the wall, and into the street below. He decided to leave through the Jewish Quarter of the old city, a warren of narrow and twisting streets with many shoddy buildings and alleys. The houses were built of gray and brown stones, pressed side by side with common intervening walls and roofs. There were many alleyways and a few courtyards. Most of the houses were worn and poor. Some housed several families.

At this late hour, the streets were dark and silent. Mounds of rubble made for many detours. The man thought that if he were caught here, he could find an excuse. He knew several women he could name, and claim that he was on his way to a late-night rendezvous. No one could check. The knights' vows of celibacy were crumbling after three months of facing death at every moment. Many of the young men secretly kept women in the town. Some not so secretly. Who would doubt him?

Now he needed to get to the Post of Auvergne, where he would fire his arrow. The wall between the Tower of St. George and the Tower of Aragon faced the camp of Ayas Pasha.

Again, he hurried his pace. He went past the Post of Aragon and St. Mary's Tower at the corner of the Post of England. He hid his crossbow again and pressed on. From time to time, he would duck into a darkened doorway or the entrance to an alley. He was breathing too hard for the slight exertion. He felt the dull thudding of his heartbeat. In the silence of the night, his heart sounded to him as if it were echoing off the walls. He rested until his breathing and his heart slowed a bit. Sweat was cooling on his skin, and it made him shiver from the chill of it. His robes were becoming progressively soaked inside and out. He pushed these distractions from his mind and moved on again, making his way directly to the fortress wall in the middle of the Post of Auvergne.

He was exactly where he wanted to be, for he had made this shot many times before. He waited in the streets below the wall for the next passing of the guard. While still hidden, he loaded his arrow into the crossbow. Then, he would need only to mount the wall, aim to the sky, and let loose his shot. He had made many practice shots during the daytime as well. Those shots he could make in plain view. All who had seen him assumed he was firing at the Turkish heathens besieging the city. After so many practice runs, he knew exactly where the arrow would fall: directly amongst the sentries in the camp of Ayas Pasha.

He pulled the arrow from its place in his waistband and checked to see that the parchment message was tightly tied to the shaft. It would not do to have it unravel in flight from the incredible acceleration delivered by his armor-piercing crossbow. He shuddered at the thought of the message tearing off the arrow shaft, fluttering slowly into the hands of one of the knights. That image in his mind melded quickly into another: his own body as it would be torn slowly to pieces on the rack if he were, indeed, caught.

He shook off the thought with a shiver, and pulled his robes tighter about him. The blackness of the garment and the blackness of the night blended perfectly. No fires were visible from the streets of the quarter. The man used this to his advantage. He was able to move off the street and climb the short, wooden ladder back onto the wall as surely as if it were noon, so well did he know this place.

The plan was simple. The guard would walk his route along the wall from the Tower of St. George to the Tower of Aragon, some two hundred yards away. The man would move as soon as the sound of the guard's footsteps were lost in the night. Neither the guard nor the man would be able to see or hear each other. He would climb the wall, take aim, and fire his message into the camp of the enemy. Then, he would be gone. It would take twenty seconds. No more.

He watched the guard turn at the Tower of St. George and begin his walk south again to the Tower of Aragon. He held his breath as the guard passed above him, the footsteps receding into the darkness, echoing slightly off the stone wall. When he could no longer hear the guard, nor see his silhouette in the night, the man made his move. Should the guard turn back now, they would still not see each other for a few more seconds.

The man vaulted up the wooden ladder, and rushed in a crouch to the wall. He could see the fires of the Turkish camp, and even make out figures in front of the tents. It was remarkable how orderly this encampment was, he thought; how clean and precise its arrangement after so many months of war and weather and death. He rushed to the wall, crossbow in his left hand, the arrow already nocked and set. The powerful trigger mechanism was cocked. He raised the bow to his shoulder, aiming for an arc that would carry the arrow towards the very center of the cooking fires in the camp. He knew that Ayas's sentries would be watching, waiting for a dark shadow streaking out of the night with a message for their Sultan. He took a last breath, let it slowly out, and prepared for his shot. As he released the last of the air from his lungs, he increased the pressure on the trigger.

The unexpected impact knocked the remaining wind out of the man's chest. He felt pain tear across his left shoulder as he crashed into the stones of the wall. Then another pain struck his shoulder blades as he landed on his back. Lights flashed before his eyes as his head impacted the rock walk. His crossbow was pinned against his chest, pressing the wooden trigger guard into his breastbone. He struggled to break free, to catch his breath. He could feel the sharp tip of the unfired arrow stuck hard against his throat.

Two gloved hands held the weapon tight against him. The man guarded the trigger with his fist. The slightest pressure would release the shaft, sending it slicing through his own throat. He might fight and struggle free, but then if the arrow flew, it could kill the knight on top of him, or kill himself. He had no stomach now for either.

He stopped his struggling, and as he heard the knight call for help, he knew that it was over. This huge knight, who happened to be on the wall for God knows what reason, would keep him pinned there like a butterfly until more knights arrived.

He let go of the crossbow and surrendered his body to his captor. Two more knights came to his side, dressed for battle in scarlet robes adorned with the white eight-pointed Cross of St. John. One knight wrenched the crossbow away, and removed the arrow with its note. The knight dashed the bow to the ground and looked for a moment at the arrow. In the few seconds it took for the him to realize what he was holding, the third knight drew near with a lantern. The knight holding the arrow unwound the tie, and opened the parchment. In the yellow light of the lantern, he read the note. Then he knelt down and brought the glow from the lamp nearer the prisoner.

As the light washed over the fallen man's face, all three knights froze. The man in black slumped back to the ground in total surrender. The knight with the lantern let out his breath and gasped, "Dear God!"

BOOK ONE

—

NEVER
THE TWAIN
SHALL MEET

1

THE SON OF SELIM

Edirne, northern Turkey, near the Greek border
September 21, 1520

Selim, *Yavuz*. Selim, the Grim.

Selim, Sultan of the Ottoman Empire, slept fitfully in his tent. He lay under a pile of silk brocade coverlets. As he rolled onto his side, a piece of parchment fell to the carpeted floor. Piri Pasha, his Grand Vizier, knelt to tuck in the sides of his master's covers. He reached down and picked up the parchment. Leaning nearer the light of the brazier, he unrolled the document. He immediately recognized the distinctive calligraphy of his master. He smiled as he realized that even in what could certainly be the last hours of the Sultan Selim's life, there had been time for yet one more poem. Piri had made sure to leave the gilded box of writing materials always close to Selim's bedside, for the master liked to write late into the night when the pain woke him.

Piri unrolled the parchment. The words were written in Persian, the language of the poets. The Sultan's hand had shaken badly. Though spatterings of ink had stained the parchment, the writing was fully legible. Piri held it closer to the warm yellow light, and read:

The hunter who stalks his prey in the night,
Does he wonder whose prey he may be?

As the Sultan's Grand Vizier, Piri Pasha was the highest-ranking official in the entire Ottoman Empire. As such, he was arguably the second most powerful man on Earth. He sat on a low *divan* in the darkened tent, watching the Sultan sleep. The coal brazier gave off a red glow that carried its heat deep into the body of his master. But, Piri himself could not get warm. The Sultan made low noises as he breathed fitfully. Now and again, Selim's eyes would tighten as a grimace of pain crossed his face.

Outside the tent, the Janissaries stood guard; two of them flanked the door, while seven more surrounded the tent. Another ring of twenty Janissaries stood at attention in an outer circle, creating a formidable wall of warriors. The young men were dressed in dark-blue jackets and baggy, white pants. Their caps were tapered white cylinders, each holding a tall, white heron's feather in its band. They wore high boots of soft, brown leather, and were armed with jeweled dirks in their belts; in the left hand some carried sharp pikes on six-foot wooden poles. All wore long, curved scimitars, inscribed in Arabic with the words "I place my faith in God."

Piri dragged the heavy brazier closer to Selim's body. The tent was warm, but still Selim shivered in his broken sleep. His body had been racked with pain for the last several months, and the Sultan now spent most of his time asleep. His doctor had given him ever-increasing doses of opium so that now his sleep was disturbed less and less by the lightning jabs of pain. Still, he would awaken suddenly and cry out in the night, as the cancer ate him from within.

Piri knew that the end was near, and had made all the appropriate arrangements. Many lives would hang upon Piri Pasha's judgment. An empire could fall with a single mistake.

Piri Pasha was the Grand Vizier of the House of Osman, rulers of the Ottoman Empire since 1300 A.D. For eight years, he had been the ear and the right hand of the Emperor. He was both friend and confidant to Selim *Yavuz*. He had, from the very first day of his duties, kept absolute faith with the trust Selim had placed in him.

Selim had named Piri Pasha the "Bearer of the Burden," for so great was his load that a lesser man would have faltered long before.

In the eight years of service, Piri had no thought but for the welfare of his master, the Emperor; and of the Empire. Now that Selim's death was near, Piri had much to do.

The story of Selim's short life had been written in blood. It was the blood of his times and the blood of his people. It was written, too, in the blood of his father and the strangled breath of his brothers. These deaths were the result of the law of Selim's grandfather, Mehmet, *Fatih;* Mehmet, the Conqueror.

An early unwritten Ottoman law had directed the newly crowned emperor to slay all his siblings, their children, and all but his own ablest son. The eldest did not necessarily succeed to the throne. It was hoped that in this way the new Sultan, by leaving only one heir alive, could prevent wars of succession that might endanger the Empire. Selim's grandfather, Mehmet, had codified this tradition in the Law of Fratricide. Under the Law of Fratricide, all the possible heirs to the throne must be strangled with the silken cord from an archer's bow. A knife or sword could not be used, for it was a sacrilege to shed royal blood. Mehmet, himself, had strangled his infant brother to death upon his own succession to the throne.

When Selim's father, Bayazid II, ascended to the throne, he, too, fell under this law of the Ottomans; but not as he had expected.

Bayazid was a more reticent and gentle man than his father, Mehmet. He was loath to carry on, as his father had, the continuous wars to expand the Empire. Mehmet had challenged the great powers of the Shiite Muslims of Persia, going to war with Shah Ismail, their ruler. The Shiite religious doctrines seemed to Mehmet a dagger at the backs of the orthodox Sunni Muslims of Turkey.

But, Bayazid had no taste for war. When he succeeded Mehmet as Sultan, he retired to the safety of Istanbul, and the Palace.

Selim was the youngest of Bayazid's five sons, and his favorite. Two of his other sons had died in childhood, and only Selim seemed suited for the succession to Sultan. But, Selim was impatient with his father, and longed to resume the wars his grandfather had started. So, at age forty, after a failed rebellion against Bayazid, Selim and his family went into self-imposed exile in the Crimea, north of the Black Sea. His wife, Hafiza, was the daughter of a

Tartar Khan. After some time, Selim was able, with the help of his father-in-law, to raise a substantial army.

Bayazid and Selim, father and son, fought each other for the throne in a great battle at Edirne, in northern Turkey near the Greek border. Only the speed of Selim's legendary stallion, Black Cloud, had allowed his escape from his father's sword. Though he lost the battle, his heroism had impressed his father's army of Janissaries. A legend began to grow around Selim's name.

As Bayazid aged, pressure began to build from the nobles of the court to send for Selim, so that Selim's succession could be assured. The Janissaries wanted nothing of the two eldest sons, whom they knew to be as gentle and peace-loving as their father. They wanted Selim. Selim *Yavuz*. They, too, longed for the return to war; to ride once more against the Infidel and drink in the heady scent of blood and smoke.

Bayazid wanted peace within his empire at any cost. So, a few months after Selim's defeat and escape, Bayazid sent for his son, asking that he return to his home in Istanbul. Selim received the letter in the depths of a terrible winter. Still, with the help of his father-in-law, he amassed an army of three thousand horsemen, and left immediately for the capital. He drove his men eighteen hours a day, in blinding blizzards and killing cold. Hundreds of men and horses died along the way, left unburied at the side of the frozen road. To save time, Selim avoided the longer detour to the bridge over the wide Dniester River. Instead, he forced his army to ford the icy waters. There, too, many frozen bodies floated away in the black current. Finally, with his army in tatters, he reached Istanbul in early April.

Selim approached the gates of the city fearing a trap. But, when the ten thousand Janissaries of Bayazid's Household Guard saw him mounted upon his famous Black Cloud, they rushed to his side, cheering and proclaiming *him* the Sultan. The soldiers surrounded his horse and fought to touch Selim's stirrups. They threw their hats in the air, and celebrated his arrival. Within a few days, Bayazid surrendered to his youngest son the symbol of power of the Ottoman Empire. He handed over the emblem of the Ottomans, the jeweled Sword of the House of Osman. Selim was now truly the Emperor of the Ottomans.

The following day, Selim walked alongside his father's litter as the old man was carried out through the gates of the city. He held his father's hand, and there were tears in both men's eyes.

The crowds followed the two men silently behind the human wall of armed Janissaries and mounted Sipahis, the Sultan's elite cavalry. After handing over his power to Selim, Bayazid wanted to return to his birthplace at Demotika, near Edirne, to spend his last days there away from the turmoil of Istanbul and the political intrigues in the Palace. As his father was carried away by the small retinue of servants and carts of personal effects, Selim and the Janissaries turned in silence and walked back to the imperial city.

Bayazid was never to have his final wish fulfilled. Three days after his departure, he died suddenly in a small village along the wayside. Some said that he died of a broken heart after being so cruelly deposed by his favorite child. But, rumors also spread that he had been poisoned on Selim's orders. Few doubted that this might be so, for Selim was capable of great cruelty, and was totally insulated from remorse when it came to protecting his succession as Sultan.

No sooner was Bayazid laid to rest in his grave than Selim set about insuring the security of his reign. Bayazid had never carried out his own father's Law of Fratricide. Selim still had older brothers with claims to the throne.

As soon as he was settled in Istanbul, Selim gathered his band of assassins—six deaf mutes, who had worked for him many times in the past. The mutes were summoned to the Palace. They gathered before the new Sultan and pressed their heads to the floor. A servant took each man by the arm and led him backwards toward the wall of the room. This way, they could not turn their backs upon the Sultan. When the six men sat kneeling against the walls and looking towards their master, Selim rose and moved toward the opposite side of the room. He took an archer's bow from its rack on the wall, bringing it in front of the mutes. He stood before them, and with his powerful hands bent the stout wooden bow tighter in its recurved arc to loosen the silk string. That this act required immense physical strength was not lost on the mutes. He removed the string from the bow and walked toward the kneeling men. Slowly he moved before them, looking into each one's eyes. From them, he saw nothing. No emotion. No fear. No love. Nothing.

He came to the end of the line. With feline speed and precision, he stepped behind the first mute, quickly wrapping the silk bowstring around his neck. He crossed his powerful hands and tightened the garrote. The big mute clawed at the rope around his throat. His legs shot out in front of him as he tried to gain his feet to find a platform from which to resist. Selim barely moved. His hands continued to tighten the snare of silk.

The mute's fingers clawed at his own neck, trying to find purchase under the cord, anything to loosen the cord and escape the strangulation. His fingers tore at his skin. But the cord was buried deep into his own flesh, and his fingers could not find their way. As he struggled, his face grew scarlet, then crimson. The veins began to stand out upon his neck. His eyes were wide with fear, and his color slowly changed to a pale blue. Small dots of hemorrhage began to break out in the whites of his eyes. Then, as if it were the changes of color that controlled his body, the strength and the intensity of his resistance began to diminish. In less than three minutes, he stopped struggling altogether. His hands came away from his neck and he buckled limply to the floor. His knees sagged, and he appeared as a puppet held aloft by the strength of Selim, the puppeteer. His skin turned gray, and the luster left his protruding eyes.

All the while, Selim had hardly moved. When the man was quite still, Selim released the garrote, unwound it from the mute's neck, and allowed the body to fall forward onto its face. He took the bow and restrung it with the silk cord. Then he carefully replaced the bow in the rack.

Selim motioned to the remaining mutes, who were led away by the servant. A moment later, four of his Janissaries hurried in from the corridor and dragged out the body of the strangled man.

The five kneeling mutes were dispatched to the quarters of Selim's two older brothers. There, the mutes carried out Mehmet's law. They strangled Selim's two brothers in their beds, with silken cords from the archer's bow. Care was taken in the struggle that no royal blood was spilled. They immediately sent a message back to the Palace. None of the mutes cared to enter the presence of the Sultan if not absolutely necessary.

But, Selim was still not content. The two dead brothers had five living sons. Selim feared that they, too, might mount opposition to his Sultanate. Their fathers had been the elder sons, and these sons might feel that their fathers were more entitled to the throne than Selim. Again, the assassins were sent out, and this time Selim went with them, listening to the struggles and cries of his nephews from the adjoining room. Some say Selim actually cried when he heard the mutes strangle his favorite nephew, the youngest, who was only five years old. But, who would ever know? The assassins, the only witnesses, were deaf and mute.

By the time Selim, himself, lay dying of cancer in his tent, only eight years into his reign, he had claimed the lives of all his nephews, sixty-two blood relatives, and seven Grand Viziers.

❧

Piri Pasha left Selim, and walked to the tent of the Sultan's doctor, Moses Hamon. Hamon had been in constant attendance for several months, as Selim's life began to slip away. The Hamon family had served the Sultans of the Ottomans for many years. In 1492, King Ferdinand and Queen Isabella had expelled the Jews from Spain. The Inquisition had steadily eroded the power of the Jews. By the time of the expulsion, thousands had been tortured to death for their perceived corruption of the new Christian principles. These Sephardic Jews emigrated to Portugal, North Africa, Europe, the Middle East, and the Ottoman Empire. The Portuguese forced baptism upon the new settlers, and the European Christians persecuted the newly arrived Jewry, as had the Spanish. Only under the Muslims was the Jewish community welcomed and able to flourish.

Joseph Hamon was one of the Sephardic Jews who landed upon the shores of Turkey in the late fifteenth century. A skilled doctor, he became the personal court physician of both Sultan Bayazid and his son Selim. Joseph's son, Moses Hamon, succeeded Joseph and became the court physician to Selim. Moses would ultimately become one of the most influential men in the Ottoman Empire, and his sons would carry on the dynasty of Jewish doctors who served the Sultans.

Hamon was just finishing his dinner when Piri Pasha entered his tent. The doctor rose from his cushions on the floor, and greeted him.

"*Salaam Aleichum*, Piri Pasha," Hamon said in Arabic.

"*Shalom Alechem*, Doctor Hamon," Piri replied in Hebrew.

Hamon smiled at Piri's courtesy in using the Hebrew, rather than the Arabic greeting. He motioned to the cushions, and the two men sat down. A servant brought in a tray of fruit and two goblets of wine. Piri waved away the wine, and instead took a bunch of grapes from the tray. Hamon dismissed the servant with a wave of his hand.

"How is the Sultan today, Piri Pasha?"

"The same. No. Worse, I think. He does not wake now. I cannot get him up to eat or drink. I think the end is very near."

"His sleep is a kindness. The tincture of opium is a blessing to those who suffer from the terrible pain of cancer. But, I think you may be right. If the Sultan stops eating and drinking, then he cannot live very long."

"Come with me, please, Doctor. I need you to assure me that he will be comfortable. And I need you to tell me when the end comes. You have served my Sultan well. As did your father, Joseph."

Hamon nodded his thanks, but he said nothing. He could sense that Piri had more to say. The silence lasted several minutes, and the men filled the time nibbling at the fruit. Finally, Piri said, "Doctor Hamon, I trust your discretion as I trust almost no one else. The Hamons have never betrayed their position in our household, and have always given us the best of care."

Hamon nodded again, and still he waited.

"So, I must ask you to bear a burden for me."

Hamon smiled. "But, *you*, Piri Pasha, are the 'Bearer of the Burden,' are you not? I have heard the Sultan call you that many times."

"Yes, I am, Doctor," Piri acknowledged with a smile. "But, I am old; and for now, I must share this heavy weight. Only you can be trusted to help me."

"Tell me what to do, and I will do it."

"First, you must wait with the Sultan until life has left his body."

"This, I can do. This is my job. My duty."

"But, you must tell *only* me, when he is dead. Nobody else must know for ten days. We must make the pretense that he lives, until I can bring his only son, Suleiman, back to Istanbul. Right now, Suleiman is in Manisa, where he governs. It will take me two or three days to get word to him, and then another five days for him to return to the capital. I must make sure that the succession is unopposed, and that there will be no obstruction to his taking the throne."

"I understand, Piri Pasha. You can rely on me."

"I know I can, Doctor. Let us go directly to the tent of Selim. I will tell you more when we have seen to the Sultan."

The two men rose, and left together.

The last months had been so difficult for Piri Pasha. Selim had been sick for years, but toward the end, the pain had intensified his anger and wrath, and many of those close to him had suffered because of it. Piri tried to intervene when his master dispensed cruel and unreasonable punishment upon his subjects. He had been able to prevent a few death sentences from being carried out. But, he could not push too far without risking his own life.

Piri knew there was nothing the doctor could do for his master. Hamon might be able to bring a little comfort to the Sultan dying in his tent. Piri and Hamon entered the tent, while the young Janissary guards remained outside. Piri led him to Selim's bedside, stepping back into the dimness to wait. Hamon kneeled on the carpet and examined Selim. He felt for the pulses, and carefully lifted each lid to gaze into the eyes. Then, he gestured for the oil lamp to be brought nearer, as he looked carefully at Selim's pupils, which were tightly constricted from the opium.

When the doctor first touched the Sultan, Piri's hand went instinctively to his sword. He had to restrain himself when *anyone* touched his master, for he was always at the ready to protect the

Sultan's person. So many years as the nearest sword to Selim had made it Piri's instinct that nobody should get within a sword's length of his Lord without Piri's express permission. There was a line in space that no one dared to cross, and it was Piri who defined and defended that line.

Hamon examined the Sultan for what seemed like a very long time. He pressed his palms against Selim's chest, and felt inside his robes for the beat of his heart. Then, Hamon placed a thin sheet of silk over the bare breastbone of the Sultan, and laid his ear to Selim's chest. He listened for the sounds of the heartbeat, the silk preventing his ear from actually touching his Sultan's skin. He touched the neck and the wrist through the silk as well, and the angle of his jaw trying to find a sign of the blood flowing through the royal vessels. Though understanding of the circulation of the blood would not reach the West for a long time to come, it was already well understood throughout the Arab world.

Next, he laid a hand upon the skin of Selim's abdomen, trying to determine a decrease in his body temperature. He lifted the Sultan's lids again. An expression of shock passed across his face. Now the Sultan's pupils were fixed and dilated. He turned to Piri Pasha, with resignation in his eyes.

Piri moved toward the bed and knelt down upon a cushion. "Well?"

The doctor cast his eyes to the ground. "I am sorry, my Lord, but our Sultan is dead."

"You're certain?" His voice was flat; devoid of emotion.

"I am, my Lord."

Piri rose so suddenly that Hamon reflexively backed away. For a second, he thought that the Grand Vizier was going to draw his long scimitar and strike him dead for bearing this terrible news.

But, Piri Pasha merely stood over him, his fists clenched. His body and his face were entirely calm. He knew exactly what had to be done, and was relieved that he could now begin. His Emperor's suffering was over, and now there wasn't a minute to lose.

"Stay with the body of the Sultan. Do not allow anybody to enter the tent, nor even view the body from the doorway." He spoke now as if to an underling; as master to servant. Hamon listened impassively. Piri went on. "Help me to put out the fire, and move the brazier away from the body, so the light of the oil lamp will be the only light in the tent."

Piri poured sand into the brazier. Hamon crouched, struggling with the heavy brazier and its still-hot cargo of coals. Together the two men dragged it to the side, away from the body. Piri looked around the tent, and moved several small articles of clothing. He arranged Selim's personal effects, so that the tent would appear as if all were in order; that Selim were alive and merely resting.

"I will leave orders for your food to be brought here by the Sultan's own Janissaries. They will leave it for you outside the tent flap. Nobody must know that our Sultan is dead. Nobody! Not for ten full days! Do you understand?"

Hamon nodded, but said nothing. His position as the respected physician in the service of the Sultan had given way to little more than that of a watch dog. He had grown used to restraining his anger, for he knew how precarious a place the Jew had in the Muslim court, and how important his position of influence was to the Jews of the Ottoman Empire.

Piri went to the side of the tent where the possessions of the Sultan Selim were stored in ornately carved wooden chests. Each was sealed with the *tuğra*, the royal crest. Breaking one seal, he carefully opened a long, slim box, and placed the cover on the carpet. Next, he unwrapped the silk cloth that swathed the Sword of the House of Osman. The weapon was encased in a silver scabbard encrusted with precious jewels. The smallest of these could keep a man and his family living in luxury for several lifetimes. He pulled the sword partially from its sheath, and held it aloft. The red glow from the lamp caught the polished steel blade and reflected the color onto the walls of the tent. Piri resheathed the sword with a loud snap, then polished the silver scabbard with a piece of silk. *Here is the power and the authority of the Empire,* he thought. *Who wears this sword at his side, rules the world.*

Piri carefully wrapped the sword again, and tied the cloth tightly with the woven silk cords. He closed the box and stood, placing the sword into his waistband, covering it with his outer robes. The Sword of the House of Osman would not leave his side until he had delivered it to Selim's only living son and heir to the Ottoman Empire. Suleiman.

Piri left Doctor Hamon in the tent and walked out through the door flap. He stopped to speak with the two Janissaries guarding the door. Both men snapped to rigid attention, and stared straight ahead. Neither looked at Piri Pasha.

"The Sultan sleeps. The *tabip* will stay with him and feed him." He had used the Arabic term, *tabip,* for "doctor." He did not refer to Hamon by name in front of the soldiers. "The *tabip* will give the Sultan the medicine he needs for his pain. See that food is brought to the tent for our master and for the *tabip*. Leave the food outside the *serai*, and call the *tabip* to fetch it. Nobody is to enter the tent except I. Not even you. No one! Do you understand me?"

The Janissaries saluted their reply and resumed their position on guard. Each of these heavily armed young men would give his life for his Sultan without a thought. Nowhere on earth was there a more loyal personal guard than the Janissaries of the Ottoman Emperor.

Piri Pasha walked through the encampment, past the tents of his men. He spoke with his servants briefly. "The Sultan is asleep now, Allah be praised, and I am going to get some rest myself. He is well guarded, and I do not want his rest disturbed. Make that known amongst you."

Finally, he reached the perimeter of the camp, where the horses were tethered, and guarded by the Sipahis, the Sultan's elite cavalry. These were the finest mounted troops in the world. Three hundred years earlier, Genghis Khan had conquered the earth from China to the shores of the Black Sea. His Mongol troops had ridden to the edge of Europe, and showed the western world a war machine the likes of which had never been seen before. The Khan's mounted troops would ride two hundred eighty miles over rugged terrain in less than three days. When they arrived at their destination, without further rest, they were ready to fight. While riding at full gallop astride their powerful ponies, they could fire their armor-piercing arrows with deadly accuracy at two hundred meters. Mere rumors of the arrival of the Khan's armies were enough to send their enemies scattering in panic before them.

Now the Sipahis would ride into battle as had the troops of the Khan. They, too, inspired such fear in their enemies that some battles were won at the news of their approach. Whole armies fled when they heard that the Sultan Selim's Janissaries and Sipahis were marching in their direction.

Two Sipahis had been waiting for word from the Pasha for several days. During that time, they never left their post, nor did they sleep for more than an hour at a time. Their food was brought to them on Piri Pasha's orders, and they were ready to move at his word.

Piri moved through the camp, appearing to refresh himself in the brisk mountain air. He showed no sign of the terrible events of this day. More than ten thousand Janissaries and Sipahis were gathered in this camp outside the city of Edirne. The night was peaceful with the low noises and stirrings of a great orderly encampment. Water carts rumbled by, and night soil was removed from the latrines. Everywhere in the camp there was complete order. Tents were lined up in perfect rows; not a scrap of garbage ever hit the ground.

Cooking fires crackled under giant copper pots. Piri could hear the quiet murmur of men talking in respectfully low voices, lest they disturb the sleep of their Sultan. Nowhere was laughter heard, for this might incite the wrath of the Pasha at this terrible moment in his Sultan's reign. Smoke drifted through the trees, and among the tents. The wind carried the smoke away from the camp, down along the fading green hills of that early autumn evening. There was a softness in the air that would soon be replaced with the cold, wet winds of winter.

Piri approached the camp of the Sipahis, and settled himself near a trough where two of the horsemen were silently gambling with wooden dice by the light of their dying cooking fire. He stood a while and watched. In their uniforms and the settling darkness, all the soldiers looked alike. The two men had been handpicked by the Pasha. One Sipahi, Abdullah, was a young sword bearer. He was the best rider in his corps, and his was the best mounted corps on Earth. The other was not a Sipahi at all. He was Achmed Agha, Commander of the Army. Achmed had pulled a cape over his uniform, and looked for all the world like an older version of the Sipahi with whom he gambled.

Piri waited a few minutes longer. He was an old man now, and felt every year of it. He never thought that this job would fall to him, for he believed that he would have died long before Selim. But, the cancer that ate at the Sultan's organs cared nothing for age, taking Selim's life when he was still in his forties.

Piri sighed in the darkness, and stretched his aching shoulders. How he longed for the peaceful life. How he wanted to return to his home and his treasured tulips. He saw himself tending his garden, perhaps adding some more roses to it this year. He wanted to see again the wonderful view of Istanbul across the waters of the Golden Horn. But, there was a job to do first. He, and only he, could protect the succession. Only he could assure the survival of the empire.

He moved toward the two soldiers. "It is much too late an *hour* for gambling such as this!" Piri spat out the word *sa'at*, hour. This was the prearranged signal that the time had come, that the Sultan was dead. The two soldiers stopped immediately. Abdullah wrapped the wooden dice in a leather sack, which he stuffed into his robes. Then Achmed Agha bowed his head and whispered, "May Allah smile upon his soul...and upon you, Piri Pasha, and upon all of us."

This high-ranking officer knew the great dangers of the next few days.

Piri took a piece of paper upon which was scrawled a few words in his own hand. Then he said, loudly enough to be overheard by the nearby horsemen, "See that the Kabarda Horses are accounted for and correct!" There was contempt in his voice. The other soldiers who overheard him believed that the Sipahis were being punished for gambling while the Sultan was so sick. This was the excuse for the men to go to their horses and leave the camp.

The two men stood up and leaped upon their waiting mounts. Nobody had noticed that their saddles were already loaded, the saddle bags packed with food and water. The two sped from the camp at full gallop. Achmed Agha would head east for Istanbul, one hundred fifty miles away. His duty was to maintain the peace and take command of the Palace Janissaries at all costs until Piri Pasha could arrive. The two would ride together for a while, and then Abdullah would turn and ride directly south across the Dardanelles at its narrowest point and into Asia to find and deliver the news to his new master, Suleiman.

Piri Pasha could not stop thinking of his years as Grand Vizier to Selim. Selim had always been so difficult. Always. The life of the Grand Vizier was not easy and often short. He might well be the second most powerful man in the world, but the price was *so* high. Though he was only in his early sixties, he was weary beyond those years. Seven Grand Viziers had served Selim before Piri, and all had been quickly beheaded in fits of anger. There was a death curse heard in Turkey in the reign of the Sultan Selim that said, "Mayest thou become Selim's Vizier!"

One Vizier had come before the Sultan and asked to know the date of his own execution. He said, "My Sultan, I need to know when you plan to kill me so that I may put my affairs in order and bid my family farewell."

Selim had laughed and said, "I have been thinking for some time about having you killed. But, at the moment I have nobody in mind to replace you. Otherwise I would willingly oblige."

The long wars had taken a great toll upon Piri, and his body now obeyed his commands only with great reluctance. Selim's military campaigns had taken the two of them to the farthest reaches of the Empire. During those years, Piri was always at Selim's side. That empire now reached from the waters of the Nile, north to the Danube; from Asia to Europe; from the Mediterranean to the Black Sea.

Now Selim was dead. It was up to Piri Pasha to assure a peaceful succession. He must carry out the pretense that the Sultan was still alive. He needed ten full days for Suleiman to learn the news, and return to Istanbul. The new Sultan must be girded with the Sword of the House of Osman at the Tomb of Ayyüb just outside the city walls. Abu Ayyüb al-Ansari had been the Standard Bearer for Mohammed, the Prophet—the Messenger of Allah. Ayyüb was slain in Islam's first siege of Constantinople in the seventh century. His tomb outside the walls of Istanbul was among the most sacred places for Muslims of the Ottoman Empire. To be seen by the people and the Janissaries to be the Sultan, Suleiman needed to be girded with the sword at Ayyüb's Tomb.

———

Piri Pasha passed the next five days making his rounds among the men, but staying as close to Selim's *serai* as he could. He paid careful attention to the gossip around the camp, for he knew it was critical that he keep control of the Janissaries and the Sipahis. He recalled so vividly the day that Selim had returned to Istanbul. Bayazid's Janissaries had turned against the old Sultan in a minute, and pledged their allegiance to Selim. They knew that he would lead them back into battle, and reward them with purses of gold and treasure looted during his conquests.

But, as the days wore on, it became apparent to Piri that tension was growing in the camp. Rumors began to spread among the men. Piri Pasha did not want the Janissaries to find out for themselves that Selim was dead. They must not hear it from anyone but the Grand Vizier. They must not feel they had been deceived. Ten thousand armed and disciplined soldiers deserved respect.

Before dawn on the fifth morning, Piri Pasha told his servants to bring him his military uniform. He would dress in the uniform of the Janissaries. He would be one of them. He washed and dressed in his own tent, and then went into the tent of Selim. He pushed aside the flaps, and saw Hamon sitting quietly by the small oil lamp reading. The air in the tent had become rank. Selim's body had begun the inevitable decay that must afflict even a Sultan's flesh. Piri moved into the tent and sat on the carpet next to Hamon. He was respectful when he spoke. Hamon could almost, but not quite, detect some conciliation in Piri's voice.

"Your job is finished here. In one hour from now, you may pack up your belongings and return to the city. I will assure your safety with a small guard to escort you home. You have helped my Sultan in his pain and for that I thank you. That you will serve his son, Suleiman, is to be expected as well. But, as you depart, speak to nobody. May Allah be with you. *Shalom Alechem.*"

Hamon rose and, without a word, left the tent.

Piri left the *serai* and walked up the small hill to the place of the *Bunchuk*, the Emperor's war standard. There, on the raised mound of earth, stood a golden pole capped off with a huge gold crescent of Islam. A carved horizontal wooden bar was fixed below the crescent, from which hung the tails of eight black horses. Tiny silver bells were suspended there as well, so light that they chimed in the slightest of breezes. Each regiment and Agha had a standard, the number of horses tails corresponding to the rank of the commander. Only the Sultan's *Bunchuk* displayed eight tails. The *Bunchuk* was the place of authority from which Piri would address his troops.

Piri moved to the standard. Immediately, the Janissaries began to congregate near him. The Sipahis stayed with their horses, reins in their hands, ready to move. The Janissaries were dressed in their full battle gear, swords and lances at their sides. They moved toward the Pasha and waited for him to speak. There was only the occasional sound of a stamping hoof on the soft earth, and the far-off nickering of a horse impatient to run. Piri waited. He tried to feel the energy of the men. At last he spoke.

"Our Sultan, Selim, is dead. May Allah smile upon his tomb."

Instantly, and as a unit, the Janissaries drew their curved scimitars in one great movement. The noise of steel against the scabbards sounded in unison. They raised the blades above their heads, and Piri found himself staring down into a sea of lethal glittering steel. The swords whistled through the damp morning air, slashing the ropes of the Janissaries' own tents. As the white tents crumbled to the ground there rose the wail and sobs of thousands of grieving young soldiers. In a moment, the camp had been leveled, and the tents lay on the ground like hundreds of piles of laundry. Where there had been a disciplined military camp, there was now only the dust and the commotion of men tearing off their white plumed hats and dashing them to the ground in their grief.

The Sipahis, too, threw their hats to the ground and cried out as if in pain from their loss. The horses stamped and reared at the cries of the men. The Sipahis held the reins tightly, never looking at the horses. Sobbing drowned all the other sounds of the morning.

Piri watched the spectacle before him. He was amazed at this display of grief from these thousands of men who had suffered so grievously for eight years under the unpredictable wrath of Selim. But, this, indeed, was what he had hoped for. The slashing of the tent cords was the traditional display of grief and loyalty at the death of a Sultan. Now, the men would follow Piri Pasha's orders. This was what he had prayed for so long would happen.

Inch' Allah. God willing.

Piri Pasha returned to his *serai* while the wailing and mourning continued through the early light. He went to the heavily guarded tents that housed the Sultan's treasure chests. He set about sealing each box carefully with the ring of Selim. Then he posted a heavy guard, giving them instructions that he was turning over command of the forces to Bali Agha, the *Seraskier,* Commander-in-Chief of the Janissaries.

Bali Agha was dressing in his military uniform. He had been combing his long, black mustache when he heard Piri Pasha's speech from the tent.

Piri entered the tent without being announced. The *Seraskier* continued wrapping his waistband. He placed his sword in its folds, and turned to face the Pasha.

"You have heard, Bali Agha?"

"I have heard, Piri Pasha."

"Then you know what you must do." Bali Agha nodded his assent. Piri continued. "You will take command of the army this morning. Strike the camp tonight, and be moving after first light. I have sealed the treasure, and it is ready to go. I will keep the seal with me."

Bali Agha showed no reaction at this apparent lack of trust. Piri continued. "Move slowly but steadily toward Istanbul. I will ride ahead, and see to the preparation for the arrival of the Son of Selim. The new Sultan and I should arrive there about the same time if my messenger gets through. I will ride in disguise until I reach the capital. I have sent Achmed Agha ahead to prepare the Janissaries and keep everything under control until we are united outside the gates of the city. Word of the impending arrival of your army will assure compliance. I know there will be spies to alert our enemies of your progress. Their news will act in our favor, for they will spread the word that your army is coming. I need but a day or two ahead of you, so move cautiously, but let no one, nothing, impede you!"

Bali Agha said nothing. When Piri Pasha had finished, the Agha stood to attention and saluted. Piri left the tent and went back to his own. Now he could mount his guard and set off for the capital with the better part of the world's fiercest fighting force close behind him. Now, he could precede his men to Istanbul, and await the arrival of the Son of Selim.

—◆—

Achmed Agha and the young Sipahi, Abdullah, had ridden hard from the encampment. At first they went towards the Kabarda Horses as they were told. But upon reaching the corrals, they turned to the east without pause. The two men pressed on in silence, bent over the necks of their mounts, side by side along the dry road. They looked like father and son as they rode, Achmed's bulk and power in sharp contrast to Abdullah's smaller wiry frame. They kept a fast lope, moving the horses steadily toward the east. For fifteen miles they rode together through the last of the summer's wheat fields and the stands of sunflowers now beginning to wilt and drop their seeds as autumn approached. People in the sleepy villages along the way were waking to the morning light as the two men sped by. Grazing animals scattered before the horses' hooves. Few trees broke the rolling terrain, but the icy northeast winds of winter had not yet begun to sweep in from the Black Sea.

At the fork in the road at another of the many identical villages along the way, the two Sipahis stopped and watered the horses. They drank from their leather canteens, and refilled them. Achmed Agha hugged the younger man, and whispered in his ear. "Ride well, my brother. Bring the Son of Selim safely back to us. May Allah go with you."

"And with you, Achmed Agha."

They rose as one into their saddles, and the Agha veered left to the east. He rode directly toward the capital, while Abdullah wheeled his horse right, south, and toward the crossing of the Dardanelles. The young Sipahi pushed his horse as hard as he dared, well aware of the animal's limits. He made sure to maintain a pace suitable for the long road ahead.

By late afternoon, the rolling hills gave way to rising terrain. Abdullah was approaching the pass to Koru Dagi, the mountain rising more than a thousand feet above the Dardanelles. This mountain pass would be the hardest push before the gentle descent to the water's edge and the ferry crossing into Asia. There would begin the final drive to Manisa and the *caravanserai* of his new Sultan. Abdullah slowed his pace to a fast lope, and pushed the horse up the steady climb.

A mile ahead of the young rider, two men waited by the side of the road. Both were dressed in long caftans of dirty, gray wool. Their boots were made of old felt, and worn nearly through. On their heads they wore black skullcaps. From a distance, it would be hard to tell the two men apart.

They, too, had horses, but theirs were nowhere in sight. The men had tied them in a small stand of trees, where the horses grazed on the scant ground cover now turning brown at the end of the growing season. The horses' ribs showed through their sides, and sores festered where the worn saddle leathers had rubbed them raw.

The men squatted in the low scrub at the side of the road. One of them squinted, looking north in the direction of a cloud of dust appearing just over the horizon. He rose and stood on his tiptoes to get a better view. After another minute, he smiled, and kicked his dozing partner. The sleepy man awoke with a start and rubbed his eyes, cursing the older one. The standing man pointed up the road to the north.

Neither spoke, but they both saw the dust now, as it resolved slowly into horse and rider. The rider had slowed to rest his horse as he climbed a steeper portion of the hill leading to the high pass of Koru Dagi.

Their plan was simple and effective. The highwaymen would wait, concealed in the brush, until a likely victim came by. If the victim was on foot, the men would emerge from the brush, their curved knives at the ready, and surround their prey. Usually, there was no resistance. They would take what treasure they could find, and ride away on their horses, only to return to the same spot some hours later. The pickings were poor on this stretch of road, but they were far from any authority, and few travelers would come back to try to track them down.

If the travelers fought, they would likely die at the side of the road, for the two men worked well together and had much practice. If the traveler were on horse, the men would leap out at the last moment, hoping to startle the mount and toss the rider to the ground. One would grab the reins, while the other pulled the rider down, if he had not already fallen. If they missed their target, they would rarely pursue the chase, for their horses were old. And the men, too, were old. Soon another rider would appear. These were patient men.

This rider was clearly in sight now. The two highwaymen crouched lower into the brush. The horse had slowed even more for the big hill. He was ridden well in hand. Surprise might not work this time, and so the two highwaymen moved into the open. They pretended to be working on something in their pack. This time they would hail the rider and ask directions, then they would spring the attack.

The Sipahi looked ahead between the ears of his mount. He saw the men at the side of the road. All strangers were a danger to him, and Abdullah became alert. He urged the horse faster, a voice within telling him there was danger indeed. He pressed his knees into the sides of his mount, digging his heels into the horse's ribs. As his speed increased, he slipped both reins into his left hand, laying his left fist onto the horse's mane. He let the reins drape loosely, so the horse could extend his neck and stretch out his stride. The horse knew this signal, and he did what the Sipahi asked of him.

The pace quickened now from a fast lope to the beginnings of a gallop. The rider calculated the distance, allowing the horse to accelerate, timing for maximum speed just as he came to the men. His right hand slipped to the handle of his long curved scimitar, and he slid it carefully out of its scabbard. His fist clutched the sword lightly as he held it to the horse's flank, out of sight.

The men saw the rider more clearly now. What they never saw until it was too late was that the brown color of the rider's clothes was dust and mud covering the light blue uniform of the Sultan's Sipahi. They moved out to the edge of the road, confused by the acceleration of the horse and rider. They had lost the element of surprise, and they were momentarily at a loss for a plan. Finally, the bigger man raised his knife in threat, hoping to stop the horse's momentum. The second man ran further ahead along the road for a second attack, should his partner fail.

The young Sipahi crouched lower over the horse's neck. The horse raised its hind end and broke to full gallop. Mud flew in brown clots off the back hooves as the Sipahi leaned low to the right side along his horse's neck. The robber reached out with his knife, ready to slash the horse's shoulder. The horse and rider moved ahead, never veering from their straight run. Suddenly, Abdullah's arm rose from his side. "I place my trust in God" flashed in Arabic on the steel of the scimitar raised high in the air. But the highwayman never saw it.

Before he could feel the pain, before the realization, the robber watched with utter disbelief as his knife fell to the ground, still clutched in the fist of his right hand. He opened his mouth to scream as the blood spurted from the stump of his forearm and the pain reached his brain. But, no sound escaped his lips as he fell to the earth clutching at his terrible wound. The severed hand held the knife tightly even as the horse's passing hooves kicked both knife and hand into the brush. The robber—now on his knees—watched the dust around him turn to a maroon jelly as he slowly bled to death from his wound.

The other man hesitated for just a second, trying to comprehend what had happened to his partner. Even before he could react to save himself, the rider was on him. So fast was the Sipahi's stroke that the man's world went instantly black. Swiftly, painlessly, the highwayman's head toppled to the ground, while his body remained standing upon his splay-legged stance for a few seconds more. Then the corpse fell forward into the dust, and his blood darkened the edges of the road.

And the Sultan's Sipahi rode on.

Doctor Moses Hamon sat on the cushions in his tent turning the pages of a new text on human anatomy. It was the very latest work on the subject, and was written in Arabic. Hamon read the language easily, since many of the most current medical and scientific research was being done in the Arab world. He spoke fluent Spanish, French, Greek, Hebrew, and Turkish. In his medical training, he had learned Latin, but never had the occasion to use the language. Now, by the light of his oil lamp, he looked through his new treasure. The illustrations were done in beautiful detail and clear lines. Some of the drawings showed new concepts in the anatomy of the circulation of the blood. In his home in Istanbul, Doctor Hamon had, over the years, amassed one of the finest book collections in the world. His volumes ranged over the fields of medicine, science, history and philosophy. Few private libraries anywhere could match the scope and quality of his.

But, Hamon's mind could not focus on the details of his new book. Instead, he churned over and over the possibilities of his future under the new Sultan. Selim was dead, and surely Suleiman would ascend to the throne without opposition. Life had been difficult as the personal physician to Selim. But, then again, it was not as difficult as it was for the Grand Vizier. At least there had not been a tradition of killing the court physician. Perhaps Selim had been afraid that he might need the skill and knowledge of the doctor, and was afraid to try a new, untested one. In a world where medicine at its best could cure very few illnesses, even the Sultan of the Ottoman Empire might not want to tempt fate.

The Hamons had fared well after Moses's father, Joseph, had come to Istanbul during the Spanish Inquisition. The Jewish population of the city blended easily into Muslim society. Their roles as merchants, artisans, and professionals made a contribution that far exceeded their numbers when compared to the other non-Muslim subjects of the Sultan. They slowly integrated themselves into the important functions of everyday life.

There had already been a tradition of non-Muslims rising to positions of power, as had the Viziers, who were mostly foreigners captured and educated by the state. The *Devshirmé*—the slave levy—provided not only a ready supply of soldiers, but of a whole class of upper-level officials as well. Every few years, emissaries of the Sultan would go out into the country and forcibly draft the young boys of Christian families, but never taking an only son. These children were brought to Istanbul where they were converted to Islam, educated, and trained. Each child was exhaustively tested to determine his particular gifts. Most of the ordinary boys were taken into the military and trained as Janissaries—or *yeni cheri*—the "young troops." Others filled more sedentary roles in the Palace. The smartest and most ambitious would enter the civil service and could, with diligence and hard work, rise to positions of great power. Indeed, the Grand Viziers themselves, without exception, were Christian converts drafted into the *Devshirmé*. This was in stark contrast to Europe, where one's birth determined one's position in later life. The Ottoman Empire was a true meritocracy.

So it was for the wave of Jewish immigrants who had been driven from Europe by the Inquisition and from the increasing levels of violent anti-Semitism that were permeating the continent. Many of the Jewish bankers had managed to bring some of their capital when they left Spain. The artists brought their skills, and the merchants reopened their shops.

As for the Muslim Sultans, they were quite willing to accept this new immigration for the good it brought to their society. Islam had a place for the *dhimmi*, "the People of the Book." Islam, Christianity, and Judaism were monotheistic religions, and shared the same god and many of the same prophets. Moses and Jesus were both revered as teachers by the Muslims. All three religions had strict laws that governed the conduct of society. The Ten Commandments were followed by both Christians and Jews, while the *Qur'an* set out the rules by which a good Muslim should guide his life. Muslims and

Jews circumcised their young sons, following Abraham's covenant with God. Neither religion permitted the consumption of the meat of pigs or camels.

Certain specific freedoms were granted to all the non-Muslims within the realm. They could own property. They could practice their religions freely as long as they paid the required religious tax.

With these freedoms came certain restrictions. They could not build new churches or synagogues. In legal matters, evidence given by a non-Muslin could not be accepted against the word of a Muslim. A Muslim could be punished, but could not be put to death, for killing a non-Muslim. Non-Muslims could not carry weapons or ride horses. But, the most egregious restraint was the prohibition against certain types of clothing, which publicly singled out the non-Muslim. Non-Muslims could not wear green clothes or white turbans. In some circumstances, they were required to wear only purple garments and purple shoes to mark them from the rest of society.

So, while the Jews and Christians of the Ottoman Empire were the Protected People, the *dhimmi*, they lived somewhat restricted lives. They paid a tribute, or tax, for the privilege of living within the empire. Idolaters, on the other hand, people who had *not* received a divinely revealed scripture, had to either accept Islam or be put to death. They were not *dhimmi*. When Hamon compared the plight of his people in Spain and on the rest of the European continent, he looked upon life under the Muslims as a gift from God.

Hamon thought about Suleiman, the heir to the throne. He had had very little contact with the young prince. Selim wanted his own doctor nearby, and Suleiman spent almost all of his youth learning the lessons of governing in the far-off provinces. Rumors at the palace were that he had become a fine young man, and that at twenty-five he was known for his scholarship, poetry and an even-handedness in dispensing justice. Yes, Hammon thought, life might even improve now that Selim *Yavuz* was dead.

Why had Piri Pasha been so worried? Hamon wondered. Why was it necessary to keep the death of Selim a secret for so many days? Surely, the Janissaries would remain loyal. They had loved Selim, of course, for the continuous military campaigns and the booty they brought. Hamon had hated the constant trips to the battlefield. He hated being taken from his family in Istanbul. His son, Joseph, named after the boy's grandfather, was in his teens, that age when he needed his father's guidance and presence. The boy would become a doctor, of course, as all the Hamons before him. With luck and his father's reputation to help him, Joseph, too, might rise to the post of court physician. He could become the doctor for Suleiman and for Suleiman's son. The dynasty of Hamon doctors could flourish alongside the dynasty of the Ottomans. *Why not?* he thought with a visible shrug of the shoulders.

Moses Hamon carefully closed his treasured anatomy book and wrapped it in heavy cloth. He put it into his travel chest and shut the lock. As he looked about the tent for any other belongings that were not packed by his servants, he heard the *muezzin* call the faithful of Islam to prayer. He pictured in his mind the many people all over the empire who were now getting ready to face the holy city of Mecca and kneel down upon their prayer mats. From every direction, Arabic words would rise into the air and affirm their most cherished belief. *There is no God but God, and Muhammad is His Prophet.*

Hamon stood alone in his tent surrounded by the sounds of the praying Muslim soldiers. Listening to the voices on all sides, he removed his phylacteries from their embroidered blue silk pouch. He placed the small, wooden cube containing the inscriptions from Deuteronomy against his forehead, and carefully wound the long leather thongs around his head to hold it in place. He attached the second cube to his left biceps and wound the leather thongs around his forearm and hand. Then, looking straight ahead into nothingness, and surrounded by the voices of the Faithful, he said, *"Shemah Yisrael, Adonoi eloheynu. Adonoi echod."* Hear, oh Israel, the Lord our God, the Lord is One.

—

Piri Pasha decided to depart under the cover of darkness. He needed all the lead time he could muster. He knew that his body could not take the pounding of the hard ride ahead as it once could; as it had done so many times on so many missions for his Sultan.

He went to his *serai*, and sent his servants to fetch a heavy robe to cover his uniform. This he folded carefully and put into his saddle bag. Next he had food and water brought to him, some of which was packed for travel. The rest he hastily consumed in the tent while he dressed. He moved out to where his guards had brought his best horse. He took the reins and mounted quickly without help. His uniform was clean and ready for the journey. He would change into his disguise as soon as he was out of sight of the camp.

Piri motioned to the guard to step aside, and slowly walked the horse through the encampment. He greeted the Janissaries with a solemn face as befit a Grand Vizier who had just lost his master. Then, he silently moved to the edge the camp, continuing over the nearby hills. He rode for less than twenty minutes, until he was sure that he was well beyond the sight of his outermost guards. He dismounted and unpacked the robes from the saddlebags. Piri quickly changed, and was soon up upon his mount once more. He dug his heels into the horse's side, and cried, "Hut! Hut! Hut!" The horse accelerated from standing to a gallop in a single step, and Piri Pasha leaned into the beast's neck. He held his knees tight against the saddle leather and steered the horse toward the City. Toward Istanbul.

The road was gentle as he started his long ride, but he was unused to riding alone. For so many years, when he rode out at night, his way was lit with the torches of a hundred horsemen, making his path as bright as the day. Now, he moved into the approaching darkness, knowing he would have to slow his pace or lose his way in the night. Worse still, his horse might stumble and fall, and Piri Pasha, himself, might be injured; might not be there to pass the Sword of the House of Osman to the Son of Selim.

As midnight approached, the old Pasha began to feel his age. His horse was strong and moved with the power that was legendary in these Arabian stallions. But, the gait was irregular, and the seat uncomfortable for the Pasha. This was a ride for a younger man and for younger bones. His thighs had ached for hours from the effort of squeezing the horse's sides to maintain his balance. Now he could barely feel his legs at all. His back was pounded by the horse's gait. His neck muscles knotted in spasm from the awkward position required of it. He could get comfortable neither at a trot nor at the lope; and a long gallop was out of the question for both him and the horse.

So, Piri Pasha pressed on, pain dominating his mind, along with the agony of realizing that he had covered only a fraction of his journey in the first night of what would now certainly be at least a four-day ride. He kept the reins tight, and satisfied himself that, *Inch' Allah*, he and his Sultan would arrive safely at the Tomb of Ayyüb together.

Abdullah covered the ground between Edirne and the coast in just over twenty-two hours. He had reached the ferry at dark on the next night after leaving the camp.

At the water's edge, the ferryman was mooring his craft to the European shore. He had just packed his few possessions and his day's meager earnings into a cloth bag. He was looking forward to a warm meal and a few hours sleep before beginning to work again before dawn.

He was walking wearily up the slope of the embankment when the Sipahi came riding hard down the same slope. His horse was lathered and covered with mud, as was the Sipahi himself. The ferryman looked up in fear as the young rider bore down upon him. He dropped his sack to the ground and turned to run for whatever cover he could find. Abdullah closed on the running man. He brought his horse up short as the man stumbled in his flight and fell sprawling to the ground.

"Get thee back to your post, old man, I will cross this water at once."

The old man remained sprawled upon the ground. He craned his neck to look up at the rider. "But, it is after dark, sir, and dangerous to be out there in the night. I cannot see, and there is no moon, and I..."

"Enough! I am the Sultan's Sipahi, and we will cross at once!"

The old man was about to protest again, but he looked into the eyes of the young man towering over him on this powerful agitated horse. "Yes, sir. At once. *Inch' Allah*."

Abdullah dismounted and walked his horse down to the water's edge, while the ferryman unmoored his boat. As they crossed the narrowest point of the Dardanelles in the darkness, a distance of less than a mile, the Sipahi dozed. They made landfall on the Asian side in very good time. The Sipahi rose into the saddle as soon as the ferry scraped the sand and rock on the Asian shore. He threw the old man a gold coin from his purse. It was worth a thousand ferry rides, at least. "Allah be with you, my friend."

"And with you," said the old man, who then lay down upon the sand to sleep a full night in Asia for the very first time in his life.

Riding as hard as the darkness would allow, Abdullah turned his horse south again for the final push to Manisa and the *caravanserai* of his new Sultan. He did not dwell upon the great history beneath his horse's hooves. Nearly two thousand years before, the young Alexander, *Sikander,* as Abdullah would have known him, had set off from Macedonia to conquer Asia. As Alexander turned south into what would become Turkey, his path was almost exactly that of the young Sipahi. Alexander crossed the water at the very same narrows, and then went by sea to the ancient city of Troy. He ordered his ships to halt, and in full battle armor, plumes flying from his helmet, he leaped into the sea and walked ashore. He drew his sword and plunged it into the soil, declaring that he would plunge the very same sword into the heart of Asia, and conquer her. He stopped at the temple and was shown a shield said to have belonged to the Greek hero, Achilles, son of Zeus. Alexander dropped his own shield, and taking up the shield of his idol, began a journey into Asia that would forever change the face of the earth.

But, the Sipahi dwelled on none of this. He first passed Çanakkale, where Selim's grandfather, Mehmet, had built the Bowl Fortress to protect the passage through the Dardanelles. Later, toward dawn, he passed the buried ruins of Troy, where Homer told of the pouting rages of Achilles, and of the beauty of Helen, and the infamous wooden horse. But, none of these ancient and historic places did the young Sipahi notice. Instead, he kept his eyes fixed rigidly upon the road ahead; his entire focus on his mission.

The road was flatter now, and the country drier. Water would be a problem unless he stopped at every opportunity. At each spring-fed creek or late-summer rivulet, Abdullah would rest his horse and both would drink together. He kept his water bottle topped off at every opportunity. He ate little from his bags, hoping to make the food last until he was very near to Manisa. He was finding it diffi-cult to stay awake in the saddle as the second night opened onto dawn. He dared not sleep, for though there was little fear of falling from the saddle—he had slept many times in such a position—there was still the threat of highwaymen. When he rode with his corps of Sipahis at his side, he could doze and wake, knowing that his broth-ers would guard his flank. But, now he was by himself, and he alone was responsible for his own safety...and perhaps that of the realm.

Abdullah pushed still further south through the historic and tur-bulent lands of Asia Minor. There were olive groves along the wayside, but he never stopped to pick the remnants of the summer's crop. Long stretches of arid, rocky ground were intermingled with green and rolling hills. He kept to the coast, for though this was longer in miles, he could push his horse harder over the flat land, avoiding the mountainous terrain of the interior. Each river they forded gave both horse and rider a refreshing bath and new energy. But, by the third day their energy was flagging badly. The horse stumbled more, and needed more rests. Once they fell together while coming down a steep hill. Only the grace of Allah had prevented the horse from rolling over on the young man and crushing him to death.

The rider knew his mount well, and allowed the horse to make decisions as to his own needs for rest. Abdullah dozed more often now in the saddle, despite the risks. He could barely hang on over the last fifty miles. The horse was bleeding from several cuts on his legs that he got from stumbling over rocky terrain. The rider began to lose sense of time and place. But, the two pressed on, the rider driven by the urgency and importance of his mission, the beast by his devotion to his rider.

Finally, on the evening of the third day, the perimeter guard at the *caravanserai* of Suleiman caught sight of a horse and rider stag-gering slowly toward them. They mounted their fresh animals and rode out to meet the intruder. Lances and scimitars ready, they rode full gallop to intercept the possible threat to their prince.

Only when they were yards away did the guards recognize the once-proud blue uniform and the sheathed scimitar of the rider as one of their own. The boy had long since lost the plumed white hat that is so easily recognized from afar. One of the Janissaries leaped from his own horse and grabbed the reins from the young man. Instantly, in his confusion, the Sipahi reached for his scimitar, but the Janissary grabbed his wrist and held him firmly in his strong grasp. "Calmly, my friend. There's no need to draw your weapon. We both serve the Sultan, Selim."

The Sipahi relaxed his grip. He had no strength left for fighting anyway, and soon realized that he was safe; that he could now deliver his message and remove the heavy weight of the mission from his back.

—

The Janissaries led the Sipahi's horse into the *caravanserai* of Suleiman. They brought the young man to the tent of Suleiman's closest friend and adviser, Ibrahim. The Inner Guard led the boy's horse away to be fed and rested. The boy staggered along with the help of the Janissary and was led into Ibrahim's tent. Word had already reached Ibrahim of the Sipahi's arrival, and he was consumed with curiosity as to what this meant.

Abdullah bowed, and then fell to his knees. Though he was meant to deliver the letter directly to the Sultan, he was unable to resist these men in front of him. He reached into his robes and pulled out the letter that Piri Pasha had given to him; safe delivery of the message was the sole purpose of this terrible ordeal.

The Janissary took the sealed letter and handed it to Ibrahim. Ibrahim stared at the Sipahi for a moment. The boy could not have been more than eighteen, and even through the mud and the grime, his beautiful clear features were striking. Ibrahim unrolled the parchment and held it near to his oil lamp. He read the message in silence, and then moved toward the door. "Bring this young man with me. We must take this to the Master at once. There will be questions, I'm sure."

Suleiman was awaiting Ibrahim, as he, too, had received word of the arrival of this unusual visitor. He was surprised at how quickly Ibrahim had come to his tent, though his own corps of advisors were already present.

"Come in, my friend. What have we here?"

Ibrahim bowed to Suleiman, and motioned for the guard to bring in the Sipahi. The young man staggered, and then knelt on both knees as he pressed his head to the rich carpet in front of Suleiman. Ibrahim handed his master the parchment, while the boy's head remained pressed to the ground.

Suleiman unrolled the document and read it to himself. Then, he looked up and read the words aloud.

"The Sword of the House of Osman awaits you at the Tomb of Ayyüb." Nothing more. There was no signature or seal.

Immediately, the advisers began to talk all at once, some rejoicing that their master was now the Sultan, and others fearing some ruse to get Suleiman away from the safety of his Janissaries.

"Ears deceive, eyes reveal," one of the advisers said to Suleiman. Many pleaded for him to remain in Manisa, and even to increase his guard.

"Send an emissary. Perhaps, Ibrahim himself," the other suggested.

Suleiman listened, but didn't speak. He looked to Ibrahim and raised his eyebrows in question. Then he asked, "Ibrahim? What do you think?"

Ibrahim looked at the note again. Then he turned to the boy, still in a position of prostration before his prince. "What do *you* say? Who wrote this message that you bring to us?"

The Sipahi raised his head, but not his body. He looked at Ibrahim, for he was afraid to meet the eyes of the Son of Selim. "Piri Pasha, himself, has written these words, and Piri Pasha, himself, has commanded me to ride and deliver the message. I have ridden for three days and nights to bring this to you. This, in the name of Allah, I swear to you."

Suleiman took a bag of gold coins from his table and tossed them to the young man. "Take him away, and see that he is fed and cared for. Let the *tabip* examine him and see to his needs; and the same for his horse."

With the help of the guards, the young man rose and backed away from the Son of Selim. He never took his eyes off the floor. Servants took him by the elbows as he was guided backward out of the *serai*. One does not turn one's back on the Sultan. He was led away to some blankets under an olive tree, while servants were sent to fetch the doctors.

"I think, my lord, that the young man is telling the truth," Ibrahim said.

"And, why do you think so?"

Ibrahim moved closer to Suleiman. He lowered his voice and said, "If this were a lure to get you from the protection of your guards, I think it would have been clearer. It would have said outright that your father, Selim, is dead; or used the name of Piri Pasha, or his seal. Instead, it only speaks only of the Sword of the House of Osman and the Tomb of Ayyüb."

Suleiman nodded and walked to the door flap. The Janissaries held the flaps apart. Suleiman walked out into the night with Ibrahim close to his side.

They walked to the olive tree where the boy was lying. "Look, Ibrahim. He has not even the strength to change his clothes or take a little food. He is so deeply asleep I doubt that cannon fire would wake him."

"Yes, and look. The gold you gave him lies on the ground next to his blanket. He hadn't even the strength to hide it in his robes. Anyone could steal it."

Suleiman nodded and returned to the tent. He told his advisers, "The Sultan's Sipahi has told the truth. My father is dead. I must go to the Tomb of Ayyüb to claim the Sword of the House of Osman. Prepare. We'll leave at first light."

⅀ 2 ⅀

THE SHADOW OF GOD

The Road from Manisa to Istanbul
September 24th, 1520

Suleiman rode easily on his brown stallion, continuing the fast pace he had kept up since dawn. He, too, would follow the level coast road, as had the young Sipahi, to spare the horses and conserve time. His body was synchronized to the rocking gait of his mount, his hands held lightly on the reins. Thousands of hours in the saddle had made him a fine and confident horseman.

He was a thin, wiry young man, with a fine black mustache. He had a long, slender neck and dark, brown eyes, shielded by thick, black eyebrows. He was said to resemble his great-grandfather, Mehmet, more than Selim, and had adopted Mehmet's habit of wearing his turban low over his forehead, which often gave him a stern and forbidding look. He was reserved and calm most of the time, only showing his father's temper when circumstances seemed to be getting out of control.

The most remarkable feature of his face was the sharp, hooked nose with its high prominent bridge, reminiscent of his beloved hunting falcons. Of course, no one dared comment about that in his presence.

Though his skin was usually pale, his hands and face were now brown from the hours of riding out in the summer sun with Ibrahim, his Chief Falconer and Master of the Horse. Over the years, Suleiman and Ibrahim had spent long days together riding through the countryside, with the Janissary guard as far behind them as safety would allow. At those times, Suleiman was tempted to spur his horse ahead, and leave the guard—and the reminder of who he was and who he was about to become—behind him, even if for only a few hours.

Suleiman was just twenty-five years old as he rode back to Istanbul to receive the Sword of the House of Osman. He had gotten his name when his father had opened the *Qur'an* at random and found the name, "Solomon," to whom God had granted "wisdom and knowledge." He became a devoted Muslim, though never a fanatic. His tolerance for the Jews and the Christian beliefs were to mark his reign in a time when there was little enough tolerance abroad in the world.

Suleiman had been away from his father and Istanbul for eight years, sent at fifteen to govern in the provinces, to learn the art of ruling as well as the many other facets of the education of a young prince. He studied history, language, law, politics, and his favorite of the arts, goldsmithing. In all those years, he returned to Istanbul to see his father only once, and never could he seek the advice and comfort that most young men found in their fathers. His mother, Hafiza, the *Sultan Valideh*, was also kept far from him, for she remained in Selim's palace. As Suleiman grew into his manhood, many eyes had watched to see how he would manage the day-to-day governing in these far-off regions of what would someday become his empire. He never liked the feeling that he was always under observation, always being tested. But, such was the lot of an Ottoman prince.

The morning grew warm. Suleiman shrugged off the heavy, gold-embroidered outer cape he wore over his white, silk caftan. He gave it to the page who rode a few yards behind him. Another page carried his jeweled water bottle and a third his fighting sword. Suleiman was dressed completely in white, except for his soft, brown, leather riding boots. His huge, white turban shone bright as the orange morning hues gave way to shimmering white light of the forenoon. The three white heron's feathers held to the turban with a clasp of rubies, emeralds, and diamonds swayed with the movement of his horse, and resembled wheat moving in a soft breeze. The heat began to rise from the sand in the road, and the dust hung longer in the air as the riders moved on.

The entourage had left the *caravanserai* before dawn, and traveled slowly throughout the day. Suleiman knew he should be exhausted already, but he was abuzz with the thought that he was now, in fact, the Sultan of the Ottoman Empire. He was soon to be the most powerful man on Earth. Only a short ceremony stood between him and the reality; nothing more than his girding with the Sword of the House of Osman.

He could hardly keep track of his thoughts. As Sultan, he would have to give up the leisurely life of a provincial governor, a life that had allowed him ample time to relax with his family and his friend, Ibrahim. His infant son, Mustapha, was one of Suleiman's greatest joys, and he treasured their time together with Gülbehar in the country. But, most of all, he worried about his future with Ibrahim. How would life in the Palace change their relationship? What role would Ibrahim play in the complex structure of his empire?

As if summoned by the Sultan's thoughts, Ibrahim appeared suddenly at Suleiman's left side. His horse was breathing hard, and seemed to have found the night's ride more draining than Suleiman's mount.

"A wonderful day is upon us, my Lord, is it not?"

"It is, indeed. I wonder what lies along this path."

"I think not much to worry about. Your guard precedes us, and they will see to our safety, surely." Though Ibrahim was only a year older than Suleiman, his large frame and barrel chest made him seem much older. He had dark hair with olive skin and deep-set brown eyes. His bushy eyebrows were always unkempt.

"That is not what I meant. There are many roads that we shall take, and they are long and arduous ones. As well as dangerous. There is *this* road that takes us to the Tomb of Ayyüb, where Piri Pasha will gird me with the sword of my ancestors. Then there is the road to the throne in the New Palace. There is where my new empire will find its home. My mother, the *Sultan Valideh*, and my *Kadin*—my First Lady—Gülbehar, the Flower of Spring, will be there. But, there are many roads after that, and I fear there will be many turnings to confuse our path. What do you think?"

Ibrahim did not answer at once, and Suleiman did not repeat his question. He knew that Ibrahim was a thoughtful man, who weighed his words carefully. The young Sultan trusted Ibrahim's judgment as much as he would from an older man. Ibrahim's hesitation was not guile, but rather the determination to be a good and true adviser to his master. The two had been together since they both were boys.

Ibrahim was born at Parga, on the west coast of Greece, to Christian parents. When he was a young child, he was captured by Turkish pirates and sold as a slave to a widow who lived near Magnesia in Asia Minor. The woman had tried to give the young boy a good education and help him to rise above his status as a slave. When Selim sent Suleiman to govern Manisa at the age of seventeen, Ibrahim's mother sent him to enter the service of the young prince as his slave, and the two became immediately inseparable.

Ibrahim was a godsend for Suleiman, whose youth had been empty of friends. Ibrahim was already a linguist even as a teenager, speaking flawless Greek, French, and Turkish, and was able to get along quite well in Italian and Persian. Both the boys loved to read, and would pass many of their hours together studying history and reading aloud to each other. Ibrahim was also a natural musician, entertaining Suleiman by singing and playing the viol for him. As the unofficial playmate and nearly a brother to the prince, Ibrahim shared all of Suleiman's education and activities. The boys would hunt together, and fish and swim. They rode horses, shot arrows, and played polo together. They even took meals together, shared the same tent, and oft times, the same bed. The exploration of their sexuality seemed natural enough, at least until the time when Suleiman would ascend to the throne. Then his attention would be expected to shift to the harem, and eventually to the production of an heir. In the meantime, life was sweet and exciting for the two young men.

As the years passed and they grew into manhood, they still passed most of their days and nights together. Over time, the differences in their station slowly became more apparent. Most of the members of the court foresaw the day when the prince would have to pay off his boyhood friend and move on to the duties of his governing.

But, that was not to be the case. Suleiman depended upon the loyalty of this long-standing friendship, and kept Ibrahim by his side. As the men loved to hunt together, Ibrahim rose quickly to the post of Chief Falconer. Later, he became Master of the Horse. Because high-court members were granted military rank, he would soon become Captain of the Inner House. But, whatever the title, Ibrahim was always Suleiman's closest friend, adviser, surrogate brother, and sometimes lover. The mores of Ottoman Turkey were not much changed from those of the warriors in ancient Sparta, where it was felt that in a fighting force, where celibacy was the norm, a man would be more likely not to disgrace himself in battle in the presence of his lover.

Ibrahim's role as surrogate brother was critical to Suleiman as well, because of the Mehmet's Law of Fratricide. Upon attaining the throne, Suleiman would have been forced to put a true brother to death. Fortunately, Suleiman had no real brothers. For his part, Ibrahim treasured his friendship with the prince equally, and not only for the riches and privilege that it brought him. He would as gladly die in the service of his friend as for his Sultan.

That dawn, as they had left the *caravanserai*, a dervish Muslim had grabbed at Suleiman's reins before the guards had set up the formal protective perimeter for the coming journey. Swords flashed from their scabbards as the Janissaries rushed to protect their Sultan. But Suleiman held up his hand, stopping his guard from cutting the old man to pieces. The dervish held onto the reins near the horse's mouth, and began to speak to his master. This was entirely improper, and Ibrahim would have stopped it had he not seen the softness for the old man in Suleiman's eyes.

"Yes? What is it you have to tell me, *Dede?*" The word "Grandfather" was spoken in a tone of respect, not derision.

The dervish spoke to Suleiman, almost chanting as if he were saying a poem or a prayer. "You bear the name of ancient Solomon, the wisest king among kings. The name of Solomon who was known all throughout the world for his wisdom."

Suleiman nodded, as the old man went on.

"You are the Tenth ruler of the House of Osman. You are called to rule at the dawn of the Tenth Century of Islam. In every age, but one is appointed to grasp the era by the horns..."

The number ten was of greatest significance to the Turks: ten is the number of divisions of the Holy *Qur'an*; there are ten commandments in the Pentateuch; Mohammed, the Prophet of God, had ten disciples; ten is the number of fingers and toes. Ten was the perfect number, and Suleiman was born in the first year of the tenth century, by the Muslim calendar, which dates from the *Hegira*, the Prophet's flight from Mecca.

Suleiman leaned down to hear the man's frail voice. But, the old man said no more. He seemed exhausted by the effort and the strain of speaking to his Sultan. He let go of the reins and moved away. Ibrahim handed a small sack of coins to a servant, and sent him after the old dervish. Suleiman looked at Ibrahim with a puzzlement on his face.

"Did this dervish speak a prophesy of my future, Ibrahim?"

Ibrahim only nodded. He was not a superstitious man, and he knew that his master was not one either. "He did, my Lord. And a propitious one at that."

"This old man has a wisdom we can only hope to achieve with time. His age is greater than yours and mine combined. Think what wisdom and experience are there in his head and in his heart. Just think of it!"

Again, Ibrahim responded with a nod.

The previous night, before they had departed the *caravanserai*, Suleiman's officers had brought copies of the orders for the debarkation and the moving of his household and family to Istanbul. Suleiman took the pen and began to sign the orders. When he looked up, he saw that the eyes of all the soldiers were on him. There was something different, and he could not put his finger on it. When he had asked Ibrahim about it later, his friend replied, "You are not the same man you were yesterday, my Lord. They know that now. And so do you. You woke yesterday as the governor of a very minor province in a very insignificant part of Asia Minor."

Suleiman looked hurt for a moment. But, Ibrahim smiled, and said, "Do not look back, Majesty. You are, indeed, fortunate. You have no brothers to race you to the imperial city. There are no enemies to draw their reins across your path. All power waits for the touch of your hand. Even Piri Pasha, Selim's Grand Vizier, waits to bend his head before the Shadow of God on Earth. With good fortune such as yours, there is *nothing* you cannot do. Nothing!"

Suleiman smiled at his friend, and turned in the saddle. He looked behind him and laughed, "Except turn *back* upon this road." Then, he spurred his horse and dashed ahead of the startled Ibrahim, down the road to Istanbul.

———

For three more days, Suleiman's small band moved north along the Aegean coast. Then, they turned east inland to parallel the Dardanelles. As they rode along, Suleiman noticed how the people's livelihoods changed with the terrain. Here they toiled to bring in crops of barley and wheat, and there they pushed their flocks of sheep over broken ground to better grazing lands. Still others tended arbors of olive trees.

Suleiman thought about these people; their hard lives. In the countryside, the Ottoman Turks lived constantly on the edge. Their meager livelihood could be wiped out with a single hailstorm, a lightning bolt, a flash flood, or any number of incurable diseases. Life was harsh, and death always in waiting. *How,* he wondered, *can I as their Sultan change their lot in life? While I live in luxury in Istanbul, these people live in rags and hovels. While I eat and drink my fill each day, they are often at the very edge of starvation. How can I change this for them? What can I do?* Suleiman shook his head and brought his mind back to the journey. There was so much for him to do, so many decisions for him to make.

As the procession neared the city, it was clear that people knew their Sultan Selim was dead, and that the Son of Selim was coming to claim his sword—to claim the Empire. The small clutches of quiet peasants grew into noisy crowds. The crowds turned into cheering mobs, until wild throngs pressed along the highway trying to get a glimpse of the new Emperor; to touch his stirrups; to see his face.

The Janissaries and the Sipahis were hard pressed to keep the crowd back. The household guard became frightened for the Sultan's safety, for they were surrounded by farmers and workers, all armed with tools of steel—farming tools that could easily become weapons. Hardly a man in that crowd did not possess at least a knife on his person, and some carried axes, scythes, and heavy staffs.

The mounted Sipahis and the Janissaries on foot formed an unbroken phalanx three deep, surrounding their master, trying to present a solid human wall within which the new Sultan would be safe. The Janissaries pressed closest to their master. The Sipahis on their war horses formed the outer ring. The horses, too, sensed the tension from their masters. They stamped the ground and snorted as the riders held them in tight rein. Only Suleiman's horse seemed oblivious to the excitement around him, walking with an even and unhurried gait. But, no attack came, and the procession moved on.

As they passed the old capital at Bursa, the Green City, they caught their first sight of the Sea of Marmara. They passed the lake near Nicaea, where Selim had returned from his campaigns in Afghanistan and Persia, and had brought home craftsmen who set up workshops to make porcelain for all the world.

Finally, the party reached the ferry station at Üsküdar across the Bosporus from Istanbul. The crowds were kept back by ten thousand Palace Janissaries who had been sent out by Bali Agha from the capital. These elite soldiers reinforced Suleiman's own guard, as he dismounted from his tired, lathered horse. Two pages led the horse away, while Suleiman walked to the waiting ferry. Through the haze rising from the water, Suleiman could just make out the landmarks of the great city. He could see the slim towers of the minarets flanking the holy mosque of Aya Sofia on the opposite shore. Barely visible were the walls and the buildings of *Yeni Serai*, the New Palace, which was soon to be his home. Eventually, the world would know this as the Palace of the Cannon Gate, the Topkapi. He stepped down into the ferry and sat upon the embroidered cushions placed for him across the rich carpets that covered the wooden seat.

His guard held the crowds back, but could not hold back the cheering and joy of his people.

"Allah bless you! God keep the Son of Selim!"

Suleiman now breathed easier as he sensed the joy of the Turkish populace at his return. The fear that had been just beneath the surface of his thoughts was quickly put to rest. There was no hostile army to bar his way; no rebellious Agha of the Janissary to stage a coup; no palace revolution to drag him down. He would be home shortly, in the cradle of his legacy. He was Suleiman, the Shadow of God on Earth.

With Ibrahim at his side, Suleiman stepped up from the ferry onto the shores of Europe; Istanbul. The City. The city of his father. The very heart of the Ottoman Empire. There was a moment of uneasy quiet, when suddenly the noise of uncontrolled shouts of joy came hurtling down the grassy slopes of the gardens. Gardeners with their sickles and pruning knives held aloft rushed to him. The Palace Janissaries leaped the carefully sculpted hedgerows, shouting for their leader, and surrounded him with their bodies in a combination of affection and protection. Soon, the Janissaries had completely sealed Suleiman off from the crowd of Turks, and were shouting in rhythmic waves, "The gift! The gift! Make the payment! Make the payment!" All pretense gone. Nothing subtle here. They were calling for the customary payment of gold by the new Sultan to his Janissaries.

Suleiman was not offended at this public display of greed and presumption. This was a time-honored tradition, and only a fool would break it. However, Suleiman had neglected to have his gold brought up with the advance party. These trim, well-muscled, and highly trained soldiers were the mainstay of every Sultan's power. They had no life outside their duty to the Sultan. Young and celibate, their entire focus was on war and the protection of their Sultan. Without this armed force, Suleiman held no power at all.

Suleiman moved to higher ground, where he could look down upon the moving mass of bodies. The crowd surged with him, as if attached to his person, but the guard kept the masses from actually touching him. He climbed up upon a small, wooden stand that had been placed there for the purpose, and raised his arms above his head in triumph. Still the Janissaries shouted for their reward. The noise made it impossible for the Sultan to speak.

Suleiman's eyes scanned the gardens for Piri Pasha. But, Piri was nowhere in sight. He felt the faintest twinge of anxiety in the depths of his abdomen, for Piri's loyalty was critical to the Sultan's power. This was the man who attended to every decision in Selim's reign. Had not Piri Pasha sent word for Suleiman to come immediately to Istanbul? Why was he not here now to greet the new Sultan?

Then, a slight disturbance occurred at the edge of the crowd, and Suleiman looked up hoping to see Piri emerge there. But when the sea of bodies parted, Bali Agha, Commander of the Janissaries, moved through his troops, climbing the platform to a step just below the Sultan. He was out of breath from his run, but he reached up to his new master and struck him lightly upon the shoulder with his open hand. This was the traditional greeting to a new leader by the Agha of the Sultan's army. Thus acknowledging Suleiman as their *Seraskier,* their Commander-in-Chief, as well as their Sultan, Bali Agha held his right hand aloft, and displayed a huge bright red apple. The crowd grew silent as the Agha began to speak. "Can you eat the apple, Son of Selim?" he shouted to the crowd more than to Suleiman.

To the Ottomans, the apple represented the traditional enemy of the Janissaries, the armies of Rome. The Pope. Christianity.

Suleiman took the apple from Bali Agha, and smiled at him. Then he turned back to the crowd, and holding the apple high, he said, "In good time. In good time."

Again, the crowd broke into shouts of joy and the fervent cheer again rose from all around the Sultan. Suleiman took a bite and tossed the apple high into the air. The Janissaries surged forward trying to catch it. Before it fell into the crowd, a scimitar flashed, and two halves of the apple came tumbling from the air.

"Make the gift, make the gift!" But, Suleiman stepped from the platform, and with his small retinue of personal guard began his walk to the Palace.

The men went silent. Bali Agha sagged with disappointment. He had hoped that Suleiman would give out the gold at that very moment. It had been the perfect time to seal the loyalty of these men. The crowd parted in silence, and the Agha followed Suleiman toward the palace.

Achmed Agha had been sitting quietly in the shade nearby. He was glad that the Sultan had shown no fear in the presence of the Palace guard, but he had hoped for more. The Sultan had missed his chance.

———

Ibrahim stirred the coals and built up the fire in the small room deep inside the interior of the palace's Third Court. The Sultan's apartments adjoined the harem, and were guarded by both the corps of palace eunuchs as well as the Janissaries. Suleiman leaned against the back of the *divan* and pulled his white silk robes tighter around him. The early fall air had chilled quickly, and the dampness seeped even into the Sultan's household. He had been silent since the episode at the ferry landing, and Ibrahim knew it was best to let his master ruminate alone on these matters. When it was time to seek Ibrahim's advice, Suleiman would speak.

The dinner plates were removed and the servants finished clearing the room in silence. Suleiman had touched almost nothing but for a few sips of fruit nectar. Even the aroma of the spiced lamb had seemed to annoy him. The pilaf went untouched as well. Ibrahim, as usual, left nothing on the golden plates nor any wine in his jade goblet.

"Eight years ago my father sent me off to govern in the provinces. To become a leader of state. To go to 'The School of the Empire.' I have barely laid eyes on him since then. I have no idea who he was, nor do I think he ever learned who I was."

"You were his favorite. That is certain."

"I am *alive*, at least. I suppose that tells me something. Do you know the last thing he ever said to me?"

"No, Majesty. I do not."

"He bid me farewell, and then he said, as if this were to guide my every decision, 'If a Turk dismounts from the saddle to sit on a carpet, he becomes nothing. *Nothing!*'"

Ibrahim listened, but did not respond. Suleiman continued, "So here I sit upon a carpet, and the reality is that until Piri Pasha arrives, and he and the Aghas gird me with my family's sword, I am 'nothing, *nothing!*'"

"You are the Shadow of God on Earth, my Lord."

"Not until I wear that sword! And that power is in the hands of *others!* How can I be the Shadow of God on Earth, when all that separates me from death by the silken cord is the whim of another man? Of other men? Why, I might be lying in one of those family graves, and another Shadow of God would rule the Ottomans. Is this the will of Allah? Is this the Plan of God? *My* power comes only from the will of a band of slaves whom my family have trained and educated, and who are loyal to us for the gold we give them? These Janissaries are the *Devshirmé*, as too are the Aghas! They are Christian children taken from their families to fill our armies. Slaves!"

Ibrahim waited for Suleiman to go on, but the Sultan seemed to have finished.

"I, too, was a slave, my Lord," Ibrahim said quietly. "I was trained for duty in the royal household. And you know my loyalty does not rest upon the whim of *any* man."

Suleiman did not respond to Ibrahim's remarks. He rose and began to pace the small dingy room. He shrugged his robes closer and scuffled his slippers along the carpet as he paced. "We trained them, we educated them. We took them from behind a plow and mounted them upon the finest horses in the world. They were starving children dressed in rags. They could neither read nor write. They had no future except for starvation and a lifelong dwindling until their deaths. Now they wear jewels in their scabbards. Herons' plumes in their hats. We made them into a fighting force that can conquer the world. And now *that* mighty weapon is poised at *my* throat! I am subject to the whims and tantrums of ten thousand slave boys, commanded by a handful of old men!

"And my father tells me that I must not dismount from my horse to sit upon a carpet! This from a man who wanted to slay every Greek Christian in the kingdom because he thought it might please Allah! That it would bring blessings upon him!" Suleiman's voice was steadily rising.

Ibrahim nodded, and then shook his head slowly in amazement as he focused on what Suleiman was saying. "And he *would* have slain them all if it weren't for Ali Djemali," Ibrahim said. Djemali had been the *Grand Mufti*, the spiritual leader of the College of Islam, and the final interpreter of Islamic Law. "Only *he* had the nerve to stand up to your father and contradict him. I think Selim believed that Ali spoke directly to the Prophet...or even to Allah, Himself. Otherwise, Ali would have lost his head along with the others. Then, of course, Ali couldn't stop Selim from slaying forty thousand Shiite heretics in Eastern Anatolia," Ibrahim went on, "just for the public approval."

"If I had only thought to have the gold with me," Suleiman said, "to have had it there at the ferry while they were cheering me. Their frenzy and their wildness could have been made to work for me. If only I had thrown a *few* bags of gold among them as a prologue to the generosity of the new Sultan. Even what gold I carried on my person would have been gesture enough."

Suddenly there was a noise at the door, and Suleiman whirled to meet the possible threat. Ibrahim dove off the *divan* and grabbed his sword by the handle, pulling it from the scabbard, which clattered to the floor. Nobody could enter the Sultan's presence without being announced. Though he couldn't articulate the thought in words, Suleiman's mind pictured a Palace coup, a revolt of the Janissaries. And his own death.

"Sultan Suleiman Khan!" the voice roared through the quiet of the palace. There in the doorway stood the only man who could arrive at the Sultan's door without escort or guard; the only armed man on Earth besides Ibrahim who could get this close to the Sultan without carving his way through the palace guard with a sword.

"Piri Pasha!" said Suleiman. It could only be Piri Pasha. Though the man looked worn and haggard, Suleiman's heart swelled at the sight of him. For, here was not a force of ten thousand Janissaries come to assassinate the new Sultan, but old Piri Pasha, his father's most trusted friend; Selim's Grand Vizier; and now, Suleiman's Grand Vizier.

Though Piri's clothes were a mess, and the man looked about to fall over from exhaustion, there he stood, a great smile stretched across his face, his arms flung wide as he trudged forward to hug his new master. He took Suleiman's hand in his and pressed it to his heart. Then he knelt and kissed the Sultan's sleeve.

"My Lord, forgive me for not being here to greet you. I hurried as fast as my strength and my years would allow. But, as you can see," he said, his arms wide, displaying his filthy clothes, "I am getting too old for such hard travel, and these bones cannot take the punishment that they once could. I took a secret way home, but even Bali Agha's huge army overtook me on the longer route." Piri Pasha's voice began to tremble with emotion, and a tears formed on his cheeks. "But, the very sight of you has given me strength. Look how you have prospered and grown! Why you were barely a lad when I saw you last. And now you are Sultan Suleiman, Emperor of the Ottomans!"

Piri snapped his fingers and two servants appeared at the doorway carrying small packages. Piri took one of the gifts, wrapped in an ornate silk brocade, and handed it to Suleiman. The Pasha waited with bowed head as the Sultan untied the ribbons. Suleiman held the gift up for Ibrahim to see. It was a brand-new ornate clock.

"To mark the beginning of a new reign, my Sultan, " Piri said.

Suleiman hugged his Vizier silently, and put the clock down. Then he turned to see what other gifts Piri Pasha had brought to him. The remainder of the packages contained the funeral clothing: a black caftan and black pants. Piri moved close to Suleiman, carrying a golden caftan, folded into a neat, bulky bundle. In a quiet voice heard only by the Sultan and Ibrahim, he said, "My Lord, under these black robes of mourning, wear this tunic of richest gold brocade. Never be without splendor about your person. These people may love you for yourself, but when they look at you, they must see the Ruler of Rulers. Unfortunately, what they see is more important to them than what resides inside you. Your royalty must always be directly in front of their eyes."

Piri motioned to his servants, who brought forth another carved box and held it out to the Pasha. He opened the lid and removed three long red-dyed heron's feathers and a large gold pin set with a giant ruby. He attached the feathers to Suleiman's turban, and handed them to the Sultan. "The time of fear had ended, and a time of hope has begun. *Inch' Allah*."

"A time of hope, Piri Pasha?"

Piri went to the side *divan* and sat down wearily. He removed his own turban and motioned for his servants to leave. Then he looked from Suleiman to Ibrahim, and back to the Sultan.

Suleiman smiled at the old Vizier. "Yes? Speak freely, my friend. 'The time of fear has ended...'"

Piri nodded and cast his eyes to the ground. "You know your father had spies throughout the kingdom. Nay, throughout the world! But, those he sent to Manisa to watch you governing there reported back to him faithfully every month." Suleiman looked to Ibrahim, who shrugged resignedly. Piri went on. "You and Ibrahim were watched, my Lord, and they reported to your father that your governing was splendid; your legal decisions just. Still, they said, you spent much time hunting and riding and sailing along the coast. Their reports described the lives of young men passing their hours idly as young men do. Your father was told that you were a wise and just judge, and that Jews and Christians and Muslims all received fair hearing from you no matter what the dispute. You have lived up to your name, Majesty, for the ancient Solomon, son of David—Allah's blessings be upon him—showed wisdom in *his* decisions and *his* judgments. And he lived to wear emeralds as well as rubies."

Suleiman absorbed the compliment. He asked Piri, "What did my father speak of when he knew he was soon to die? Did he ask of me?"

Piri Pasha hesitated, then sadly shook his head. "As I was with your father constantly before he died, it is I, alone, who heard his last words. Surely it is right that you should know what he said."

Suleiman waited, and Piri continued. "He said to me, 'I have no journeys left to make, save to the hereafter.' Nothing more passed his lips until he died. I'm sorry, Majesty, but your father did not convey any other words to you." Piri stopped. He thought he had gone too far in lecturing his new master on the wildness of youth.

He said no more, but rested his gray beard upon his chest as he slumped with fatigue down lower on the *divan*.

"No, Piri Pasha. Do not fear or be sad. You have given me hope, and it is my prayer that Allah will give me the strength to rule wisely and justly. The 'time of fear' I hope is buried forever."

Piri rose from the *divan* and knelt before Suleiman, who had now put on the black robes over the new gold tunic. Ibrahim placed the new turban upon the Sultan's head. The three red heron's feathers moved gently as the Sultan walked about the room. Piri quietly backed through the door, and then hurried from the palace. As he walked, he greeted the courtiers gathered there. He repeated again and again that now there was, indeed, "A Second Solomon" in the New Palace. He whispered to the Aghas of the Janissaries, and hugged many old friends. Outside the gates of the palace, the crowds heard the words repeated, "The time of fear has ended. It is a time for hope. There is a Second Solomon on the throne."

Suleiman and Piri Pasha were both dressed in their mourning clothes of black. The silent crowds could see gold brocade showing beneath the new Sultan's robes, just as the Pasha had advised. They rode side by side out through the city gates, and awaited the arrival of the funeral cortège that had made its way slowly from Edirne. As the simple casket came into sight, Suleiman and Piri dismounted, handed their horses over to the waiting pages, and fell into step behind the casket. Four Janissary officers and four Sipahi officers carried Selim's casket. The hill leading to the burial place was lined with fires that had been lit to protect the fallen Sultan from evil. As dictated by long-standing tradition, the body was taken from its casket by the eight officers, and in a simple ceremony, placed in a bare hole in the ground. There was none of the pomp that one might have expected for the funeral of the world's most powerful leader.

Suleiman and Piri stood by the graveside with lowered heads. The crowd was silent. Janissaries and Sipahis stood at attention as the shroud-wrapped body of their late Sultan was lowered into the ground. Their eyes were locked straight ahead, and there was now none of the wailing and crying that had erupted at Edirne when Piri

Pasha had told them of the death of Selim. They were Suleiman's army now, and they paid their respects to Selim with military decorum.

Suleiman continued the ancient custom with the words that were said over the graves of other fallen Sultans. "Let the tomb be built, and a mosque joined to it. Let a hospital for the sick and a hostel for the wayfarer be joined to the mosque." And with this, he mounted his horse and turned back toward the city with Piri Pasha. Then, he stopped for a moment, as if he had forgotten something. He turned back to the crowd and the army. Nobody had yet moved, all waiting for the Sultan to make his exit. He raised his head, as if a new thought had come to him. He added, "And a school...yes, a school. Over there." Suleiman pointed to the ruins of an old Byzantine palace. There were marble and stone and old columns strewn across the ground in disarray, ample building materials, he thought, for a start. "Yes, right over there."

He and Piri remounted their horses and began the slow traditional walk outside the city walls. Ibrahim pulled up behind them and rode quietly in their wake. They proceeded past the crowd and the armed soldiers to the Tomb of Ayyüb, where Suleiman would, at last, be girded with the sword. Though Piri Pasha was the architect fully responsible for all the events leading up to this moment, he would actually be just a spectator at the symbolic climax to the day.

They reached the place of Ayyüb's Tomb and dismounted yet again. Piri and Ibrahim stood aside, as Suleiman alone crossed the open plaza. The small mosque was dwarfed by the walls of the city. It appeared as an ornate miniature monument to Abu Ayyüb al-Ansari, the companion and standard bearer of the Prophet, Mohammed. There, a wizened old man with a long white beard waited for the Sultan. He was the spiritual leader of the Mevlevi dervishes. By tradition, only this man could present the Sword of the House of Osman to the new Sultan. For centuries, the Mevlevis had been at every girding ceremony since the Osmanlis ruled Turkey. No Sultan had ever taken power without this symbol and rite.

The old man was dressed in peasant's robes, which were in stark contrast to the priceless curved sword he now held aloft. Without lowering the sword—still in its jeweled scabbard—he took Suleiman by the hand and led him to the raised platform, where the crowds could better see the moment of the girding. He placed the sword into the belt of the Sultan, turned to the crowd, and with Suleiman's hand still firmly in his, said, "We, who believe from of old, give to thee the keys of the Unseen. Be thou guided aright, for if not, all things will fail thee."

There was silence in the crowd at this great moment, all wondering what lay in the heart of the new Sultan. Rumors of his governing in Manisa had reached the city, but few knew the soul of the man. They had all suffered terribly under the reign of Selim, the Grim. Suffering was an expected part of life for the majority of Ottoman Turks. How much, they wondered, would they suffer under this new Sultan?

Only a few people in the closest part of the crowd heard what the frail old man had said, but all had seen their Sultan girded with the Sword of the House of Osman. Many wondered whether he would raise the sword again and set out on more unending military campaigns as Selim had done; or would he use his power to help ease and enrich the hard life of the ordinary Turk? A chant began to rise among the spectators. At first, Suleiman could not make out the words. He craned his neck forward, trying to hear the words of the people.

The voices grew louder, until the entire populace seemed to be chanting together. Over and over they offered the advice commanded by tradition to their new Sultan: "Be not proud, my Sultan; Allah is greater than thee."

Suleiman nodded slowly, then turned the palms of both hands toward the sky to affirm the sage advice of his people.

The procession moved away again toward the Palace. Ibrahim looked at Piri Pasha, as the old Vizier seemed to grow taller in his saddle. It was as if someone had taken a heavy stone off the old man's back. Now, Piri could stand erect and breathe freely. Ibrahim wondered if he were destined to compete with the Grand Vizier. Piri had served Selim well for eight long years. He was the devoted and wise servant that every Sultan prayed for. *Can Piri truly transfer all that loyalty to the Son of Selim?* Ibrahim thought to himself. *He is old and frail, and Suleiman needs someone strong and full of energy...* He would not let himself complete the thought, *like me.*

Piri had done exactly as Selim had ordered. The peaceful succession to the throne was accomplished. Now he only hoped to live out his days in peace, tending his tulips and his roses at his home across the Bosporus. With luck, he would never wear *his* sword again, unless commanded by his Sultan. *May the Sultan never need my sword nor my services again, Inch' Allah.*

But, Allah had different plans for Piri Pasha.

Piri and Suleiman began their ride back to the New Palace. Ibrahim rode with them. After a while, as the shouting of the crowds diminished, Piri turned to the Sultan and said, "My Lord, the first acts of your office will be remembered by all the people more than anything else you may do. This is the time to show them who is the man living inside the robes of their Sultan; the man who wields the Sword of the House of Osman."

Suleiman did not answer, his mind acknowledging the fact that Ibrahim had said almost exactly the same words to him.

Piri knew this was a Sultan who could take good advice. After about ten more minutes, Suleiman turned to Piri Pasha and said, "I have heard that there are more than six hundred merchants here from Egypt who have been rotting in my father's prisons. I am told that they have committed no crime other than that of angering Selim. See if this is true, and if so, free them. They may then stay within our city and resume their trade, or they are free to return to Egypt. Make this happen."

Piri nodded. Suleiman went on. "Also, it has come to my ears that there are officers in my army and an admiral of the fleet who have taken terrible liberty with the laws of the Empire. They have cheated and stolen. They have meted out unjust and harsh punishment to those they should be protecting. Bring them to trial, and if the charges are true, have them publicly beheaded. The people must know we are a nation of law." Piri made note of this, too. He knew exactly which high-ranking officers and which admiral were soon to publicly lose their heads.

"Do you know, my friends," he said to both Piri and Ibrahim, "the *Kutadgu Bilig*?" Neither Ibrahim nor Piri answered. "Almost five hundred years ago, the Turkish ruler of the *Karakhanids* wrote on the ideal principles of government." Ibrahim smiled and nodded as he remembered reading this with his master. Suleiman continued, "He wrote, 'To control the state requires a large army; to support the army requires great wealth; to obtain great wealth the people must prosper; for the people to prosper the laws must be just. If a single one of these is neglected, the empire will collapse!' We will see that the laws are just, and that our people prosper, and that our empire does not collapse."

Suleiman would make good his words. Though he was to become known in Europe as Suleiman, the Magnificent, his own people would call him *Kanuni,* the Lawgiver.

A while later, the procession approached the gates to the city, and Suleiman saw the Janissaries guarding the entrance.

Suleiman leaned over toward Ibrahim and whispered, "The payment! The payment!" mimicking the cries he had heard at the ferry. "Yes, we will make the cursed payment!"

Piri and Ibrahim both laughed aloud, secretly relieved that Suleiman had remembered without their having to remind him again.

"For my personal guard, each man will get exactly what Selim has paid them. No more. For the rest of the army, give every man a bonus in keeping with his station."

When the payment was announced, Suleiman could not tell whether the Janissaries were pleased or not. His guards stood impassive at their posts, and nothing revealed their thoughts. Their eyes were fixed straight ahead at attention, and they saluted their Sultan as he passed. They were a splendid army, Suleiman thought as he rode past, dressed in perfect uniforms of blue cotton, topped with white, felt hats. Their swords, polished and honed, gleamed in the bright light. But, who could read their hearts? How could this new Sultan forget that in the flash of a sword stroke, they had turned against his grandfather, Bayazid, to follow Selim?

⚜ 3 ⚜

THE GRAND MASTER

Marseilles, France
September, 1521

The stagecoach careened down the muddy road toward the harbor, its six horses lathered and blowing as they struggled to keep their footing on the treacherous surface. The horses were covered with a layer of caked mud mixed with the foam that sprayed from their mouths. The coach, too, showed the scars and marks of the difficult overland journey from Paris to Marseilles.

The driver leaned back hard against the reins, straining to keep the horses in hand and control the speed of the coach as they pulled into the final run for the port. He ran the horses onto the old wooden wharf and reined up abruptly in front of two knights dressed in full shining battle armor, immaculate scarlet surcoats, and broadswords hanging at their sides. Both men paced nervously, stopping only when the coach stopped at the edge of the wharf.

Almost before the wheels had stopped, the righthand door swung open. Philippe Villiers de L'Isle Adam, Grand Prior of the Order of the Knights of St. John in France, jumped to the ground. He, too, was dressed in full battle gear with identical surcoat and markings. Older than the others, he had a weathered face and long, white hair hanging down nearly to his shoulders.

The journey from Paris to Marseilles was long and difficult. Philippe's bones ached from the pounding, and his joints were stiff from inactivity. He had allowed stops only to change horses and to buy food for his drivers. The route had been treacherous. Several times they had nearly ended their journey in a collision. At night, as now, there were no lights along the way. The wars between Charles V, the Holy Roman Emperor, and Francis I, of France, had brought chaos to the region. The roads remained unprepared, and bands of undisciplined soldiers roamed the countryside.

But, after more than four days of travel, Philippe debarked safely at the wharf, where his heavily armed knights awaited him.

"Quickly, my Lord," said the captain of the knights, "the ships are ready. We can sail on the next tide, which is only an hour away. Your knights are all aboard. We have sufficient food and water for the trip."

Philippe stared into the dark night, but could not see the waiting ships. His mind recoiled at yet another long journey. He did, however, welcome the relative comfort of this large ship. "What ships are waiting here?"

"The *Sancta Maria,* my Lord, the largest ship of our fleet. The one we captured from the Egyptians, and rearmed at Rhodes. And we have four smaller escort galleys, heavily armed with knights and cannon."

The carrack, *Sancta Maria,* was the flagship of the Knights of St. John, and was one of the most heavily armed sailing ships afloat in the world. It was the sea-going headquarters for the Grand Master of the knights, as well as a formidable platform for cannon, men, and supplies. This ship had previously been the *Mogarbina,* captured from the Egyptian Mamelukes in 1507 at a battle near Candia in Crete. The treasure on board alone had been worth the fight. She was longer and sleeker than the old round ships, and had four tall masts with square rigged sails. A large cabin, perched high in the stern, served as both meeting room and captain's quarters. Her new powerful cannons could reach out and destroy whole cities while staying out of range of shore batteries. She could carry a crew of over two hundred fighting men. The *Sancta Maria* was a machine of war.

Philippe nodded as he remembered how powerful his new ship really was. He quickly stepped into the small tender waiting at the dock. As the band of knights rowed into the darkness, he breathed easier than he had since he left Paris nearly five days before. The departure from Paris was so fast...so painful. He had no time to do what needed to be done. *Never enough time,* he thought.

The summons had been delivered to Philippe in Paris by two of the Knights Hospitaller of St. John, who had been dispatched from the island fortress of Rhodes by the Grand Council. The note informed Philippe that the Council had elected him Grand Master of the Knights of St. John on Rhodes. The former Grand Master, Fabrizio del Caretto, had died eight months earlier, in January, after a long illness. The letter went on to warn Philippe of several problems he would have to face in very short order. "The election was not easy, my Lord," the note read. "Of the three candidates, you and Thomas Docwra of England were separated by only one vote. And while Thomas Docwra took his defeat with the equanimity and nobility expected of a Knight of the Order of St. John, the third candidate—Chancellor Andrea d'Amaral—did not."

Philippe realized that this was, indeed, a serious matter. D'Amaral was an arrogant and difficult leader, immensely unpopular even among his own men.

The letter went on, "To make matters worse, d'Amaral did not receive a single vote, and has retired to his quarters at the Inn of Aragon, where I understand he is brooding over this perceived insult."

D'Amaral was Portuguese by birth, and his relationship with the French-born Philippe was tenuous at best. Most of the time it was intensely hostile. As Chancellor and head of the *langue* of Spain, d'Amaral wielded much power. His anger and pouting could do a great deal of harm to the unity of the knights.

Philippe had just turned fifty-eight years old when he was summoned back to Rhodes. He was a big man, over six feet and nearly two hundred pounds. He was well muscled, and wore a full, white beard. His silver hair made him look older than he was, but the rigorous physical conditioning of the knights kept him fit and active. His face was distinguished by high cheekbones, and a sharp, aquiline nose. He moved with a gracefulness unexpected of such a large man, and his quick reflexes had been finely tuned after decades of fighting alongside his brother knights. He wore his long, scarlet cloak with the white, eight-pointed cross of the Knights of St. John over the left breast, and another cross in the center of the back. He carried his broadsword in the leather belt at his left side, handle tilted forward, always within easy reach of his right hand.

From the earliest days of the crusades, the Knights of St. John had established fortifications at several places along the Middle East and Asia Minor. Their mission was to provide food and shelter for pilgrims to the Holy Land, as well as hospitals for the sick. During the five centuries of the Crusades, the Muslims had driven them from one stronghold to another in the Holy Land. Their worst defeats came after long and costly battles all along the Mediterranean coast, at Jerusalem in 1187, at Krak de Chevaliers in 1271, and then again in 1291 at St. Jean d'Acre, when they were driven from their last foothold. Nearly all of the knights perished in the flames of Acre, including their leader, William de Henley of England. Only seven of the Knights escaped. The survivors fled to Cyprus, where they began to rebuild the Order of the Knights Hospitaller. Finally, in 1309, they landed on the island of Rhodes. There, they were to remain for over two hundred years, tending to the sick and making life generally miserable for Muslim vessels sailing the Mediterranean. They preyed upon shipping between Africa and Turkey, took slaves, and amassed huge fortunes in booty.

Philippe was born of noble lineage, a kinsman of Jean de Villiers, who had been at St. Jean d'Acre at the time of its defeat by the Muslims in 1291. Philippe followed his family's tradition of service to the Order. He joined the Knights of St. John when he was still a teenager, arriving at Rhodes just after the terrible siege of 1480. By age forty-six, he was Captain of the Galleys, and at age fifty he was elected Grand Prior of the *langue* of France. For eight years, he led the *langue* from his quarters in Paris.

The knights, nearly five hundred of them, came from France, Provence, England, Aragon, Auvergne, Castile, Italy, and Germany. Each lived in a separate inn, or *Auberge*.

That they were perceived by their Muslim neighbors as nothing more than pirates did not appear to influence the activities of the knights. They continued to raid and plunder virtually all the shipping that passed near their stronghold on Rhodes. The knights were expert seamen, and they had little difficulty in taking almost any prize that caught their eyes. The location of the fortress at Rhodes gave them the perfect starting point for ambushing the Ottoman merchant fleets that plied the waters between Africa, Asia Minor, and Europe. They controlled several other islands in the region, where they kept lookout posts and small bands of knights and ships. The knights could board merchant vessels at will, taking the cargo and the ship itself. The enemy crews would be kept as slaves for the knights or sold off in the slave markets of Africa and Asia Minor. There seemed little the Muslims could do to stop the slaughter.

In 1480, Suleiman's great-grandfather, Mehmet, the Conqueror, attacked Rhodes with a massive armada. He hoped to destroy the knights and reclaim the Aegean as his own Ottoman Lake. But, the siege was repulsed, and Mehmet's troops returned to Istanbul in disgrace. Mehmet died on the way home, just fifty miles from the city. When Suleiman's father, Selim, died in Edirne in the fall of 1520, he was preparing a fleet and armies to attack the knights again.

With the enemy in full preparation to attack Rhodes, Philippe was on his way to lead the Knights of St. John in the defense of their island.

———

Philippe stood in the stern of the small tender and reflected quietly on the problems that he would have to face with Andrea d'Amaral as his Chancellor. The quarrel between Philippe and d'Amaral had started eleven years earlier, when both were lower-ranking Knights of St. John. In 1510, Suleiman's grandfather, Bayazid, had attacked Portuguese shipping from a naval base at Laiazzo, in Asia Minor, north of Cyprus. There the Sultan was resupplying his ship builders with timber from the rich forests of Edirne, near the Greek border. The knights had hoped to destroy the Turkish fleet, which had been harassing the lucrative trade routes in the Red Sea and the Indian Ocean. Then they would destroy the Sultan's ship-building base at Laiazzo.

The Order dispatched an armada from Rhodes to attack the Sultan's naval forces and then to attack the base itself. D'Amaral commanded the oared galleys, which were the main striking force of the fleet. These three-tiered vessels were low and sleek. Their oars gave them complete independence of movement. They were wholly free from the vagaries of the local winds. The galleys were armed with a pointed bowsprit for ramming the enemy near the water line. Boarding planks with grappling hooks held the enemy ships fast. The armored knights would fire a salvo of arrows, then scramble aboard to destroy the enemy in hand-to-hand combat with their heavy broadswords. Some of the galleys had small cannons mounted in the bows as well, but the main striking power came from the knights themselves. The principles of battle were those of land warfare carried out on a sea-going platform. As commander of the galleys, d'Amaral had technically been the commander-in-chief of the entire naval force.

Philippe was Commander of Ships, by which was meant the sail-powered vessels. These larger vessels carried knights as well, but additionally were heavily armed with cannon. They had superior firepower, but were at the mercy of the winds. The oar-powered galleys could maintain their maneuverability in calm waters, but were handicapped in high winds and rough seas.

It was the difference between these two kinds of ships that brought the commanders into open conflict. The two met aboard Philippe's flagship the night before the planned attack. Philippe was dressed for battle, his sword hanging as always within reach on a wooden peg near the door. The men were alone in the main cabin. Philippe sat at the side of the small table bolted to the wall. D'Amaral stood, rather than sit on the edge of Philippe's bunk bed. D'Amaral was a large man, heavy boned and broad. He had a huge chest and arms, which he used to good advantage in battle. He was dark-skinned and had shining black hair that covered his ears and neck.

There was just enough room to move about the cabin, and d'Amaral kept pacing the entire time. The strain between the men was apparent even before d'Amaral had insisted on leading the attack into the protected harbor with his galleys. The argument had reached its second hour, and both men were feeling the strain.

D'Amaral spoke again, his voice weary and tense. His tone was that of an exasperated teacher lecturing a backward student. The implication was not lost on Philippe. D'Amaral said, "We can be in and out of there before the Turk knows we are upon them. We will row in under the cover of darkness and take them in the night. Why, my knights and guns will have it over in minutes. Your ships can bombard the shore and their ships, set fire to the land base, and destroy all the timber they have. We will be gone before dawn!"

Philippe let him finish and then said quietly, "And what of these capricious winds of August. They shift hourly. My ships could enter that harbor and be becalmed in a moment." D'Amaral began to object, but Philippe raised his hand and went on. "Worse yet, we could sail in, and a change of wind could blow us into the range of their shore batteries. You would get out to sea, and my men would be slaughtered. I cannot allow the risk, and neither would the Grand Master risk our most powerful forces to the chance changing of an August wind."

"Grand Master d'Amboise is in Rhodes, and I am here! In command!" D'Amaral was red-faced and furious. His fists were clenched and some spittle showed in the corner of his mouth. He could barely contain his fury, and Philippe thought for a moment that d'Amaral might actually attack him.

Philippe remained completely calm as he spoke, and this infuriated the angry d'Amaral even more. Philippe continued. "I will not allow the pride of our fleet to be jeopardized by an irresponsible attack on uncertain ground. My ships will not be allowed to fall under the shore batteries of the Turk and Mameluke!"

The argument raged for several hours more. Though d'Amaral was technically in command of the entire fleet, somehow Philippe prevailed in the end.

The very next day, the knights' ships sat at rest outside the harbor, a decoy target too tempting to be passed up by the Turk and Mameluke commanders. They rushed out of the harbor at first light to meet the knights in open water. In moments, the battle turned to a one-sided slaughter.

The knights met the onrushing forces with a few deadly salvos of cannon fire from their big sailing carracks. Next, the knights' galleys closed with their own cannon fire, and then moved in to grapple the enemy ships. Just before the knights boarded, the archers sent thousands of arrows streaking into the sky and down onto the waiting bodies of the Turks. Chain was fired from the cannons, shredding the rigging and sails of the Turkish ships. When the knights boarded, the fighting was fierce. But, the Sultan's armies proved no match for the knights. After two terrible and bloody hours, the Turks surrendered eleven ships and four galleys. The survivors of the enemy were taken prisoner, and the Sultan's nephew was killed while in command of one of his own fleets of galleys.

Then, Philippe's ships closed upon the harbor. Just out of range of the batteries, they took all the time they needed to methodically level the fortifications and destroy the entire base with cannon fire. Finally, a band of knights went ashore where, after killing or chasing off the remaining defenders, they set fire to the Sultan's large store of ships' timber.

The knights then set sail for Rhodes with the newly enlarged fleet, manned in part by some of the captives chained to the oars. As they began the journey toward Rhodes, some of the Order's spies in the area sent word of a large Egyptian fleet seen heading south from Gallipoli to try to engage the knights on the open sea. Though, again, d'Amaral wanted to stay and fight, Philippe prevailed, and chose to run.

"Andrea, we are in no position to engage a large fleet now. Our men are weary, and many of the ships have more prisoners on board than knights. They would betray us in a fight, or at best hamper us. Let's just slip away in the cover of night, and return to fight another day."

The knights had always preferred to man their own galley oars with free men upon whom they could depend. The Turks used slaves, and only the lash of the overseers' whips and their manacles kept the prisoners at the oars.

So the knights returned to their fortress on Rhodes, and Philippe's judgment was vindicated. Few knights had been killed, and the Order's fleet was enlarged in both ships and slaves. Philippe's reputation for judgment and skill was greatly enhanced.

Only d'Amaral tasted the bitterness of defeat in Philippe's victory. It was a taste he swore never to forget or forgive.

—

Philippe continued to stare into the darkness as his men rowed towards the waiting ship. Finally, out of the night, there appeared the outline of his great carrack, the *Sancta Maria*. Just off each side lay anchored two war galleys, their gun ports uncovered, and their knights standing at the ready. A platform on the outer decks was built over the rowers' oars, providing a deck from which the knights could leap aboard the enemy ships. The knights were in full battle dress and armed. They stood atop the fighting platforms waiting for their new Grand Master.

Philippe was relieved as he boarded the ship that he would not have to face d'Amaral until he arrived in Rhodes. He needed time to think about Paris, to resolve his doubts and his sorrows. He could recover from his hard journey from Paris in this easy sail to his island fortress. So he thought.

—

The small flotilla weighed anchor an hour later. The outgoing tide sped them southeast on their course toward the tip of Italy. From there they would continue around the southern end of Greece to Rhodes.

Philippe stared into the darkness. The blackness of the sky merged with the surface of the water so perfectly that the ship seemed to float in a void rather than upon the sea. He felt a tightness in his chest as his mind drifted back to Paris. Had it been only five nights ago that he had said good-bye? So much had happened, so much distance traveled, that it seemed to have taken place in another lifetime. He ran his fingers through his beard, combing out the salty dampness that had already settled in the gray hairs.

He moved toward the rail of the raised afterdeck above his cabin, and stared out over the stern. In the silence, a small wake troubled the black water and reflected some of the receding lights of Marseilles. Within a few minutes, the lights flickered, dimmed, and one by one extinguished themselves in the sea. Alone in the darkness, Philippe surrendered, letting his mind drift back to Paris. Try as he might, he could not find relief from the anguish that pressed upon his chest as if a boulder had been placed there. He took deep breaths of the salt air, consciously slowing his breathing, trying to lighten his heart.

He had known that the day would come. For years, while he was still Grand Prior of France, he lived with the knowledge that he was the most likely of the Knights of St. John to be called to the position of Grand Master. D'Amaral's and Docwra's names would surely be proposed. Others, too, would be considered. But, Philippe knew, his own election to Grand Master was almost certainly assured.

When the messenger came to his door, Philippe knew that his world was about to change. Long before he actually stepped into the role of Grand Master, he would confront pain such as he had never known; pain of which he never dreamt. Paris and all that filled his life there was now behind him and would never be the same again. Less sure was whether he could make amends. Would Hélène ever forgive him? Would he ever see her again?

Three days later, the little fleet was sailing the channel between Malta and Syracuse at the southeast corner of Sicily. The weather was deteriorating, and the ships had closed ranks for an approaching storm. Philippe stood next to his helmsman as they beat into the increasing easterly wind. His long, gray beard was wet and salty with the spray. His black mantle was heavy and sodden from the rain.

"It will be good to see our island again, eh?" he said to the helmsman.

"*Oui, Seigneur.* It has been too long. And this weather will worsen surely." Though they spoke in French, the man's accent was clearly Portuguese. It was not lost on Philippe that his helmsman was a countryman of d'Amaral. The old man gripped the long, wooden tiller lightly, his hands callused from years of holding the hard, rough surface. The long, wooden pole curved down and back to the stern, where it was hinged to the center-line rudder.

Philippe looked at the coming storm and said, "You're right about that storm, *mon vieux*. My old bones told me of this storm many hours ago. And by the feel of them, it will be a strong blow. There is also a great deal of lightning in this weather. See there? Dead ahead of us?"

"*Oui,* I do my Lord. But, these winds and the seas give me no choice. We will have to run through it, and hope to be out the other side in good time, *grâce à Dieu.*" God willing.

"*Peut-être, mon ami, peut être.*" Philippe said absently. Perhaps, my friend, perhaps.

The storm strengthened, and the lightning grew closer, hardly an instant between flash and sound. Several shafts of blinding flame struck the water between the boats, and the noise made even the experienced sailors nervous. Most of the crews were on deck, so they could be available in the event one of the ships or shipmates needed help; and, so that they would not be trapped below in case their ship foundered.

The crew stood facing into the wind, as the old helmsman tried to hold his course. Philippe stood back from the helm, balancing carefully as the ship split the oncoming waves. Each crash of the hull against the sea shuddered through the wooden keel. The lightning kept intensifying. Suddenly, the blinding flash and the noise of one stroke of the lightning came simultaneously. The scotoma blinded most of the men for almost a minute, as the smell of ozone overpowered the salt air. St. Elmo's fire lit the rigging of the other ships and danced in brilliant green flames around the spars and shrouds.

When his vision cleared, Philippe could not believe what he saw. He was surrounded by the dead bodies of nine men, including the helmsman, who had been talking to him just seconds before. The clothes of the men were charred black and still smoking. The smell of ozone now mixed with that of burnt clothing and flesh. Dark blood ran from the corner of the helmsman's mouth, and the helm moved freely in the thrashings of the sea, bringing the ship into the wind. Neither Philippe nor the remaining knights could hear a sound, for the blast of the lightning bolt had temporarily deafened everyone on board the *Sancta Maria*. No one spoke. The knights stood in a circle around Philippe and their nine dead comrades. Not a man moved.

Then Philippe met their eyes, all fixed upon him. No, not upon him, but upon his hand. For there in his right hand was the handle and guard of his sword. There was smoke coming from the short stub that remained of the blade. The rest of the sword lay in ashes at his feet. Its very substance and being were nothing but a few blackened cinders of steel on the scorched deck where lay the bodies of nine of his brave knights. Some of the molten steel still glowed orange, branding a blackened scar on the wooden deck.

Philippe's hand burned, the pain radiating upwards into his shoulder. He tried to release the hot sword handle, but his fist would not open. The muscles of his forearm were frozen in spasm so that the handle of his destroyed sword remained tight in his involuntary grasp.

In that instant, a legend was born. Though Philippe was never to hear of it directly, the men believed that this was a prophesy from God. It was a sign that Philippe Villiers de L'Isle Adam had been sent by the Almighty to lead the Knights Hospitaller of the Order of St. John to victory over the Muslims. The new Grand Master had been baptized in fire from heaven. They had all seen it, and nobody could deny it.

Philippe returned to his cabin on the *Sancta Maria*. He settled down on his bed, trying to find a comfortable place for his burned hand, but failed to do so. It still throbbed, though the surgeon had assured him that he would fully recover from the burns. He closed his eyes and tried to sleep. As his body relaxed, he realized with some surprise that the events of the past few days had so consumed his attention, that this was the first time since leaving Paris that his mind had not been at least partially preoccupied with thoughts of Hélène. As he fell into the first really deep sleep in days, sleep protected by the presence of his ship and his knights, he saw her face again, looking at him as he left her apartment in Paris for the very last time.

73

⇥ 4 ⇤

THE PALACE OF THE CANNON GATE

The Topkapi Palace, Istanbul
September, 1521

"Take this letter at once, and see it delivered directly into the hands of the Ambassador, himself. Release it to no one else. Is that clear?"

"Yes, Majesty." The Janissary rose from his knees and took the letter from Suleiman. He placed it securely in a leather bag at his waist, and backed through the door. There he retrieved his sword and made for the exits from the Palace.

Ibrahim was surprised to hear the Sultan have a conversation with a person so far beneath him as a Janissary. Normally, there was almost complete silence in Suleiman's presence, except for his closest advisors or his Viziers. A centuries-old Ottoman tradition held that in the inner recesses of the Sultan's Palace, silence must be observed. The world of the Sultan would be free from the cacophony of random noise generated in the streets of the Empire. To ensure this, Suleiman had adopted a language of hand signals called Ixarette. He learned this from two mute gardeners in his inner court. The sign language obviated the need for any conversation with his servants, and served to accentuate the magnitude of the separation between the Sultan and his servants. As time went on, Suleiman became more dependent upon Ixarette, and verbal conversations with anyone other than his close advisers were rare.

Suleiman sat on the *divan*, drinking fruit nectar from his favorite jade goblet. Generations of Ottoman Sultans had drunk only from vessels made of jade, because the court scientists believed that most poisons would discolor the delicate stone. Suleiman swirled the liquid and cursorily examined the walls of the goblet. It remained a rich translucent green.

"Well, Ibrahim? What think you of our letter?"

Ibrahim smiled and nodded. He rose from the *divan* and began to pace. Suleiman allowed Ibrahim this annoying habit, for he knew it settled the man and helped him see through the various possibilities of a problem.

Ibrahim thought for a moment and said, "This letter must be sent. The *Qur'an* tells us that we must warn our enemy and give him an opportunity to surrender to us. Yes, the letter is necessary."

Suleiman nodded his head slowly. "But, it will have no effect. The knights will never surrender their fortress without a battle. But, I've done everything the *Qur'an* requires of me."

The two men were in the Sultan's Privy Chamber, now made up for the daytime as an audience room.

"Do you worry for the safety of the young soldier who carries the letter, my Lord?"

"Yes. You never can tell what the Infidel will do when bad news arrives. Do you remember what happened to my envoy to Hungary? All he did was bring news of my accession as Sultan."

"Yes, I do. Poor man, he was rewarded for his troubles by having his nose and his ears cut off! Only by the grace of Allah—and our court physicians—did he survive at all. But, I think, my Lord, that the Grand Master will know your meaning quite well. This 'Letter of Victory' cannot be misconstrued as anything but a threat. Though I, myself, am as yet undecided as to the wisdom of the venture."

"Why? Have we not covered ourselves with glory since we took the White City of Belgrade? Did our armies not show the world that we cannot be stopped? Have they not seen Suleiman, the warrior, equal to their wildest comparisons with Selim? So, now, why not Rhodes?"

"I fully agree that the Infidel knights need to be driven from the island once and forever. They have preyed upon our trade and shipping for far too long."

"Too long? They have been pirates upon our Mediterranean and Aegean routes for two hundred years!"

"Forgive me, Majesty, perhaps I spoke too mildly. Yes, they have been pirates, or *corsairs* as their new Grand Master would put it, upon our trade routes for two hundred years. Why, I have heard that sea called the 'Lake of the Knights of St. John.' And we've lost many millions in treasure and trade to their war galleys. Not to mention the enslavement of our people. Yes, we must make it an Ottoman Lake once again."

"It's fully time that they were stopped," Suleiman interrupted. His father, Selim, had never been happy with the knights' location between Istanbul and Egypt, and had been preparing to attack them when he died. "My war with Hungary was an extension of my father's war, and I needed it to take command of my armies. *Really* take command. If it were not for Belgrade, I would still not know how much I could depend upon the loyalty of the young troops. You think it was a whim that I took the pay of a Janissary for myself?"

"No, my Lord, I do not." Ibrahim recalled the day in detail. It was a wonderful display of the Sultan's cunning and perception.

Piri Pasha had wanted Suleiman to be seen as the true leader of the Janissaries. He had told the Sultan, "These young men are restless, Majesty. They long for battle. They live for nothing else. They have no families, no wives. Their only friends are each other. They live in camps, and train day in and day out to fight and to kill. And when there is no war, there is no extra gold. No reward. No glory. It's bad for them in the city, where they chew the bitter roots of drill and discipline and eat indoors at the kitchens instead of outdoors, as in the war camps. You must lead them. They must see *you* as their *Seraskier,* their Commander-in-Chief!"

The next morning, the *yeni cheri* were drummed to assembly. They were shocked to see the Sultan not upon his horse, but walking on foot among them. This was unheard of. They drew to attention, and squared their ranks in preparation for the morning march and drill. Usually, on these paydays, the Janissaries would rush wildly at the Paymaster, forgetting all discipline. But now, the

Sultan was among them. There would be no chaos. The officers and men were at rigid attention. The ranks were arrow straight. Although there were more than five thousand Janissaries gathered there in the huge Second Court of the Palace, not a sound was heard. Not a man spoke, nor moved. In the stillness, even a whisper would have been heard by everyone.

Suleiman walked in front of his troops. He wore his battle dress instead of the gold brocade and silks in which he usually appeared in public. His boots and hat resembled those of the Janissaries. He moved to the head of their columns, and then lined up with his men. Together, they all waited for the Paymaster's distribution. The Sultan was going to be paid as a non-commissioned officer in the Janissary Guard!

Bali Agha, *Seraskier* of the Janissaries, stood to the side and smoothed the long black mustache that hung below his jowls. He nodded to Ibrahim, who was waiting off behind the troops, mounted on his restless black stallion. The only sound now was the stamping of his horse's hooves and the occasional snort of breath from its flared nostrils.

Suleiman nodded to the Paymaster as he received a handful of silver *aspers*, and slipped them into his leather pouch. Ibrahim knew that these young men would now willingly die for their master. The Sultan was not a Sipahi, nor a galley-man. He was a Janissary! He was one of them. A Janissary could walk past the Sipahi horsemen now with pride, for the Sultan himself would go to war with them.

Almost immediately after ascending to the throne, Suleiman had led his troops to Belgrade. After three months, the city had fallen to Suleiman's army. The twenty-five-year-old Sultan had his first great victory, and the kings of Europe began to tremble as the news reached them of the might and bravery of the armies of this Son of Selim. In less than six months, the Sultan had returned with his armies to Istanbul, weighed down with treasure and slaves. All of Christianity waited in terror to see where his armies would turn next.

"Yes, Majesty," said Ibrahim. "That was a day, indeed!"

Suleiman smiled at his friend. "Indeed."

A servant entered the room and knelt at the doorway. He touched his head to the floor. Then, without rising, he began to converse with the Sultan using the hand signals.

Though Ibrahim was well versed in the Sultan's hand signs, he rarely used them in Suleiman's presence. He understood that the servant was announcing the Steward of the *Hazine,* the Treasury. Suleiman signaled for the Steward to be admitted to the room. The servant backed away, and the Steward entered. The old man was attired in a rich caftan of silk brocade and a white turban adorned with crimson herons' feathers. He knelt with great difficulty on the carpet before the Sultan, and pressed his head to the floor. Suleiman bid the Steward to rise, and extended his arm. The old man touched his forehead to the Sultan's sleeve and rose from his kneeling position. Ibrahim could see the pain in the man's eyes as his arthritic knees struggled with the ceremony of greeting the Sultan.

"Majesty," he began, "if it pleases you, I should like to take you and the Captain of the Inner House on a tour of the Royal *Hazine.*" The man kept his eyes bowed and waited for a response.

Suleiman inclined his head toward Ibrahim, who smiled and nodded. The Sultan turned back to the Steward and said, "Very well. Let us see what the House of Osman has, after so many years, stored for us."

The Steward bowed from the waist, and led the way from the Sultan's quarters. The small group left the Sultan's Privy Chamber, where the Janissary guard immediately formed their protective human wall around the Sultan. They left the royal quarters and walked directly to the Treasury.

The guards remained in formation at the entryway as the three men entered the multi-domed stone building. When they reached the store rooms themselves, Suleiman felt for the first time an uneasiness at the weight of the responsibility of his office. He could feel an almost physical mass pressing him into the stone floor. Ibrahim noted the look on the Sultan's face, but said nothing.

"First, Majesty, we should see the emblem of your power." He reached into one of the shelves and removed an obviously heavy bundle. He carried it with both arms to a wooden table, and set the package down. Then, he carefully untied the silk cords and unwrapped the brocade cover. He spread the cloths out on the table and stepped back, revealing to Suleiman the sword of Suleiman's great-grandfather, Mehmet, *Fatih*. The great jeweled weapon was massive in its bulk, and Suleiman realized that only a man of immense power could wield such a weapon in battle. The blade had a very slight curve, less than that of the traditional scimitars of the Janissaries. The great sword represented the power of one of the Sultans of the Ottoman Empire.

Suleiman began to sweat in the small room. He stepped forward and placed his hand on the carved hilt of his great-grandfather's weapon. The flickering light of the oil lamps bounced off the jewels and the shining metal blade inscribed in Arabic.

"I Place My Faith in Allah," Suleiman read aloud.

The Steward and Ibrahim waited for the Sultan to take the sword in his two hands, and heft the mighty symbol of the Empire. But, Suleiman merely ran his hand lightly over the surface of the weapon and then turned away. He nodded to Ibrahim, and then signaled the Steward to move on.

The Steward rewrapped the sword and placed it back in its niche in the wall. At the next station, the Steward said, "Here, Majesty, are some of the garments worn by your ancestors. The great Sultan, Murad, adorned his turbans with these herons' plumes, and these golden robes and caftans. Your own father wore these robes hanging here." He pointed to several robes displayed on wooden dummies. "They are of the finest gold filaments that can be found anywhere. Selim wore all these at one time or another," and he pointed to rows and rows of splendid clothing of every color and description. It was not uncommon for the Sultan to wear one of these priceless garments only a single time.

The men moved slowly among the treasures, as the Steward pointed out gifts to the Ottoman Emperors from the monarchs of Europe; clocks in gold and ivory; swords and knives encrusted with precious stones; finely tooled and bejeweled leather saddles with silver stirrups; chests of gold paid as tribute from foreign princes; a ruby-covered flyswatter; porcelains from as far off as China; a carved ivory belt buckle.

"It seems a pity that these treasures should remain here in the darkness," Suleiman commented to Ibrahim. He turned to the Steward and said, "See that these dishes are brought to the Palace and used. Make a list of anything of practical use, and see that it finds its way to my quarters. And the gold ducats from Venice, have them counted and shipped to the arsenal at Tophane. I want that sum to go to the cost of building the cannons that will arm the ships."

The Steward bowed, acknowledging his orders, then led Suleiman and Ibrahim to a deeper recess in the *Hazine*. The room was darker than the rest, lighted only by two small oil lamps. In a corner were hung several garments on simple wooden racks. Each was made of heavy white felt, trimmed in rough black lambskin. They were a far cry from the opulence and grandeur of the robes of Murad, Mehmet, and Selim. Even the casual lounging clothing that Suleiman was wearing seemed a stark contrast to the simplicity of the garments on the rack.

"These are...?" Suleiman asked.

"These, Majesty, are the clothes of the very founders of the Ottoman Empire: Osman, himself, and Ertoghrul."

A silence of deepest respect filled the room, as Suleiman and Ibrahim stared at the clothing. The Steward dared not speak, but waited for the two men to inquire about the history of the clothing. Surely they must have heard the story a thousand times before, as had every child growing up in the empire of the Osmanlis. Their families would have told them how more than two centuries earlier, the warrior chieftain, Ertoghrul, wandered with his tribes over the vast plains and mountains of Asia Minor. Hoards of nomadic peoples had traveled from the steppe of Asia, driven west before the armies of Mongols.

Suleiman would have been taught the history of the tribes led by Ertoghrul; of the years of starvation and decimation; of their wanderings and their pain. He would have learned how Ertoghrul kept his people together and alive through all the hardship.

Suleiman's mother had told him the great legend of the founder of the Osmanli clan. In a bedtime ritual when he was young, Hafiza had recounted over and over again how one day Ertoghrul witnessed a battle raging in the nearby plains. A large force of horsemen seemed to be on the verge of destruction when, for his own reasons, Ertoghrul led his people down into the valley to the aid of the nearly defeated horsemen.

When the battle was over, Ertoghrul learned that he had rescued the Sultan Kaikhosru, leader of the Seljuk Turks, who was about to be defeated by still another Mongol invasion.

The Seljuk Sultan rewarded Ertoghrul with a small parcel of land in central Anatolia, which became the first step in building the Osmanli fortune; this was the beginning of a warrior tribe that fought for whatever army they chose to aid, sometimes the Seljuks, sometime the Byzantines; an army stopped by no hardship that fate could put in its way; an army that ultimately would dominate the entire mass of Asia Minor, and culminate under Mehmet *Fatih* with the conquest of Constantinople, seat of the Byzantine Empire. This small tribe of nomads would rise to an unimaginable power, and extend their realm even into the heart of Europe. This was the beginning of the Ottoman Empire.

But, the Steward did not have to repeat any of this to the Sultan. Suleiman was well aware of every detail of the story. He knew that he was the tenth in a line of extraordinary leaders. He was the tenth Sultan of the House of Osman. None had ever faltered before the tasks necessary to perpetuate, strengthen, and enlarge the Empire. Suleiman stood before the crude robes of his forebears, and wondered if he would have the resolve and the skill to extend his empire through still one more generation of Sultans.

Ertoghrul wore these robes almost fresh from the bodies of the animals that bore them, he thought, *while Selim's tailors spun gold into garments. Each of my ancestors has had the strength to move forward, and each had weaknesses that could have brought down their kingdoms. Murad had been wildly reckless in his conquests. Yet he succeeded in building an army hitherto never seen on the face of the Earth; my father, Selim, was cruel beyond belief, yet he prevailed to conquer territories on the scale of Alexander; the unbroken theme of conquest and expansion of our empire lived through the strength—not the weaknesses—of my ancestors. Where will I fit in this fabric of history? What will my son think when he is brought here by the Steward of the Hazine? Will he remember a father who fought to extend the Empire? Will I closet myself in the Palace as did Bayazid? How will they remember me? The Warrior? The Lawgiver? The Lover? The Goldsmith? The Poet? Can I be all of these? Any of them?*

Ibrahim waited quietly as his master pondered the future of the Empire. The Steward kept his eyes downcast, waiting for the Sultan to stir. Finally, Suleiman raised his eyes once again to the felt and sheepskin clothing hanging before him. He touched the garments lightly, feeling the age-hardened felt and the still soft wool. He nodded, then turned on his heels and left the *Hazine.*

By 1521, life in the New Palace was reaching a grandeur and splendor under Suleiman that had not been imagined by his predecessors. What had been Constantinople—the City of Constantine—under the Byzantines of the thirteenth century, was now Istanbul, home of the Ottoman Sultans. Though the city had acquired different names from the many people who lived there—some 100,000 in all—the one most commonly accepted now that the city was in Muslim hands again, was a Turkish version of the Greek words *eis teen polin:* "into the City." For the citizens of Turkey it was, indeed, the City. Their City. Istanbul.

This was the most multinational capital city in Europe. Its streets resounded with the sounds of Greek, Italian, Bulgarian, Serbian, Persian, Turkish, Arabic, Albanian, French, English, and many more current languages of trade and commerce.

Shortly after capturing Istanbul from the Byzantines in the mid-fifteenth century, Mehmet built the Palace of the Cannon Gate, what would later be called the Topkapi Palace. But the citizens of Istanbul would still call it the New Palace for many decades to come. Selim had expanded the city's role as the center of the Islamic world. But, the pomp and ceremony that surrounded the Sultan had been secondary to the issues of religion and war. Suleiman knew well the words of the Prophet: "Do not drink in vessels of gold or silver, and do not dress in silks and brocade, for they belong to the Infidel in *this* world and to you in the *next.*"

But, when he ascended to the throne, religious as he was, the words of the Prophet were forgotten. The Shadow of God on Earth began to live a life of riches that would eclipse most of the treasure houses of the world.

The Palace was an enormous walled city in itself. It sat overlooking the Bosporus, perched on a hillside with gardens sweeping down to the sea. The windows of the Palace were described as the Eyes of the Sultan, through which he could see the outside world.

There were stables for four thousand horses. A hospital was located there, and kiosks where professional letter writers were paid to write petitions for people with grievances to submit to the Sultan or his Viziers. There, too, the Sultan's decrees were written and circulated among the people. The First Court was the starting place for the many processions that were so popular among the Ottomans. At the funeral of Mehmet II, a guard of 25,000 mounted soldiers and two hundred personal pages lined up to accompany the dead Sultan to his grave. Yet this enormous crowd did not fill the First Court. The atmosphere was always charged and exciting. It would not have been out of the ordinary to see an elephant or a leopard being walked by a keeper. Suleiman's accession celebration included a parade of elephants and giraffes.

To the left, in the Second Court, was the *Kubbealti*, the Imperial *Divan*. This was the meeting place of the Viziers and high officers of state. Four times each week, after morning prayers, the Viziers would meet and debate public policy. There, too, they would hear the complaints and lawsuits proffered by the citizens of the state. Every Turk was said to have access to this system of justice. The system was fast and decisive. Disputes were settled and judgments handed down on the spot, without further deliberation or appeal.

The Tower of Justice was a small room above the *Divan*, curtained from view. The Sultan could sit there secretly and listen to the deliberations of his advisors and his judges. The beauty of it was that those below never knew if the Sultan was listening or not. But, when displeased, he could sentence a person to death by stamping his foot, or merely opening a latticed window directly above the *Divan* chambers. The victim would be immediately led away to be strangled, beheaded, or stabbed to death at the Executioner's Fountain, just to the left of the Middle Gate.

Nor were women exempted from the Sultan's wrath. They would be spared the violence of strangulation. Instead, they would be tied into a sack weighted with stones and thrown into the Bosporus to drown. Their bodies would wash out to sea with the tide.

Even the Viziers, themselves, did not know when the Sultan might be listening. They, too, could be subject to his wrath if they behaved badly. Viziers were in constant danger, no matter how high their rank. Very few died of old age, and even fewer survived to retire from office. If they displeased the Sultan, their heads were cut off and displayed upon white marble columns in the First Court for all to see. Often, the written charges against them were displayed beneath the severed head, the execution order signed in the handwriting of the beheaded Vizier, himself. If there were no more room for severed heads, smaller organs such as noses or ears of the less exalted were displayed instead.

Behind the Imperial *Divan* was the entrance to the Royal Harem, where the quarters for the Sultan's women were situated. At one time, there were over four hundred rooms in the harem. The population varied between two hundred women in Suleiman's time to over nine hundred during the reign of some of his ancestors.

Suleiman's quarters were extensive, and were directly adjacent to the harem. This allowed him easy and unobserved access through a secret passageway to his mother, Hafiza, whose room was immediately adjacent to his on the other side of the harem walls.

Within the many rooms of the Sultan's quarters were numerous fountains bubbling day and night with tumbling cascades of water. These were placed as much for the purpose of preventing eavesdroppers from listening to the conversations of the Sultan as for their esthetic effect.

Suleiman's bedroom served as his sleeping quarters at night, and was converted into the Royal Throne Room during the day.

When the Sultan was ready to retire, fifteen chamberlains would precede him to prepare the way.

In the morning, the bedding and canopy were folded away in the corner of the room, and the throne occupied the place of honor. In the Throne Room, protocol was at its strictest. The Sultan, alone, was permitted to sit, while all others in attendance, no matter what rank, remained standing motionless with hands folded in front of them. Emissaries were led by armed guards into the presence of the Sultan, where they made three prostrations. Then, they might be allowed to kiss the Sultan's hand or, more likely, the hem of the Sultan's caftan. Lower-ranking supplicants, their foreheads still pressed to the floor, might reach up and place the Sultan's booted foot on top of their proffered neck as a sign of submission before retreating.

Suleiman finished eating his fruit and began to pace. Ibrahim could see his master grow restless, and did not finish his thoughts about the war aloud. There would be time for that when the Sultan called for a *Divan*.

"We have been trapped within these walls too long, Ibrahim. Arrange for us to go out and ride north to Edirne for a hunt. Near the Maritza River, I think. A small party of Janissaries and bearers. We will camp there for a few nights, and stay as long as the hunting is good."

Ibrahim bowed, and made his way from the residence.

As soon as Ibrahim was gone, the servant appeared. He pressed his head to the floor and knelt before the Sultan. "I have done as you have ordered, Majesty. The Sipahi you sent for is here now," he signed. A few minutes later, the Sipahi was announced and entered the room. He, too, pressed his head to the floor, and waited for instructions to rise before moving.

"You may kneel," Suleiman said. They spoke with words, as only the household servants had been taught to use Suleiman's sign language. "So, you have proved the faith that my Grand Vizier placed in you. Piri Pasha told me that he picked you to deliver the message of my father's death because he knew you would be stopped by nothing short of your own death. And you did well. He also told me that you accounted yourself bravely at Belgrade. This is good. You bring honor to your colleagues and to the Sultan."

Abdullah said nothing. He looked toward his Sultan's feet, and was afraid to raise his eyes. He barely breathed.

Suleiman looked at the young man and was struck by his physical beauty. Now dressed in the clean-pressed uniform of a Sipahi, he was a far cry from the muddied, exhausted lad that had shown up at the *caravanserai* at Manisa. Suleiman continued, "I have another mission for you. But, this must always remain a secret between the two of us. No matter what the outcome, you will speak to nobody about it, and you will carry out the task completely alone."

The boy still did not look up, but merely nodded.

"My Captain of the Inner House, Ibrahim...you know of whom I speak?"

"I know Ibrahim, Majesty."

"Yes, I am sure you do. Then you will have no trouble recognizing him when he leaves the Palace?"

"No, Majesty."

"He has been seen leaving the Palace at odd times about once a week. Late at night, when everyone else is long asleep. He can do this because of his position as Captain of the Inner House. But, still I have been told of this." Suleiman moved from the *divan* and began to pace. The Sipahi remained motionless. "I want you to wait at the Palace entrance every night, until you see him leave the Inner House. Then follow him, but take care that he does not see you. Do not underestimate Ibrahim for his fancy clothes and high position. He is a powerful man, and could kill you before you knew what struck. In any case, follow his every move. Find out what he is doing in these secret outings. Then report back to me. Do not confront him under any conditions. And, if you are found out, you will say nothing to anyone. Is that clear?"

"Yes, Majesty."

"Good. Then be off, and do not return until you have completed the task."

Abdullah pressed his head to the floor again and backed out of the chamber. Suleiman remained standing, deep in troubled thought.

The Sultan could not sleep. Long into the night, his thoughts were disturbed by the possibility that his closest adviser—his closest friend—might be a spy. Ibrahim was, after all, Greek by birth. Was it not possible that after all these years he was a spy for the Greeks? Worse yet, could he be a spy for the Knights of Rhodes? *It seems I have not a true friend in the world,* Suleiman mused. *Anyone close to me could be there for the profit they might gain. Any friendship can be tainted by the possibility that it is my power and wealth that attracts. The curse of the Emperor!*

He moved from his bed and put on a heavy robe over his sleeping clothes. He summoned his servant and sent him ahead to announce his arrival at the harem. Then he waited for word that his mother, Hafiza, was ready to receive him. Of all the people who wielded power in the Topkapi Palace, few came close to the *Sultan Valideh*, the Queen Mother. The *Sultan Valideh* ruled the harem, to be sure. But, her influence went far beyond its bounds. As the mother of the Sultan, she was his confidante and advisor. She was the one person on Earth he could trust with anything, any thought.

The Chief Black Eunuch arrived and bowed before Suleiman. He was a huge man, well muscled, as well as obese. He wore a scarlet-red caftan, completely edged with white ermine. His turban of white silk was almost three feet high. In his golden cummerbund, he wore a jeweled dagger in a gold and jeweled scabbard. The Black Eunuch had complete responsibility for the conduct of the harem, and even the power of life and death when it came to harem discipline. He had been in his position since the days of Selim, and nobody with a shred of sense would cross him.

All the eunuchs of the palace—white and black—had suffered the terrible pain and indignity of surgical procedures that made them suitably safe as harem guards. The closer to the Sultan's women the guard might be, the more severe the surgery. Ordinary slaves who merely attended the harem as servants underwent castration. Guards who might need to spend the night in the harem had their penis removed as well as an extra precaution against despoiling the Sultan's treasures. These surgical procedures were extraordinarily painful and dangerous as well. Most of those selected for the position of eunuch died as a result of profuse bleeding or severe infections. Of those who survived, many felt that death would have been preferable. To be the person selected as the Sultan's Chief Black Eunuch was a mixed blessing, for the price of such power was considerable.

The eunuch bowed to Suleiman, and turned in silence to lead his master to the quarters of the *Sultan Valideh*. They left the Inner House and proceeded through the secret passageway to the harem. There, over two hundred women were quartered as slaves in luxury for the personal use of the Sultan. The Turks had learned polygamy from the Arabs, and many of the Sultans spent huge amounts of money and time in the maintenance of the harem. While his great-grandfather had felt the need for a harem with over nine hundred women, for Suleiman the traditions of polygamy were an anathema. He was relatively modest in his activities there. Among his two hundred slaves, many were merely children, and others were older women—perhaps twenty-five years old—who would be married off to Palace widowers in search of mothers for their own children.

Suleiman followed the Black Eunuch into his mother's elaborately ornate quarters. In the large marble-walled room, the Queen Mother lived a life of unparalleled opulence. Her quarters were guarded by twenty black eunuchs, and she was attended day and night by a staff of more than fifty serving women. Her rooms were adjoined by a heated marble bath chamber, and gave out onto an enclosed garden, where flowers and trees were tended by her own gardeners. Most of the harem girls lived three or four to a room, in small cubicles, and attended by about fifteen servants per room.

When Suleiman entered the chamber, Hafiza was seated on the *divan*, and was dressed and washed as if this were a mid-afternoon visit, rather than so late in the night. Her eyelids were darkened with *kohl* and her nails painted reddish brown with *al Hanna*. Her skin was hairless, for each day the servants meticulously plucked and scraped each body hair. Hafiza's servants spent many hours of every day and every night washing and scrubbing her face and body. Her skin was oiled and massaged, and delicate scents from the Far East were applied to her hair.

As soon as the Sultan entered, the servants backed out of the room, leaving the two alone.

"I'm sorry to disturb your sleep, Mother. I thank you for receiving me at so late an hour." He bent over and kissed Hafiza on her forehead, and she in turn touched him lightly upon his cheek with her fingertips. Suleiman was comforted by the familiar scents of his childhood.

"It's nothing, my son. I'm here for you always." Hafiza, now forty-two, was aging with a grace and vitality that went with her high station. "What is troubling your sleep, my son, that you are up and about so late?"

"There is enough in my mind to keep me awake for the rest of my life. I hardly know whom to trust. It seems to me that everyone around me, everyone except you, could have something to gain from me. And, thus, their counsel might be tainted by their greed. I don't know who is my friend and who is not." He decided not to mention his worries about Ibrahim, because he knew his mother would lecture him again. She was not happy that his childhood friend had risen so high in the ranks of the imperial household. She feared that Ibrahim would rise still further under the reign of Suleiman, and the thought did not sit well with her. She had always looked upon Ibrahim as nothing more than an educated playmate to keep her son company.

"This is the burden inherent in being Sultan of the House of Osman. Were you the head of a smaller state, your burdens would be less. But, as you command the mightiest empire on Earth, your burden is the heaviest on Earth as well. Your mistrust is proportional to the burden."

"Was it so with Selim? Did he awaken at night with terrible indecision? Did he haunt the corridors of the palace as I do now?"

"Your father was Selim. He was Selim *Yavuz*, the Grim. Selim, the Terrible. Selim, the Protector of the Faithful. He had so many titles.

But, my son, he was Selim and you are Suleiman. I think you are well named, for the Solomon of the Book was very wise, as you are.

"Never was a son so different from his father. If I had not bore you, myself, I would wonder who your father really was." Suleiman looked uncomfortable, and shifted on the *divan*. Hafiza moved and sat next to him. "Do not lose any sleep over *that* question. Your father *was* Selim. Of that there is no doubt. But you are made of different stuff, and you must not fear to be the man you are. Do not try to be Selim. You will fail. I know you went to Belgrade to show the people and the world that the House of Osman rests in strong, decisive hands. And to show the Janissaries that you are not Bayazid."

She placed her hand on top of his and gently tightened her grip. In all the world, only she and Suleiman's consorts had the privilege of touching him this way. She thought of how the rules that surrounded him and protected him were the very rules that isolated him from ordinary human kindness. "But, you must be true to yourself. You are a lawyer. A poet. A lover of the arts. A goldsmith. You are gifted at crafts and at hunting. And you are kind and just." Suleiman nodded, but did not respond. "Yes," she continued, "I know you are given to some outbursts of anger and rage. Perhaps that is where you and your father share the same blood. But, where he would strike out and kill for the slightest reason, you restrain your anger, or recant after reflecting upon it. *There* is the difference between you."

"What was it like for you, Mother? You lived with him, as I did not. I barely remember him save for a few days here and there, between the wars and my going off to Manisa."

"It was much like that for me as well. He was away fighting during most of our life together. I stayed at the Old Palace and took care of you when you were little. I saw him between military campaigns. But, I did see a different man than you did. And I saw some things that nobody else saw."

"Such as...?"

"He was always good to me, and I think he loved me well enough. I am one of the few people in this palace who is not a captured slave. That's unusual, don't you think? You know I was a princess before he found me. A Tartar princess at that. My father was Mengli Giray, the Khan of a large and powerful army. He was your grandfather as much as Bayazid was, though no one would dare say that out loud. And so the blood of Genghis Khan also runs in your veins. My life was good before your father took me as his bride. And it was good afterward."

"And how did he treat you here in the harem? I have heard that he took many of the odalisques to his bed. Did that not hurt you?"

"My son, that is the way of our Sultans. That you do not follow in the footsteps of your father or your great-grandfather in that regard is of no consequence. It is your choice, and I think at least the *Kadin*, your First Woman, Gülbehar, the Flower of Spring, may give thanks to Allah for that. It's too bad that Gülbehar has not learned to read," she said as an afterthought. "She would love the poems you have written. She keeps them in a silk brocade bag, as her own treasure."

Suleiman nodded and said, "Yes, I think she would."

"You know," she went on, "I always was amused at the way the Sultan has to follow the rules and traditions that an ordinary man is not bound by. Why, the ritual Selim followed just to spend the night with a woman was hardly worth the trouble. He would have to arrange on the day before to send for the Black Eunuch, and tell him of his desire. For the *next day!* A girl would have to be chosen to 'Walk the Golden Way' with the Sultan. The girls would be bathed and dressed and lined up in the main courtyard of the harem, while Selim walked before them. Sometimes on horseback—since he was the only one allowed on horseback beyond the *Bab-i-Salam*, the Gate of Salutation.

"But, usually he would just walk in front of the line," and she laughed, "pretending faint interest. He would greet each girl casually with the Black Eunuch walking three paces behind him. He would banter with the girls, and when he found one he liked, he would take a silk handkerchief from his robes and place it upon her shoulder."

Hafiza pantomimed the parade, playing the parts of the Sultan, the Black Eunuch, and the girls. Suleiman suppressed his laughter, but he could not help smiling at her story. He had always loved his mother's storytelling. "A handkerchief! Really!" she said. "Then, as if they were merely out to take the afternoon air, and as if the girls were just another row of trees in the garden—or should I say a row of roses—he and the Eunuch walked on together and admired the wild animals. They would feed the peacocks and chase the ostrich. Sometimes an elephant was there to amuse them. Or a leopard." Hafiza was gaining momentum, and Suleiman had almost forgotten why he had come to the harem.

"Later—perhaps he has lost the urge by then, I imagine; it is so late after all—he goes to his bed, and tells the servant to bring the girl to him, that she might return his handkerchief. The eunuch brings the girl and the handkerchief—praise Allah that he gets his handkerchief back!—and the Eunuch is dismissed until it is time to return the girl to the harem." She giggled again, and said, "Yes, praise Allah for the handkerchief. The next day the girl is sent a dress and a few *aspers*. A gold dress if she has made him *very* happy. And maybe an extra maid or two to wait upon her. Then he will stay in the *serai* for several days, perhaps sending for more girls if he wishes, until he either returns to me or back to war."

She paused, realizing that she may have gone too far in making fun of a custom that her son, too, might continue. Then she thought, *But, I am the* Sultan Valideh, *and I can say what I will. I am not afraid to offend the Sultan. He is still but my son.* Suleiman became serious. He was feeling the pain and shame that his mother must have felt. "And didn't this hurt you, Mother?"

"My son, it is not easy for a mother to talk of this to her child. But, your father is dead, and you are a grown man now, with your own *Kadin*. You are the Sultan." She thought for a moment, hard pressed to reveal more emotions to her son. In the harem, the women sought each other for comfort and advice. They were so completely cut off from the rest of the world that they formed a tight bond of friendship with each other. Though they were competing for the Sultan's attention, there was an undeniable sisterhood of great strength. And though they lived lives of idle luxury, the emotional price they paid was very high. "So, yes, I will say it. I loved your father. But, I did not welcome his presence in my bed."

Ottoman Sultans did not marry their women. There was no ceremony to bind them together as there was for the ordinary Muslim. The *Kadin* could be displaced by another woman at any time. The greatest security came only to the woman who conceived the Sultan's favorite son, thus becoming the *Sultan Valideh*.

"He may have written love poems or war poems to me." Hafiza said, "but, he was not kind, nor gentle, nor considerate of my feelings when he came to my bed. So, for me it was of no consequence if he stayed many nights in the harem with one of the girls. That was just so many nights he was not here with me. As long as I was the *Kadin*, I bore what I had to. I was seventeen when I gave birth to you, but I became the *Sultan Valideh*, and my position became secure because my son was the heir to the throne. I don't know if there were other women who bore the Sultan's child, and if there were, I don't know what became of them. Perhaps your great-grandfather's law intervened. I'm sorry if this hurts you, my son. But, it is the truth."

Suleiman, again, was quiet while he pondered his mother's words. It had not been thoughts of the Sultan and the harem that had been keeping him awake. Now there was much more to roil the waters of his mind. He had come to speak to his mother of affairs of state. Now he was mired in the sensuality of the harem. Of his father. Worse yet, of his mother!

"Thank you, Mother," he said as he gently touched her cheek, "but no more of this. This is not why I am here. I have always valued—no, treasured—your advice. And I am in need of it now. Tomorrow, I meet the Imperial *Divan* to advise me as to the matter of the Knights of Rhodes. These Infidels have harassed our trade routes between Istanbul and Egypt for longer than I care to think of it. They have disrupted the trade with the East, and have stolen treasure that is ours. They kill and enslave our sailors, and capture our ships and galleys." Hafiza watched her son grow agitated, though he maintained an outer face of control and calm. "They rule from their fortress on Rhodes and hold power over us. We are the strongest force on Earth and this handful of Christians strikes at our heart without fear or remorse

"But, my council is divided. Some oppose a war against the knights. They point to the siege laid by Mehmet, forty-two years ago. They say that if Mehmet, the Conqueror, could not take Rhodes, then neither can we. Surely you have heard talk of this?"

"Yes, I have. And I have no information to help you with a decision, my son. I am your loyal friend, but I cannot guide you in this. No mother wants to see her son go off to war. But, that is a woman's point of view. If we women ruled the empire, I should think there would be fewer wars by far. A great pity *we* do not rule."

Suleiman got up and began to pace in front of his mother. She remained completely calm and silent. "Men rule the world, Mother. We govern and we go to war. Women will never rule."

Then he let out a long sigh, as if releasing all his frustration into the air with his breath. He turned to Hafiza and asked, "Do you believe in the prophesy of dreams?"

"I do."

"Then hear this one that I dreamt last night. In the dream, you were already dead, though you still appeared to me as an apparition. You spoke to me in the dream and assured me that victory would certainly be mine; that I *should* join the battle."

"Suleiman, I don't know what this dream means. Dreams may tell the truth, and they may deceive. If I were dead in your dream, and I am not dead in this life, then does that mean the dream is true or misleading? I have no idea. Do not decide such an issue on what may have been the result of a troubled mind at the time of sleep. Or too spicy a piece of lamb for your dinner. Go to your *Divan*. Take their counsel and weigh it carefully. Then make your decision and, having made it, stand by it with all your might."

Suleiman bowed his head, and hugged his mother. "*Salaam Aleichum.* Peace be upon you, Mother."

"And upon you, my son."

<hr/>

Suleiman sat on the *divan* in his Privy Chamber. He had heard a great deal about the man who now sat upon the cushions directly opposite him. "I think my father introduced you to me many years ago. On one of my brief visits to the Palace," he said.

Moses Hamon, now Chief Physician to Suleiman, sat on his cushions in front of the Sultan. He answered, "Yes, Majesty. I remember it very well. You had returned from Manisa to greet your father on his return from one of his campaigns. You met us outside the city. I recall your riding a wonderful brown stallion."

Suleiman smiled and nodded. "Yes. Indeed, I ride him still."

"My caravan passed by," Hamon continued, "and your father stopped me to present me to you. He was very proud of you. He would have been pleased to see that your ascension to Sultan was so smooth."

Suleiman nodded, and said, "My mother tells me you served our family well. The Sultans of the House of Osman have not wanted for excellent physicians since your family landed on our shores so long ago. When the king and queen of Spain expelled the Jews from their land, they did us a great, if inadvertent, service."

"You are very kind, Majesty."

"*Inch' Allah*, I will never have need of your services," Suleiman said with a little laugh.

"Believe it or not, Majesty, others have said that very thing to me. Everyone wants to have a good physician and never have to use him."

Suleiman smiled, and said, "You have a family here in Istanbul?"

"Yes, Majesty. My wife and son live with me when I am home, which I hope will be more frequently now. My father, Joseph, died in Damascus. He had served as Royal Physician to your Grandfather, Bayazid, and to your father as well. He accompanied Selim in the military campaign against the Mamelukes in Egypt, but died on the return journey."

Suleiman said, "I knew him only slightly. I was away most of the time, and he was kept close to my father's side. But, all of the Court spoke well of him. And your son?"

"My son is named for his grandfather, Joseph. He needs me now. There is much for me to teach him that he will not learn in school. One of the most important parts of scholarship is the process of handing it on to the next generation. As important, I think, as the practice of scholarship itself."

"Your people have always placed great emphasis on education, have they not?"

"Yes, Majesty, we have. We believe that there is no better tool to insure success than an education. Jewish parents will do almost anything to ensure that their children are educated. And, of course, the professions have the greatest appeal. Most areas of business and trade are closed to us. For centuries, we have not been permitted to own land. All over Europe, there have been proscriptions against our participation in any but a few livelihoods. In our family, we would consider nothing less than entering the medical profession. To learn. To serve. To heal the sick when we can. These are gifts from God. At the moment, this palace is served by sixty-two physicians, of whom forty-one are Jews"

Suleiman nodded, but did not speak. Hamon went on. "As long ago as the reign of your great-grandfather, Mehmet, the court employed the greatest physician of his day, Jacob of Gaeta. He was a Jew, though I think he converted to Islam in the later days of his life. He even became a Vizier before he died."

"Turkey is a good place for your people. The Christians, however, have not adjusted to change so easily. They still look to the time when they will overthrow the Muslims, and force their ways upon everyone."

"My people were slaughtered in Spain, and then again in Portugal," Hamon said. "The Inquisition has spread all over Europe, and the Christians have made it clear that Jews will not survive in their lands."

"My ancestors have looked at your people with different eyes, Doctor. We think of you as our *rayas*, our flocks. My ancestors were nomads, shepherds. The Ottomans know the value of culling a flock, but not destroying it. The European Christians think that they should rule a country where everyone is of one religion. The king of the country thinks he should determine the religion of all his subjects. The rest are killed if they do not comply. We see your expulsion from Spain as the killing of a fertile ewe. You have come here with a fecundity of skills and knowledge. Why would we want to destroy such a gift?"

Hamon did not answer. He looked down at the carpet, and tried to detect whether the Sultan was leading him into a discussion that might become dangerous. Suleiman went on. "Tell me, Doctor Hamon, what do you see in our city that you think should be changed? Though I try to get out among the people as often as I can, it's not possible for me to experience the real world. I am protected from violence by my guards. But, they also protect me from the truth. What do you see out *there*?" he said gesturing to the window overlooking the gardens and the Bosporus.

Hamon considered for a moment and said, "Majesty, I too have some trouble finding a way into the real world. My position as Court Physician places me within the Palace most of the time as well. But, there are things I *have* seen and heard that might be fit for your consideration."

"Please, Doctor, feel at ease, speak truthfully with me. You are not in danger. My family has depended upon your family for our lives, have we not? I would have us continue in such a mutually rewarding friendship. Come. Tell me what advice you have for me, that I may rule with wisdom; that I might help your people as well."

Hamon thought for a moment. Then, he looked directly into the Sultan's eyes and spoke. "Majesty, what you say is true. My people have found a home within your empire that we had never dreamed of. We came here with only our skills and knowledge, and were accepted into your world. It has not been easy, but we have not asked for an easy road. Only one that we might travel with hard work and diligence. The taxes we pay for the right to practice our religion is a value beyond measure. In Spain and Portugal, we prayed in cellars, in secret. The penalty for discovery while talking to God was death. A cruel and painful death, at that. Now we follow our own religion in the midst of Islam, and we are by-and-large left in peace. Our taxes exempt us from military service as well, and that too is a blessing for us, so that we might follow our own choice of profession. We have never been a warlike people."

"We have no need for conscripts from your people, Doctor. My armies are more than filled with the tribute children of the *Devshirmé*."

"If I had to ask for anything from you, it would be to consider one source of terror that still pervades the lives of my people."

"And that is...?"

"The Blood Libels, Majesty. From time to time, my people have been accused of the crime of ritual murder; usually accused by Christians, I might add. There is no truth to these accusations, for murder has no place in Judaism. This problem was addressed by your great-grandfather, Mehmet *Fatih*, when he issued a *firman* requiring that these cases be tried not by governors or judges, but by the Imperial *Divan*, itself. This would free the court from local politics, and I might add, superstition and bigotry against the Jews. But, increasingly, our people have been tried in local courts, by justices easily influenced by the people they serve. Majesty, would you consider reissuing the *firman* of your great-grandfather, thus giving royal teeth to the law that is now being honored in the breach?"

"This seems reasonable, Doctor. My position as leader of the Empire must rest upon a system of justice that reaches all my subjects. If the Christians are propagating Blood Libels against *any* of your people, whether here in the City or in the provinces, they will be stopped. Your people will have the protection of my court. Remember that when cases are heard in the Imperial *Divan*, whether I am in the room or not, *my* will rules. It will be done as you have asked."

Hamon bowed his head, and said, "Thank you, Majesty. That will be a great gift, indeed."

Kanuni, the Lawgiver, nodded his assent, and Moses Hamon backed out of the room.

—

Before convening the *Divan*, Suleiman went to morning prayers at Aya Sophia. In the great mosque, he sat on a small balcony above the throngs of people. The Janissaries tried to remain discreetly hidden, but their presence was felt. Armed men among the Faithful were evident. After the prayers were finished, the reader stood near Suleiman, turning his body and his voice toward the Sultan. In his right hand he held a sword, and in the left the *Qur'an*. Upon seeing the raised sword, the closest of the Janissaries moved nearer the Sultan. Though he made no overt motions, he placed himself between the reader and the body of Suleiman. Then, the sword ceased to be a threat. With both the sword and the *Qur'an* held aloft, the reader began to intone a prayer. "The mercy of Allah, all pitying, all compassionate, be upon the Sultan of Sultans, the Ruler of Rulers, the Shadow of God on Earth, and dispenser of crowns upon Earth, Lord of the Two Worlds, Lord of the White Sea, and the Black Sea; Sultan Suleiman Khan, son of Sultan Selim Khan." The huge congregation knelt on their prayer mats, foreheads pressed to the floor, and prayed together.

When the prayers were finished, Suleiman rose to leave. The guards kept the crowd in place as the Sultan left the mosque. He walked to his horse and mounted it as his personal guard held the horse's reins. Piri Pasha rode silently on the Sultan's left.

The crowd was always huge and overjoyed to see the Sultan so close up. Suleiman rode with a quiet dignity, his horse well in hand.

Ibrahim rode a few meters behind the Sultan. He smiled to himself at the sight of the ruler of the Ottoman Empire astride this wonderful horse, with its neck arched, muscles rippling beneath his shiny coat, nostrils flared. He wondered if even Suleiman knew why he was able to maintain such easy control over his usually energetic Arabian stallion? Did the Sultan know that the horse had been starved for nearly two days? That the stallion was suspended off the ground all night long, from leather webbing under his abdomen, hauled aloft by ropes and pulleys to keep the animal hanging in the air unable to sleep at all? That the magnificent animal was all but exhausted and could barely make the walk from the palace to the mosque and back? No wonder he was such a docile beast.

Just as he was asking himself these things, Ibrahim saw the Sultan turn and nod his head, smiling to his closest friend and confidant. And Ibrahim flushed, ashamed at keeping even something so trivial from his master.

On the short ride back to the palace, as was his custom, Suleiman distributed thirty-two pieces of gold to people in the crowds that lined the way. Every morning, his servant would place the same number of gold coins into the pocket of his caftan so that the Sultan might make gifts to the people wherever he went.

His rides to and from the mosques, as well as his other ventures into Istanbul, were the only time Suleiman had any contact with his people. His routine behind the palace walls was so insulated from the daily lives of his subjects that he felt a detachment that troubled him. He longed to know how the ordinary Turk lived out his days. On these little journeys into the city, he often ignored Ibrahim so that he could notice what was happening around him. Ibrahim understood just what the Sultan was doing.

On this occasion, as they passed a small market, Suleiman noticed a disturbance taking place to his right. The mounted troops drew nearer to the Sultan, but Suleiman waved them off. Only Piri stayed close to protect his master's back. A local policeman was in the process of arresting a citizen for drinking a new prohibited drink that had recently arrived in Istanbul from the Arabian Peninsula. The man saw the Sultan's procession and shouted to Suleiman.

"Help me, my Sultan. You are *Kanuni,* the Lawgiver. Help me, Majesty, for I have committed no crime."

Suleiman turned his horse and walked slowly toward the man and the policeman. His guard followed close behind, and the crowd gathered to hear their Sultan's judgment. Whenever the Sultan would stop, large crowds would press closer, making the Janissaries and Sipahis nervous and alert. They hated these unofficial changes in plans, for the situation was always unpredictable. The guards rested their hands lightly on their swords as they moved closer to their master. Suleiman had to motion them out of the way so that he could talk to the two men.

"My Lord, I have done nothing," the man repeated

Suleiman looked to the policeman. The officer looked very nervous and his face flushed. He let go of the arm of the man he was arresting and bowed low to the Sultan.

"My Sultan, this man has been drinking coffee. It is a corrupt drink. It is called 'the black enemy of sleep and copulation.'"

"My Lord," the man interrupted, "there is no law against this drink. I have been told that this drink comes from Mokha, in the land of the Prophet. Indeed, a holy man discovered it. Did

Mohammed, the Prophet of Allah, forbid us this drink? Does the *Qur'an* forbid it?"

Suleiman laughed and said, "A thousand years ago, at the time of the Prophet, there was no coffee. How, then, could the Prophet forbid its use?"

The man shrugged and looked down at the ground.

Suleiman went on, "Do you think that the Prophet of God would sit in the streets and drink coffee?"

Without looking up, the man answered in a barely audible voice, "No, my Sultan. I do not."

"No, indeed. And should we all not try to follow the path of the Prophet in our daily behavior?"

"Yes, Majesty, we should."

Suleiman nodded his head again slowly. He paused to think a moment, and then turned to the policeman, who was now looking proud and vindicated.

"Free him!" Suleiman shouted at the startled policeman. Then he turned his horse and rode on toward the palace. Ibrahim spurred his horse and moved up on the right, next to the Sultan. He did not speak. Finally, Suleiman asked, "Well, Ibrahim, have we done justice today? Has *Kanuni* acted with mercy and wisdom?"

"Oh yes, my Lord. That man did not deserve to be imprisoned for drinking coffee. Actually, I, too, have had a taste of it."

"Have you? And what was it like?"

"I liked it. It did keep me up late at night. But, as to copulation...I can't see that it hurt anything."

Suleiman laughed. "Then I see that we shall have to make a very clear ruling on this, lest all my outings turn into a court of appeals."

When Suleiman entered the *Kubbealti*, the Assembly Room of the Ottoman Council of State, all the members were already waiting. The *divans* that lined the wall were empty, as no one would be seated before the Sultan entered and took his place. The undercurrent of hushed conversation stopped with the Sultan's first step into the room. The center aisle cleared and the crowd became a tableau frozen in the moment; all the heads were bowed low, all eyes cast to the ground. The Sultan was joined by Piri Pasha at one elbow, and by his Second Vizier, Mustapha Pasha, at the other. The Viziers accompanied the Sultan to the throne, and then took seats at a level just below him. This was a special meeting, since in addition to the counselors of state, the room was almost completely filled with the Sultan's military commanders.

Ibrahim sat at his Sultan's right hand. He sat alone on a *divan* that could have seated three. This was a tacit statement by the military and the council that, though Ibrahim had the ear and the confidence of the Sultan, he was still an outsider.

Suleiman remained quiet for a moment, surveying the room carefully. He had made his own decision regarding Rhodes, and had dispensed wholly with the opinions of the Council of State. Now he wanted only the advice of his generals and Ibrahim on how best to conduct the coming campaign. The faces before him represented all the military might and experience that his empire could muster. These were the men upon whose judgment and strategy he would rely. Suleiman had learned much from his experience at Belgrade. But victory on Rhodes could be his only through the advice of these men.

Piri Pasha sat directly to Suleiman's left. He was, to his own dismay, still the Grand Vizier. He would rather have been the "recently retired Grand Vizier." It would now be a long time before he would relax in his tulip garden by the Bosporus, he thought. *This Sultan will have me back to war for certain.* Suleiman looked into the eyes of Piri Pasha. If he sensed his Vizier's discontent, he made no sign. "I am glad to see you looking well, Piri Pasha. And it pleases me that you will serve as the leader of my government as you did for my father. May Allah grant us continued victories under your banners."

Piri smiled and nodded to his Sultan. *"Inch' Allah."*

Still talking to Piri, Suleiman continued, "May *your* ancestors ride with us into battle, my friend!" Suleiman was referring to the fact that Piri Pasha was a direct descendent of one of the most revered and important people in the history of Islam, Abu Bakr. Piri was a blood relative to the close companion, father-in-law, advisor, and successor to the Prophet, Mohammed.

THE SHADOW OF GOD

"My Lord, I hope that I may always ride into battle with you. For few Grand Viziers are privileged to die at the side of their Sultan. Fewer still are blessed to die in the service of Allah, peace be upon His name."

Suleiman nodded solemnly.

Piri smiled and went on, "I am sure you have heard the story of the Grand Vizier who asked a dervish Sheikh, 'Who is the greatest fool in the world?' The dervish replied, 'Why *you*, oh mighty Vizier. You have done everything in your power to attain your office, even though you rode past the bleeding head of *your* predecessor, which lay upon the same spike as the bleeding head of *his* predecessors!'"

Suleiman laughed, though the room remained silent. A few heads turned to look at Achmed Pasha, who was thought to have designs upon Piri's job. Achmed kept his eyes on the Sultan.

Piri spoke again. "Our Sultan's victory at Belgrade should have made two things clear. First, the *ferenghi*, the Europeans, are afraid of us. They cower now, even as we speak, and wait to see where we will turn our mighty armies next. Each of their kings prays to their Jesus that it will be the *other* whom we attack." Suleiman smiled at his Vizier.

"Secondly, the Belgrade campaign made it clear that they will *not* come to the aid of each other. I strongly suspect that they will not come to the aid of the Knights at Rhodes. They may send a few more soldiers, and some food and weapons. But, they will not come to reinforce the island in strength. Their Pope, Adrian, has, our spies tell us, refused money or men in their defense. And the Venetians will not use their fleet to obstruct us. Though they have no love for us, they know that they are vulnerable should they incur the Sultan's anger."

Suleiman said nothing, but waited for Piri to continue.

"*Against* that, my Lord, is the fact that this Rhodes is the best-built and the best-defended fortress in the world. These knights have shown incredible bravery against many onslaughts. Even your great-grandfather's troops—may Allah's blessings shine upon him—were not able to breach their walls. Though they are a nest of vipers and should rot in Hell, we should not underestimate their bravery and determination in battle. In the past, they have either died bravely, taking many good Muslim soldiers to their deaths, or they have been victorious, slaughtering the innocents of battle, the women and children. Even their women fight in the end. It is told that two hundred years ago they slaughtered six thousand Turkish captives, and that one crazed English woman beheaded one thousand of them with her own hands! In victory or in defeat, there will be much Turkish blood on the sands of Rhodes."

The Sultan bowed to Piri and turned his attention to Mustapha Pasha, who was sitting next to Piri Pasha on Suleiman's left. He was a huge man with full mustache and a great black beard, which hung down over his chest. Suleiman had appointed Mustapha Commander-in-Chief of all his armed forces. Mustapha was also Suleiman's brother-in-law, married to the Sultan's eldest sister, Ayse. The men had had a long and close relationship years before Suleiman ascended the Ottoman throne. Mustapha was now Second Vizier, and nobody doubted his ability to function both as a military leader and as Suleiman's confidant. He was brave to the point of recklessness and absolutely fearless in situations where other men faltered. He was known for his furious temper, and his soldiers made very sure that his orders were carried out to the letter. More than once he had waded into battle, driving his soldiers forward, shouting and cursing and beating them with the flat side of his scimitar.

"Well, Mustapha, my *Seraskier*? What say you to our plans for these knights?"

"Majesty, those Sons of *Sheitan* have disrupted our lives long enough. Your great-grandfather was correct to try to weed them from their Island of Roses. And your father, may Allah smile upon his tomb, would have attacked them had he not been prematurely cut down by the cancer. These knights have captured eight other Dodecanese islands surrounding Rhodes. They use the islands as lookout posts and ports for reinforcing their fleet. I fear that they will expand their sphere of power further. Even now their lookouts and galleys on the island of Kos betray our movements and harass our ships. I am for our immediate departure. Sultan Selim had started the building of the necessary fleet, and we need only to complete that job. Our cannon foundry at Tophane has turned out the most formidable weapons ever made. With them, we should reduce the knights' fortress to rubble within days. I am ready when your Majesty tells me he is ready."

"Very good, Mustapha. Prepare your troops. When I send word, you will sail with our fleet directly to Gallipoli. There, you will join forces with the *Kapudan*, Admiral Pilaq Mustapha Pasha, and his ships. I will try to get Cortoglu and his smaller fleet to join you there."

"Cortoglu? The pirate? Forgive me, Majesty, but Cortoglu has failed us in the past, and I fear he might again. He fights for himself and his own profits, and I think we might not be able to depend upon him. His men do not respect him. He rules only by the terror he instills in his crews. He made fools of us when he let the new Grand Master slip by his fleet near Malta." Cortoglu had attacked Philippe's fleet many years before, when Philippe was a commander of ships. But, under Philippe's command, the knights' small force escaped under the cover of darkness, leaving Cortoglu raging and swearing at the empty horizon.

"What you say is true enough, Mustapha. But, I think we can make good use of his ships and his men. They will add strength and numbers to our fleet, and his duties will be merely to harass any of the knights' ships that try to come or go from the island. He will intercept messengers and blockade reinforcements from reaching the island. This would free up your men and ships for more important duties on the island. I plan to use you and your troops against the ramparts of Provence once we are established there. Should Cortoglu fail us, he will meet a pirate's end. His head will end up upon a pike as would any man's who fails in his duty to us."

The *Divan* was quiet. It was clear that Suleiman wanted each of his Aghas to make a stand and declare himself. There would be no avoiding this conversation.

"Bali Agha, my 'Raging Lion.' You are quiet today. Do the wounds you received in Belgrade still trouble you?"

"No, my Sultan. I am healed. These knights will know they have fought, indeed, when they feel the steel of my Janissaries. They shall drown in a sea of their own blood, and we shall bring you their heads upon the tips of our swords for your pleasure. If need be, the bodies of my Janissaries will be but the stepping stones for their brothers march into the breach! We are the Sons of the Sultan!"

Suleiman nodded and let out another of his rare laughs. "I can always look to you for enthusiastic killing, Bali Agha. We will all aspire to the level of commitment and ferocity that you display. And we all know that this is no charade spoken from the safety of the *Divan*. With you at their head, your Janissaries will perform. *Inch' Allah*, it will be just as you say."

Suleiman turned to his right and looked at Achmed Pasha, his Third Vizier. Achmed was an Albanian, and had risen in the ranks by pure fierce ambition. He was a devious man, and his colleagues knew him to be overly proud and often envious of the Sultan's affection for the other Aghas. Achmed had risen rapidly after the war at Belgrade, for his troops performed well. Suleiman had made him *Beylerbey*, regional Governor, of Rumelia. But, he now recalled him to Istanbul for this new war that was pending. The other Aghas all knew that Achmed eyed the post of Grand Vizier. Whether he would live long enough to see that dream was another matter.

"My Sultan, the men and I are ready to serve you. Anywhere. Any war. We will see that these knights know that the strength of Allah is with us; that under the Banner of His Prophet, our swords wield His might."

Suleiman turned and smiled as he looked at Ayas Pasha. He knew Ayas to be prudent and generally fair. Most of all, the man would set his sights upon a task and plow straight on until it was completed. But, Ayas Pasha was an undistinguished leader of men, and Suleiman weighed this thought in the total equation. "And you, Ayas Pasha? What do you say?"

"Majesty, if we are to rid ourselves of these Hellhounds, there is only one way. They must be attacked in force and for however long it takes us. Your Empire will not be safe as long as this nest of vipers is secure in our midst. They have had two hundred years to fortify Rhodes, and they have succeeded well. Your great-grandfather, may the blessings of Allah be upon him, laid siege to that island with fewer men than necessary to do the job. Also, he fought the war from his ships rather than from land. We should also remember that your people will support this venture. There is a strong contingent of merchants in Istanbul who threaten insurrection unless the pirates of Rhodes are destroyed. These merchants have lost so much to the knights' predations, they would gladly give whatever funds are necessary to support our armies. I believe if we commit our entire military to the task—army, navy, cavalry—we cannot fail."

The Sultan's eyes fell next upon Qasim Pasha, the son of one of Bayazid's slaves. He commanded a huge feudal force of Sipahis. His men were given fiefs of land in exchange for their services. They provided their own horses and their own weapons in return. He was respected by all the fighting men for his valor and his ferocity. He was a quiet man and dependable. "Qasim Pasha? Are you ready to go to war against the Infidel?"

Having seen the mind of the Sultan, Qasim Pasha had no chance to dissent, for everyone had shown unequivocal enthusiasm for this attack. 'Yes, my lord. I, and my men, are ready to leave forthwith."

"Very well. You have all spoken your truths. Now leave the *Divan*, and make ready your men and supplies." The men bowed low and backed out of the room. Only Piri Pasha remained. Suleiman waited until they were alone, and then motioned Piri to his side. Piri remained standing before the Sultan and did not speak.

"Piri Pasha, there is something on your mind. Share it with me."

"My lord, I have heard these men. They serve you well, and they all have fought for our Empire with no small success. Even Cortoglu as naval *Seraskier* is wisely placed, no matter what the others think. He is bent upon revenge against the Grand Master, de L'Isle Adam, for humiliating him in the Malta Straits. Cortoglu has a strong will, and a long memory for such things. He will be of value, though probably a source of great irritation as well.

"But, duty demands that I offer a word of caution: we have only just returned from Belgrade, and our treasuries are strained with the debts of war. We brought back many slaves and a good deal of treasure. Another war will cost us dearly, I'm afraid, in both men and gold. These knights have been a thorn in our sides for two hundred years. Though I would be rid of them, too, would it not be wise to take our time and rebuild our strength in all regards before we set out on this undertaking?"

"My old friend, I know you speak from your heart. But, I also think that your heart is older than mine, and perhaps tired of these campaigns. I know you loved my father well, and served him loyally. He kept you far from home for eight long years. You would be well and truly content to stay in your garden by the sea, and tend your tulips and roses in peace." Piri nodded wearily as the Sultan spoke.

Suleiman continued. "But, I need you now even more than did the Sultan Selim. I have nobody I can trust as he trusted you. Ibrahim, even though he has been with me since my wild youth, is still untried and not ready for the post of Grand Vizier." Piri raised his eyebrows at the realization that the Sultan had even *considered* Ibrahim for such a post. To elevate a childhood playmate to such a position was beyond possibility from Piri's point of view.

"Majesty, you have many fine leaders and fighters among the Aghas. I will admit that there are one or two less well suited for the post of Grand Vizier than the others. Ayas Pasha would not last long, I fear, in such a position of power."

Suleiman cut him off. "There are none other in this *Divan* who can bear this responsibility. The Grand Vizier is not only a soldier, but he must be loyal to a fault. As you have been. And as I *know* you are. The Grand Vizier must be wise, not only in the making of war. Any of my Aghas can do that. No, Piri, I need the wisdom that age alone can bring. I honor your experience and the store of knowledge that you bring to this post. I am fortunate to be the heir not only to the Empire, but to the Grand Vizier who served my father so well and wisely. I need you for my teacher as much as for my Grand Vizier."

The Pasha sagged in resignation, then quickly pulled himself together. "There are more things that you must know, my Lord. Permit me."

Suleiman nodded for Piri to continue.

"Our spies tell us that the knights already know of your father's preparations for war. They have seen the large fleet that your father built before he died, and they must have seen our continued preparations. They cannot ignore the threat to their island and they are making preparations to reinforce their defenses. Possibly, they may have already sent for more men and arms from Europe, though I think they will have little success in that regard."

"Have we captured any of the Christian spies?"

"No, my Lord. We have not. With so many merchants passing through our ports and cities daily, it is doubtful that we would learn much anyway. I think that there are Greek sailors and others who report to the knights as part of doing business. It is not necessary for them to have a full-time spy here. Any passing ship plying its trade could learn much about our preparations just from observing us as he sails by."

"And what can we learn about the knights?"

"My Lord, this is what I have come to tell you. It is of greatest importance that you know what your father has already done."

"My father? Tell me, Piri. All of it."

"We have good intelligence that the knights are fully aware of our plans, and that they are at this moment preparing their defenses. Fortifications are being strengthened and supplies are being stockpiled. The Greek Rhodians are preparing to retreat into the city and aid the knights. They are ready for a long siege."

"And how do we know such things?"

"We have a spy, too, my Lord."

Suleiman clasped his hands and leaned forward, elbows on his knees. "Who is this spy? Is he reliable? How often do we hear from him?"

"Your great-grandfather was handicapped by lack of information. Selim knew this. So when he became Sultan, one of the first things he did was to find an agent he could plant among the knights. Though he knew it would be many years in the future, he still believed that some day he would go to war. He planned well, my Lord. And carefully. For the eight years of his reign, we received communications almost every month. The information was written or verbal, and was sent by trading ships that plied the seas and stopped both at Rhodes and Istanbul. And it has always been reliable."

"Who is this man?"

"I am not sure, my Lord. I know only that Selim always trusted the man's information."

Suleiman stood and began to pace the room. It seemed odd that he, the Sultan, would know nothing of this from Selim; but that Piri Pasha had to tell him of it. Then, again, he had almost no contact with his father, and this spy was not needed while Selim was still alive.

"Can we contact this man?"

"No, my Lord. Selim felt it would endanger the man to have messages coming from us. This spy makes all the contacts, and it is always through different channels."

"When was the last time we received information?"

"Just this month. He sent a parchment with the captain of a trading ship that was bound from the East to Istanbul. But, I am not sure that all he tells us is accurate. The information from our other sources say that the new Grand Master from France is old and frail. That his health and mind is failing. Other reports tell us of a strong and able leader who fights alongside his men. They also tell us that the defenses are in poor repair, and easily overwhelmed; that the knights have not taken in sufficient arms or provisions. This, too, is at odds with what we hear from Selim's spy. And there is yet another spy who seems to be very well placed. But, we have no idea who he is."

"How can this be?"

"We only know that other messages come from time to time telling us in detail of the preparations the knights are making. It is always written in the same hand. It arrives on different ships, and is delivered to the Janissaries in the First Court. But, we have no idea who sends them. We believe the second spy as well, because the information he sends tends to agree with the messages we receive from Selim's spy. Whenever one of our merchant ships lands there, we get good agreement with the information in these mysterious letters. Perhaps it all comes from the same man, and is written in a different hand to obscure his identity. Or it could be that these men do not know each other's existence. We just have no idea."

"And what have these mysterious letters told us of late?"

"That the walls are in *good* repair in most places, but that there are some gaps, and that we might make use of these selected weaknesses in the defenses. But, more important, they say that some of the stores of gunpowder have been stolen and hidden by night where they will not be found."

"Why?"

"Well, the powder has been accounted for, and listed by the quartermaster. It is thought by the knights that there is powder enough to last a year. The Grand Master thinks that we will not last the winter. He calls us a 'summer army,' and thinks that we will retreat as soon as the weather turns bad. My lord, that is exactly what happened when Mehmet laid siege forty-two years ago."

Piri stopped speaking and waited. Then he went on, "Forgive me, Majesty. I must say this because it is part of the Grand Master's plan. He thinks he can just wait us out, and we will be driven off the island by the coming of the cold winter rains. But, you see, when we lay siege, there will not be enough powder to last more than a few months. This the knights will not know for quite a while. When they discover the loss, it will be too late, and they'll have to surrender. At the same time, the battlements on Rhodes *are* stronger than ever. The knights have expected us to attack and they have made ready for it. Their new Grand Master is neither old nor frail; rather, he is strong and determined. But, it is also true that there is little hope for support from the *ferenghi*, their brothers in Europe. This is just as we have suspected."

Suleiman remained silent, and so Piri went on. "But, from purely a military point of view, this attack seems imprudent. For us to move this huge field army to a small island with virtually no source of supplies is dangerous. The knights are very skillful at sea, and it is possible that they could cut us off from our supply lines in Anatolia."

"Go on."

"And, Majesty, our greatest strength is in the power of our mounted troops, the Sipahi. Our cavalry is virtually indestructible. They have terrorized some of the finest armies in the world and defeated them easily. But, in a siege against a fortress surrounded by deep ditches and high walls, they will be useless. They will merely sit in the camps and consume supplies. We will be fighting without the help of our strongest asset. Why not return to Europe and continue up the Danube to Vienna? There we could secure our position and eventually take over the whole of the continent. After that, Rhodes could be strangled with the silken cord of isolation."

Suleiman considered Piri's words carefully and long. He settled himself down on the *divan* and took some fruit from a bowl. Piri waited while the Sultan ate a handful of the grapes.

The Sultan turned to Piri and said, "Piri Pasha, you have spoken well, and I believe what you say is true. About this spy, I care not. Whether his information is good or not matters little. If this Philippe Villiers de L'Isle Adam is wise or not; if he is old or not; if he is frail of mind or not; none of this matters to me. I am the Sultan of Sultans, and I fear nothing. My armies fear nothing!"

Suleiman took several long breaths and resettled himself in the *divan*. Slowly the Sultan composed his thoughts and said, "We are well prepared for this siege. We have over one hundred thousand troops ready to fight this pitiful band of knights. How many can they muster to defend this stronghold of Hellhounds? Five hundred knights? Perhaps a thousand mercenaries? And the Greeks? Maybe a thousand?"

Piri nodded as the Sultan spoke. They both tallied the numbers in silence. Then Suleiman said, "So we will face two or three thousand armed men? Let us say five thousand at the outside. We will still outnumber them by twenty to one. And we will have the capability of resupplying our forces by sea, while they are penned up on their small island like so many rats."

Suleiman went on. "Our victory at Belgrade assured the gateway to Europe. But the knights on Rhodes still strike at the trade routes that supply my Empire. My great-grandfather was humiliated by his defeat at the hands of these knights. My father's next campaign was to be their destruction. Do not forget that my father left me an armada of over three hundred ships, which are this very moment preparing to leave Gallipoli for Rhodes. There are ten thousand engineers, miners, and sappers ready to destroy the fortress walls.

Between our miners and our new siege guns, the fortress of Rhodes will crumble. Our men will pour into the city like a pestilence. Then what will their knights do?"

Piri bowed his head and remained in this position. There was no way out now. There would be no tulips for him to tend. There would be no sultry nights overlooking the Bosporus from his gardens. Now there would be war on the Island of the Roses. And a terrible war at that. Only Allah, Himself, could know the outcome.

Abdullah, the young Sipahi, waited every night for a week. He stood guard in the shadows of the many trees that lined the gardens of the New Palace. His eyes never left the exit from the Inner House. For seven nights, all he ate was flour with water and spices, as he waited in the shadows of the trees. He barely slept, catching a few minutes here and there as he leaned against the Palace walls in the cover of the gardens. Since nobody knew of his orders from the Sultan, he was also required to perform his daytime duties of training and mounted drills along with his company.

Finally, well after midnight on the seventh night of watch, a figure appeared in the doorway, back-lit by the oil lamps from within. The man looked about, and then made for the corridor of shrubs that led from the Inner House. At first, Abdullah could not be sure it was Ibrahim, for the lighting was poor. But, after the man took a few steps, his gait made it certain that it was he.

The Sipahi followed Ibrahim through each of the Palace gates, staying in the cover of the nearby walls. At first Ibrahim seemed to be walking toward the Mosque of Aya Sophia. But, when he reached the front of the mosque, he passed by the doors and headed away from the water toward the center of town. For nearly an hour, Ibrahim went farther away from the Palace. He seemed to make several circles in his path, but Abdullah stayed close. It was easier for the Sipahi to go undetected once they were in the city, because even at this late hour there were more people in the streets than there had been at the Palace grounds, and the boy could blend into the crowd. His uniform and sword were hidden in the outer robes that he had thrown over his shoulders.

Finally, Ibrahim stopped his circuitous route and made straight for the poorest section of Istanbul. The Sipahi watched as Ibrahim looked among the bodies of men sleeping in the gutters and against fountain walls. Eventually, he found one in particular that he seemed to recognize, and shook the man awake. The man had been drinking, and still held the empty bottle in his hand. Ibrahim shook the man some more. Abdullah watched as he took the man's arm and pulled it over his own shoulder. Then Ibrahim rose from his crouch and dragged the man to his feet. They stood uneasily for a moment, as the man regained his balance. Ibrahim placed both arms around the man's body and hugged him tightly.

Then, the two staggered to a nearby fountain that ran weakly with cold water. Ibrahim sat the man on the cobbled street and propped his back against the fountain wall. He painstakingly removed the rags and washed him delicately with water from the fountain and a small bit of soap he took from his pocket. He threw away each piece of the torn and dirty clothing, replacing them with simple clean cloths he was carrying under his own robe. Finally, when the man was dressed and cleansed, Ibrahim again hoisted him to his feet and helped him along the road. Abdullah moved in closer now, because he was sure that Ibrahim was so busy, he would never notice he was being followed.

The two men moved painfully along the streets of the city, finally stopping in front of a boarding house. Ibrahim took some silver *aspers* from his pocket and placed them in the man's pouch. Then he opened the door and helped the man inside. Abdullah waited for a long hour in the cold night. Finally, Ibrahim returned to the street again, alone.

Abdullah went back to the Palace and got there before Ibrahim. He stationed himself once more at the exit from the Inner House, and watched as Ibrahim returned for the night.

The Sipahi didn't go to the Sultan with the news right away, for he hadn't really learned enough in that one night. He continued his vigil, and was able to follow Ibrahim on three more nights over the next two weeks. Each time, Ibrahim would find the man in a different place. Sometimes he would be sleeping in the boat repair sheds along the Bosporus. On another night, he would be near the steps of Aya Sophia. Always, the man was drunk, and always he wore rags. Each time, Ibrahim repeated the same process. He would gently wash the man and change his clothes, feed him, and then put money in his pockets and find a place to stay for the night. Sometimes Ibrahim would remain inside only a few hours; sometimes the whole night. Each time Abdullah watched these events, he was able to get closer and closer, until finally he could hear the words that Ibrahim spoke to the man. After the fourth foray, he left his post for good, and reported to his Sultan.

The Sultan's party had left Istanbul four days earlier, and had ridden west and north to Edirne on the border with Greece. They made camp at Suleiman's favorite hunting site on the banks of the Maritza River. Suleiman loved to spend August and September away from Istanbul in the more pleasant climate of the north. At the chosen campsite, his servants set up miles of gardens, planting roses and wild quince. The tents were elaborate and lacked nothing that could be found at the Palace itself. Though he took a minimal security force, there was no lack of servants in his camp. His *caravanserai* was set up in almost the exact pattern of the Topkapi Palace.

His quarters were at the center of a perimeter guarded by the Janissaries. There were plush carpets and *kilims* covering the ground, and the walls of the tent hung with artwork brought along from the *Hazine*. There were fountains and gardens, as well as an outdoor throne set under the shade of a large tree. The orientation of the Sultan's *serai* was such that Suleiman could watch both the sunrise and sunset from his chair outside the tent. He and Ibrahim had spent the hours talking together of the old days; of the period in their life together when there was ample time for reading and music and hunting. Ibrahim always had writing materials handy with which to take down his master's dictation, in case the Sultan decided to write a poem.

When they arrived back at the camp on the day of the falcon hunt, Suleiman sent for lunch to be served outside under a tree. Ibrahim retrieved his viol, and quietly played old Greek tunes in the shade. Neither spoke. Both seemed to be longing for the simpler days. While his friend played, Suleiman still wondered uneasily to himself about what secrets the young Sipahi would learn about Ibrahim.

They were finishing a lunch of cold yogurt and dried fruit when a servant arrived. Suleiman signaled for the servant to speak.

"Majesty," he signed in Ixarette, while kneeling before Suleiman. "Your mother, the *Sultan Valideh*, has arrived. She has asked that you visit her in her tent when it is convenient."

Suleiman nodded.

The servant went on. "And, Majesty, the Lady Gülbehar has also arrived, and she, too, wishes an audience."

Suleiman raised his eyebrows and glanced at Ibrahim. Ibrahim merely shrugged. The servant was dismissed, leaving the two men alone once again.

"Well, a visit from the *Sultan Valideh* and the *Kadin*, Gülbehar. Quite a day this will be. I'm glad we had the hunt this morning, Ibrahim, for the rest of the day will not be so restful. Why do you suppose we are graced with such visits as these?"

"I'm not certain, Majesty."

"Yes, well, I'll go see my mother first. The *Kadin* can wait."

Ibrahim rose as Suleiman left his place and walked between the rows of Janissaries toward the tents reserved for the harem.

He kept to the crimson carpeted path between the privacy wall, which was hung with row upon row of priceless tapestries. At the entry to the harem, Suleiman was met by the Chief Black Eunuch, who bowed low at the Sultan's approach. Suleiman acknowledged the eunuch with a slight nod of the head and continued toward the harem's entrance. There were six Janissaries guarding the doorway. They saluted as to a fellow officer, then bowed as to their Sultan. Suleiman passed into the court of the harem and made his way directly to his mother's apartment. Several of her servants scurried ahead of the Sultan to announce his arrival.

Hafiza was sitting upon several cushions placed on the carpet. She was dressed in a satin jacket, and her hair was being set by servants with several clasps of jewels. At Suleiman's entrance, the maids dropped to the floor, then quickly rushed backwards from the room.

When they were alone, Hafiza turned to her only son and lowered her head in a small bow. She reached out her hand, which Suleiman took and touched to his own forehead. Then the two embraced and touched each other's cheek in a gentle kiss.

"Ah, Mother. What are you doing in Edirne? I thought you were going to remain in the City."

"We were all so jealous that you should see the coming of autumn here on the Maritza River, while we sweltered in the last days of the summer. So, here we are."

"And who exactly are *we*? "

"Gülbehar is here with me. And enough of the harem to attend to our needs...and yours, if you so desire."

"And how many exactly would that be?"

"Not quite a hundred, my son. That should do, I think."

Suleiman laughed at his mother's extravagance. A hundred women in the harem meant twice that many in servants and cooks and guards. But, he could not say anything to reprimand his mother. He never would.

"And Gülbehar, how is she?"

"She is waiting to see you. She'll tell you herself. Your son, Mustapha, stayed back at the Palace. He has been sniffling again, and we thought the trip might be dangerous for him, with the air changing and the winds starting to blow here. Not good for children to have too many changes in climate."

"Yes, Mother. I miss him, though. Perhaps we'll go back to the City a few days early so that I can see him. It's been a bit too long for me. And when we go to Rhodes, it may be very long indeed before I can see him again."

Hafiza frowned, but said nothing. She was not in favor of still another military campaign, still more Turkish lives lost in battle. But, she kept silent because she knew that her son was intent upon dislodging the Infidels from their island. And, since the Shadow of God would be constantly protected by his Household Janissaries, he would never be in any real danger. It was one thing for the leaders of the knights to fight alongside their men, but certainly not the Sultan.

Suleiman started to sit down, but Hafiza shooed him away like a badly behaved child. She waved both hands in a gesture of dismissal, something no one else in the Empire could do.

"No. No. No," she said waving both hands. "Go to Gülbehar, and be with her. I think she has a present for you."

"A present?" His eyes lit up like a little boy. "What could that be?"

"You'll have to go to her and see for yourself."

Suleiman smiled and hugged his mother again. He bent and kissed her on the top of her head, happy to smell the familiar rose fragrance that he had known since he was a little boy, a fragrance that meant home.

———

As he entered Gülbehar's quarters, Suleiman was struck at how excited he had become at the surprise appearance of his family. He was a little sad that Mustapha was not there, but in his heart he knew that this would give him more time alone with Gülbehar. Unlike his father, his grandfather, and his great-grandfather, Suleiman did not make many visits to the harem.

Suleiman walked quickly into Gülbehar's room to find her sitting quietly on the *divan*. Clearly, she had been waiting for his arrival; her maids were nowhere to be seen. She was dressed in a fine silk robe, her hair done up in jewels, perfumed in a scent totally different from that of Hafiza. As Suleiman crossed the carpet to her, Gülbehar slipped to her knees and pressed her head to the floor. Suleiman took her hand and led her back to the *divan,* where he sat next to her. She remained silent, but never took her eyes off his. He was happy to see a look of intense joy and love in her eyes.

Before bidding her to rise, Suleiman took a moment to look at his First Lady. She was tall for Circassian, and more slender than most of the women in the harem. Her light willowy hair and fresh clear skin had brought her the nickname, Flower of Spring. Suleiman smiled at the sight of her and touched her gently on the top of her soft hair. As she rose, he could smell her perfume permeate the air around him.

Gülbehar let go of his hand and reached down to pick up a packet from the carpet. It was flat and wrapped in crimson velvet, stitched in gold edging. She handed it to Suleiman and said, "I found this for you, Majesty. I hope it will make you safe." She lowered her eyes and waited for him to open it.

Suleiman smiled, and admired this woman who would find a gift for a man who owned nearly all there was to own in the world. What could she have possibly found that he didn't already have?

He undid the package and dropped the wrapping to the floor. Inside was a white cotton pullover vest with short sleet sleeves. It was freshly pressed and completely free from wrinkles. On the vest was painted a pattern of small squares in black ink. Hundreds of them, both front and back, each with an Arabic symbol or words inside. The entire front and back of the vest was covered in this writing. Even the sides under the arms were inscribed with letters and words.

Suleiman held it up to the light. It was thin and fragile looking, and though he could read the letters, he had never seen anything quite like it before.

"What is this, Gülbehar? What have you found for me?"

Gülbehar laughed and took it from him. She held it by both shoulders and presented the front to him. "It's a medicinal shirt, Majesty. I got it from a holy man who told me that he had a dream in which the Prophet—may His soul rest eternally in peace—came to him and gave him directions for making this shirt. He recited sacred names and words that will protect you. He says it will even turn away bullets and arrows. It is truly magical, my Lord. You must wear it when you next go into battle."

Suleiman took the shirt and held it up to his chest. "It will fit nicely under my robes and even my armor. I will wear it whenever I go to war. And for this wonderful gift, I thank you. And I thank the Prophet, may his soul rest in peace, for sending the holy man this dream."

He put the shirt aside on the *divan* and took Gülbehar's hand in his. "Who but you could find such a gift for me? Thank you. And, what of Mustapha?"

"He is well, my Lord. He walks and he runs away from his guards at every chance. He tries to hide from them, and they pretend they can't find him. He is a love and of course he misses seeing his father, but I feared bringing him here to you. He is still just a baby, and may become sick on such a trip. Better that he stay at the Palace for now."

"Yes, the *Sultan Valideh* told me. But, I am pleased you are here, and we'll all be back in the City before long anyway. Have your dinner, and I will send for you later. You will spend the night with me. It's been too long." Suleiman kissed Gülbehar's cheeks and rose to leave.

As soon as he was gone, Gülbehar's maids rushed into the room and began preparing her for her night with the Sultan. She would be bathed and perfumed. Hairs would be plucked and scraped and dark brown kohl applied to her eyelids. She would wear a sheer silk gown sewn with gold, a gift Suleiman had given her after her last night in his bed. Pearls would be woven into her hair.

After all the preparations, she would remain in her tent, sitting on the *divan* with her maids in attendance, quietly awaiting the summons from her Sultan.

—

Abdullah entered the Privy Chamber of the Sultan. He pressed his head against the floor, then rose as Suleiman bid him to speak.

"You have been gone for four weeks, young man. I hope you have news for me that will put this matter to rest. "

"I hope so, too, Majesty. I followed the Captain of the Inner House as you instructed me, for four nights over as many weeks. He never did actually catch me, though on one night he looked in my direction for a very long time. I think he would have fought with me, but he feared for the safety of the man with him."

"What man? You get ahead of yourself. Start from the beginning."

And so the young Sipahi collected himself, and told the story of each of the nights in detail; how Ibrahim always found the same derelict man sleeping in different parts of the city; how he would bathe and clothe him; how he would buy him food and shelter; and how he would sometimes stay the night with him.

Suleiman stirred uneasily. "And? The man? Did you find out who he is?"

"I did, Majesty. On the last visit, I took it upon myself to get very close and listen to them talk. It was the very last night, and I followed them into a poor restaurant in a shabby part of the city. They sat at a table near the window, and I crouched beneath the outside sill all through their supper. I could not hear all of what they said. At first there was only talk of the sea. It soon became apparent that the man had been a sailor. From Greece, I think."

Suleiman raised his bushy eyebrows. "How did you know he was from Greece?"

"Because, Majesty, though they spoke mostly in Turkish, the old man had a heavy Greek accent. I heard him talk of his days at sea, and how he wished he could sail away from here. Then he would talk in a language unfamiliar to me, but I think it was Greek. I have learned a few words of Greek when I was at your schools, and it sounded thus to me."

"So, this Greek sailor, who was he? A spy? Is my Captain of the Inner House selling my plans to a Greek sailor? From Rhodes perhaps?"

"No, Majesty, he was not. The Captain of the Inner House is not a spy. This, I know for certain. For many times on that night he called the man, 'Baba.' This poor old man was his father."

Suleiman sat quietly in his tent, after a light dinner of lamb and rice. He reclined on a nest of cushions in the middle of the dimly lit room; he was warmed by the heat of a coal brazier. The Sultan was just taking a taste of lemon sorbet when a page announced himself and entered the room. He knelt, pressing his head to the floor. Suleiman signaled for the page to rise and waited.

The page signed that the *Kadin* Gülbehar had arrived in the Sultan's quarters from the harem, and was being escorted by the Black Eunuch. Suleiman nodded and dismissed the page with a wave of the hand.

There was a short interval before Suleiman heard muffled footsteps in the corridor, followed by the appearance of the Chief Black

Eunuch. The eunuch bowed and announced the arrival of the *Kadin*. Putting down the remains of his sorbet and adjusting his robes, Suleiman signaled for Gülbehar to be brought in.

She entered the room unattended, having dismissed her maids at the entrance to the Sultan's quarters. In an ancient Ottoman ceremony, Gülbehar knelt at the door and then crawled the several yards to the Sultan's *divan* in silence. She placed her forehead to the carpet while reaching up, taking Suleiman's ankle in her hand. As an act of submission to his power and her own vulnerability, she placed his foot upon the back of her neck, holding it there for several seconds before releasing it.

Suleiman reached down and without a word took her hand in his. He pulled her gently to her knees and guided her to the cushions beside him. He was touched at her preservation of the traditions of subservience. In the several years of their relationship, Gülbehar had quickly become more informal in his presence. She was allowed free access to his presence, often arriving with little notice and in many cases no escort at all. But those were the days of Suleiman's governorship in Manisa before he had ascended to the throne. Somehow, from the day of his girding with the Sword of the House of Osman, without specific agreement, their relationship changed. But, here in his tent, Suleiman, relaxed with his *Kadin*, fell into the role of lover.

Suleiman felt Gülbehar settle onto the *divan* and nuzzle her body closer to his. Her thigh was warm against him, a faint taste of her perfume barely detectable on her skin. Not a word passed between them, for they had done all their talking earlier in the day. There was little for Suleiman to discuss with Gülbehar outside of the well-being of their baby son and heir, Mustapha.

Now, in the silence of the encampment, the couple tried to feel completely alone. Suleiman, more than Gülbehar, had learned to ignore the reality that there were dozens of armed men and servants within earshot of him at all times. Though the tent walls were thicker and more opulently draped than the ordinary military tent, sound still traveled beyond the limits of his privacy. For Gülbehar, it was hard to relax knowing that her words and sounds would be overheard. The Sultan had always lived his life in such a protected environment, but his eighteen-year-old *Kadin* was still learning.

For what seemed like a very long time, Gülbehar waited for her master to respond to her presence. She could feel his body slowly relax against her and soon she was close enough to detect the faint scent of spiced lamb. She herself had not eaten that evening, so that there would be no unnatural taste on her tongue or breath. Everything in her day had been carefully designed to please the Sultan. Her future, her whole life, and the life of her child could rest on the whim of this man who had nearly two hundred other women waiting to please him.

Suleiman let out a long sigh, signaling to Gülbehar that he was relaxed and ready for her attentions. She responded to this minute invitation by easing out of her caftan, revealing a rose-colored gauze top that showed the hint of the curve of her breasts and the suggestion of her nipples. Suleiman looked into her eyes and smiled. He placed his hand on her thigh and gently stroked her through the silk layers of her long gown. She in turn placed her hand for the first time that night on Suleiman's thigh and gently caressed him in return. She could feel his response to her approach in the slight increase in the depth of his breathing. She continued to stroke him until she could feel his erection growing beneath his loose-fitting pants. She stopped for a moment and leaned away to blow out the oil light nearest the *divan*.

She reached up and started to undo the pearls that held her hair high on her head. The jewelry snagged for a moment, and Suleiman took her hands away to help her himself. The feel of her soft hair aroused him even more than her touching him. When the jewels were free, he dropped them to the floor. Her hair fell around her shoulders and he kissed the top of her head, smelling even more strongly the scent of her perfume.

Gülbehar pulled at a coverlet that lay nearby, covering both her legs and Suleiman's. Then in the very dim light of the room, she undid the buttons of her top and let it fall away. Suleiman bent down to kiss her bare breasts as she slid the rest of the way out of her many layers of silk. When she was completely naked, she pulled the coverlet higher over her body and enveloped them both in a silk cocoon. The Sultan undressed himself and dropped his own clothing at the side of the *divan*. They stopped for a moment, holding each other quietly, motionlessly. Still, not a word had passed between them.

Gülbehar relaxed her hold on Suleiman, sliding slowly beneath the coverlet. As she disappeared from sight, Suleiman gave in completely to the feelings that were washing over him. As he felt her mouth and tongue explore his body, all the thoughts of his empire and his coming war faded away.

Gülbehar took her lover into her mouth as she wrapped her arms around his waist. Her fingers explored his back and his buttocks. In the briefest time, Suleiman burst with the pent-up longing that had gone so long unsatisfied. When he was finished, Gülbehar crept up next to him and held his sweating body to hers. She felt him sleep awhile and she slept, too. Sometime later, she woke to feel Suleiman caressing her in the darkness of the room, the only other lamp now extinguished. She responded to him and he grew aroused again and quickly entered her. The two made love through the night, like new lovers. They slept again, and when the morning light brightened the roof of the tent, Suleiman found himself on his cushions, beneath his silk coverlet, naked and relaxed, and alone once more.

⚜ 5 ⚜

THE STRONGHOLD

Rhodes, the Fortress of the Knights of St. John
May, 1522

When the newly elected Grand Master, Philippe Villiers de L'Isle Adam, finally reached the island of Rhodes on September 19th, 1521, he was put ashore at the Commercial Port, near the Tower of Naillac. He looked up to the battlements where most of his youth had been spent. Philippe had been born of a noble family in Beauvais, France, in 1464. He was a kinsman of one of the Order's most famous Grand Masters, Jean de Villiers. It was de Villiers who had been in command when the knights were driven from their fortress at St. Jean d'Acre in 1291.

Philippe was inducted into the Order of the Knights of St. John as a teenager. Thus, many years before, as a fledgling knight, he had arrived at that very spot, when the fortress was barely recovering from the damage inflicted during the terrible siege of 1480, by Mehmet, the Conqueror.

On the day Philippe returned to his beloved Rhodes, he stood in the shadows of the giant stone walls and prepared to take command of the strongest fortification on Earth. Now, only a year later and a few miles away, Suleiman's armies, the largest force of fighting men in the world, along with nearly three hundred ships of war, were preparing to bring the battle back to Philippe's island home.

The fortress was situated at the northeast end of the island of Rhodes. The island itself was oblong, pointing from southwest to northeast, some forty-five miles long and twenty miles wide. A ridge of mountains ran up the middle of the island like a spine, the highest of which rose to nearly four thousand feet above the sea. The port city of Rhodes, itself, was served by two separate man-made harbors. Pointing to the north like an open mouth was the *Porto Mercantile,* the Commercial Harbor. Its entrance was guarded by the Tower of Naillac on the mainland and the Tower of the Windmills on the outer side along the artificial stone mole. The opening was barely three hundred yards wide, and easily protected with a massive chain and log booms. A second, smaller harbor to the north was the *Porto del Mandraccio,* or the Galley Port. It was across this port that in ancient times stood the legendary Colossus of Rhodes, one of the seven wonders of the ancient world. The Colossus long gone, this smaller harbor was now defended with chain and booms.

Surmounting the harbors on a small hill was the fortress itself. The city was just under a mile square. The walls were of heavy stone, guarded at intervals by towers. For two hundred years, the Knights had reinforced the walls and the defenses of their city. After their successful defense against the siege in 1480, the knights had worked even harder at modernizing and strengthening the fortifications.

Many of the changes had been made to keep up with the latest advances in siege warfare. The original thin curtain walls, designed before the development of heavy cannon fire, merely prevented soldiers from climbing into the city. The new walls had to withstand a constant barrage of huge stone and iron cannonballs, now in general use by the Turks. So, the old walls were thickened and replaced by massive bastions over forty feet thick. The bastions were projections in the fortress walls that allowed wider fields of fire to cover the approaches to the city. Each *langue* had responsibility for a portion of the defenses, and its wealth dictated the degree to which the position could be strengthened. The already huge ditches, or dry moats, were widened and deepened around the entire fortress. The moats were then encircled by a second perimeter of moats.

The guard towers, which were formerly designed for observation and the occasional use by archers, were pushed out and angled in front of the bastions. The defenders could rain down a murderous crossfire of both arrows and gunshot upon the attackers who might try to breach the walls. Boiling oil had been generally replaced by modern weaponry, and attackers trying to scale the walls would be slaughtered by an enfilade of arrows and shot. By the time Philippe had taken the reins of command, there was not a fortress in the world better able to withstand a prolonged attack.

On Rhodes, as elsewhere throughout the world, the knights were organized by their home countries, divided into *langues*, or the "tongues" for the languages they spoke. There were the *langues* of England, France, Germany, Auvergne, Provence, and Italy. Aragon and Castile comprised the *langue* of Spain.

Though France was by far the most dominant of the *langues*, most of the men spoke several languages fluently. A great rivalry existed among the knights of the different *langues*. Jealousies arose from the great differences in the financial resources available to each. France was the richest, and their *Auberge*, or inn, was the most opulent. Responsibility for the fortifications on Rhodes were also divided among the *langues*, and there, too, were major differences. The defense posts of the French were the most lavishly built, while weaknesses riddled the posts of the poorer *langues*, such as England.

The French knight, Jean de Morelle, first encountered the young Greek woman, Melina, in the market outside the city walls. Melina was struggling with a heavy basket of fruit, and Jean had helped her load the basket onto a donkey.

It was the first time Melina had seen this particular knight. She paid little attention to the many men who sauntered through the streets of her town with their black capes and swords. Though the knights had been in Rhodes for two centuries, she still considered them intruders. Rhodes was *her* town. All the occupying forces over the centuries could not change that.

Without offering much in the way of conversation, Jean had secured the basket to the back of the donkey and prepared to lead the animal for her. While he was busy loading the animal, she examined the craggy good looks of the knight. His face seemed more weathered than his real age would suggest. She knew that all the knights served terms in the galleys and the great ships of their Order. Perhaps so many years of service at sea in the galleys had done that to him. He had dark brown hair and blue eyes. When he looked at her it was hard for Melina to meet his stare. Something made her want to turn away. She fussed with the donkey's halter so as not to stare into his eyes. *Why does this knight make me so uncomfortable?* she wondered.

The two walked back into the fortress together, Jean still leading the donkey. *She must be Greek*, he thought. Her black hair, dark eyes, and olive complexion were strong indications of her heritage. They spoke briefly in Greek, and she had no accent. But, then again, neither did he, and he was French.

Jean followed Melina through the narrow, winding streets. Finally, they turned into the Jewish Quarter and onto the street of the synagogue. The *Kahal Kadosh Gadol*, the Holy Great Congregation, destroyed in the siege of 1480, had been rebuilt with the help of the knights as a reward for the aid the Jewish residents of the island had provided during that siege. Mehmet's forces bombarded the Jewish Quarter from the sea, pounding it with stone cannonballs without let-up for five weeks. The walls of the fortress itself had been reinforced with the rubble from the destroyed homes of the Jews.

The Turks had then entered the Jewish Quarter through a hole in the walls. But, just as it seemed inevitable that the Turks would overrun the city and slaughter the knights and the Jews together, something happened. For no apparent reason, the Turkish army turned and fled from the city. The Jews and the Christians could only believe that their victory was a divine intervention; that they had been saved from the Infidel by the hand of God. But, the friendship between the Christians and the Jews on Rhodes was not to last long.

After the turn of the sixteenth century, relations deteriorated. The Christian intolerance for the Jews that swept through the mainland of Europe finally washed ashore in Rhodes. Grand Master Pierre d'Aubusson ordered all the Jews expelled from the island. They were given fifty days to sell their possessions and leave. They were also forbidden to settle in Turkey, for fear that the Jews might be used as spies for the Muslims. They could only remain on the island if they accepted baptism, and converted to Christianity. But, the hardest of d'Aubusson's decrees was that which forced baptism upon all the children of the Jews regardless of the parents' decision to stay or to leave. Those who left were sent by boat to Nice. Others would be tortured and killed.

The reaction of the Jews to this decree was immediate. The people flocked into the streets, tearing their clothes and wearing them inside out in protest. They covered their bodies with the ashes from their cooking fires, their screams of anguish filling the air. Their leaders pleaded with d'Aubusson, who responded by having all the remaining Jews who had not converted cast into a deep pit. There they stayed without food or water until only a handful remained alive. At the end, these faithful few died repeating their most important prayer, *Shemah Yisrael, Adonoi eloheynu, Adonoi echod.* Hear, Oh Israel, the Lord, our God, the Lord is One.

The irony was that in the years to come, the knights would continue their piracy on the Mediterranean, and take many shiploads of slaves. Among the slaves they captured were large numbers of Jews. And, by 1522, the Jewish population had reached an even greater number than had been killed or expelled by Grand Master d'Aubusson.

Jean and Melina walked past the synagogue and turned into the next street where her house was located. It was sandwiched between the two houses on either side, and made of rough stone, with small shuttered windows. Every house in the street was almost identical to each of its neighbors. The street was paved with small black and white pebbles. Jean noticed some flowers growing in a small patch of uncobbled street just outside her door. "Did you plant those?" he asked.

"No, they're wildflowers," she said in Greek.

Like you, he thought. He wondered why a Greek was living in the Jewish Quarter, but said nothing. Then, he smiled at her and touched the brim of his hat. *"Au revoir, Mademoiselle."* With that, he turned and walked back toward the *Collachio.*

Melina watched from the doorway as he walked down the street. She liked the way the black cape with the white cross outlined his broad back and wide shoulders. He seemed to her a strong man, and he moved more gracefully than she had expected him to. As he turned the corner, Jean paused to look back. She could just make out a smile on his lips. He touched his fingers to the edge of his hat once more. Then he disappeared around the corner. Melina closed and bolted the door behind her, her face lit by a smile.

Two weeks later, Melina was walking from the market to her home. It was a Sunday, and she had just bought a few more vegetables. Jean was leaving the *Auberge de France* to take up his nursing duties at the Hospital of the Knights. He rounded the corner of the *Loggia*, and took a long detour to walk past Melina's house. He slowed as he passed her door on the chance that he might see her again. He had been making this detour several times a day, in hopes that their paths would cross. At night, he could see the glow of light coming from the cracks in her shuttered windows, and his imagination pictured her sitting beside a small fire. He longed to knock on her door, but he never did.

Melina had just turned into her street when she saw the knight walking slowly past her house. He looked over his shoulder to her doorway, and then sped up again. She smiled, for it was clear that he was hoping to see her. Then, when he resumed his pace toward the hospital, he caught sight of her. They were both smiling as they approached. When they were a few yards apart, Jean stopped and took off his hat.

"*Bonjour, Mademoiselle,*" he said.

"*Bonjour, Monsieur le Chevalier.*"

They stood in the narrow street for a moment, both at a loss for words. There was really no easy way for either to say what was on their minds. Finally, Melina said in French, "Thank you for helping me the other day. It was very kind."

Jean cocked his head and nodded. "*De rien.*" It was nothing.

Melina could think of no words to say to this stranger, so she smiled and turned to go. Jean quickly said, "*Mademoiselle.*" Then he stopped, and just looked uncomfortable. She waited. Finally, he said, "I am on my way to the hospital. On Saturdays I work there until Sunday morning."

"All night?"

"Yes. Sometimes there are a few hours to sleep. But, usually Doctor Renato has a great deal for us to do. Right now, there are a great many patients to care for. Sometimes there are not so many."

"And what do *you* do there?"

He laughed. "Anything. Everything. Oh, not surgery. But, I help. Last time, it was very quiet, and I merely made bandages and fed the patients. Sometimes I help the *docteur* in his surgery. Sometimes I change the dressings. Anything that he is too busy to do."

Melina took a deep breath. She hesitated, and finally, summoning all her courage, said, "Is there work that I could do there, too?"

Jean just looked at her. He stared into the blackness of her eyes. He was shocked at her boldness. Finally, he came back to the moment and said, "*Bien sûr!*" Of course! "There are many things you could do. Especially for the women there. They need a great deal of help that we knights cannot give them. Mmmm. Yes, please. I would be most grateful for your help. And, I am sure, so would Doctor Renato."

Without another word, Melina and Jean turned and began the first of many walks together to the hospital.

The Chancellor, Andrea d'Amaral, walked into the chamber of the Grand Master without being announced. Philippe ignored the intentional insult and looked directly into the Portuguese knight's eyes. He waited long enough for d'Amaral to make the pretense of a bow, and then said merely, "Yes, Chancellor?"

"This message has just been delivered to us, Grand Master. I am told it is from the Sultan Suleiman, himself."

Philippe raised his eyebrows. "Delivered how?"

"It was brought to the embassy in Istanbul, and thence by sea with our courier. It has just this hour been given to me." D'Amaral took the two steps necessary to reach out and hand the rolled message to the Grand Master. Then he bowed very slightly again, and stepped back.

Philippe finished what he was doing and looked up. "Have you read this, Andrea?" Philippe used the man's Christian name as a small offering of friendship. There had been so many years of enmity between the two that he felt the time should come when they were more than just civil. They were the two ranking leaders of the Knights of the Order of St. John, and this feud was destructive. Their knights might be forced to choose sides one day, and that could only hurt the Order. He knew that d'Amaral had not read the scroll, for the seal was still intact.

"I have not, Grand Master." D'Amaral would not return the first-name familiarity offered him. This was not lost on Philippe.

"Very well. Stay a moment and I'll read it to you. Please sit." He broke the seal and unrolled the scroll. At the top of the page was an elaborate golden monogram, the *tuğra* of the Sultan Suleiman. Beneath the *tuğra* was the letter, written in Turkish and French. After a moment, Philippe began to read aloud.

Suleiman, the Sultan, Shadow of God on Earth, and by the grace of God, Sovereign of Sovereigns, King of Kings, most high Emperor of Byzantium and Trebizond, and very powerful King of Persia, of Arabia, of Syria, and of Egypt, and Lord of Jerusalem,
To Philippe Villiers de L'Isle Adam.
I congratulate you upon your new high position and rank. I hope that you will rule in peace and prosper. I announce to thee that following in my father's footsteps, I have captured the most powerful of fortresses of Belgrade, and have taken many other well-fortified cities. I have destroyed them by sword and fire, reducing them to ashes and slavery. I shall myself return in triumph to my court at Istanbul.
10 September 1521

Philippe looked up at d'Amaral. He said, "It's signed with a very elaborate drawing and seal, which I assume is the mark of the triumphant Sultan, Suleiman. So, what do you think of this?" he said handing the scroll to d'Amaral.

"It's a threat. Of course. They call this a *fethname*, a 'Letter of Victory.' But, how serious he is, I'm not sure. Surely he hasn't forgotten his great-grandfather and the siege of 1480?"

"I'm sure he has not. In fact, I think that is why he is so anxious to take back Rhodes. That siege must stick in his throat. I am told

Mehmet called us 'The most damnable of the *Kuffar*. Sons of Evil. Allies of *Sheitan*.' No, I would say he has not a lot of good will toward our Order."

D'Amaral nodded slowly, deep in thought. "I heard that his father, Selim, was preparing a fleet to sail against us, too. Only his death stopped him from attacking us. Now, it would appear that the son will try to best his great-grandfather and his father, too."

"And what do we do now, Andrea?"

"Continue to strengthen the fortifications, and proceed as if he were already on his way. Which, for all we know, he may well be. And we answer him directly and with no question of our intent. For, I swear to you this day, Grand Master, that we shall be shedding Turkish blood before very long."

Philippe thought for a moment, then called for his attendant. The young knight appeared a moment later and stood to attention before Philippe.

"Prepare to leave at once for Istanbul. I have something for you to deliver to the palace of the Sultan Suleiman." The young man's eyes widened. Philippe continued, "Take another knight to accompany you, and let nothing get in your way in the delivery of this message." The knight saluted, and turned to prepare for his mission.

Philippe took out paper, pen and ink, and slowly wrote his reply. D'Amaral watched in silence, as the older man carefully penned a terse and unequivocal letter. When he finished it, he applied his signature and read it to the Chancellor before rolling and sealing the message.

Brother Philippe Villiers de L'Isle Adam, Grand Master of Rhodes,
To Suleiman, Sultan of the Turks:
I understand your letter, which has been presented to me by your ambassador. Thank you for informing me of your recent victories. I congratulate you and your army. The prospect of a peace between us would please me. I can only hope that your deeds and words coincide.
Peace be with you.
Philippe Villiers de L'Isle Adam.

Philippe applied his seal to the letter, and then handed it to d'Amaral. "There's *our* 'Letter of Victory.' Let's see what he makes of that."

D'Amaral took the letter. "I will see that the two knights deliver this letter with due haste, my Lord." D'Amaral started to leave, then hesitated a moment, and turned to Philippe. For a long moment the Chancellor remained silent.

"Andrea? Is there something more?" Philippe asked.

"My Lord," d'Amaral began, slowly, "if we are correct, and the Sultan does try to make good Mehmet's attack upon our fortress, what will we do?"

Philippe could not believe what he was hearing. This was not the question that should be asked by the Grand Chancellor of the Knights of St. John. "What are you asking me, Andrea? Is there any doubt what we must do?"

"My Lord, a moment, please. The Sultan can raise the most powerful army on Earth. We have information that there could be as many as three hundred ships...perhaps more in his fleet. Some say his armies number more than one hundred thousand. Some say *two* hundred thousand. And these are not conscripted rabble. These are trained fighting men. Professional soldiers, like us."

Philippe waited, but d'Amaral said nothing more.

"What would you have us do?" Philippe asked. "Pack and run before this hoard of Infidels? Should we turn over our island and our fortress without a fight? I cannot believe I am hearing this question from you, Andrea."

D'Amaral winced at the Grand Master's words. But, he did not back down. "My Lord, our Order has seen the wisdom of strategic retreat many times before. When others have chosen to die in their cause, our leaders had fled before superior forces and lived to fight another day. We have faced defeat at Jerusalem. At Krak de Chevaliers. At Acre. This would not be the first time our Order has fled to reestablish itself elsewhere. Is it better to fight to the death of the last knight, and see our Order vanish from the face of the Earth? Is this not exactly what the Sultan wishes? Think of it. There may be a hundred thousand trained men against our handful of knights and a few mercenaries. The slaughter could be beyond anything we have ever imagined. And the people of Rhodes. What of them?"

Philippe breathed in and out deeply. His face grew red, and d'Amaral realized that he had gone too far. Philippe said, "The Chancellor does not need to instruct the Grand Master on the history of our Order. Of the battles we have lost, and the brothers we have buried, I know all too well. These souls are not the least burden on the heart of a Grand Master. And of the fortresses we have vacated, the flights of our Order, I am also all too well aware. Do not presume to lecture me on the duties of my rank. We will defend our island and its people. My knights are up to the task. This is the best-fortified city in the world, and our knights the most skilled and devoted army. We will show the Sultan exactly why his great-grandfather fled before our walls, only to die in Damascus on the way home. Mark me, Chancellor. Suleiman will learn what it is to challenge the Order of St. John and the Power of Christ. "

Andrea stared into Philippe's eyes. "Very well, my Lord. As you wish." The coldness had returned to his voice. Philippe realized then that there would never be an end to the hostility between them. As the door closed behind d'Amaral, Philippe thought, *So be it, Andrea.*

As soon as d'Amaral had left, Philippe sent for his lieutenant, Gabriel de Pommerols. He had fought beside de Pommerols for many years, and had the deepest faith in him. De Pommerols arrived within minutes. He had been at the *Auberge de France,* the residence of the French Knights, only a short walk from the Palace of the Grand Master.

He removed his hat and bowed. "*Seigneur?*"

"Come in, Gabriel. I have just dispatched two knights with a letter for the Turkish Sultan. There is little doubt in my mind that he means war, and we could be looking at a long and difficult siege." De Pommerols remained standing and silent. Philippe continued, "I have an important mission for you. You must leave at once for France. I will send two galleys to accompany you, and a sufficient complement of knights to assure your safe passage. We need to recall all the knights of the Order who are now away from Rhodes. But, that is secondary. I need you to go to King Francis and deliver a letter. We need reinforcements of men and arms and any money that he can give us to buy supplies. Please sit down, and I shall have a formal letter for you in a moment."

Philippe sat down at this desk, and unrolled a clean piece of parchment. He dipped his pen into the ink stand and began to write. He read aloud as he wrote so that Pommerols would know the contents of the letter.

"Sire: You should know that the Turk has sent letters in which, under the guise of peacemaking, he informs me that he has taken the city by force."

Philippe looked up to see de Pommerols' reaction. "I shall appeal, as I said, for money, troops, and supplies. But, I am not sure of the disposition of Francis toward our plight. He has much to keep him occupied right now. Make ready for this trip, and I shall have this letter brought to the *Auberge* as soon as I have finished with it."

Pommerols nodded, and rushed from the Palace.

Jean and Melina rode west, side by side along the north coast road. They had left the city early in the morning to avoid the inevitable late-summer heat. The days would soon start cool and clear. But, as this mid-day approached, the sun would heat the ground and the air, and the days would become distinctly uncomfortable.

Soon, they were well along the lower coast road, heading to the south. The sandy beaches below them were covered by the high tide, and a light chop was roiling the water. Just after they left the city proper, they ascended the steep cliffs on the north side of the island. Mount Saint Stephen rose gently above them on their left, its grassy slopes still wet with dew.

Melina tapped her horse's sides, and increased the walk to a trot. Jean clicked his tongue, and his horse joined the pace.

"Why are you hurrying, *Chèrie?*" he asked.

"I want to be in the shade of the valley before it becomes too hot." They had been riding for about an hour, and were nearing the turnoff that would bring them inland to Petaloudes.

"Where are you taking me? "

"To Petaloudes. It is very special for me. My father used to take the whole family there. Especially this time of year." Her voice cracked, and Jean reached across and touched her right hand with his left.

"I know, I know. It will never be the same without them. It cannot be."

Melina squeezed Jean's hand, and smiled at him. "I love this place. You will see why. In a minute."

They turned off the coast road at Kalamonas and headed south toward the interior of the island. The land became hilly and greener as they rode on, the air growing warmer and more moist. The road descended several valleys, and then climbed again before finally petering out at the bottom of the last valley. It narrowed to a single-lane horse trail, and eventually nothing was left but a small path in the woods.

Jean dismounted, and helped Melina from her saddle. They led the horses single file along the shady path. Melina showed the way, and Jean could see that she was very familiar with the narrow winding trails. They crossed a small brook, stepping on the stones that lay in the shallow current. Finally, they entered a cool, sun-dappled glade with a stream running through it.

She took Jean's hand and walked him to the edge of the water. "Sit here a moment, and I'll be back." Before she left, she helped him out of his boots and pointed to the water. Jean let his feet hang into the stream as Melina went back to the horses. When she returned, she was carrying the lunch they had packed, and a bottle of wine. Under her arm, she held a small blanket, which she spread out next to Jean. She sat down, took off her boots, and dangled her feet in the water alongside his. She rubbed her foot lazily over his, and put her arm through his arm. He took his arm away and put it around her shoulders. For a moment more, neither spoke. The only sound was that of a few crickets, and the burbling of the water over the rocky bottom.

"So this is your secret place?"

"Yes. Mine and many others. But, on most days, you can come here and be all alone. Especially if it's a work day such as today."

"It's wonderful, Melina. I'm glad you brought me here."

She smiled and kept staring at him.

"What is it?"

Her smile widened.

"What?"

She opened her mouth and began to laugh.

"What are you laughing at, woman? Tell me."

She reached up and kissed him on the mouth. Then she pulled back and laughed out loud. "You don't know, do you?"

"Know what?"

"Look about you, my love. Just look."

Jean looked at the trees and the flowers. He glanced at the water running over their feet. "What? You're maddening! What?"

"*Petaloudes!* The name of this place! It means 'Butterflies!' This is the Valley of the Butterflies!"

"And?"

"Clap your hands. Hard."

Jean looked at her with puzzlement.

"Clap them! Go ahead."

Jean cupped his hands and made a single loud clap. All at once the ground and the tree trunks seemed to dissolve into a blur. In a second, there were hundreds of thousands of brown butterflies swarming into the air. It was as if someone were shaking out a giant mottled brown blanket. The butterflies moved as a unit, as if their wings were tied together. As they settled back, they became waves of cloth rippling to earth. As fast as they had appeared, they blended with the trees and the earth, and were still again. Only now did he see that the entire glade was carpeted in brown butterflies. They were so well camouflaged that they were invisible to the casual eye. Once you knew they were there, however, you couldn't miss them.

"By Jesus, there must be millions of them. Millions!"

Melina laughed again, and hugged her knight. "Yes. Millions. They're here this time of year, for about two months. They fly at night and sleep in the day. Unless some boorish French knight disturbs their sleep. Are they not wonderful, Jean?"

"They are, indeed. As are you. And...I'm famished. Let's get to that lunch."

Melina opened the cloths that wrapped the food and took out several pieces of cold chicken. She placed the wine bottle in the stream and gave Jean some fruit. Jean cut a piece of apple and gave it to Melina. Then, they proceeded to feed each other for the next hour.

When they were just beginning to finish the wine and some dessert cheese, Jean said, "We are so blessed to have found each other. Who could have thought that we would stumble on each other in the market the way we did; and from that chance meeting to this?"

"If you had not been prowling about my front door every day, our 'chance' meeting the second time might not have happened."

"Good thing I did, isn't it?" He pointed to the stream and the butterflies and the remains of the lunch. "'It's a dream, *n'est-ce pas*? Who could have known? Some years ago this could not have been. We knights have all sworn vows of celibacy. The past Grand Masters would not have tolerated anything such as this."

"I should think not."

"The rules were very strict. The young knights had to go about in groups of twos and threes, and not just with their friends, but with whomever the Master has ordered. Chaperones, you see."

Melina laughed, and asked, "Have we any chaperones lurking about today?"

"No. But it was strict then. No women were allowed to make the beds in the *Auberges*. Still aren't. Or wash our hair. It is even written that we must not sleep naked, but fully dressed in wool!"

Melina laughed, and squeezed Jean's arm.

"And, hear this," he said, "for we all have it memorized. 'If a Brother—may it never happen—falls into fornication because of the strength of evil passions, if he has sinned in secret, let him repent in secret and impose on himself a suitable penance.'"

Melina roared with delight, and rolled back upon the blanket. "Oh, Jean, have you repented in private? Have you?"

"But, wait, wait. It gets better yet. 'If the fornication is *known* and *proved*, the knight is to be beaten by a superior, very severely with whips and sticks, and excluded from the Order for a year!'"

Melina grabbed Jean's shoulders and pulled him down on top of her. He struggled to pull free, but she locked her arms around his neck and held tight.

"*Sacré Coeur! Mon Dieu!* Why woman, what will you make of me?" he said imitating the accent of the Grand Master. "Have you no shame! Where's my whip?"

Melina held fast as the two grew quiet. She kissed him lightly on the mouth, and he sank onto her.

"But, times have changed. And so they should."

"Thank God for that," she whispered.

"We were never meant to be monks to live our lives in cells. Cut off from life. Our mission to serve the poor and the sick is of itself enough for God, I think. Why chain us to such an unnatural oath?"

"It's unnatural, Jean. Men and women were not made to live apart."

"I swear I would have left the knights for you, my love." Jean paused. He seemed lost in thought, so Melina did not interrupt him. "Do you know why I take the extra duties at the hospital?"

Melina shook her head. "It's because it troubles me when I see what our Order has become. Oh, yes, we still serve the poor and the sick. But, we're really just pirates. We sail these waters and take booty whenever we please. We attack every ship we can, and make slaves of its crew and passengers."

Still, Melina said nothing. Jean continued. "We are no better than that fiend, Cortoglu, about whom the Grand Master rages all the time. This was not our calling. Why, we have been on this island for more than two hundred years. This place is a paradise. There are crops and fruits to feed everyone here.

"The climate is kind. And, we straddle the richest trade routes in the world. From this place we could be legitimate tradesmen, and sail these seas as honest merchants instead of..." Jean shook his head. "Slavers."

Melina gently touched his lips. "You should be careful who hears you say these things, my love. This is treasonous talk."

"But, our Order has become something other than that which I joined so long ago. I have no heart for these things. I don't know what I should do. I have sworn an oath. And, as far as caring for the sick and defending our city, I have no problem. But, the next time I am ordered to serve my time in the galleys...I just don't know."

Melina had no answer for Jean's dilemma. She said, "Jean. Will they leave us alone? Will this go on? Will the Grand Master allow us to live as we have?"

"We cannot hope that he would sanctify a marriage. He may turn his back upon his knights living with women on the island, but a true marriage performed in the church would violate the oath we swore. He has sworn the same oath. But there is some talk in our *langue* that he left a woman of his own behind in Paris. I don't know if this is just soldiers' gossip or if there's truth in it. But, if it is so, it could explain a great deal. Hélène, I think she is called."

Melina pulled back and looked into Jean's eyes. "Explain what?"

"His singlemindedness of purpose. It is almost as if he has thrown himself into this new position with such fervor as to extinguish all thoughts of Paris. To work and punish himself with long hours and dangerous missions to expiate the guilt he feels for breaking his vows to God."

"I hope such guilt will not cloud his judgment, Jean."

"I, too. But, as for our marriage, he will never relent. He would never sanctify it. For I, too, have broken my vows."

"Is there nothing we can do?"

"If it means so much to you, could not the Greek priest marry us in the privacy of his church?"

Melina looked away. She seemed not able to meet Jean's eyes. He pulled her back and kissed her again. "What is it, *Chérie?*"

"Oh, Jean. It's much more complicated than you know. I have not had the heart to tell you before now, because I didn't want to add to your burden. I didn't think it would matter. Only that we were in love. That would be all we needed to be happy."

"And?"

"Jean, it is more than my being Greek and you a Latin."

"Then it's time you told me. What is it?"

They sat up together, side by side. Melina dangled her toes in the cool water, and Jean stared off at the pattern of the butterflies on the trees and the ground. Then she began.

"Jean, my family is not from Rhodes. It's a very long story, but we came from Spain. We were Sephardic Jews."

Jean sat up straighter and stared into Melina's eyes.

"My father and mother fled during the Inquisition. All their family were killed. They, alone, survived to come here. They went to North Africa first, but things were hard there. So they joined a fishing fleet, and sailed here as part of the crew. My mother worked as the cook. They landed in Lindos first, but could not find enough work. They had spent their whole lives in the city. My father was a banker. He lost everything, and started in Lindos as a fisherman. But, they could not make a living, so they moved to the city and lived in the Jewish Quarter. My father fished and did various jobs as a laborer. My mother worked at whatever she could. Eventually, she got a good job in the silk factory. I was born right in that little house near the synagogue."

She paused and stared across the little stream. Jean waited for her to continue.

"Things were fine for a while. Then the Grand Master—it was d'Aubusson then—ordered all the Jews off the island. My parents were among the few that refused to leave and refused to convert. He ordered all the Jewish children seized from the parents and baptized. I was taken from them when I was only an infant, so I don't remember them at all. I know they died in that horrible pit. But, I'm sure they kept their faith to the end."

Jean reached over and squeezed her hand. The tears were flowing freely now. Melina looked into Jean's eyes, and saw that he was crying as well.

"They died as Jews, Jean, and I was given to a family of Christians. I was baptized, and raised as a Christian until I was twelve. Then my adopted father died, and a year later my new mother grew ill. They were always very kind to me. I thought they were my real parents. Just before she died she told me the story; of my real parents, and that I was born Jewish.

"When my adopted parents died, I had nobody left in the world. No brothers or sisters. All my real family were killed in Spain or killed here on Rhodes. When I heard the story, I couldn't believe it. So, I went around asking everyone I could find. This is a small island and a small community. Nobody would tell me anything. Finally, I went to the synagogue and talked to the rabbi. He confirmed everything. Everything. All at once, I wanted to be myself. My true self. So I asked the rabbi if I could once again become a Jew. He told me he could teach me many things about Judaism. It seems that the religion requires that in order for the child to be accepted as a Jew, the mother must be born a Jew. So, I was really already a Jew, and needed only to be taught the ways of my family."

Jean pulled Melina close to him and wrapped her in his arms. She placed her head on his shoulders and continued to tell her story.

"I'm Jewish, Jean. All my grown life I have hated the knights and the Christians. I hated them as a Greek whose island they invaded. I hated them as the Christians who tortured and killed my people. I just wanted to be a Jew and to wall myself up in the Jewish Quarter. I managed to find the house where I was born, and the family who lived there took me in. They made me part of their family. When they died, I stayed on. And then you found me. Oh, Jean, how I hated the knights and what they stood for. But, when you came along, I was so lonely. I had nothing in my life until I saw you there. God had brought us together, my love. I know he has."

Jean sat quietly, collecting himself. He dried his eyes, and said, "It doesn't matter, Melina. None of it matters. I fell in love with *you*. Not the Jew or the Greek or the Christian. By God, my own Order would have shunned you anyway because you were Greek Orthodox, and not of the church of Rome. It's absurd! Nobody has challenged my right to remain out of the *Auberge* at night. It's no secret that I live with you, yet none dares mention it to me. So we will keep our house, and I shall stay a knight. And damned be he who tries to get in the way of us."

Melina put her head against her lover's chest, and they both lay back upon the grassy bank. They slept the early afternoon away. Then, damp with the sweat of sleep, they awoke, in the cool of the setting sun. Jean undressed, and then helped Melina remove her clothes. They left their clothes among the butterflies that carpeted the glade, and together, holding hands, they slipped into the cool stream. The chill rippled their skin as they slid down into the cover of the running water. Jean could feel Melina's cool, wet skin slide beneath his fingertips. Neither spoke, but held each other as the gentle current of the water washed over them. They felt each other's bodies grow warm with their longing. After some time, they left the water and made love in the sand at the edge of the little stream. Both of them were waiting for the arrival of the two new lives that were already growing to term in Melina's womb.

———

The Grand Master strode into his chambers and threw his cape and sword on the bed. He removed his gauntlets and the remaining elements of his formal uniform. A servant had filled a golden flagon with red wine, which now stood half full at a bedside table. Philippe drank the rest of the wine, and cut himself a slice of cheese and bread that had been placed there as well. He looked over a few notes of paper that were on his desk, and then threw them down again. Finally, he slumped into a large stuffed armchair, and put his feet up on a footstool. A servant entered the room.

"Get Antonio Bosio in here at once!" Philippe shouted.

The servant turned and sped from the room without a word. The windows were open, and the spring breeze delighted Philippe. He got up again and began to pace the room. From time to time, he glanced out of the windows set in the thick stone wall of his Palace. He looked into the large walled courtyard of the Convent, which took up nearly a quarter of the walled city of Rhodes. From the other side of his rooms, he could see the water. He was grateful that his quarters gave out onto the expansive view of the sea.

Philippe became impatient, and poured himself some water from a pitcher. Then, because there was little else to do, he cut some more bread and cheese. There was fruit on the table, but he was really not that hungry.

There was a knock at the partially open door, and his Servant-at-Arms, Antonio Bosio, entered the room. Bosio stood at attention near the door until Philippe motioned him to come in and sit down.

"I cannot take a single more of these ceremonies, Antonio. I have been paraded around Rhodes from one dinner to another. Received one ambassador after another. These formal receptions make me obese and nearly drunk with the toasting and the good wishes. And the processions in the afternoon heat. Don't the Rhodians have work to do? Crops to get in?"

"Yes, *Seigneur*. It's tiresome. But, the ceremony is part of what defines you for these people. For the Greeks as well as for the knights of our Order. And you must be seen face to face with each of the holy fathers—the Greek as well as the Latin."

"It's wonderful to see the old shipmates, and knights who have stood beside me in battle. They are old friends and it lifts my heart to see them again. But, if I have to sit through one more Te Deum or Mass, I will truly have calluses on my buttocks."

Bosio smiled and nodded to Philippe. "I think we can safely say that the worst is over, my Lord. We seem to have run out of bishops—Greek and Latin—as well as Piliers of the *langues*, bailiffs, judges...who is left?"

"I still need to review the reports with the Treasurer, and inspect the troops. But, the inspection will be a pleasure. It is good to see the knights in their battle dress and their weapons."

"And let us not forget the inspection of the Hospital," Bosio said.

"Yes, actually I was looking forward to that. I'm anxious to talk with Doctor Renato and see how well prepared he is."

Philippe took up his broadsword, placing it carefully on his hip, assessing himself in a small wall mirror as he did so. When he had adjusted his uniform, he motioned to Bosio. "*On y va!*" Let's go! "We have some daylight left. Let's visit the good doctor and his staff."

The two men walked side by side, in a military cadence. They left the Residence of the Grand Master, and proceeded toward the hospital, which was located at the eastern end of the Street of the Knights, farthest from the Palace.

As Philippe and Bosio proceeded through the city, small groups of Rhodian citizens greeted them: a tip of a hat; a military salute; a word of greeting. One group of men had congregated near the doorway to the Inn of France when the Grand Master walked by. Philippe raised a gloved hand in salute, but the men merely glared at him. He touched Bosio's shoulder and turned toward the small group. Bosio started to protest, but it was too late. Philippe had stepped over to the men and was saying something that Bosio could not hear. The tallest of the men stepped forward and confronted Philippe directly. Bosio rushed to Philippe's side, his hand on his sword. Without taking his eyes from the man, Philippe raised a quieting hand toward Bosio, but Bosio held his place at Philippe's right. He was not going to allow even the gesture of violence against the Grand Master. As Bosio took up his position he heard Philippe say, "...and we are your allies, are we not?"

The man blew a puff of air through his pursed lips, contemptuous of Philippe's words. "You are nobody's allies but your own, monsieur. We have been on this island long before you came, and we shall be here after you leave. The Turks would not be bothering us if it were not for you. If you were not here, they would leave us in peace. We could trade with them, or with anyone else in these waters. But you...*you* bring down the anger of the Turks upon our island. Then you burn our farms and destroy our houses..."

Philippe interrupted. "If we did not burn the outlying farms and destroy the houses, the Turks would use them. We would be providing them with food and shelter...something we cannot do in a siege..."

"If you would take your knights and just leave us, there would be no siege!" the man shouted. The others began to mutter and grumble in agreement. Bosio sensed that the situation might be getting out of hand. He did not want to fight with the Rhodians. They would be sorely needed in the coming months.

"Grand Master," Bosio whispered, "we must hurry. We have no time for this."

Philippe hesitated, then reluctantly turned. He hoped that these were only a few who felt this way inside his city.

———

The Hospital of the Knights was a large and imposing building, completed in 1484 by Grand Master d'Aubusson. The stones had been taken from the ruins of an old Roman building on the same site.

As they entered the ward, Doctor Apella Renato recognized the uniform of the Grand Master. He jumped to his feet and faced Philippe. When Renato stood, he was as tall as the Grand Master, himself. And the Grand Master was well over six feet. Bosio broke the embarrassed silence, and said, "I am sorry to have startled you, *Dottore.* But, *Permettez-moi de vous présenter, Le Grand Maître, Philippe Villiers de L'Isle Adam."* Please allow me to present the Grand Master.

Renato brought his heels together and bowed deeply to the Grand Master. The men shook hands, and he replied, *"Enchanté de faire votre conaissance, Seigneur.* 'I am pleased to meet you, my Lord.' Let me show you our hospital."

They left the doctor's office and walked through the ward. Beds were lined up neatly on either side against the walls. Philippe was heartened to see the absolute cleanliness of the room. All the floors and walls had been neatly scrubbed, and the beds were freshly made. There were no dirty dressings or any sign of garbage, as he had seen in so many other hospitals around Europe. The air smelled of disinfectant, but he could not place the odor precisely. Before he could ask, Renato said, *"Seigneur,* as you can see, there are none of your knights here at the moment. Happily, when we are not fighting, the knights stay healthy enough. Most of these patients are farmers or people of the town. A few are travelers who took ill while nearby or while visiting our island."

They stopped at the foot of one of the beds, and the doctor walked to the side near the patient. There was an elderly man lying in the bed, wearing a white gown. The stump of his arm was heavily bandaged. A knight was finishing with the old man's dressings and taking away the soiled bandages. Next to him, a young woman, her back to Philippe, was holding the old man's hand.

Gesturing to the knight, he said, "My Lord, *permettez-moi de vous présentez le Chevalier, M. Jean de Morelle."*

Philippe nodded. "Yes, I am well acquainted with Monsieur de Morelle."

"Oh, of course." Renato turned to the woman and smiled. But, he did not introduce her to the Grand Master. Melina continued to tend to the old man, and silently thanked the doctor for leaving her out of the introductions. The less the Grand Master saw Jean and Melina together, the better, Renato thought. No need to flaunt their relationship. Jean took the dressings away, and moved on to another patient. Melina remained with the old man.

Philippe moved closer to the old man. As he did so, Melina sensed his closeness and looked toward him. As their eyes met, she could see the Grand Master wince. His eyes locked upon hers, and narrowed almost as if he were in pain. His breath stopped in his chest, and his hands balled into fists. His whole body stiffened. She could not hold his gaze, and turned back to the old man. When she resumed wrapping his dressings she could feel the eyes of the Grand Master still on her. Her hands began to tremble, and she could not stop them. She began to make a mess of her work.

For his part, Philippe could not tear himself away. His heart was racing. Small droplets of sweat began to glisten on his lip. He tried to calm himself. He was sure the beating in his chest could be heard in the room. Surely the woman had sensed his emotions, for she had turned from him and he noticed that her hands were shaking badly.

How can it be? he wondered. *How could two women look so alike, yet be unrelated? It is almost as if she were a twin. Hélène's twin.* Philippe's mind was already back in Paris.

His rooms in Paris had been nearly dark except for the small candle guttering in the last of the wax. Soon it would be out, and the room would be completely black. The summons to come to Rhodes as the newly elected Grand Master lay on the floor next to his bed, where it had fallen hours earlier. He had read it so many times that he could recite it by heart. Some of words were partially obscured, for they were wet with the salt moisture of tears.

Hélène had read it through before she had thrown it to the ground. She rolled back on the rumpled sheets of their bed and buried her face in the pillows. Philippe leaned over her and tried to take her in his arms. But, she pulled away, and sought refuge at the edge of the small bed. There was nowhere to go.

"It's a summons I cannot ignore, Hélène."

Hélène said nothing.

"I must go, and I don't know when I will be coming back."

Hélène rolled over onto her back, pressing alongside Philippe and holding on to him tightly. Her dark hair was in cascades, tousled and wild. She was still wet from perspiration and now from her tears as well.

"Can't I go to Rhodes with you, Philippe?"

Philippe closed his eyes and shook his head slowly back and forth. *"C'est impossible, Chérie. Impossible."*

Hélène let go of him, and turned away once again.

Nothing is possible now, he had thought. *And never can it be again.* Then the candle had sputtered for a last time and the room was black.

———

Philippe could feel the stares of everyone around him.

"My Lord?" Bosio asked, "are you unwell? Is it the odors, perhaps?"

Philippe brought himself back to the present and moved closer to the old man. He forced his eyes away from Melina and cocked his head, as if he had not understood what Bosio had said.

The old man looked up at the Grand Master and his Servant-at-Arms, but made no signs of recognition.

"This farmer was injured while harvesting his crops," Renato told Philippe and Bosio. "He cut his hand badly, and developed an infection that nearly killed him. Only when he was suffering from a gangrene did his family bring him from Lindos to our hospital. Unfortunately, I had to amputate the arm below the elbow. That was over a month ago, and we've had a stormy time of it." He turned to the old man and said in Greek, "Haven't we, *philo moo*?" My friend. The old man smiled and nodded slightly. But, there was a persistent sadness in his eyes.

"He will live now, thank God, but life will be difficult for him, I'm afraid. It's hard to be a farmer without your right hand, and he has no family other than his aging wife. His sons were killed right here during the last siege. Now, who will care for him?"

The Grand Master stood stiffly erect. "God will care for him, *Dottore*, and we shall be the arms and the hands of God. Make sure that this man and his wife are well provided for, Bosio. If necessary, bring them within the city walls and provide them with shelter. Their sons died in our service. We will see that this old man and his wife do not suffer for that."

When they reached the end of the ward, Philippe put out his hand and said, "Thank you, *Dottore*. I am very pleased to see what you've done here. Though we spend a good deal of our time in the military pursuits of the knighthood, you know that our main task on Earth is to care for the sick. Make sure that you always have enough of my knights to maintain this level of care. We will provide you with whatever you need." Then his voice lowered, and he spoke to Renato in a tone of confidence.

"Now hear me well. As you know, we expect the Turks to attack this fortress. I don't know when that may be, but we must be well prepared. My knights will take care of the preparations for the battle, but you must prepare for the possibility of many wounded and sick. We may well have another siege here, and I fear it will be far worse than the last one. Send now for whatever medicines you may want. Herbs, dressings. Opium. Yes, especially opium. Anything you need, have it sent for at once."

"I will, my Lord. But, in calculating my needs, for what period of time shall I plan?"

"I think you should lay in supplies that would last you for a year."

Renato's eyes widened at the words of the Grand Master.

Philippe and his Servant-at-Arms turned from the ward and made their way back to the Palace.

Renato went back into the ward and found Jean cleaning instruments at a basin. Melina was with him, drying and sorting the clean instruments.

"You have met the Grand Master before, then, Jean?"

"*Oui, Docteur.* I have. He makes it his personal business to know every one of the knights. And since we are of the same *langue*, I see him often. In fact, I am one of his officers."

Renato nodded, and began helping Melina. "And you, my dear, have you met him before?"

"*Non, Docteur,* I have not. I've seen him at the ceremonies, but we have not met." She tried not to meet Renato's eyes. Something in the Grand Master's behavior had badly unsettled her. She could not explain her feelings, so she said nothing more of it.

"Yes. Quite right. There is no way that he could know all the Rhodians, is there?" Renato said.

"I suppose not," Melina answered. She looked to Jean for help, but he continued his work without joining the conversation further.

Finally, Renato turned to leave. He stopped at the door and said to them both, "Jean. Melina. I care for both of you. You have served me well here, and I need all the good help I can get. There is good reason for me to suspect that I will need you even more before very long. You know you have nothing to fear from me. You and Jean are a wonderful family. Your secret—if it is still a secret in this small village—is safe with me. I would never do anything to put you in harm's way." He seemed about to say more, but thought better of it and left.

Melina turned to Jean and said, "Does he know?"

"Who?" Jean said, looking at the disappearing back of the doctor.

"Not Doctor Renato. Of course *he* knows. The Grand Master. Do you think the Grand Master knows?"

"We are not the only lovers on this island. Many of the knights have women in town. As long as it does not interfere with our duties as knights, the Council and the Grand Master seem to ignore us. But, does he actually *know*? I have no idea. We can see that Renato has no intention of telling him."

"I like him. He's a very good physician. He seems to care for all the patients with equal fervor. It makes no difference to him whether they are knights or Greeks; Muslims, Christians, or Jews; he treats them all as if their lives were a precious thing."

"I know nothing of him, do you?" Jean asked.

"Only that he was here when I first moved to the city," Melina said. "I hear he came about eight years ago. That he was a Jew, and has converted to Christianity. The Latin Church of the Knights, I think. No family here. But, I don't know where he came from."

Jean said, "I have heard him speak fluently in French, English, and Greek. I have also heard him speak Turkish to some of the patients here, but I don't know if it is good Turkish or not, since I don't speak it myself. He seems to have traveled a lot before he came here, though. He has spoken of things in Spain and Istanbul. And a lot about Greece."

"Well, he has been very kind to the two of us. I like this work. He has even paid me for my time with food, and a few things I might need at the house. He's a fair man."

They finished cleaning up in silence. Just before the evening bells, they left the hospital together and walked back to the street where Melina lived. Renato watched them from his window as they disappeared around the corner of the winding street. He nodded, and smiled to himself. Then he went back to his new anatomy book.

———

Philippe stood at attention on the balcony of the palace. He was flanked by the Piliers of the eight *langues*. The Knights of Justice were lined up to his left, and the Knights of Grace were to his right. All the remaining knights of high rank, including the Chaplains of Obedience and the Servants-at-Arms, stood on the wide open staircase that led to the large courtyard below. D'Amaral and his servant, Blasco Diaz, stood apart at the very edge of the massive stone staircase.

The main force of the knights, some five hundred in all, were lined up in front of each *Auberge* in full military dress. Their usual black capes were replaced with scarlet battle surcoats bearing the eight-sided cross of St. John in white, both front and back. They wore black leather boots, and their broadswords hung almost to the ground from their left hips. Each carried his black steel helmet under his right arm, and wore chain-mail gauntlets that reached above the elbow. At their sides were oblong, leather-covered shields that came to a point at the ground.

The knights stood at attention in perfect rows at the entrance to each *Auberge*. When they were all assembled for the review by the Grand Master, the Street of the Knights looked like a military parade ground.

In the *Loggia* between the Street of the Knights and the Palace of the Grand Master were gathered the mercenaries and the remainder of the militia of Rhodian Greeks organized into separate fighting units. In all, three thousand armed men stood ready to defend their island fortress from the more than one hundred thousand Turkish troops of Suleiman's army that were now traveling across Asia Minor.

At the Grand Plaza in front of the Palace, the citizens of Rhodes were gathered; another three thousand women, children, and aging men who sought refuge within the city walls. When the army and the crowd were fully assembled, Philippe moved to the front of the balcony. The crowd became silent, though most would not be able to hear what he said.

He spoke slowly in French. "Knights of St. John. People of Rhodes. You all are aware of why we are here. An army of Muslim Turks is preparing to invade this island that we call our home. The knights of our Order have lived here with you for more than two hundred years, serving the poor and the sick. We have fought off many small and large armies in the past. We will do so again. Though our numbers are not as great as that of the Muslim, we are well prepared for what they might do. Our fortifications have been strengthened. Supplies have been stored. Our knights are superior warriors to the hoards that the Muslim emperor brings with him. We have burned or destroyed all sources of food and shelter that are outside the city walls. For many of you, that will mean a hardship when this is over. But, after we have defeated these Turks, all of us will work together to restore our island. To restore your homes and your lands."

Then in a solemn voice he declared, "There must be no thought of surrender, for death is far preferable to a life in chains. God Almighty will see that we will prevail."

Then, the Grand Master raised his arm and signaled for the procession of the knights to begin. He stood with several of the higher-ranking knights: Thomas Docwra, Antonio Bosio, and John Buck at his back. Thomas Scheffield, *Seneschal* of the Grand Master, stood off to one side. The knights assembled in front of their Inns began to march in columns of four toward the Palace of the Grand Master. They proceeded along the Street of the Knights to the *Loggia,* and then into the plaza in front of the palace. The mercenaries and Rhodian Militia fell in behind the knights. Soon the square was packed with men at arms greeted by the cheers of the citizens assembled along the Palace walls. Voices in Greek, Italian, French, Spanish, and English rebounded off the stone walls. Prayers were murmured quietly by old men and women who had not forgotten the bloodshed and horror of the siege of 1480.

"Well, Thomas? Antonio? This is an army to be reckoned with, is it not?"

"Yes, my Lord," said Antonio Bosio.

Philippe turned to Thomas Docwra, who had remained silent. There was a slight smile on Docwra's lips; almost a smirk.

"What is it, Thomas?"

Docwra let out a small laugh. "This is indeed a mighty army, my Lord. In fact, if we stay here long enough, it might equal the armies of the Turk!"

Philippe smiled, but Bosio looked puzzled. "What are you saying, Thomas?" Bosio asked.

"Unless my eyes deceive me, those knights of the *langue* of Germany and of Auvergne have already marched by us twice!"

John Buck remained quiet, but a smile appeared on his lips as well.

Philippe interceded quickly.

"Yes, yes, Thomas. But, no more of this. I thought the sight of a few extra knights on display might hearten the spirits of the people. A show of force is all the better if the force is large."

"Yes, but...."

"Enough. These people need all the strength that we can give them. A small deception such as this will harm no one. Let us finish with these ceremonies, and return to the real preparations."

⊰ 6 ⊱

THE WAR CAMP

Üsküdar, Turkey
June, 1522

In the fields outside the walls of Istanbul, the morning mist was just burning off. The summer was beginning to show its strength. It took only an hour or two for the daylight to warm and dry the air. Motes of dust rose and hung in the stillness, kicked aloft by the movement of men and animals.

Barges and *caïques* were making hundreds of trips back and forth across the Bosporus, ferrying men, horses, and tons of supplies from Istanbul to Üsküdar, a mile away across the water. The energies of tens of thousands of men and women were concentrated on the building of a temporary encampment in preparation for the coming battle at Rhodes.

The Sultan's tents were erected first; strong, sturdy, white, red, and blue tents of heavy felt and sail canvas, supported by huge center posts as thick as a ship's mast. The tents provided shelter and comfort in even the most extreme climates. Along with their functional structure, the tents were also decorated with hangings and paintings fit for a museum. Some had several rooms, and many carried regimental banners. There were carpets on the floors and *kilims* hanging on the interior walls. Instead of camp cots, there were *divans* and thick beds for the ranking officers.

The Vizier's tents ringed the Sultan's. Janissaries surrounded the Viziers' circle. The remainder of the military spread out in concentric rings. Courtiers were at the periphery with the tradesmen, as were the food markets and supply wagons.

One man's *serai* stood between the Grand Vizier and the Sultan. This was the tent of Moses Hamon, for the Chief Court Physician was always placed close to the Sultan. The dozens of other military physicians were camped near the field hospital at the edge of the Janissaries' camp.

In front of Suleiman's pavilion, the Janissaries erected the Imperial *Bunchuk*: the Sultan's war standard with its gold crescent and seven black horses' tails. The banners of the various regiments were hoisted into the air, and one by one the elements of the Sultan's armies appeared.

The Janissaries were the first to assemble in the camp, setting their tents in the usual defensive perimeter about the Sultan's Household Guard. Their encampment was precision itself, and nowhere could a visitor find the slightest scrap of garbage or disarray of any kind. It was a far cry from the armed camps of the *ferenghi*, which would reek with excrement within days of encampment.

The daily martial drills of the Janissaries approached, as closely as possible, the real conditions of battle far more than those of any army in the world. The violence was realistic, and injuries were commonplace. The *tabip* were very busy treating the wounds sustained in practice. When the troops were not at their drills, Suleiman insisted upon complete silence in the camp, just as in the Palace.

At the center of each Janissary regiment was a massive copper cooking pot nearly as tall as a man, and the regimental banner. The cooking pot was the symbolic assembly point of each regiment, as cherished as the regimental colors. The men would gather there to receive their meals and to greet their officers. The fine food that was provided for the Janissaries was legendary. Even the ranks of the officers were named after the kitchen positions. Sergeants were Head Cook, and corporals were called Head Waiter. So important was the place of the regimental cooking pot in the campaigns of the Ottomans that it became the rallying point for rebellion as well. Traditionally, when the Janissaries had serious grievances to air, the men would topple over the cooking pot and spill their dinner onto the earth. This was their way of expressing displeasure with the decisions of the Aghas or even the Sultan, himself. The act was a declaration that his fiercest soldiers would no longer eat the Sultan's fine food. The military power of ten thousand highly trained and armed men gave the Sultan and the Aghas cause to pay close attention.

Though fed richly in the war camps, in times of continuing battle or forced march, the Janissaries reverted to a meager diet. They carried leather sacks of flour, salt, and spices. Twice a day, they would mix this with water and eat it uncooked. The mixture swelled up in the stomach, and relieved their hunger even if it provided little in the way of nutrition. They carried a small ration of butter and dried beef to supplement the meals of spiced flour before going into battle.

The Sultan's Household Cavalry was a force of Sipahis heavily armed with lance, bow, and sword. In contrast to the armies of the knights, who depended upon the weight and mass of their broadswords to crush and overpower the enemy, this cavalry used the slim, razor-sharp steel of their curved scimitars to slash their way through the battle lines. Instead of the shock techniques of the massive attacks employed by western armies, the Sultan's troops relied on precision and perfect coordination to cripple the enemy before the kill.

From the Crimea and Ukraine came the fierce horsemen of the Tartar Khans. Each led a string of stout, rugged ponies clad in richly woven saddle cloths. The men appeared too large for the small animals, but the appearance belied the strength and endurance of these short-legged beasts. Each man was armed with the short thick bow, with designs inherited from the days of Ghengis Khan. Any of these men could match the most deadly feats of battle of that legendary army from the steppe of Asia. This light cavalry was used as an advance raiding party to pin down the enemy and return with intelligence as to their numbers and deployment. Their reputation was so fierce, and their coming was so feared, that enemy armies would often disperse and flee before a single arrow was fired.

Arriving after the Tartars came the Sipahis, led by *Beylerbey,* Qasim Pasha, the Provincial Governor of Anatolia in Asia Minor.

Their strategy was to ride as one huge mass of man and horse into the center of a line of infantry. Then, just when it appeared that they were going to strike at the center of the enemy force, they would unleash a huge barrage of arrows while still at full gallop. The arrows would rain down from the sky like hail, and inflict serious damage on the defenders. Holes would appear in the enemy ranks where there had once been a solid phalanx of soldiers. The Sipahis would finish the battle by cutting down the remaining troops with their scimitars, in a furious charge of their horses.

Finally, Ali Bey, the Agha of the Azabs, arrived in the war camp. The Azabs were the marine irregulars, who, as in many armies of the time, would serve as cannon fodder for the Sultan. They would attack the enemy on foot, rushing into the breaches in the defensive walls created by the Sultan's artillery bombardment. Their strength was in their numbers, and they were expendable. All too often their bodies served as stepping stones for their brothers-in-arms, the Janissaries.

With the arrival of the last of the soldiers, as the departure became imminent, some the merchants and craftsmen disappeared back across the Bosporus, to resume their normal trade in Istanbul. A large number, however, would follow this huge army all the way to Rhodes, setting up at the battle camps just as they had in Üsküdar. Commerce and trade would go on even in the midst of furious battle.

When the armies were finally assembled and ready, the Sultan would be notified and word sent to prepare for his procession to the war camp.

—

The Sultan left the Palace with a huge retinue of more than six thousand horsemen in his Imperial Guard. They were mounted on Arabian thoroughbreds, and armed with bows hanging from their shoulders and quivers bursting with arrows. They also carried a mace and a jeweled scimitar, and wore headdresses adorned with black-dyed feathers.

Behind the Imperial Guard came the Janissaries in their light-blue jackets and feathered headdress as well. Then came the rest of the court, the servants, spare horses, and more of the household guard.

All marched in with unnerving silence, the only sounds being that of the stamping of horses' hooves and the padding of the soldiers' boots. There was none of the banter and ribaldry of western armies in the field.

Suleiman followed behind this impressive army, dressed in full battle gear, adorned with the finest silks and brocades. He wore a high white turban with diamonds and rubies that held his treasured heron's feathers.

When the Sultan rode into battle, the sacred green banner of the Prophet, Mohammed, was taken from its vault in the Palace and its forty layers of protective silk cloth unwound from around it. The Muslims carried their holy banner into battle as the Children of Israel carried the Ark of the Covenant. The precious banner was displayed at the vanguard of the Sultan's armies throughout the war until victory was achieved. As it was paraded through the streets of Istanbul, the people bowed low, crying out blessings in the name of Allah.

Other relics, captured from Mecca by the previous Sultans, were also taken to war. Along with the Prophet's banner was the twin-pointed Sword of Omar. For a Muslim *Gazi* to die under this banner and sword in a *jihad*—a holy struggle—was a guarantee for entry into Paradise on the Day of Reckoning. These soldiers would fight the nonbelievers exactly as had the Prophet.

The armies were assembled. Everything was in place. The war camp was complete. It was time to go to war.

Suleiman reclined on the *divan* in the Imperial Tent. The usual guard had been posted both inside and outside the great silk wall. There was silence throughout the tent as the Aghas waited for the Sultan to begin.

"Now then. All is ready," he said finally, as if in the middle of a thought. "This morning after prayers, I called upon Abu-Seoud, the *Sheik ul-Islam*, our Ancient of Islam. As prescribed in the *Qur'an*, I have asked the Sheik to issue a *fetvà*, a ruling, as to whether our war was a holy one, and whether it is incumbent upon good Muslims to follow us into this war. As it is also written in the holy *Qur'an*, I have offered the enemy the opportunity to surrender, and have received no reply from them. The *Sheik ul-Islam* tells me that our *jihad,* our struggle, against the Infidel *is* just, and that Allah will watch over us in the holy battle. Those who die in this cause will find a direct path to the side of the Prophet, may Allah smile upon them.

"It has been our custom to officially declare war by arresting the ambassador and throwing him into our jail. Unfortunately, the knights have recalled their ambassador." The Viziers smiled at the Sultan's small joke.

"Piri Pasha, tradition dictates that you will receive a new and gallant stallion selected from my own stables. He is caparisoned as befits the war horse of my Grand Vizier. You will find a new saddle of the finest leather. And in your quarters this moment is a scimitar with a handle covered in rubies and emeralds...soon, I hope, to be set off with the blood of Christian knights."

Piri bowed his head and remained silent. He would miss his soft saddle and his older, gentler horse, so comfortable to ride in *its* old age.

"Ferhad Pasha, I have a special task for you to complete before your troops join us against the knights. The *Shiite* dog, Shah-Suwar Oghli Ali Bey, is inciting rebellion in Siwas. Go to Persia at once, and destroy this affront to Allah, this menace to our authority. Bring me his head, and the heads of his children, and leave no one alive to trouble my thoughts or my kingdom while I am at Rhodes."

Ferhad Pasha bowed low and backed out of the tent.

"The rest of you will all disembark at Rhodes out of range of the knights' batteries. For I am sure that the Grand Master has sighted us in his guns by now. He will not miss many shots once we are in range. We will encircle the fort in the crescent of Islam from north to south; from sea to sea. We will not make the same error that my great-grandfather made, that is, to wage this war from the water. And, more importantly, I will lead the attack in person. Make no mistake. We will remain on that island until our mission for God is completed!" Still, the Aghas remained silent.

Suleiman waited for comments, but there were none. "The battle plan is simple and effective. We shall cut them off from resupply. We will destroy the walls with cannons and mines. Our troops will enter the city through the gaps in the walls that our miners will create, and our superior forces will cut to pieces whomever remains alive when we enter the fortress. There will be no prisoners. There will be so survivors."

Suleiman looked about the room, and fixed his gaze upon each of his generals in turn. All met his eyes, but again none spoke.

"Now, return to your men, and make ready to move towards Rhodes. May Allah be with you."

Two days later, the camp was struck. The armies of the Sultan began their march south and west across Asia Minor towards Marmarice. The fearsome procession left in separate groups to cross the Anatolian landscape and regroup at Marmarice for the short overwater crossing to Rhodes.

Suleiman and Ibrahim rode side by side along the rolling hills of Anatolia. Behind them rode the Sultan's three pages. One carried Suleiman's water bottle; the second, his cloak; and the third, the Sultan's bow and arrows. Following close at hand, both fore and aft, were the usual guard of Janissaries.

"You have been very quiet this day, Ibrahim. What's on your mind?"

"There is nothing, my Lord. I was just thinking what a pity that we are traveling on such a mission. What a wonderful journey this would be if we were here to hunt and fish and rest by these beautiful lakes and streams."

Suleiman nodded. "There will be time for that when we retrace these steps some weeks from now. After we have driven the Infidels from their lair. Their very existence offends me, Ibrahim. These faithless devils have haunted my dreams. Their Crusades to capture our Holy Lands have gone on now for five centuries, and I cannot think how many Muslim lives have been taken by the Sons of *Sheitan*. They slaughter our men and our children. They rape and torture our women. Life has no meaning to them. They are animals, and we must slaughter them with as little thought to it as stepping on a scorpion. There will be no end to this until they are all gone from our lands." Suleiman looked ahead into the far distance and said, "I think we should find a place to stop for the day. Our armies are only a short day's ride ahead, and I do not wish to overtake them."

"I will send a Janissary to scout over there, and find us a suitable place to spend the night."

Ibrahim spurred his horse and rode off to find the officer in charge of the household guard. Suleiman kept his horse at a slow walk. He was relieved to be freed from the worries about Ibrahim's nighttime excursions. He would never mention a word of it to Ibrahim. Now, his mind was still on the enormous task of coordinating the world's largest fighting force.

Ibrahim sat with his back against the tree while his master arranged himself on the pillows spread out on the carpet in the grass. They both faced the lake, staring at the changing colors of the late afternoon. They had eaten lunch in the tents of the temporary camp. The two had ridden out together with a small guard of Janissaries and archers. The guards stationed themselves out of earshot of the Sultan and Ibrahim; but they were never out of sight of their master. Neither was there a gap in the circle of soldiers who ensured the safety of the Sultan.

"I've heard you and Piri disputing the relative virtues of the Europeans, Ibrahim. How do you find so much to argue about?"

"I have lived among many of them, my Lord. Indeed, I was born in Europe. But, Piri—who has *not* spent time there other than during the attack on Belgrade—loathes them. He tells me," Ibrahim said laughing as he accurately imitated the stuffy accent of Piri Pasha, "'they do not know how to breed proper horses, nor how to grow tulips or roses.' And with that I cannot disagree. He also despises their cities. In Belgrade, he remarked that their houses were dark and damp. They would hover by the fires and see no daylight unless they had to. And they never bathed! The reek of them was obnoxious. He says they only cleanse their insides with wine, and with this I agree as well. Their cities are stinking and foul. The streets run with excrement."

"And if all of this is true, then with what do you disagree?"

"Actually, my Lord, I agree with almost all of it. I just *like* to argue with Piri Pasha."

They both laughed at this, and then Suleiman said, "There is much to despise in the *ferenghi*." He looked over at Ibrahim, placing his hand over his friend's hand. There was a moment of silence and even, Suleiman thought, some tension. He removed his hand, and then turned away again. "Don't worry, Ibrahim. You are not a European to me. When you came to Turkey, and converted to Islam, you became one of us. I know you bathe every day. And you drink little wine. Some things forbidden to us in the *Qur'an* are unforgivable sins. Others..." Suleiman did not finish the thought.

Ibrahim was uncomfortable with his own thoughts. The physical relationship that had seemed normal when they were both young teens now impinged upon the friendship of the grown men. Ibrahim shook his head, as if to drive out the old memories of their intimacies, and changed the subject. "I think that it is the conflict between Islam and the Christians that enrages Piri Pasha most. "

"Of which conflict does he speak?"

"Oh, many. Perhaps all of them. He railed last night about how the Christians can buy their way free of sin with money given to their church. As if their sacred souls might find salvation for sale."

"This is true? They can do this?"

"Yes, my Lord. But, I tell Piri that there are more things in *common* between our faiths than there are differences. Do we not all worship one God? Do we not share the same Prophets? Believe in the same Book? The Holy *Qur'an* tells us how to behave. That we must not kill or steal or cheat or lie. It is a guide to take us through our lives. And are not the laws that guide the Christians—nay, even the Jews—the same. They call them Commandments of God. But, they are the same as the rules recited by the Prophet, and recorded in the Holy *Qur'an*."

"I think I will leave this debate to you and Piri Pasha. At this moment I have no heart for it. My rage against the knights on Rhodes pervades all my thinking. Yet I cannot easily rest even while I direct my energies to the coming battle."

"But, why so, my Lord?"

"I have left a household in upheaval, Ibrahim. I do not know what I shall find when I return." Ibrahim already knew every detail of the story that he was about to hear. He had many sources of his own within the Topkapi Palace, and nothing escaped him. As Ibrahim rose in the power structure of the court, he set out a network of informants to keep him apprised of the intricacies of the court. But, now he settled back in the grass, and let his master and friend talk of what troubled him.

"My life with Gülbehar has been just what I have wanted. You know that I am not like my father, Selim. Nor am I like the Sultans before him. They used the harem to satisfy their desires, and thought little of the *Kadin*, the favored woman. But, I do not feel the need for so many women. I think I have made more visits to the harem to see my mother, Hafiza, than to visit Gülbehar." Both men laughed. "Perhaps it is because I spent so many years in the provinces, away from the Palace and the harem."

Ibrahim nodded. The days in Manisa were the most treasured for the two young men. Those times were the freest either of them would ever be.

"I was only eighteen when Gülbehar was captured," Suleiman went on, "I was drawn to her immediately. She was beautiful, and so fair that I named her Gülbehar, the Flower of Spring. Her hair, her light skin, her eyes were so different from most of the women in the harem that she stood out immediately.

"Indeed, she has pleased me much, and has borne my first son, Mustapha. I cannot think of anything that has brought me more joy than his smiling face." Suleiman paused, and took some grapes from the bowl at his feet.

"I have watched you together, my Lord, and there can be no doubt of your feelings."

Suleiman was quiet for several minutes. He stared across the lake, and continued to eat a handful of grapes. Only his eyes betrayed his troubled thoughts.

Ibrahim knew exactly what was coming. He would not offer any information, but he would not lie to Suleiman if pressed. The Sultan went on. "Another woman has found her way into my life. She was captured in a raid into Galicia near the border of the Ukraine. She immediately captured the attention of the harem, for she was full of energy—and, I think, more than her allotment of mischief. The Keeper of the Linen called her *Khürrem*, the Laughing One. And the name has stayed with her."

Ibrahim knew all of this. In fact, he had heard of this young woman even outside of the Palace. Some of the Europeans in the international and diplomatic society of Istanbul knew of her budding relationship with the Sultan. They had taken to calling her *La Russelane*, the Russian. Over the years, this was corrupted into *Roxelana*. But, for those within the guarded walls of the Palace, she was always *Khürrem*, the Laughing One.

"She was a Christian, of course. The daughter of a Greek Orthodox priest, I'm told. But, she has a fire about her that stirs me beyond my good judgment. I find myself listening to the counsel of my loins instead of the logic in my mind. If I were a Sultan who took to bed the hundreds of girls living in the harem, then she would be one among many. She would get her gold dress and a few jewels, and I would not be troubled this way. But, in truth, I have little experience in this regard, for a Sultan of the Osmanlis. I feel out of control in my own household."

Ibrahim listened without comment. He knew that he and his master had now entered still another era in their relationship. Suleiman's son, Mustapha, was the next heir to the throne of the House of Osman. While the Sultan occupied himself with expansion of his empire and the succession to the throne, Ibrahim would spend his energy and his considerable intelligence toward the consolidation of his own power. Though Piri Pasha was the Grand Vizier, Suleiman still relied heavily upon Ibrahim's advice. This was the legacy of growing up as inseparable friends. While Piri had the title and the power that went with it, Ibrahim still had the ear of the Sultan. And Piri was old.

The Ottoman Sultans rarely married or had any official ceremony recognizing the union between the Sultan and the bearer of his children. There was only the titular position of *Kadin*, First Girl; or *Hasseki*, the Chosen Lady. Though the position of *Kadin* might change with the whims of the Sultan, no religious or legal rite sanctified the union. Even the children of such unions would not stand in the way of the Sultan's whims.

Suleiman interrupted Ibrahim's musings. "There is a naiveté about her that beguiles me. Yet when I look into her smiling eyes, I feel somehow that she is mocking me! Me! The Emperor of the Ottomans!" Suleiman laughed at this, and Ibrahim smiled quietly.

"My Lord, I have seen this *Khürrem* of whom you speak. She *does* stand out among the harem girls. There's no doubt about that."

"She comes to my room from the harem," Suleiman went on, ignoring Ibrahim. "And she performs all the rituals of the approach with care. The Black Eunuch has instructed her well. She knows to make the prostrations at the door, and to approach the bed by touching the coverlets to her forehead. She comes bathed and perfumed, but without jewelry, and slips into my bed with the silence and grace that is required. But, once there, my friend! She does things to me that I have never known. Things that I never dreamed, nor have I heard done before. Her lips! What she can do with her lips! *And* her tongue! I feel I am an adolescent boy in her presence. And by the time the African comes to take her away before dawn, I am of little use until noon. I can only lie in my bed and think about her next visit."

"Why do you fret so now, my Lord? This is a usual thing in the household of a Sultan. Your mother, the *Sultan Valideh*, still rules the harem. She is a wise and strong woman. Surely she will maintain control over these girls?"

"Yes, my friend. Hafiza rules the harem. But, there is something about this *Khürrem* that makes me lose my judgment. Already she has asked me to send Gülbehar and Mustapha away to the provinces so that she may stay with me more often. And, as I prepared to leave for the war camp, she told me that she thinks she is going to have a child. Though she made no scene at my going, as Gülbehar did, I have a feeling that, in my absence, these two women will clash, and that my mother may not be able to contain them. What do you think? You are always wise in matters such as these."

Now, Ibrahim had no choice but to voice his opinion. "My Lord, I have seen you and your son together. And I have seen you and the Flower of Spring together. There is, indeed, much to worry about should the Laughing One bear you a child. Especially a son. For then you will be faced with the Law of Fratricide that you have inherited from Mehmet. I cannot bear to think about your having to order *any* of your children strangled. Forgive me, my Lord, if I speak harshly. But, there is a lot to fear. You have told me that this woman takes away your reason when she takes to your bed. The House of the Osmanli cannot be ruled by passions such as these. I see in the eyes of *Khürrem* a thirst—no a *plan*—to gain control of the palace. Only you can stop this, for it is beyond the capabilities of the *Sultan Valideh*—strong and wise as she is—to stop it. I only want your reign to remain free from the intrigues of court that plagued so many Sultans before you."

"From your lips to Allah's ear, my friend."

Trying to draw Suleiman away from the Palace intrigue, Ibrahim said, "Anyway, my lord, what need is there to build more palaces or cities, for they will be only ruins in short order?"

"So, then," Suleiman asked, shifting away from the uncomfortable subject along with Ibrahim, "what is it that *does* endure?"

"Wisdom...and the music that I play for you."

Suleiman smiled and nodded. He looked at the animals grazing in the fields and added, "And these Angora goats!" With that he burst into laughter, and Ibrahim laughed, too. It took several minutes for the two old friends to calm down. Finally, Ibrahim looked at his boyhood friend, and said wistfully, "Aye, my Lord, truly."

In the early morning of July 11th, several weeks after Suleiman sent him on his mission, Ferhad Pasha rode unannounced into Suleiman's camp as the Sultan was preparing to proceed toward the sea.

The small band of riders, Ferhad Pasha and four of his own Janissaries, dismounted outside the curtain-wall, and walked to the *serai* of the Sultan. They waited in the cool morning air outside the elaborate pavilion. The Sultan's servant emerged first and held his hands up, palms facing toward Ferhad, signaling the Pasha to remain where he was. The Sultan would come out to meet him.

In a moment, Suleiman strode through the tent door dressed in his riding clothes of white silk. He walked towards his waiting guests. When he saw Ferhad and the Janissaries, a huge smile broke out across his face. All of the Sultan's household guards stood at attention, but pleasure beamed in their faces as well.

Suleiman stepped back one pace and admired the presents that his Pasha had brought from Persia. There in the ground before Ferhad were planted four iron pikes. And upon the point of each was a fly-blown human head, mouths and eyes open. In the morning silence, the nickering of the horses dominated the moment, and only the buzzing of the flies as they crawled across the gray faces of the dead called attention to the nature of Ferhad's gift to his Sultan. The heads had begun to decompose in the summer's heat. The eyes were shrunken and shriveled. They stared with an opaque blindness at the Sultan.

"Shah-Suwar Oghli Ali Bey, my Lord," Ferhad extended his hand palm up, and bowed toward the first head, as if introducing two strangers, "and his three sons." Ferhad and his Janissaries knelt down on one knee, and bowed low in the dew dampened grass. "At the service of my Sultan."

Suleiman told the men to rise. He instructed his page to bring some gold coins and reward the Janissaries. "Feed these men," he ordered. Then he turned to Ferhad and said, "Come, my Pasha, we will celebrate your return with breakfast in my *serai*. You will be tired and hungry, I'm sure." Ferhad bowed his head again, and followed the Sultan into his tent.

The armies continued along the remaining two hundred miles to their embarkation point near Marmarice, within sight of Rhodes some twenty miles across the water. The huge armada of over three hundred ships and one hundred thousand men would require several more weeks to disembark and set up their camps on Rhodes. Then, when all was in place, they would await the arrival of their Sultan, Suleiman, and the siege of Rhodes would begin.

⚜ 7 ⚜

THE GATHERING STORM

The Island of Rhodes
June, 1522

On the eighth of June, just after dark, the sentries on the rampart of Italy looked to the northeast, where they saw signal flares. There was no pattern or code. From the distance, the flares seemed to come from the Turkish coast near Marmarice across the water. This was the narrowest point between Rhodes and the Asian mainland. Only twenty-four miles of open water separated the knights from the armies of Suleiman.

The news of the flares was brought to the Grand Master at once. "Send three galleys, with full fighting complements of knights. Take no chances. Approach as if to battle. These might be our own ships in trouble. Or it might be a trap to test our mettle."

The guards left, and spread the word. Within an hour, three galleys left the Mandraccio and headed north. Before dawn, the three galleys were back. No shots had been fired. No fighting engagement made. The captain of the small task force ran up the small hill from the Mandraccio. He entered the fortress through St. Paul's Gate, and made his way left along the Street of the Knights. The narrow, cobble-stoned street was still dark and wet as he hurried under the imposing walls of the Inns. At the Inn of Provence, he turned right and made his way to the Palace of the Grand Master. He saluted the knights on guard, and took the main stairs two at a time.

Philippe was waiting in the anteroom of his quarters. With him was Thomas Docwra. Both men were restless and visibly ill at ease. The captain was winded from his run. He still wore his fighting armor. His outer cape was wet from the salt spray and the light rain. He bowed, and pulled from his black cloak a rolled parchment, tied and sealed with the *tuğra* of the Sultan, Suleiman.

Philippe knew this seal well, as he had seen it when he had received Suleiman's Letter of Victory. He knew before even opening it that this letter would be more direct. The Sultan had already issued the formal warning required by his religion. The *Qur'an* required that notice be given and time allowed for the enemy to surrender before an attack. That time was well past.

He took the letter from the captain and motioned to the table where a late dinner and wine had been set. "Help yourself, Captain, while I see what the Sultan has in store for us."

"Thank you, *Signore*. This message was delivered to us at sea. The flares had been sent up by the Sultan's galleys a mile off shore. No trouble finding the hulk in the dark for all the stink of it. By God, they're heathens! I think they delivered this letter off shore so that we would not see what forces they had on land. But, I can tell you that the fires that burned in their camps numbered in the thousands. This is no small raiding party. This is a major invasion, *Signore*."

Philippe nodded silently, broke the seal, and removed the silk ribbon. He tossed the ribbon into the fire, and read aloud:

The Sultan. To Villiers de L'Isle Adam, Grand Master of Rhodes, to his knights, and to the people at large.

Your monstrous piracies, which you continue to exercise against my faithful subjects, and the insult you offer to my Imperial Majesty, oblige me to command you to surrender your island and fortress immediately into my hands. If you do this, I swear by God who made heaven and earth, by the four thousand prophets which came down from heaven, by the four sacred books, and by our great Prophet Mohammed that you shall be free to leave the island, while the inhabitants who remain there shall not be harmed. But, if you do not obey my order at once, you shall all pass under the edge of my invisible sword, and the walls and fortifications of Rhodes shall be reduced to the level of the grass that grows at their feet.

Philippe handed the document to Docwra, who read it slowly again. "This son of a whore doesn't know what he's up against!" Docwra said.

"Indeed, he does not, Thomas," Philippe said calmly. "Make preparations as if the attack were to come at once. We will send no reply. That may buy us some time, for if we reply to this...this obscenity," pointing to Suleiman's letter, still in Docwra's hand, "he will set out at once. Instead, let him wait for our reply. Surely he will hope for an easy victory by our surrender. He has not forgotten the losses suffered by his great-grandfather. Unless he is truly insane—which I doubt he is—he will want to take an easy victory from us. While he waits for our reply, Thomas, go out this very moment and declare martial law on the island. Send word to whomever is still outside the walls to hurry here at once and bring whatever weapons, food, and clothing they may have. Leave no food or shelter out there that might give comfort to our enemy. For, it's possible that we may not leave this fortress again for many months to come. Alert the knights that we shall meet before dawn to make our final plans to defend the city. And I shall see that the final strengthening of the defenses is carried out as speedily as possible."

"*D'accord, Seigneur. Tout de suite.*" Yes, my Lord. At once. As Docwra turned to go, he paused and said, "One more thing, my Lord."

"Yes?"

"There is a Florentine ship's captain by the name of Bartoluzzi. He is here in Rhodes, and I spoke with him about the possibility of a prolonged siege. He had a suggestion that we might want to consider."

"And that was?"

"Well, he noted the large number of ships moving in and out of our ports. He suggested that we commandeer some of them and turn them into fire ships. That we load them with explosives and send them out among the Turks *before* they are debarked on the island, to set as many of their fleet ablaze as possible. He even offered to lead the attack with his own ship. We might severely damage their supply line and decrease the numbers of men that we have to face on shore."

"Thank you, Thomas. And thank Captain Bartoluzzi for his idea and his brave offer. I have given a lot of thought to whether we should engage the Turks on the water. There is no question that we have the superior fleet in terms of skill and seamanship. We could do great damage in a conflict at sea. But, the numbers here are so overwhelming in terms of ships and men set against us that even if we were to strike them in a surprise attack, I fear the loss of lives and ships would, in the end, be too much for our small force."

Docwra nodded.

Philippe continued. "A good idea, Thomas, but I think we should conserve our limited supply of men and powder for a more certain battle behind our walls."

Docwra nodded again. He left the anteroom and sped from the Palace. Philippe turned to the captain and said, "Finish your meal. I think this may be the last hot, unhurried dinner you will eat for a very long time."

The captain, unable to contain himself, gulped down the remaining food and wine and, with a bow, hurried from the Palace.

Philippe was alone for the first time in many days. The comings and goings of his staff, the preparations, the battle plans, and the interminable details had all conspired to leave him barely a minute to himself. The sudden emptiness of the room and the unusual quiet bore down on him with a heaviness that caught him by surprise. He slumped into his great oak chair, rubbing his eyes. He moved his papers to the side and stared down at the ancient oak table, dark and scarred with age. He tried to close his eyes and rest, but sleep would not overtake his thoughts. Again his mind wandered—as it had almost every hour of his waking days and nights that were not fully occupied with the business of war—back to Paris; back to his rooms across from *L'Isle de la Cité*.

He had been standing in the darkness, staring at the flying buttresses of the great cathedral of Notre Dame de Paris, then almost four hundred years old. The great stone edifice was shrouded at its base with the light mist coming off the river, a few orange lights flickering at the rear of the building. It had been...how long? Ten months? *Could it be only ten months?* he asked himself. It was the night the message had come from Rhodes. He had been elected the new Grand Master. The night had been calm, and it was after midnight when Hélène came to him. She often came late at night, when the chances of being seen were least. Sometimes she could stay through the next day, holding every moment together as if it might be their last. *Ten months!* he told himself. *Surely not.*

And when would he see his Hélène again? Another ten months? Ten years? Ever? What was she doing now? This moment. Was she with another man? Would she wait for him on the slight chance that he would return? Philippe could not follow the thought through to completion. Each time he pictured her—her young and lovely body—in the arms of another. Sometimes a stranger. Other times he would see her in the embrace of one of his knights. He would squeeze his eyes shut, as if denying himself vision could possibly erase the image in his mind. And, of course it never did.

His first meeting with Hélène had been so innocent. Nothing could have told him. Nothing could have warned him. Only the feeling in his chest, and the unfamiliar sensation in his groin when he saw her for the very first time.

Philippe was walking through the *Jardins* one early April afternoon. The Parisians had flocked to the streets with the first taste of warm weather. The winter had been particularly severe, with spring gray and damp day after day. As he moved among the groups of families out for a quick break from their toils, he was drawn most strongly to the couples walking quietly in the bright warmth of the day. His heart felt heavy with the knowledge that he was destined by his vows to God to forever walk alone. For all the camaraderie and honor inherent in his knighthood, there was still an emptiness that he could not ignore. On days such as these, he could not deny his yearning for the physical and emotional connection with a woman.

Hélène had been sitting near a fountain, tossing small pebbles into the water. Her eyes never left the water as she watched the ripples spread and disappear. Philippe stopped to stretch his back. He looked up at the sky, and let the sun warm his face. When he resumed his walk, he saw her sitting alone. She had dark eyes, nearly black in the bright sun; long dark hair hung down in loose curls over her shoulders. She was slender, and, even sitting, Philippe could see that she was rather tall. Philippe guessed her to be about twenty-five years old, though he would later learn that she was nearer thirty-five. She was perched on the edge of the fountain, with her legs tucked back under her. On the ground just behind her was a woven basket with some bread and fresh vegetables. Philippe was torn between his powerful instincts to walk nearer and introduce himself, and the knowledge that his knight's vows of celibacy made such a meeting improper; impossible that it could lead anywhere. But, how he wanted to taste the sweetness of just a few moment's innocent conversation with this lovely woman.

Hélène continued to stare at the water, completely unaware of Philippe's interest in her. Philippe shook his head, as if to drive his unthinkable urges from his mind, when his attention was taken by the sound of feet running along the coarse gravel path behind the woman. He turned toward the noise in time to see a tall man dressed in rags. The man was running flat out in Hélène's direction. Instinctively, Philippe's hand went to his sword—an épée, shorter, lighter, and faster than the broadsword he carried into battle. He stepped forward to protect this woman so peacefully engrossed in her thoughts.

The running man bore down upon Hélène. Philippe closed the distance between them, trying to insert himself into the man's path. In that slowing of time that happens in such moments, he could see a frenzy in the man's eyes, dirt embedded in the heavy layers of clothing. Sweat poured down the man's face—a face covered with stubble and several open sores—as he ran toward the woman. He never looked at Philippe, but closed steadily on Hélène. Philippe drew his sword at the very instant the running man closed the last few feet that separated him from Hélène. The man stooped low without slackening his pace, and Philippe thought he was about to tackle her. The man's arm shot out and snatched at the basket sitting on the ground, just as Philippe leapt to close the gap and shield the woman from the attack. Philippe held his sword in his right hand, blade low, trying to impale the running man before he made contact with Hélène. At the very same moment, the man swerved. Grabbing the basket and changing direction like an antelope, he veered away from Philippe and Hélène.

Philippe maintained a protective arc with his sword, creating a safe zone around Hélène that no one could invade. But, his great bulk had gained too much momentum, and he could not prevent himself from crashing into her as she sat unaware on the edge of the fountain. Philippe slipped on the gravel as he tried to slow himself down. His shoulder struck her back, knocking her off the edge and into the shallow water. Hélène shrieked at the painful blow and the surprise. Too late, Philippe reached out with his free left hand to grab at her right arm in an attempt to keep her from falling into the fountain. His bare sword hand still wrapped around the handle of his weapon smashed into the gravel, abrading the skin along all four knuckles as his full weight came to bear upon the supporting arm.

Hélène, thinking she was under attack, swung her elbow back toward Philippe, catching him squarely across the bridge of his nose. There was a loud crack as two small bones broke under the force of Hélène's blow. She slid off the edge, propelled in part by her own strike against Philippe, landing up to her waist in the cold water. When she turned to resume her defense, Philippe was kneeling in the gravel, holding his right hand to his face. His sword hand was still supporting his body. As he turned toward Hélène, she could see the blood running between his fingers and down his sleeve. She pulled herself to her feet and was about to resume her own attack when she saw the sword in his hand. She stopped where she stood in the fountain, now afraid for her life. She never noticed that the food basket was gone. This was no petty *voleur,* no thief. There before her was a knight, sword in hand, blood streaming from his nose. Hélène was truly frightened now. She had been attacked by this stranger whom, from the looks of it, she had seriously injured. She took a step back deeper into the fountain, maintaining a safe distance from the injured knight.

Philippe collected himself and stood, wincing as he pushed up on his injured sword hand. He resheathed his sword, and drew a handkerchief from his pocket. He turned to Hélène as he held the handkerchief to his nose. He wiped away the blood, still grimacing slightly from the pain in his nose and his hand. *"Pardon, Mademoiselle. Je vous en prie,"* Excuse me, Miss, I beg of you. "I was unable to stop the thief who stole your basket." He turned to his left, and could see only the small crowd slowly gathering about them. There was, of course, no sign of the thief. "He has gotten away, I'm afraid. *Je suis désolé."* I am so sorry.

"Thief?" she said. "What thief?"

Philippe pointed to where the basket had been and said, "Your basket. I'm afraid it's gone. But, thank God you are all right."

The two stared at each other for a moment. Only then did Hélène realize what had happened. At the same time Philippe saw what he had done to the young woman, and after an awkward moment the two began to laugh. Philippe reached out and took her hand as she stepped out of the fountain, soaked through from her toes to the bottoms of her breasts, which were now outlined beyond any hope of modesty. Hélène stepped from the fountain and began to shiver. Through her chattering teeth she said, *"Je suis désolé aussi, Monsieur le Chevalier."* I, too, am sorry, Monsieur Knight. "Your nose...and your hand. I'm so sorry."

Philippe covered her body with his surcoat, and helped Hélène back to her small apartment near the market. He started a fire for her to help ward off the cold, and made some tea while she changed into dry clothes.

So Philippe had met the young woman. They met often after that, clandestinely at first. Usually, they stayed at her apartment, but after a few weeks the secrecy began to weigh upon them. Their affair took on a seedy feeling. They began to go out into the streets of Paris more and more openly. Though Hélène could never be seen at formal functions of the Knights Hospitaller, she was content to bide her time with Philippe. They didn't discuss the future at all.

It was now nearly three years since Hélène had broken Philippe's nose and captured his heart. And he loved her more every day. *Where,* he thought, *is Hélène now?*

Philippe found himself staring again at the oak desk, and his real world closed in once more.

As Philippe returned to the present, Gabriel de Pommerols, a lieutenant and countryman of the Grand Master's, rushed into the anteroom. He was breathless, and paused a moment to collect himself. Then he removed his helmet and bowed to Philippe. Philippe motioned him to the table. Pommerols removed his cape, gloves, and sword, and sat down opposite Philippe.

"*Seigneur, un moment, je vous en prie.*" My Lord, a moment, please.

Philippe waited silently for de Pommerols to get settled. As they waited, Thomas Scheffield entered the room. As *Seneschal*, the officer in charge of domestic relations and ceremony, he would naturally be privy to all important communications with the Grand Master.

Sheffield nodded to de Pommerols and took a seat beside him. "I heard of your arrival, Gabriel. What news of the reinforcements?"

"*Doucement*, Thomas." Gently. Philippe held his hand up, giving de Pommerols a moment more.

Finally, collecting himself, de Pommerols said, "My Lords, I have very little good news to tell you. Though we have gotten word to all the knights who have been away to come home at once, the rest of my mission has been a failure." Philippe and Sheffield looked at each other and then back to de Pommerols. Neither spoke. Sheffield toyed with the knife at his belt, while the Grand Master sat quietly with his hands folded in front of him.

De Pommerols went on. "Pope Adrian will send us neither money nor men. He refused us even after he heard the pleadings of Cardinal Giulio d'Medici. The Cardinal is a member of our Order, my Lord, and even his tears had no effect on the Pope. His Eminence says that he can spare neither troops nor money at this time. He says that he needs all his resources to fight the French armies now harassing him on the very soil of Italy."

"And of England? What news there?"

"Henry of England will send no help either. He needs money for his domestic wars and extravagances." De Pommerols looked at Thomas, expecting disapproval for speaking of his sovereign this way. "I'm sorry, Thomas, but it is so."

Sheffield nodded. This was not news to him. His loyalty after so many years was to his brother knights more than to his king. He had only lived a few years on English soil, and since he joined the Order, he had not been home at all.

"Henry is at this moment claiming many of the lands and estates of our own knights. He is taking them on various pretexts, but in reality he needs the incomes, and he's jealous of the power we have gained abroad."

Philippe waited a moment, and then asked, "And France?"

"Chaos rules Europe, my Lord. As Holy Roman Emperor, Charles is worried about this heretic Martin Luther. Luther's following is growing larger by the day, and he divides the people of the Church. Charles is at open war with Francis. Francis is at war with Italy. Everyone fears to send us money or men that they might need themselves. They send us only their prayers and their good wishes. I am afraid, my Lord, we can look only to ourselves for our salvation."

"And to God. But, I expected nothing of them. I had only hoped. They have a long history of looking on and doing nothing. Only a year or so ago, when the Turk attacked Belgrade, the King of Hungary sent to Europe for help. Indeed, they should have feared that the loss of Belgrade would bring the Sultan's armies to their very doorstep. But, they did nothing. The princes of Europe hoped that the Turks would be turned back without their help. Now they quiver in fear of another Turkish attack. Buda, Prague, and Vienna will fall to the Sultan as surely as did Belgrade. But, they fight among themselves and send no aid to anyone. No. We must expect no help from anyone but ourselves and God Almighty."

Philippe rose from the table and walked to the window. He looked out over the walls toward the sea. The sky was clear, and only the occasional fair-weather clouds dotted the expanse of rich blue. White caps blew off the surface of the ocean and wisps of spray were visible from the window. He thought of his peaceful island and its incredible beauty. The crops of fruit and the roses. The mountains and the clear streams. Now, after forty-two years of relative peace, the blood of his knights and of the Rhodians would once again stain the streets of his city.

The Grand Master waited in his private chambers for the arrival of Antonio Bosio. By now, the Servant-at-Arms had proven himself able to handle the most difficult and dangerous assignments. The man was inventive and determined. Little could stop him once he had made up his mind on any given task.

When the Grand Master was provisioning the fortress for the lengthy siege to come, he had assigned Bosio the task of getting as much wine as might be needed for at least one year. The wine would be necessary as a medicinal as well as a libation. Bosio went out in a galley with a full complement of heavily armed knights. In short order, he negotiated fifteen shiploads of wine bound for various Mediterranean ports under a Venetian flag. Venice was trying hard to stay neutral in the coming conflict with Turkey, fearing that Suleiman might turn his armies on her instead of Rhodes.

After Bosio had diverted the Venetian ships to Rhodes, he then enrolled the foreign crews to fight as mercenaries for the knights. In spite of the Venetian neutrality, he was able to conscript five hundred expert archers from Crete. They were all off-loaded disguised as wine laborers and merchants, and quickly organized into a fighting force.

Shortly thereafter, Bosio boarded the ship of Master Bonaldi, a Venetian, bound for Istanbul with seven hundred casks of wine. With a little persuasion, Bonaldi eventually volunteered his services as well as the wine.

Less-willing accomplices were also boarded on the high seas. Domenico Fornari, a Genoese sailor, was bound for Istanbul from Alexandria with a load of grains. Eight miles from Rhodes, Bosio boarded his ship, and was able—after several uncomfortable hours for Fornari—to convince the man to serve the knights.

Philippe paced the floor as he waited for Bosio. There was a loud double rap at the door, and Bosio appeared in the doorway. Philippe nodded impatiently, summoning Bosio into the room. "Sit down, Antonio. I have a dangerous mission for you."

Bosio smiled, moved to the desk, and sat opposite Philippe's chair. Philippe remained standing. "I have received a good deal of intelligence that Suleiman has recruited expert miners and sappers from his lands in Bosnia. These mines, along with his very powerful artillery, is surely what he intends to use to destroy our defenses. The walls were well reinforced these last months, and I think artillery alone will not breach them. But, if he has the time to dig beneath the walls and set mines, there might be the danger of a breach. Especially in some of the weaker fortifications such as the Bastion of England."

Bosio listened in silence. He had no idea where this was leading, or what his job would be.

Philippe continued. "There is a Bergamese engineer named Gabriele Tadini da Martinengo. Have you heard of him?"

"Yes, my Lord, I have."

"Well, my sources tell me he is a genius in the arts of mining and countermining. He is working as Engineer General and Colonel of Infantry for the Governor of Venice in Crete, the Duke of Trevisani."

"Trevisani will never let him go, my Lord. Venice is committed to staying out of this war. They are afraid of Suleiman's armies more than they are afraid of their hostile neighbors."

"Yes. Quite. But, this Tadini; he is, from what I hear, a soldier of fortune. My sources tell me he is bored in Crete. He is a military genius and a ferocious fighter. I suspect that the right person could convince him to join our side in the coming battle. They tell me he longs for battle, and could be turned."

"And you would like me to 'turn' him?"

"Exactly."

"Where is he right now?"

"He is still on Crete, in Candia, not far from the Bay of Mirabella. I have sent inquiries to see if he might be able to come of his own accord. Somehow, Trevisani heard of my offer and forbade Tadini to join us. On pain of death."

"So, Tadini knows we want him. And from what you tell me, he seems inclined to join us. I would have only to provide a way?"

"Exactly. But, it would be dangerous for you both. If the Duke's guard were to catch you, you would surely hang. Both of you."

"We will not be caught, my Lord. I assure you of that. When do I leave?"

"Tonight. There is a galley in the Mandraccio with a full complement of knights. Most of them have sailed with you before. Provisions are on board. Here is a letter under my seal for you to give to Tadini. It will guarantee his wages and his rank, as well as safe conduct should he wish to leave us." Philippe handed Bosio the papers.

"I will be back with Tadini, my Lord. You have my word."

"God speed to you both."

Bosio's galley hove to just off shore, not far from the cliffs near the Bay of Mirabella. The night sky was lit only by the starlight, and the wind was light. Bosio and the knights waited on deck as the galley's oarsmen held water. They dared not anchor, for they were poised to move in an instant. Bosio squinted into the darkness. He watched the beach in the direction of Candia.

The meeting three nights earlier had gone well. His galley had pulled near shore at Candia. He had been put ashore in a small boat and was met—as planned—by two old friends, Scaramosa and Conversalo. Bosio trusted them both with his life. In the middle of the night, they took Bosio to Tadini's quarters. Tadini read the letter from Philippe, and without a moment's hesitation had wrapped his arms around Bosio and lifted him off the ground. He kissed Bosio on both cheeks, and then turned to his two companions and said in Italian, *"E tu due? Son con noi?"* And you two? Are you with us?

"Of course, Signore," Scaramosa replied, "but we cannot stay here now. *Andiamo!*" Let's go.

"Signore Bosio. Give me three nights to gather my things and prepare for our escape. These men need the time, too. We must also make a diversion for that night, so nobody will know we are gone for several hours. That will give us time to meet you. Once we are on the galley, I am confident that your fine crew will get us safely out of here and off to Rhodes."

He hugged Bosio again with an exuberance that he just could not contain. Two more kisses were planted on Bosio's cheeks before Tadini let him go. "We will show those Muslims a thing or two about mining, eh? I have a new invention I am anxious to try. The Sultan will regret his little expedition, and wish he had stayed in Istanbul. This, I can promise you."

—

As the galley neared the entrance into the Mandraccio, Philippe recognized the shape and the uniform of Antonio Bosio standing atop the ramming sprit in the bow, waving wildly to the small gathering on the pier. Standing next to him was the man that Philippe could not recognize but was so anxious to meet. The galley hove to, the lines cast ashore. Greetings were shouted in French and Italian. The camaraderie was contagious, and soon all the knights were greeting their brothers from the galley.

Tadini extricated himself from the embraces of the knights and turned to the Grand Master. He took Philippe's extended hand and knelt down on one knee. He bowed his head and kissed the Grand Master's gauntlet. Then he rose and burst into a great wide smile. "Gabriele Tadini da Martinengo, *Seigneur. À votre service.*"

"*Benvenuto, mìo amico.*" Philippe's Italian was passable.

"*Si, Signore. Con tutto mi cuòre.*" Yes, my Lord. With all my heart.

Philippe turned to Docwra and the knights and said, "Leave us now. We will celebrate the arrival of these brave men tonight at dinner at the Inn of France. For now, I have great need to speak with Brother Tadini at my quarters." Philippe had called Tadini his brother, indicating to the crowd that they had just welcomed a new knight into their ranks.

—

It was June 26th, the Feast of the Corpus Domini. The first ships of the main force of the Turks were expected to pass just offshore before the city of Rhodes. As the midsummer morning sun moved over the walls of the fortress, the palace gates suddenly opened, and the procession began. The Grand Master was mounted upon a magnificent charger, whose muscles rippled beneath its carefully groomed white hair. The horse was in full battle armor, his rider was completely covered in his own ceremonial armor of gold, which glistened in the sun, making it difficult to look directly at him.

The Piliers of the eight *langues* who rode behind the Grand Master were also dressed in their finest battle armor. The Piliers were the senior knights in each *langue*, and held traditional posts in the Order. Docwra, himself of the *langue* of England, was the *Turcopilier*, or Commander of the Light Cavalry. As he moved along the Street of the Knights he passed the *Auberges*, the Inns, of the other *langues*. At the Inn of Italy, the Admiral of the Fleet moved alongside Docwra. Then as they passed the Auberge de France, the Pilier who served as Hospitaller joined their ranks. The three moved on and were joined by the Marshal from Auvergne and the Grand Commander from Provence. As they approached the *Loggia*, the open court at the end of the Street of the Knights, they were met by the Grand Conservator from Aragon and the Grand Bailiff from Germany. The seven men walked quickly in a tight knot through the *Loggia*, where a number of knights were drilling and preparing for the coming war.

As the day progressed, they would grow distinctly uncomfortable in their heavy hot outfits. But, for the moment they were a splendid spectacle that gave heart to the citizens of Rhodes.

Five hundred knights followed on foot, dressed in their scarlet battle surcoats with the white crosses of St. John on the left front breast and in the center of the back. They carried their broadswords and battle shields as they filed past the crowds gathered in the city. Within the walls of the city, the town was bursting with people and animals. Nearly the entire population of the island had sought refuge from the oncoming Turks, bringing with them farm animals and pets, food and household provisions. Many side streets were blocked with carts and supplies. Dogs wandered the alleyways looking for food and for their lost families.

In spite of the crowding and the discomfort, the knights and the citizens were happy to proceed with the festival day. They needed to show themselves, as much as the Turks, that they were not afraid.

As the Grand Master proceeded past the crowd at the entrance to the *Collachio*, the Convent of the Knights, trumpets announced his passage and drums marked the time of his march. At a signal from within the Street of the Knights, the highest windows of all the Auberges of the various *langues* were thrown open, and hundreds of flags began to wave in the morning sun. The yellow lilies on a blue background marked the Inn of France; golden lions rampant were flown from the Inn of England. All the *langues* displayed their colors, the crowds cheering the display of each in turn.

In the procession, the knights marched by country. There were only nineteen knights from England on the island, and they formed their own small phalanx. Their force of only nineteen knights, led by *Turcopilier* John Buck, was combined with the knights from Aragon. Throughout the history of the Order, the Knights of Provence had traditionally taken on the defense of the most dangerous outposts. On Rhodes, they would continue the tradition with the defense of the vital Tower of St. Nicholas. The French fielded the largest body of knights, with over two hundred of them marching behind the Piliers.

As the knights passed the entrance to the city, they received blessings from their spiritual leaders. In a show of solidarity, the Latin Bishop, Leonardo Balestrieri, and the Greek Archbishop, Clement, stood shoulder to shoulder making signs of the cross and murmuring prayers for the knights and their city.

As the parade left the city, the crowds followed them through the outer streets and into the nearby countryside. From across the blue water they all could see the massive armada that was heading their way. Hundreds of ships of war under full sail were plowing a white foam on the water's surface. By noon, the Turkish ships were clearly in view, and it would be hard to find anyone on Rhodes who did not resonate significant fear at the sight of this enormous battle armada. In a few moments, the brave knights, the citizen militia, and the mercenaries realized the pitiful size of their own army compared to the hoard of men and supplies that was bearing down on their island home.

As Suleiman's fleet passed the tip of the island and began their turn southeast to their debarkation point at Kallitheas Bay, a deafening roar filled the air. Many of the citizens thought they were under attack, and ran for cover. Horses shied, and the riders struggled to maintain control. Then smoke appeared on the wind, coming from the battlements of Fort St. Nicholas, which guarded the mole at the end of the Galley Port. When all eyes turned there, the knights and the Rhodians could see a second volley fired from their city at the Turkish fleet. They began to cheer and throw their hats into the air. A few people could see the splash of the cannon shot landing well short of the ships in the choppy seas. The Turks knew to keep out of range, and the knights at the fort knew they could not reach the ships. The knights wanted only to show the Turks what welcome was in store for them. For their part, many of the Turkish sailors had heard stories of the destruction that the knights' cannons had inflicted upon the Turkish fleet in 1480. Rather than responding with cannon fire, the Turks bombarded the Rhodians with music. From the shores, the knights and the citizens of Rhodes could just make out the sound of trumpets and drums; of bosuns' whistles and tambours; of cymbals and pipes.

Then, as if to accentuate and complete the picture of the Turkish fleet, a terrible smell began to reach the island. At first, the people began to look about them for the source, for it smelled like an overflowing sewer. The knights who had experienced battle against the Turkish galleys realized at once where the smell had come from. The onshore breeze had brought to Rhodes the dreadful odors of the Turkish galleys themselves. For, the slaves that manned the oars were chained to their places, their excrement puddled in the scuppers of the ships they rowed.

Then another sound made its way to the shores. Carried across the water, amid the trumpets and the drums, was heard the rhythmic crack of the galley-master's whips as they snapped the air over the backs of the slaves at the oars.

Philippe paused at the top of the hill and brought the procession to a halt. "Well, Thomas," he said to Docwra who was riding at his right, "they are here at last. I wonder when we will again stand upon this promontory."

"Soon, I hope, my Lord; to watch their sails retreating whence they came."

"A brave thought, Thomas. Let us hope God has that plan in mind as well."

With that, he wheeled his horse and led the band of warriors back into their walled city. Nobody in the crowd could help but wonder when they would emerge again.

BOOK TWO

—

TWO
STRONG
MEN

⊰ 8 ⊱

THE SULTAN'S ARMY

The Island of Rhodes
July, 1522

By mid-July, after weeks of shuttling supplies from the Turkish mainland, the entire army and navy of the Sultan had landed at Rhodes. It was decided that the mass of the Ottoman Army would land on Rhodes together in as great a show of strength as possible. Suleiman would wait in his camp at Marmarice, on the shores of Asia Minor, twenty-four miles away, until his army was fully deployed. Only then would the Sultan proceed to Rhodes for the beginning of the siege.

Their spies had told the Turks that the knights were preparing to defend the island completely from within the fortress. But, Mustapha Pasha wanted no surprises. Though he planned to land his men and equipment fully six miles from the city, at Kallitheas Bay, he did not want to be ambushed while his ships were being unloaded and vulnerable to fire from a shore party. Mustapha's fears turned out to be well founded, for though the knights had committed to defending their island from the fortress, they sent out small parties of knights to harass the Turks.

In groups of ten or twelve, the knights would exit the city secretly after dark. They made their way along the walled gardens and behind the destroyed dwellings of the outer city. The knights knew the terrain intimately, while the Turks were still learning their way.

Jean de Morelle commanded the first such raiding party. Five knights from the *langue de France* and six more from Provence slipped through the St. John's Gate between the Posts of England and Provence. They followed the shadows of the walls through the ditches, and emerged to the far northwest side. There, they mounted their horses and made a wide counterclockwise arc, bringing them to the road between Kallitheas Bay and the main storage depot of the Turks.

When they reached the small wooded section they had chosen for their cover, they split up. Jean said, "Pierre, take your six men around to the rocks over there, and wait for the next party of Turks to arrive. If there are more than thirty of them, do nothing. But, if they are mostly load-bearing slaves and a moderate guard, wait until they have completely passed your position. Then charge down upon them from behind. They should flee directly ahead on the road. The rocks will prevent them from scattering to the sides. We'll wait to take them from the front, in their panic. Christ be with thee."

"And thee." Without another word, Pierre signaled his men, and rode off in the direction of Kallitheas Bay. After riding less than twenty yards, they disappeared into the darkness of the night. Only the soft patting of the horses' hooves remained hanging in the night air, and the occasional metallic sound of sword and scabbard. In another minute, there was only the sounds of the night; the rhythm of the crickets and the rustle of the leaves moving in the negligible breeze. Jean and his four men split into two groups, flanking the road. They hid in the cover of the sparse woods, invisible.

And they waited.

The horses barely moved, but stood facing the road under light rein and a reassuring hand upon their necks. The knights whispered words of comfort to the animals. *"Doucement, mon brave. Doucement."* The horses, lulled by their masters' voices, settled in to wait as well.

Thirty minutes passed, a long gap in what had been a steady flow of traffic along the road by daylight. Jean whispered to the knights at his side. "I hope this doesn't mean that the Turks are waiting to send a large, heavily guarded force."

The other knight had only just murmured, *"Oui,"* when a noise was heard in the distance.

At first Jean could hear the loud voices of his men shouting and cursing in French. He could hear the screaming and panic in the darkness; strange voices and a language he did not understand. Then, the lower-pitched sounds of horses' hooves came to him just as the first of the fleeing porters appeared out of the darkness, racing down the road toward the knights. Most had dropped the heavy bundles and were running as only the terrified can run. Others held onto their loads, reflexively clinging with both hands to the tump lines around their foreheads.

Every man in the road was running straight ahead of the galloping horses. Before the porters were within sight of Jean, the slowest of the porters was cut down by the knights. Bodies covered the roadway, headless, dying before hitting the ground. The wounded staggered on, driven by fear and the faint hope of escape, bleeding to death as they stumbled along. One by one, the knights rode them down, slashing and stabbing with sword and lance.

Within minutes, the pursuing knights had to slow their pace so that horses would not trip over the bodies of the dead and the wounded, or the scattered bundles of supplies lying in their path. It was too dark to risk injury by jumping the horses over the obstructions.

Pierre's assault began to lose its momentum, the fleeing porters gathering strength from the sense they were, at last, outdistancing the pursuing enemy.

Just as the survivors were regaining their hope, they heard a cry in the night.

"Allons-y! Jean shouted to his tiny band. He spurred his horse forward. The four knights dashed into the middle of the road and wheeled to their left to form a solid wall. The porters stopped short, standing in the middle of the road like frightened deer.

Without a second's pause, the knights rode into the remaining Turks and cut them down with their swords. Not a porter or guard survived the attack. Not a single knight was injured.

Both groups of knights quickly surveyed the scene, killing off the wounded as they begged for their lives in Turkish, or prayed for salvation from Allah in Arabic. When the slaughter was finished, Jean signaled for the knights to retrieve the enemy's weapons. This done, the knights disappeared into the bush, leaving the road empty and quiet once again.

Jean led his men back the way they had come, entering the fortress through the same hidden passage. They tended to their horses and gathered at the Inn of France. Philippe had joined the other French knights for a late meal, and was awaiting Jean's return.

"So, my Lord!" Jean said to Philippe. "There are several less porters and Turks on our island tonight. They have gone to their God. Not a survivor to tell the tale."

"Well done, Jean," Philippe said. "Any of our men hurt?"

"Not a scratch, my Lord. Not one."

"Thank God for that. If only the rest of our battles will be so easy. Somehow I doubt it."

The men grew curiously quiet at the Grand Master's words. Each realized that the porters' fate could easily be theirs in due course. They finished their meals in silence rather than celebration, and returned to their posts.

For Suleiman's army, the process of landing troops and equipment was immense. Day and night, without let-up, ships crossed the few miles of open water between Rhodes and the mainland. Men unloaded uncountable tons of food, shot, powder, and cannon. Mortars were brought ashore; picks and shovels; timber and draught animals; cooking utensils; and, of course, the Janissaries' huge copper cooking pots. Tents were stacked for later use; dried meats and grains unloaded and stored. Extra guns, swords, pikes, and bows and arrows were set aside to replace those that would inevitably be lost in the battles ahead.

Almost immediately the heaviest cannons were set up in preparation for the bombardment of the city. The biggest were placed on a hillside opposite the Post of England. Another was aimed at the Tower of Aragon, and still another at Provence. It was Mustapha

Pasha's plan to begin the bombardment immediately, to cover the unloading of his men and equipment. He wanted the Sultan to arrive and see what wonderful destruction his new artillery could produce. Before Selim died he had built a massive new foundry across the Bosphorus at Tophane. The newest technology and metallurgy was employed to build cannons more powerful than had ever been seen before. Some of the biggest guns became so hot they could fire only once per hour. But most could hurl a stone ball with a circumference of over nine feet more than a mile with great accuracy.

But as the first of Mustapha's massive cannons opened fire, the Commander-in-Chief tasted the metallic bitterness of things to come. For, no sooner had his elite batteries opened fire, and almost before Mustapha breathed the first fumes of spent gunpowder, the batteries of the knights replied in kind.

In the months before the siege, many of the knights and the citizens of Rhodes wondered why so much powder and shot was fired for practice. It seemed to them a terrible waste of their limited supplies. But not one of those shots was wasted. The best artillerymen had been dispatched to locate every possible firing point that the Muslims might use to besiege the fortress. They marked every point on every hill that seemed a suitable firing place. They then set out stone targets and marked each of those spots. At that point they began to systematically fire at each target until they could consistently, with a single ball, strike a direct hit. Each and every possible Turkish cannon mount could be destroyed by a single shot from the knights' batteries. They had recorded the amount of powder, the weight of the ball, and the angle of elevation of the cannon. They would correct for windage at the time of firing. They would waste nothing. The Turks would have almost endless supplies of shot and powder, and the knights would make do with what they had stored already. But every time one of the knights' batteries fired, the Sultan would have one less cannon and several fewer artillerymen with whom to fire back.

The first of the Turkish cannons struck the walls with little effect. The forty-foot-thick reinforced bastions swallowed the cannonballs with barely any noticeable effect. With Gabriele Tadini in command at the battlements, the knights' cannons immediately roared back, and destroyed each of the three of Mustapha's heavy guns in a single volley, killing most of the men in the artillery crews. Those who survived the blasts fled, and did not stop running until they were well out of range of the knights' batteries.

Mustapha met with his officers on the first night of the disembarkation. They sat in his tent, alone except for the usual Janissary guard at the door.

"I'm grateful that the Sultan was not here to witness this day. We have lost three of our finest cannons. Those were cast at the great arsenal at Tophane, in the very presence of the Sultan, himself. Lost to a single volley! It is clear that they have sighted in on the best of our firing positions. The Grand Master is no fool, Infidel though he may be. We must take every precaution from here on. And the Sultan must be protected from harm."

"Mustapha Pasha, if I may?" It was Qasim Pasha who spoke.

"Yes, Qasim?"

"There is more worrisome news. We had been told that the knights would stay within the walls, and we would have to bring the fight to them. But, they have—as we expected—sent out small war parties to harass our troops. There have been no real engagements; only small groups of five and ten knights who appear out of the dark, and sweep down upon our soldiers while they unload and store supplies. While our men are working, the knights cut them down with their swords and then disappear again into the bush or hide in the rocks. These small raids have killed more than a hundred of our men already!"

"May Allah have mercy upon them."

"May He indeed. But, Mustapha Pasha, we have heard talk of mutiny among some of the mercenaries and the irregulars. We need to assign Janissaries to guard the workers, and Sipahis to chase the knights when they strike."

Piri Pasha broke in. "Indeed. Let that be so. But, let's not talk of mutiny. If there is dissent, let the officers find the men and have them punished quickly and publicly. A few beheadings in the center of the camp will stop any mutiny before it goes any further." The Aghas nodded their agreement, and there was a general murmur of approval. "Furthermore, I think we should risk no more cannon or shot until we are ready for the actual siege. The Sultan has said repeatedly that he wanted to be here in person when the attack begins. Then we can fire sixty or eighty cannons at once, and overwhelm the knights' pitiful artillery." Again, the Aghas agreed.

"We will await the orders of the Sultan, himself," he continued. "In the meanwhile, we will set up his camp out of range of the knights' guns. There is a villa that the knights abandoned but did not destroy. We will set up the Sultan's *serai* next to that, and he will decide whether to take over the villa later, or live in his own tent. For now we will deploy the troops in the crescent formation around the city as the Sultan has ordered."

The Aghas left the tent and returned to their troops as the disembarkation continued. It would last for almost two more weeks.

On July 28th, 1522, the fourth day of Ramadan, Suleiman's ship dropped anchor in Kallitheas Bay. He was put ashore in a tender and was immediately surrounded by his own battalion of Janissaries, who had arrived with him. Mustapha's Janissaries waited further up on shore. The Sultan was dressed entirely in white. His high turban had the customary egret's feathers fixed with a jeweled clasp. The band assembled to greet the Sultan as he took his first steps on the island of Rhodes. Their trumpets, cymbals, and drums sounded as soon as the Sultan stepped onto the beach. Several cannon salvos were fired to salute him, and the Sipahis formed a pathway between their horses.

In full battle gear, Mustapha Pasha waited on the sand for the Sultan. As he moved toward Suleiman, the Janissaries parted to make way for him. Ibrahim was one step behind the Sultan and remained there as Suleiman moved on shore to greet his *Seraskier*, his Commander-in-Chief.

"Mustapha, my brother! You look fit and ready for battle." Suleiman strode towards his brother-in-law and the two gave each other a hearty hug. "It looks as if you have things well in hand."

"It is going as planned, my Lord. The troops have debarked and all the equipment has been sorted and stored. This very day the Aghas are deploying in the crescent around the fortress as you prescribed."

"And where is my Grand Vizier? Where is Piri Pasha?"

"He is preparing for your arrival at the camp, my Lord."

"Have the knights engaged us as yet?"

Mustapha began to stroke his mustache again, and Suleiman scowled. He knew his brother-in-law's nervous habits well, and was instantly aware that something was wrong.

"My Lord, for the most part they have stayed within the fortress. All the citizens are within as well. There have been some sorties by small bands of knights harassing our troops. But no big battles as yet."

"And what of the skirmishes? How did we fare?"Mustapha's initial enthusiasm had been tempered by reality. He knew now not to deceive his master. "Not well, Majesty. We have lost nearly a hundred men in the first few days. We have killed none."

Suleiman's lips tightened. Mustapha had wanted to bring news of Turkish victories, not of these petty deaths in hit-and-run ambush. "There is more, my Lord."

"Yes?"

"On the first day, we set up cannon at three sites suited for maximum artillery effect. But, as we feared, the knights have sighted the best of the locations."

"And?"

"And our cannon were destroyed, my Lord. One volley each from the fortress scored direct hits on our batteries. The cannons were shattered and the men killed. A few escaped, but it is clear that we will have a difficult time against this fortress. The knights are skilled and well prepared. The fortress reinforced beyond imagination."

Suleiman did not answer. All his dreams of arriving in triumph with an overpowering unstoppable force were dwindling before the battle had truly begun. Suleiman did not want to show his anger in front of the parade of Janissaries and Sipahis on the beach, so he kept completely still.

"Majesty, we have eighty more large guns to deploy. I think that when they are in place, and we begin bombardment simultaneously with all our weapons, it will have a devastating effect. The knights are not capable of responding to so many positions firing at them at once."

Suleiman nodded. He motioned Mustapha to follow him, and then walked the few steps to his waiting horse. The Janissaries and Sipahis quickly formed the ring of protection around the Sultan, and the procession began its march to the encampment some two miles nearer the city.

Mustapha rode at Suleiman's side. Ibrahim held his position a few steps behind his master. Both Ibrahim's black charger and Suleiman's brown one were edgy and difficult to control. After waiting inactively at Marmarice, the seven-hour boat ride did nothing for the horses' temperaments. They skittered and moved sideways in the sand. Both riders had to rein in tightly to keep the horses on the trail.

The trail from the beach was difficult. There was no direct road from the bay to the city. The party had to cover rough rocky ground over several substantial hills before reaching the main road.

"How far is our camp from the fortress itself, Mustapha?" The Sultan was preoccupied, and seemed to be focusing on controlling his mount.

"It's over a mile west of the city, my Lord. Well out of range of the knights' batteries. There is a villa that was not too badly destroyed by the knights. It lies on the slopes of Mount Saint Stephen, and has a view of both the sea as well as the city. It is also well out of range of the knights' batteries. We have set up your camp there, and repaired most of the damage. But, I thought you would be more comfortable in your own *serai*, rather than in the stinking pigsty used by the knights. There is a villa nearby, abandoned by the Sons of *Sheitan*. They have no sense of cleanliness, my Lord. They live here much as they do in Europe. Open sewers; garbage everywhere. Until this morning, there was a foul stench at the camp, but our troops have cleaned the area, and I am sure it will be to your liking now."

Suleiman nodded. His mind was still on the early defeats of his forces. He said no more as the procession turned onto the main road at Koskinou and headed north to the camp.

—

Piri Pasha waited in his tent at Suleiman's camp. He had been feeling sick since his arrival on Rhodes, and the task of setting up the command post had been more fatiguing than in the past. This time, his heart was not in it. He knew that these knights would not surrender so easily. Other armies trembled in fear at the approach of the Ottomans. But, here on Rhodes, the knights showed none of it. This would, indeed, be a long and bloody campaign. For the first time in his long service to his Sultans, Piri Pasha was in doubt as to how the battle would end.

When his servant brought news of the impending arrival of the Sultan, Piri dressed in his military uniform. He wore the new jeweled scimitar that Suleiman had given him as a present in Istanbul. Then, he sent for his new horse. This, too, was a present from the Sultan, though Piri longed for his old comfortable familiar mount. The new horse had just a bit too much energy for the old Vizier. *This is a mount for a young Sipahi,* he thought, the first time he had ridden the horse. *My fat bottom has grown used to the soft rolling gait of my own horse.*

Piri walked his horse from the encampment, and proceeded down the road to meet the Sultan and escort him into camp. As the huge procession came into view, Piri took a deep breath and dug in his spurs. The stallion broke into a cantor, and Piri held the reins tightly to keep the animal from breaking into a full gallop. He squeezed his knees into the horse's sides to maintain control. It would not do to rush headlong at the Sultan. It might spook the Sipahis or the Janissaries guarding the procession. And, it certainly wouldn't do for the Grand Vizier of the Ottoman Empire to fall off his horse.

As he approached the vanguard, Piri waved his hand in the air. His blue caftan flapped in the wind, and twice he had to reposition his tall turban so it would not fall off. *I am becoming a parody of an old Grand Vizier,* he thought. *Though, I should be happy to grow old. There are not many Grand Viziers who have lived long enough to become old and fat!*

Suleiman loosened the reins on his horse, and with scarcely a flicker of his boots against the horse's flanks, the animal sped to a controlled cantor. The Sultan passed a few of his guard, and rode up to meet Piri alone. Mustapha and Ibrahim waited in their place in the procession. They knew that the Sultan wanted to greet his Vizier alone, and perhaps would vent some of his anger on the old man instead of them.

But this was not the case. The sight of Piri gave Suleiman some hope that his armies would rally and conquer these knights in short order. Somehow, seeing his father's Vizier riding toward him, Suleiman felt the power of Selim and the old guard that was so successful in battle. Surely Piri Pasha would make it right.

"Piri Pasha!" Suleiman shouted. "How wonderful you look upon that horse. It suits you well."

The horses stamped and shifted from side to side as the riders approached each other. Suleiman's horse circled in place as Piri's moved sideways to avoid the other. The horses gradually calmed down enough to allow the men to close the gap and reach out to clasp the other's forearm.

Piri smiled and made a gallant attempt to look martial and strong. "My Sultan! It lifts my heart to see you safely here. Allah smiles upon you. Now we can begin, at last, to drive the vipers from our realm. Now you are here! Now we can begin!"

Then Piri waved to Ibrahim, who had just ridden up to where the Sultan's horse was standing.

"*Salaam Aleichum*, Piri Pasha."

"*Aleichum salaam*, Ibrahim."

Suleiman looked carefully at Piri Pasha. He rode alongside the old man, and realized now that his own initial enthusiasm had clouded his vision. The Grand Vizier was not the man Suleiman knew at Belgrade. He was certainly not the man who rode at Selim's right hand for eight years. Piri's face was wan and gaunt. Though he was obese, he had the look of a starved and hungry man. He had new bags under his eyes, and the eyes had lost their sparkle. *Could this be the same man who greeted me at my serai in Istanbul?* thought Suleiman. *Is this the man who will lead my armies to victory over the Christian dogs?*

The Sultan felt a heaviness in his chest. He looked back to Ibrahim. Ibrahim nodded sadly. Though no words were spoken, the lifelong friends had read each other's minds. The party formed back into line and continued along the short way into the camp of the Sultan. Piri moved his horse closer to Suleiman. "Majesty, a word if I might."

"Of course. Are you not my Grand Vizier?" Suleiman made his voice especially light to hide the pain he was feeling at the sight of Piri.

"Majesty, we need your presence here to deal with a problem before it gets out of hand."

"And this problem is?"

"The Janissaries. They are very unhappy about this campaign. I fear they could get out of control, unless you act quickly."

"More tipped cooking pots on the horizon?"

"That, and worse, Majesty."

"Be specific, Piri."

"They have never been in favor of this campaign. They knew from the start that it would be long and difficult. You know that they love to go into battle, defeat the enemy quickly, and return home burdened with booty."

Suleiman nodded. Piri went on. "They have been grumbling since we arrived on the island. No, even before. They stomp around the camp. They swagger, they curse. There have been fights."

"What do you think I should do about it, Piri? I think you have something in mind."

"If I may, Majesty. You are officially a Janissary. You are a non-commissioned officer in their ranks. One of them. I was there when you took your pay from the Paymaster. They would have died for you on the spot that day."

"And?"

"Go among them. Dressed in your battle clothes. Tomorrow at dawn, review the troops as a Janissary, yourself."

Suleiman thought for a moment. "Why tomorrow? The battle begins at dawn. Why not right now?"

"Now?"

"Yes, now. Send ahead to the camps. Have the men assembled. There is no better time than now. You're right, we will stop this discontentment before it starts. They will long for battle when I am done with them."

"Yes, Majesty!" Piri sent his personal guard ahead with the instructions. Then, he and Suleiman stopped at the roadside. A tent was quickly set up, and the Sultan's wardrobe brought to the roadside. His servants dressed him in the full battle gear of his Janissaries. His loose tunic was light blue, and his pants white. He wore a steel helmet wrapped in white silk and topped with the white feathers of his men. He mounted his horse, and was immediately joined by Ibrahim and Piri Pasha.

"Now, let us see these unhappy Janissaries of mine. Come Ibrahim, stay close by my side with Piri. Before the sun sets over that damned fortress, we will have the cheers of a hundred thousand men to send us off to battle."

From the ranks, the Janissaries appeared, led by their military band. Drums and cymbals sounded in the afternoon glare. Trumpets and flutes blared their salutes, and rebounded off the walls of the city. From every camp came cheering throngs of soldiers: Janissaries and Sipahis rushed to greet their Sultan. Azabs and archers, miners and sappers poured out of their tents to see Suleiman, *Kanuni*. They pressed Suleiman's guard to touch his stirrups. Everywhere the bands played and the crowds roared with delight. The knights on the battlements heard the music, and thought that the Turks were massing for an attack. They knew from their sources that Suleiman's armies *always* preceded a major attack with drums and trumpets and fanfare. This was to be the last time that they would hear such music without having to pay for the pleasure in blood.

Suleiman's procession moved past the walls, post after post; tower after tower; rampart after rampart; always just out of cannon range. His procession was dwarfed by the massiveness of the walls and the overpowering depth and width of the ditches. His armies appeared tiny beneath the bastions of stone. For the remaining hours of the day, Suleiman rode with his entourage from sea to sea in the giant crescent that encircled the city.

At dawn on the following morning, July 29th, 1522, the battle for Rhodes would begin.

⊰ 9 ⊱

FIRST BLOOD

The Fortress of the Knights of Rhodes
July 29th, 1522

The sun had just appeared over the eastern Mediterranean Sea. Rays of pink light reached from the horizon to touch the parapets of the Port of Italy. As the minutes passed, the sky brightened and the light ran down the battlements of the fortress, coloring the pale brown walls with a rosy hue. Soon the warmth of the summer sun began to perfuse the air. The guards on the walls rotated their necks to ease the aching that had beset their muscles after a night of staring into the darkness at the encampment of the enemy. They stretched and waited for their comrades to come and relieve them of their duties. Breakfast would be waiting at each *Auberge*. A few hours sleep would be welcome.

As the morning watch appeared on the ramparts, the knights straightened their uniforms for the formal changing of the guard. Each *langue's* captain greeted his fellow officer, and passed on the orders of the day. As the men formed up for the exchange, a series of blasts shook the air. Instinctively, the knights ducked and took shelter behind the walls. The noise intensified, coming from all sides at once. Several of the blasts struck the walls directly below the guards. The stones at their feet reverberated with the impact. The guards huddled behind the wall trying to maintain discipline and assess the extent of the attack.

Within moments, it was clear that a massive artillery barrage had begun, and that *all* the ramparts of the fortress were under fire simultaneously. Though the knights were unaware of the actual numbers, more than sixty of the Sultan's cannons were firing stone balls up to nine feet in circumference and weighing hundreds of pounds, from points all around the city.

As the impacts became more closely spaced, dust and rubble flew up from the walls. Some of it blew into the city on the winds that came in from the sea. Several stone balls flew over the walls and into the city itself. The huge cannonballs crashed into the cobblestone streets and smashed on impact into sharp, flying shards. People began to run in panic; some to their homes, others to the nearest *Auberge*, seeking safety in the quarters of the knights. The knights themselves ran to muster at each of the *Auberges* before proceeding to their assigned posts.

Chaos in the city increased. Thousands of panicked citizens impeded the progress of the knights and the civilian militias. Though they had waited for this day for many months, the actual start of the barrage was nothing the people could have envisioned. The massiveness of the attack and the constancy of the barrage was beyond imagining. Few could have conceived of such a force of arms aimed at their city. Even the few knights and citizens who remembered the siege led by Suleiman's great-grandfather forty-two years earlier were shocked by the force and violence of these huge new weapons.

The first casualties of the war came within a few minutes of the start of the barrage; four citizens of Rhodes lay dead. These were not knights fighting on the parapets, nor were they artillerymen responding to the Turkish fire. Rather, they were a small family, seeking the safety of their home; the shelter and refuge they had known for seventy years. Dead were an old man and woman in the center of the Jewish Quarter. Hiding on their bed, they held tightly to their two grandchildren and prayed. They affirmed the unity of God, as they had every day of their lives. *"Shemah Yisrael, Adonoi elohehu. Adonoi echod."* Seconds later, after they had bolted their door and huddled together on their only bed, a stone ball smashed through the roof and crushed them all beneath its massive weight. The door of the small house was blocked by the cannonball as it rested upon the dead bodies of the family.

Neighbors tried to rescue their friends, but they found no way to enter the house. The only window was filled with stone rubble, and the cannonball wedged the front door tight. Three knights paused on the way to their battle stations, but it was instantly clear that there could be no survivors in that pitifully crushed little house, for the ball itself practically filled the entire room. *"Je suis desolé, monsieur. Ils sont déjà certainement morts,"* the knights said to a pleading neighbor who was trying to rescue the family. I am sorry, Sir. They are already certainly dead. The knights saluted and hurried to their stations, leaving the neighbors wringing their hands in despair.

In the Palace of the Grand Master, the *Piliers* and lieutenants were converging on the meeting room. Philippe was standing at the great oak table. The windows were shuttered against the attack, the room lit by candles. For the knights rushing in from the bright daylight, it took a moment for their eyes to adjust to the dim lighting. Thomas Docwra was speaking to Philippe as the others arrived.

"They have formed a crescent around the walls. Complete encirclement, as we expected. Our scouts are trying to find out the exact deployment, as well as the numbers of men in each camp. So far, we have counted nearly sixty cannons firing from about twenty positions around the city. They seem to be concentrating the heaviest fire on our weakest walls."

Philippe was distressed to hear this information, as it suggested that the Muslims had learned about the relative strengths and weaknesses of the city. "How severe is the damage so far?"

"It's too soon to tell, my Lord. Most of the cannonballs have been swallowed by the walls. They have penetrated the outer stones, but they are lost in the earth and the inner reaches. Thus far, there are no serious breaches."

John Buck, Philippe's lieutenant, had been listening to the Grand Master and interrupted. "They have been at it only a few minutes, my Lords. Already there is some damage to the Bastion of England. However, we are now returning fire, and I think we'll inflict some heavy damage to their batteries within the hour. Our positions are well aimed, and the Muslims are only firing for effect, making corrections. I hope we can destroy many of their cannon before very long."

Gregoire de Morgut rushed into the room. "My Lord, we have had our first deaths." The other knights stopped talking and turned to Morgut. "I was coming from the *Auberge*, and some of the knights told me of a house in the Jewish Quarter that was hit directly with a large stone. It crushed four people to death. They tell me that the stone ball was massive. Bigger than any we have seen before."

Philippe looked at his knights. There was silence in the room. Then, d'Amaral and his servant-at-arms, Blasco Diaz, came in together. They walked to the head of the table and waited there in silence.

"Chancellor," Philippe said, acknowledging d'Amaral.

"Grand Master," d'Amaral replied.

Then, turning away from the Chancellor, he said, "Our presence is required out on the battlements," Philippe said to all the men gathered. "We need no further planning. The battle has been joined, and I doubt there will be much letup for some time to come. Get to your men, and make sure that the militia and the mercenaries perform as we have trained them. Andrea, muster the Inns of Castile and Aragon, and lead them yourself. We need all of the officers at the forefront of this battle."

"*D'accord, Seigneur*," the Chancellor said. He nodded to Diaz, and the two hurried out to the battle.

"For the moment," Philippe continued, "we need to see just how the Muslim plans to execute this siege, and most of all, to keep the citizens calm. Urge those who are not fighting to stay indoors and keep out of the way."

The knights bowed and hurried from the room.

John Buck remained behind. When all the knights had left, he approached the Grand Master, who was pouring over the diagrams of the city's defenses.

"My Lord?"

Philippe looked up, surprised to see his lieutenant still there. "Yes, John?"

"My Lord, I have a man waiting outside whom I think you should see."

"Yes? What's this about?"

"He is Basilios Carpazio, from Karpathos; a Greek fisherman, and he has a plan that may help us."

"What plan, John? What does he want to do?"

"Let me bring him in, my Lord. He will tell you."

Buck left the room, and in a moment he was back with a short stocky man dressed in fisherman's clothing. He was darkly complected, with black hair and dark brown eyes that looked black in the dimness of the room. He wore a heavy mustache, with a stubbly growth of black beard that covered the rest of his face. There was the smell of raw fish in his clothes. His boots were worn and old. He stood before the Grand Master with his head bowed. He held his black fisherman's cap in front of his waist, and worried it with both hands.

Philippe addressed the man in Greek. *"Kalimera, philo moo."* Good morning, my friend. "What is it you wish to tell me?"

The man hesitated. He kept squeezing his hat tighter and tighter. Then, he looked to John Buck for assurance. Buck nodded and said, "Go on, tell the Grand Master your idea."

The man looked into Philippe's eyes. After a few seconds he began in Greek.

"My Lord, I have spent many years fishing off the coast of Turkey, and have spent a great deal of time at the markets there selling my catch. So, I speak fluent Turkish and am familiar with their ways. I could take some of my men and circle the island. Then, with a catch of fish in the hold, I could come ashore near their camp and sell the fish at the market. They have already set up a small city filled with merchants. Mostly Turkish. But, some others. I would not be recognized as a Rhodian Greek there. I could listen and move about to learn what I can for you. After we have sold the catch, I would come back around the island, and land off shore on the north coast again, then return here."

"Do you think you might have trouble with the blockade?"

Basilios laughed. "No, my Lord. Their navy is commanded by fools. We move in and out every night, and our small boats are nearly invisible. We can easily avoid them. And, if they stop us, we are merely fishermen with no weapons. We pose no threat to them."

"John?"

"I think it is worth the risk, my Lord. These are brave men to volunteer for such a mission. I think we should let them try. Are there specific details you wish for them to discover?"

"Yes, actually there are. The Turks have begun a determined effort to erect an earthwork facing the Tower of Aragon. It would be good to know exactly the purpose of this structure. See if you can bring me information on this." Philippe paused, and then said, "Very well. I thank you for your bravery. May God be with you."

"Thank you, my Lord." With that, the man turned and left the palace.

—

Jean and Melina finished boarding up the two small windows of her house. As he finished wedging the thick boards in place, he said, "I must hurry now, *Chèrie*. I'm late for my post. When I leave, bolt the door from within, and make sure you recognize the voice of anyone trying to gain entry. Remember, should the cannon barrage get nearer this quarter of town, take the girls and get under the oak table. I have placed it next to the strongest wall in the house, where it is connected to the house next door. That should give you two walls and the table as well for protection." He took Melina in his arms and kissed her. Then he turned to the small cradle where his two babies were asleep despite the noise and the chaos outside. "They're so beautiful, *n'est-ce pas?*"

Melina smiled and squeezed his arms in response. She tried not to shed the tears that were welling up in her eyes. She was afraid to speak. She was so frightened now that she had Jean and the two girls to worry about. Finally she murmured, "Be careful, my love."

Jean buckled his armor breastplate and reached for his sword and cape. As he placed the sword belt around his waist, the whole house trembled from the impact of a nearby cannonball. Both he and Melina staggered from the blast, and the babies began to cry in their cradle. Melina rushed to the twins and took them in her arms. She sat on the floor next to the heavy oak table, prepared to slide underneath in case of a closer hit.

"Oh, *Mon Dieu*, Jean. What will happen to us? This is only the beginning."

Jean knelt down and held Melina and the babies all together in his broad arms. "You must try to stay calm, my love. This will be the worst. They will try to inflict the greatest damage early on. They are hoping that we will lose faith and surrender."

"And will we?"

"No, we will not. These Infidels are savages. It's better that we die in battle than become their slaves. I've told you before what happens to those they conquer. The men are slaughtered, and the women and children taken as slaves. Death is far, far preferable to life as a slave to the Muslim."

Melina began to cry quietly as she held her two babies. The thought of her helplessness to protect them overwhelmed her. "When you are out there fighting, where shall we find safety?"

"If the cannon fire gets to close, take the babies to the hospital. Doctor Renato will keep you safe there. The hospital building is strong, and partially protected from the cannons by the terrain. Just go there and stay. If I don't find you here, I'll look in the hospital next." He kissed Melina and each of the babies. Then, he put on his cape and helmet and left the house. As he closed the door, he said, "*Au revoir, Chèrie.* Be sure to bolt the door behind me."

And he was gone.

It was just after dark on the first day of the siege. The cannons had fired without letup since early in the morning. Miraculously, there was little damage to the city. Most of the Turkish batteries were trying to make breaches in the wall to allow the Turkish foot soldiers to storm the city. Very few of the stone balls or mortars were aimed into the city itself. The forty-foot-thick walls absorbed the shot with little damage. In fact, the only casualties that whole first day were the family killed in the Jewish Quarter early in the morning.

As the night grew dark, Basilios Carpazio and his three comrades climbed aboard their little boat, slipped their mooring, hove to, and rowed quietly out of the Galley Port into the darkened Mediterranean Sea. His mate was Nicolo Ciocchi. The two men had fished the waters around Rhodes together for thirty years. Nicolo was a big man, over six feet tall and two hundred ten pounds. Years of pulling in the heavy lines and nets had hardened both men. With them were two brothers, Petros and Marcantonio Revallo, ages nineteen and twenty-one. The boys had worked for Basilios for the past four years, and were almost part of his family.

They rowed further out into the sea and drifted with the land breeze until they were well clear of the shoreline. Then they hoisted their sail and set out for the northern coast of the island. They beat to windward for a little under an hour. When they reached their favorite fishing grounds, they dropped their nets into the sea and set about fishing just as they did almost every day of the year that the weather allowed.

A few hours before dawn, they pulled in their nets for the last time. Their small boat was nearly full. With the load secure, they came about, and ran before the wind back to the northern tip of Rhodes. They circled the city and headed toward shore to the south of the harbors. They put ashore at the beach just behind the encampment of Piri Pasha. There, the small army of merchants had already set up a market and a thriving trade was going on. Tools and clothing were being repaired. Off-duty soldiers were buying rations to eat, and enjoying some time near the water. There were artillery crews as well as small groups of Janissaries and Sipahis tending to their weapons and their horses. The merchants came from all over the Mediterranean. There were Turks, Arabs, and Anatolians. Even some Egyptians and Persians had made the journey. The conversations were in every language, and voices bargaining for price broke loudly into the black predawn air.

The four men loaded the fish into wicker baskets and began ferrying them up to the marketplace. They set the baskets down, and while Marcantionio stayed to sell the catch, Basilios and Nicolo wandered together in the crowd. Basilios had the best command of the Turkish language, though Nicolo could get by in Turkish heavily accented with Greek.

The others began to mingle with the crowd, buying a few items to eat and drink from the stalls along the beach. They would sit at tables and slowly sip from their cups while they listened to the conversations of the Janissaries and the Sipahis.

After about an hour of casual information gathering, Basilios said, "This is not enough. We need more specific details. I think we need a few of these soldiers to come back with us and tell the Grand Master directly what the Muslim plan is." He raised his bushy black eyebrows and smiled at Nicolo.

Nicolo looked at Basilios out of the corner of his eye, and then smiled at him as well. He nodded his head and finished his drink. The two men began to mingle again with the crowd of soldiers along the beach.

"We will need to lure them to the boat. I think they'll be less suspicious if I'm alone. They'll be braver if they are not outnumbered. Go back and get Marcantionio and Petros."

Nicolo went and got the boys. Basilios moved in among the soldiers. Three Janissaries were sitting on a rock drinking from leather bottles. They seemed a little drunk. Alcohol was forbidden to the Muslims, but many of the soldiers drank when in the field. This was especially true of the Muslim *Devshirmé*, who were forced conversions from Christianity, as were nearly all of the Janissaries.

Basilios moved closer to the men without looking at them. He sat down on the sand with his back to the soldiers. He reached into his coat and pulled out a long dagger. This was a new weapon, an armor-piercing dagger, inlaid with gold and reinforced in the center of the blade. It was much longer than the usual knife carried by fishermen, but shorter than the curved scimitar of the Janissaries. It had proven itself a good tool and a fine weapon on more than one occasion.

He began to polish its blade, whistling quietly as he worked. He never looked at the men. He overheard them talking about their war. When they stopped, it was clear from the conversation that they had noticed the knife. They spoke in Turkish, and Basilios understood every word.

"An odd knife, that, isn't it?" one of the men said in Turkish. There was some low murmuring, and then Basilios heard the thump of two feet hitting the sand. He was alert and tense, preparing to fight if the young soldiers decided to try and take the knife from him. He watched out of the corner of his eye as the shadow of the Janissary moved closer over the sand. Then, a voice said to him in Greek, "What have you there, old man?"

Basilios did not turn his head to answer, insulting the Janissary in his own way by speaking without looking at him. "It's a knife. Surely a Soldier of the Sultan can see that."

"Speak civilly to me, *old man*. You speak to a Janissary of the Sultan."

Basilios turned and rose. He towered over the young man, who stepped back, laying his hand on the handle of his scimitar. No fuss would be made if he killed this fisherman on the spot. A perceived insult to his Sultan would be sufficient cause.

Basilios bowed his head and took his cap off. He was much taller than the young soldier, and fifty pounds heavier; fifty pounds of muscle. He held his hat in his hands and slouched to make himself less threatening, as he spoke deferentially to the Janissary. He never looked at the others who were still sitting on the rock. "Forgive my rudeness," he said, "but I did not know who was talking to me. I'm sorry."

The Janissary relaxed his grip on the scimitar and moved closer. "So what kind of knife is this? It is neither sword nor knife, but somewhere in between. A bastard!" He laughed, and his comrades laughed as well. They were laughing at Basilios, but Basilios remained calm and subservient.

"It was made especially for me, sir. It's useful when you're faced with a sword but can manage to get in close. I can reach a man's throat with this, while the sword becomes useless at close range. Yet, I am still out of reach of my enemy's short knife. It can also pierce armor! See the slit down the middle—this groove is reinforced." He lowered his voice, and spoke as a conspirator. "It has proved its value a few times already."

"Let me see it. Hand it to me."

Basilios pulled away and pretended to be afraid of giving over his knife.

"Hand it to me!"

He gave the knife to the Janissary, who seemed impressed with it. The soldier made several sweeps through the air and then tossed it to his friends. They, too, seemed impressed.

Basilios heard the soldiers bantering in Turkish about killing the old man and keeping the knife. Basilios crouched fractionally lower and prepared to strike. He said, in Turkish, "I have more of these at my boat. I could sell them to you very cheap."

The Janissaries talked among themselves in Turkish again, and Basilios had difficulty hearing the words. He could not tell whether they wanted to come and buy knives for all of them, or just kill him and take the knives.

Then the leader of the three said, "Let's go. Show us your long, armor-piercing knives." Basilios led them down to the beach and walked along the water line. He kept to the soft pebbles near the water's edge, hoping that the bad footing would hinder the Janissaries more than him in the event of a fight. As he drew near his boat, he could see nothing of his mates. He hoped that they were there in the shadows, but had no way of knowing if they had made it back yet. As he got within a yard, he could see a lone basket of fish in the sand. Did the boys bring this back or had it been left there all along? He had no idea. The odds now were getting a little tight for him.

"Over here, sir. Right this way."

The three Janissaries were right behind Basilios as they came to the basket. Basilios walked to the side away from the boat. That way, if his men were hidden, they could strike from behind. If they were not there at all, he would have a half-step lead in running from the soldiers.

The young man leaned over the fish, and then pulled away in disgust. "Those are fish! Where are the knives?"

"Right here," Basilios said, as he pulled his own knife from his belt.

The leader immediately perceived the threat and drew his scimitar. He pointed the tip of the blade straight at Basilios' throat and stepped forward, closing the distance. There was no hope for Basilios now. He could neither fight with his shorter knife, nor could he run.

There was a movement in the boat. The two other Janissaries turned to confront the danger, but they were too late. Both slumped to the ground as the two wooden oar handles simultaneously swept into their temples. They fell in a heap together on the wet sand. Before the third man could attack Basilios—before he could even turn his head—Nicolo's ax severed the young man's head from his body. As the boy fell forward, his scimitar grazed Basilios' thigh. The Janissary fell into the sand next to his unconscious comrades, his blood covering their new blue uniforms as his heart continued to pump for a minute more.

Basilios staggered back, grabbing at his thigh. He took off his neckerchief and pressed it into the bleeding wound. The blood stopped, and he said, "Quickly! Get all three of them into the boat. We don't want to wait a minute more."

Marcantonio and Petros dragged the bodies of the two unconscious Janissaries over the gunwales of the boat and dumped them into the scuppers. Nicolo took the dead boy by his collar and belt and heaved him into the stern. Then, Basilios limped into the boat, and as he cut the mooring line with the Janissary's scimitar, he plucked the severed head from the beach by the hair and impaled it upon the blade.

"A gift, for the Grand Master." He threw the head and the sword onto the pile of fish and grabbed an oar. Together, the men rowed the boat back into the black night. Once well off shore and hidden by the darkness, they set sail north again, for their secret route to the city.

Only a drying stain of blood was left on the sand to inform upon them. As the morning wore on, the incoming tide washed away the last traces of the dead young man.

⁓

Melina was terrified for her babies. The only sounds she heard were the crashing of the cannonballs that entered the city and the screams of her neighbors. Animals began to panic at the noise and the flying stone chips. Their anxious screams added to the din. With little light in the small house, Melina became increasingly frightened.

The walls closed in on her. She began to fear that she might be killed and the babies left alone for days while Jean was defending his post. She had no idea when he might be able to check on them again.

By noon, the house was beginning to heat up in the fierce July sun. With the doors and the windows bolted and shuttered, it became difficult to breathe. Melina fanned the twins as they slept. Ekaterina and Marie were like two little dolls in a toy bed. They even slept on the same side and held the same little arm stretched out, with the other curled near their heads; two tiny fencers in the *en garde* position.

Melina could hardly believe her good luck twelve months ago when she had discovered that she was pregnant. By then, she and Jean had been living permanently in her little house. Nothing had been said to Jean by the Grand Master, or even the knights of his own *Auberge*. Somehow the preparations for war and the huge amount of work that needed to be done had made their own relationship of little importance to the rest of the inhabitants of the city. Many of the knights had women in the town. Some lived openly with them, while others slipped back and forth between their inns and their lover's houses after dark.

When she discovered her pregnancy, she knew Jean would be thrilled as well. They had not yet married. The war and the threat to their lives had made a formal ceremony seem insignificant just then.

Neither of them had considered the possibility of twins. When she went into early labor, Jean called the Jewish midwife from the Quarter. He and the midwife stayed with Melina for the first hours. When there was no progress after the first day and night, Jean became alarmed.

"Stay with her," he told the midwife. "I am going to get Doctor Renato."

Melina had tried to stop him, but he insisted. The midwife was horrified. No male doctor would attend a woman in labor. She would have protested, but she, too, was alarmed for her patient, and actually relieved. By the second day of labor, she actually wanted to share the responsibility with someone else. She knew that women who remained in labor for more than a day or two after their water broke often became sick and died of a fever shortly thereafter.

Jean had hurried down the *Calle Ancha*, the Broad Street of the Jewish Quarter. He went through *Calle de Los Ricos* and *Calle de Los Locos,* the Streets of the Rich and the Crazy. Finally, he left the Quarter and hurried to the *Collachio*. He turned right into the Street of the Knights and ran to the hospital. He took the massive staircase two steps at a time, and went directly to the ward. Renato was bending over a patient, changing dressings on an abscess that he had drained the prior day. He was surprised to see Jean running into the ward.

"What is it, Jean?"

"It's Melina, *Dottore*. She has been in labor now for more than a day. And still there is no sign of the head. The midwife is of no use. Can you come? Please?"

"*Bien entendu!*" Of course! "Wait here a moment, while I get some things."

Jean waited in the ward while Renato fetched his bag of surgical instruments. The two hurried from the hospital and back down the Street of the Knights. Jean led the way, for Renato rarely left the hospital, and had never been to the couple's little house.

"Jean," Renato said, as they hurried through the streets, "this must remain between the two of us."

"Doctor?"

"I mean that I will do everything I can for Melina. I love her and you too dearly to let anything go undone. But, it's a grave crime in these idiotic times for a man to...to...see the private parts of a woman in labor. It is madness, but even a doctor may not do this. This very year a doctor in Hamburg—Wartt was his name, I think— was burned at the stake for doing such a thing. He wanted to help a poor woman in labor who he thought was dying. He dressed in woman's clothing and went as a midwife. But, they caught him and burned him for the crime. I will help you, of course. But, we must keep our silence. And the midwife, too. I know her. She will not betray me. I have helped her before."

"*Merci*, Doctor. I know what it means for you to do this for us, *merci beaucoup.*"

215

When they entered the room, Melina was quiet. The midwife stepped back against the wall. Renato ignored her and went directly to Melina. He lifted the gray wool covers and pulled back the sheets. Jean turned his head to the wall. He could not look at Melina as she was so intimately examined by another man; even his trusted friend, Doctor Renato.

As Renato examined Melina, she began to groan and then cry out as the contractions resumed against her partially opened womb.

"Bring that lamp closer," he called to the midwife. Jean, by this time, was sitting on the floor in a corner. He was sweating more than Melina, and had buried his face in his folded arms. He prayed aloud as the doctor and midwife tended to his love. He found himself alternating between the Latin prayers of his youth and the unfamiliar Hebrew prayers that Melina had taught him. He wanted God at his side now, and it didn't matter whose God.

"Closer!" Renato shouted. "There! Hold it right there."

He wiped his hands on a damp towel and reached between Melina's legs. She cried out louder, but Renato persisted.

"There! There's the problem!" He turned to Jean. "There are *three* hands in there, Jean. Therefore, there will be a fourth!" And he laughed. Jean looked up, but what the doctor had said made no impression on him. He only heard Melina's cries. Then, in the midst of her pain and tears, she too laughed, as she realized what the doctor had said.

"Twins, man! Twins!" He slowly inserted his fingers into Melina's womb and took gentle hold of the little hand. Then, as carefully as he could, he used both hands to maneuver the little child until its crown of black hair was showing. Melina pushed, and Renato said, "Harder, my dear, harder!"

Melina cried out and pushed again. The little black patch of glistening wet fur grew larger, and then, without warning, there was a forehead and ears and a slightly squashed nose. With a rush, the baby fell into Renato's hands. She was so slippery that he nearly dropped her.

"Over here, woman! Take this child and hold it while I get the other one out. We cannot deal with this umbilical cord yet. I must get the other child out quickly."

He handed the first baby to the midwife, who swaddled it in a bit of clean cloth and held her to the side, as far as the umbilical cord would allow. Renato placed his hand back into Melina's womb, which was considerably more dilated and roomy now. He probed around and found a foot. He maneuvered the foot as he had the arm, and rotated the baby around to prevent it coming out feet first. "I'm sorry for this, *Querida*, but I don't want to take the risk of entangling the two cords. The baby might strangle before I can get her out."

Jean was still praying wildly, almost oblivious to the scene in the room. His time in the hospital had taught him no skills relating to childbirth; virtually all the babies born on the island were born at home. None had ever come into the hospital, at least while Jean was there.

"Don't push just yet, Melina. Hang on, and pant if you need to. Pant like a puppy in the heat. I need to get the head down before you push any more." Renato continued to work, as Melina puffed her cheeks and panted as fast as she could. The reflexes in her laboring pelvis were telling her body to push, and it was all she could do to fight it. The sweat poured from her forehead and trickled down her neck. She kept glancing at Jean, who was trembling at the sight of his wife and the one baby in the room. *Pauvre Jean!*

"Now! Now push!" Renato shouted in Greek. He had the baby's head in his hand and was pulling gently from side to side. First the right shoulder came through and then, very slowly, the left. As soon as the head and shoulders were out, the baby flew into the doctor's arms. The cords were slightly tangled, and Renato placed the second child on Melina's abdomen. He took two strings of sinew and tied each cord twice. It took no more than thirty seconds to complete the four ties. Then he took a knife from his pocket and cut each cord between the ties.

The midwife took the children away from the foot of the bed and placed them next to Melina. She tapped Jean on the shoulder several times before she could bring him back from his prayers. She very nearly had to drag him to Melina's side. He knelt by the bed, and was about to ask if the babies were all right when two wonderful cries filled the room simultaneously. He put his head down on her breast, hugged Melina and his twin girls, and sobbed.

"A few minutes more," said Renato. "As soon as the afterbirth is delivered, I'll leave you in the care of the midwife. There is much to do in the hospital. I think we have a single afterbirth for the two babies, so it will be hard to tell the little girls apart. Better to name them now, and find some mark on their bodies to tell the difference."

Then, with a gushing noise, the single afterbirth was propelled from Melina's womb, attached, as Renato had predicted, to the two cords. A large volume of blood and clots followed the afterbirth, sliding off the sheets and onto the floor. To Jean, the pink stain on the sheets looked like the trail of a wounded animal. He couldn't bear to think of Melina's blood spilling onto the floor, like the blood of the men he had killed in battle. So, he turned away and buried his face again in Melina's breast. Melina cupped his head in her arm and comforted him like a third baby.

Renato dropped the placenta into a bucket, and began to massage Melina's lower abdomen. He could feel the muscles of the womb begin to contract under his fingers, and he called to the midwife. "Here, keep massaging until the bleeding has stopped." Then he turned to Jean, Melina, and the girls and put his hands on the babies' heads. "You are very blessed, Jean and Melina. Two lovely little girls. I wish you all great joy."

"I don't know how to thank you Doctor. What you have done for us..." Jean began to weep again.

Renato put his arms around the big knight and hugged him. "This is what I do, Jean. This is my work. And, by the way, I have offended the Law once again."

"How?"

"Well, we are not supposed to interfere with the position that 'Providence' has decreed for the baby. These imbeciles quote the Bible to us: Genesis 3:16. 'In sorrow thou shalt bring children.' They take it to mean that the women must suffer, and that babies shall die while we stand idly by doing nothing. But, I tell you that God did not give me the brains and the hands to do such work, and then expect me to stand aside when I might help. If that were the case, then why would He have given the world doctors at all? We are here to intercede, to help our fellow man...and woman. God bless you, Jean. Stay with Melina as long as she needs you. There are many knights who can take your place this night. *Adieu.*"

He turned and left the room. Both Jean and Melina shuddered at the reality that their moment of joy would soon be replaced by the realities of the terrible conflict.

Philippe, Thomas Docwra, John Buck, Antonio Bosio, and Gabriel de Pommerols were gathered around the large oak table in the meeting room of the Palace. The bombardment had continued all day. None of the cannonballs had reached the Palace. The windows were still heavily boarded and the air was heavy and hot. Dust stirred up by the blasts drifted in through cracks in the doors and the men had a hard time suppressing their coughs. The five were engrossed in the battle plans, and were marking the drawings of the fortifications to delineate the weak points that needed repair. From time to time, a messenger came in to bring them up to date on new damage and repairs.

Just before dark, as the servants were clearing away some of the meal that the knights had eaten during their war council, a messenger came running into the room. It was one of the knights from the *langue* of Italy.

"*Scusi, Signores,*" he said catching his breath. "The fishermen have returned with their catch."

Philippe looked up at the knight standing in the doorway. "Their catch? What fishermen?"

The young knight stepped aside, and in marched Basilios with his three mates. Philippe rose from his seat and gasped. "God Almighty!"

Basilios smiled, and held aloft the scimitar upon which he had impaled the severed head of the Janissary. Behind him came Marcantonio, Nicolo, and Petros, dragging along the two others. The prisoners were bound at the elbows with their hands behind them. Their legs were hobbled with heavy ropes, which allowed only small, mincing steps. Both were gagged with filthy rags used to clean the fishing boat, and their uniforms were ragged and wet with salt and sand. They reeked of dead fish, and all wore identical caps of crusted blood, where they had been struck over the head. One of the young men seemed unable to focus his eyes and staggered as he walked. It was only because Marcantonio supported him that the he did not fall to the ground in his stupor.

"What have we here?" Philippe said, now smiling. "You have had a successful fishing trip, *Monsieur* Basilios?" He walked around the table and looked at the beaten bodies of the Janissaries. "I hope they are well enough to talk to us."

"They only just awoke, *Signore.* I think your inquisitors will have better luck with them than we could."

"Yes, I should imagine so. Antonio, have these men taken away, and see what they have to tell us. Waste no time, though. If they are unwilling to answer all our questions, put them right to the rack. They'll talk soon enough, and we have no time for foolishness. *Allez!*" Bosio and the three fishermen left the room dragging the prisoners behind them.

Then Philippe turned to Basilios and said, "And what did *you* learn, my friend?"

"I overheard a few of the soldiers talking, my Lord," Basilios said. "There were only a few conversations about the battle and the troops. I could not learn a great deal, which is why I thought to bring you these men instead. But, what I did hear may be of some help. The morale among the Turks is very bad. The cavalry can see that they will be of little use here. They are angry that they will not be able to fight. The Janissaries are worried that there will be a long battle; many months, and perhaps into winter. It is clear that they cannot just walk into this city and kill us. So, they are brooding, too. They like fast campaigns. In and out. Home to their Istanbul with gold in their pockets. They see that there is little here to plunder anyway. So they grumble in their drinks, and brood."

"Excellent. Any more?"

"Not really. The Aghas are disappointed in the effects of their artillery. There was talk in some units of mutiny. But, others dismissed that. The Sultan would waste no time with mutineers. They would be killed on the spot, and others sent to replace them. But, of numbers and strength I learned nothing. Nor of tactic aside from the obvious bombardment and siege. I am sorry, my Lord."

Philippe walked around the table and placed a hand on Basilios' shoulder. "You have nothing for which to be sorry, my friend. You have done well. Even better than we hoped for. These young Janissaries will be talking in a few minutes. They are trained to fight and die for their Sultan. But, they have not been trained to lie upon the rack while their body is slowly torn apart. They will all talk to us. In good time. Thank you for your service. Get you and your men some food and drink, and some rest. You have done well."

"Gentlemen," Philippe said, turning to his knights, "we have fished some treasure here today. Basilios has done very well, indeed." The fishermen left.

The four knights returned to the drawings of the fortress to resume their work. And the bombardment continued.

Jean stood with his men on the wall near the Palace of the Grand Master. They looked north and could see the camp of Bali Agha and his Janissaries come into being. The white tents seemed to grow like mushrooms in a forest, but in perfect order and alignment. The encampment was just out of range of the guns, but Jean could see the figures moving about and preparing for battle. He knew that soon he would be locked in hand-to-hand combat with the men moving in the fields beneath him.

But, his mind would not stay focused on the fight. He kept thinking of Melina and the twins. *I should have taken them to the hospital before I left. Renato would have seen to them. That little house is no protection. The hospital has thick walls, and is surrounded by other buildings as well. They would be safer there than in the house. Damned! Why didn't I move them?"*

He forced his thoughts back to his men and began to try to discern what strategy the Turks were setting up. So far, there had only been the incessant cannonade. Though the barrage had been relentless, at the close of the first day remarkably little real damage had been done to the knights' fortress. Moreover, the deadly accuracy of the knights' own batteries had decimated the Sultan's cannons. Though the cannons did not fire exploding missiles, the sheer weight and mass of the stones did incredible damage. In the first days of the siege, the Turks would lose nearly half of their large cannons and many hundreds of skilled artillerymen. The Turkish batteries were completely exposed to fire from the fortress. The knights were well protected by their thick walls. The gun ports were splayed to allow for a wide field of fire without losing their protective cover.

Not all the knights were as sanguine as Jean. For many of the younger ones, this was their first time under fire. Their training, with its emphasis on swordsmanship and horseback riding, did not prepare them for the terror that filled them as they waited for the next monster stone to descend from the sky. Many of the lads were crouched beneath the walls, and huddled together for comfort. Some even whimpered and quaked, oblivious of the scorn of their brother knights.

Jean saw three of his younger knights huddling beneath the St. Paul's Gate. He turned to one of the Servants-at-Arms and said, "Get those men up here! Spread them out. Don't they know that clustering together only means that all three could be killed with a single shot?"

Jean was trying to decide whether he should go back now and move Melina and the babies to the hospital. Just as he was turning to leave, he saw Gabriele Tadini, their master miner, climb up onto the battlements. "Gabriele," he shouted, "over here!"

Tadini turned. When he saw Jean, he waved and walked toward him.

"*Bonjour*, Jean," he said. "We are off to an excellent start, are we not?"

"I'm not sure what you mean by excellent, Gabriele. We are taking a great deal of cannon fire, and there seems to be no letup in the barrage."

"Yes, yes. But, they're doing very little damage, really. Most of their balls are being eaten by the walls, and the few that landed within the city have done very little harm to the buildings and to the people. And, for our part, we have done well. Why, my batteries have destroyed at least twenty-five cannons. The accuracy of the batteries means that we have destroyed their weapons with very little expenditure of our own powder and shot. Oh, yes, have you heard?"

"Heard what?"

"The Janissaries. The ones the fisherman captured. One of them had little stomach for the rack. He told the inquisitor a great deal. Most important," he explained, "is the earthworks that we see across from Aragon. It will be a massive ramp, to bring in cannon. They plan to make it higher than the walls, and fire down into the city."

"But, how? That would be totally exposed to our fire. They could never complete it."

"I think they could, my friend. The Sultan doesn't care how many lives it takes. Once he has a battery above our walls, he could decimate us with his field of fire."

"And the Grand Master knows of this?"

"*Bien entendu.* It was he who told me."

"What will he do about it?"

"He considers this the greatest threat to the city at the moment. He is sending a large force of knights to continuously harass the workers. Sorties. Cannon. Muskets. Even arrows. You see, when *we* build trenches to attack a fortress, we zigzag the approach to protect the miners and the sappers from fire coming from the walls. But, see? They dig straight trenches directly at us. It's quicker, but the loss of lives from our fire will be massive. We'll just keep pouring it into them, even if only to slow them down."

"I see your point, Gabriele. But, I can't stop thinking of Melina and the twins. As soon as possible, I want go back and move her to the hospital."

"Good idea. But first, come with me. I want to show you something. Then you can bring your family to safety. It's on the way."

Jean and Tadini walked along the perimeter of the walls. They skirted the Palace of the Grand Master and walked past the Post of Germany and the Post of Auvergne. From there they walked south past Aragon to the Post of England. They stood together in front of St. Anthony's Gate and looked out toward the encampment of Qasim Pasha.

"Look there," said Tadini, pointing to the south. "The Turks have begun to dig their trenches toward the walls. They are too far out for fire from our *arquebuses*, and a little too close for our cannons. But, soon they will be in range, and we will be able to open fire from the walls and the towers."

"They'll be slaughtered. There's no protection at all down there."

"Quite right," Tadini said, "It's just as I told you. They are fooled by the fact that they have not yet come under fire from the walls, so they're digging straight trenches that offer no protection. It will bring them in faster than digging a zigzag pattern, but by nightfall, or early tomorrow, they'll be close enough for us to fire on them. We'll fill the ditches with their bodies."

"Is this what you brought me here to see?"

"No. Not entirely. This Bastion of England is in poor repair. Their King Henry has sent virtually no money or knights. I think the Turks have found this out. And, though the Turks may not know it, there are only nineteen knights in the *langue* of England. I fear the Turks may be successful in making a breach here, and then with so few knights to defend this area, they could enter the city *en masse*."

"Can you not stop them? Stop the mining?"

"I will be doing all I can. My men are preparing the vents and the tunnels to counter-mine them right now. But, still there is always the possibility that we might fail. Or, that we might be occupied elsewhere at the time. Pick your best men, and prepare them for the possibility. You would be a mobile force and respond wherever you are needed. I'll speak to the Grand Master to get approval. But, I think it might be critical that you are ready for this eventuality."

Jean nodded. *"D'accord."* I agree.

Tadini turned to go. He said, *"Au revoir, Jean."*

"Addio, Gabriele." Jean descended into the city and ran back to Melina's house.

The situation in the city had deteriorated since Jean had first entered the streets earlier in the morning. The Rhodians were in a state of serious panic. Most had not yet been born during the siege of 1480, and even those who remembered the earlier siege had not been exposed to such powerful weaponry. The streets that had been practically empty before were now filled with men and women shouting and crying for help. Though there had been little damage considering the massiveness of the attack, the noise and the flying debris had sent fear through the town. People ran about the streets looking for strong stone buildings in which to hide. The knights of Aragon had been sent to guard the entry to the hospital because there had been a surge of citizens trying to enter the protection of its massive walls and heavy roof. Renato had to block the doors and call for help from the knights, so that his wards would not be over-run. In the small streets, dogs were running wildly about, and the cattle that were penned up were shrieking and kicking at their enclosures, insane with fear from the noise and the fires that burned in the streets. Only a handful of incendiary bombs had exploded inside the city itself, and they merely burned themselves out without setting fire to any of the stone houses.

Jean made his way through the winding maze of houses and shops. He stopped a group of three knights from the Inn of Aragon and said, "Get these people off the streets! Return them to their homes. They will be safer there. Do it at once!"

Then, he began to run toward the Jewish Quarter and the small street where Melina's house stood. As he rounded the final corner to their home, he watched in horror as a cannonball landed directly on the roof connecting his and his neighbor's house. The huge stone ball crushed both the houses and sent thousands of fragments of stone flying in all directions. Jean felt the sting as a shard of slate from the roof struck him in the forehead. His hand reflexly flew up to protect his eyes. When he pulled it away, it was covered with blood. He ignored the wound, for his whole being was focused on the devastation; the two little houses were mere piles of stone and wood. Their common roof sagged from the impact, making a slate saddle between the two structures. Cries came from within his neighbor's house, where the force of the ball had collapsed all the walls. The large intact hemisphere that rested on Melina's house had crushed the walls to powder. It lay there in the center of the roof like a fist from the sky.

Jean could feel the tears welling in his eyes. His sorrow overwhelmed his anger as he ran the last few yards to the pile of rubble. He began to claw at the debris, trying futilely to make a hole to the interior. He cried out, "Melina! Melina!" Why had he let Tadini detain him? Why hadn't he moved them as soon as the barrage had begun?

But, it was no use. He could not find a place to enter the house from the street. Then, he remembered the alley that separated the house from the next row to the rear. He scrambled up over the fallen front wall and made his way along the roof tiles. The horrid stone ball lay in his path, and he clawed his way around it. Blood trickled into his right eye from the wound in his forehead. He swiped at the jellied clots to clear his vision.

In his mind he saw images of the babies and Melina crushed to death beneath the oak table. *Why didn't I take them to the hospital? How could I leave them?* His guilt drove him forward, and he began to pry loose the roof tiles where the stone ball had broken through the rafters. He found several tiles loose enough to remove and threw them over his shoulder. Finally—it seemed like hours to him—he made the hole large enough to squeeze his bulky frame through the gap. His armor held him up as he lowered his legs through the opening. With his feet dangling below, he took off his sword and the breastplate. Finally, he was through. He dropped the few feet to the floor. As he crouched in the small space between the crushed roof and the floor, he called out Melina's name again and again. There was silence in the tiny room. Motes of dust circulated in the air and Jean began to cough.

When his eyes adjusted to the darkness, he could make out the oak table near the wall. The massive stone was pressing the rafters down upon it, and the table itself was flattened to the ground. Jean's eyes filled with tears, and a sob gathered in his throat as he saw the pieces of a small rag doll caught under the edge of the table.

He crawled to the table and clawed to get a grip beneath the edge. Blood blurred his vision. He shouted their names. "Melina! Ekaterina! Marie!" Over and over, he called them, whimpering,

"What have I done?" Jean pulled and strained at the table. His fingers became bloody again as he tried to raise the impossible weight.

Suddenly the room became completely dark for a moment as a figure blocked the small opening in the roof. Jean turned in time to see the shape of a man drop through the opening to the ground behind him. He whirled reflexively, more to protect his little family than himself. The man rushed at Jean, knocking him to the floor. Two strong arms wrapped around his body and held him tightly.

"Jean! Jean! *Arrêtez! Arrêtez!*"

Jean struggled to break free of the powerful grip. He tried to drop his right hand to his dagger, still in the scabbard in his belt.

"They're gone! Jean! *Écoutez-moi!* They're gone!"

Jean went completely limp, and slumped to the floor. John Buck, Philippe's lieutenant and *Turcopilier*, released his grip and sat in the dust next Jean. He realized that Jean thought he meant that they were dead. "*Non, mon ami.* They're not here. Listen to me. They're fine. Melina took the babies to the hospital. They're safe with Renato. She asked me to come and find you, so you wouldn't be worried."

Jean sat on the floor, still panting. The two men sat together in silence for a moment. He wiped the tears from his dusty face and hugged John Buck. Then, without a further word, they rose and climbed back into the daylight. Jean recovered his armor and gloves. The two men climbed down from the roof and walked back to the street.

They had reentered another world. The air was filled with the blast of cannon, and the shattering of stone as the huge balls impacted the walls and the city streets. Stone fragments flew past them. People seeking shelter from the barrage rushed wildly about the streets.

Slowly, he and Buck became aware of the cries for help coming from the house next door. There seemed to be people trapped inside. Jean turned to help.

Buck put his hand on Jean's shoulder. "*Va-t-en, Jean. Allez-y!*" Go on, Jean. Go away. "I'll get some knights to help these other people. Go to the hospital and see Melina. It'll be all right."

Jean stood and hugged Buck with both arms. Then he turned and hurried back through the Quarter to the hospital to see his babies.

⁓

Earlier in the day, Melina could not bear being in the small, dark room anymore. She had gathered the twins and what clothes she could carry, and left her home. She rushed to the hospital and brought the babies to the second floor. There she found Doctor Renato on his rounds. She went to his side and said, "Excuse me, Doctor, but I need your help."

Renato turned, surprised to see Melina there holding her three-month-old babies in her arms. He took the bag of clothing from her and set it on the floor.

"What is it, my dear?"

"Oh, Doctor Renato, please can we stay here? The cannons and the noise are terrifying us. I am so afraid for my babies. Please let us stay. I would be able to keep watch on the twins, and perhaps I can help when the casualties start arriving."

"Why, of course, Melina. You're always welcome here. Take the babies to the room at the end of the ward. There are no windows, and it's surrounded by inside stone walls. They should be completely safe there even if a cannonball were to hit the hospital directly. You'll be able to see them and look in on them as much as you need to. And, yes, I certainly will need your help very soon."

Melina hurried to the room and placed her babies in a makeshift bed on the floor. She surrounded them with blankets and soft cloths. Then she propped the door ajar. With Ekaterina and Marie sleeping, she went back in the ward to help Doctor Renato.

Over the next hours, she would find herself completely occupied with her work in the hospital ward. She snatched the time necessary to feed and care for her babies. It was immediately obvious to her that working in the hospital with Renato was to be the only way she could keep her babies safe and preserve her sanity during the days of terror.

⁓

Jean accelerated his pace as he neared the hospital. He was practically running by the time he ascended the outer stairs. He rushed into the ward. He saw Renato crouched over a wounded citizen. Blood was running onto the stone floor and puddling near the man's feet. Jean knelt down next to the doctor and, without a word, reached out to help hold pressure against the badly lacerated leg. The old man had been cut by a shard of stone as he ran through the streets. The impact had torn through his skin and muscle, breaking both bones beneath the knee. Renato would have to complete the cannon-inflicted partial amputation as soon as he had stabilized the injured man. It took a moment for Renato to realize that it was Jean who was assisting him. He turned his head toward the little room, and nodded. Jean looked over his shoulder at the closed door. Renato called for help, and another knight came to relieve Jean. Jean rose, placing a hand on Renato's shoulder. "Merci, *Docteur*."

Renato nodded again and returned to his work. Jean walked down the center of the ward, calming himself as he went. He paused outside the room and took a long breath. He said a silent prayer of thanks before entering the small room.

When the door swung open, Melina involuntarily jerked awake. She had fallen asleep while nursing the babies. Ekaterina and Marie were still sucking loudly at her breasts as Jean knelt down on the makeshift bed. He straightened the blankets and helped Melina adjust her position. Then, without a word, he slid down on the blanket next to his little family and held the three of them in his arms. He put his cheek against the top of Melina's head and smelled her hair. It was so familiar to him that it brought tears to his eyes. Even the grime and the dust of war could not disguise the feel and scent of the woman he loved.

"What's happening out there, *Chèrie*?" Melina asked after a few minutes.

"Not good. Not at all. The Turkish cannons are firing without stop. We destroyed many of them today, but they just replace them as fast as we destroy them. This hospital is going to be filled with wounded by tomorrow morning. And we have not even begun to fight. When their soldiers try to enter the city—as they surely will—there will be more wounded and dying."

Melina cuddled closer to Jean and held her babies tighter. They had stopped feeding, and were now fast asleep in her arms. Still she did not put them down, but contented herself to hold them while Jean held her. She would hold onto this tiny island of comfort. If only a few minutes of peace and warmth could be hers that night, she would gladly embrace them.

⤙ 10 ⤚
THE END OF THE BEGINNING

Rhodes
July and August, 1522

Suleiman struggled to contain his anger. The losses of his cannons and so many of his finest artillerymen was staggering. Though he could not blame his Aghas, his frustration and rage needed an outlet. Though the knights were the obvious target, his Aghas bore the brunt of his anger as they stood before him.

"*This* is how I am greeted? *This* is what you have to show me? My best artillerymen slaughtered at their guns? Half my fine cannons lie shattered and melted in the sands of this accursed island?"

Nobody answered. Not even Piri Pasha could bring himself to meet the Sultan's eyes. This was what he remembered so well from the days of Selim. Was this Selim's blood boiling in the veins of the son?

Suleiman stood with both fists clenched upon the desk top, elbows locked, supporting his rigid body as he glared at each of the men in turn. He breathed deeply several times, and then, incrementally, began to relax his muscles. Slowly he regained control; his face began to soften, and the tight string of muscles in his neck disappeared. His fingers uncurled and he pushed himself away from the table.

Piri looked around the tent. The eyes of the other Aghas would not meet his. All of the Sultan's generals were backed up to the wall. They stood with their hands folded in front of them, eyes cast down to the carpet. Each stared at his folded hands. Still nobody spoke.

"Well, it seems as if our mighty cannons are little more than thorns in the sides of the knights. Pinpricks! We cannot count upon them to bring down these walls. Mustapha, what is the disposition of our miners and sappers?"

"Majesty, we have begun to dig. I have directed the miners to run their ditches straight to the walls. It will move more quickly, this way, than having to run angled ditches. They have dug deep trenches, and we have covered them with wood and shields to protect the men from gunfire from the walls and the turrets. But, it is very slow going. I have poured thousands of slaves and even some Azabs into the work."

"And how are they progressing?"

"They are almost through the first, the outer ditch. They have to cross a high escarpment and then the second, inner ditch. But, as they get closer, they also get within range of much more accurate fire. Much of the time they are exposed, and the losses, I am sorry to report, are heavy."

"How many dead?"

"More than five hundred dead and wounded in this first week of digging, Majesty."

Suleiman recoiled at this information, and turned his back. After a few moments, he returned to the table. He motioned the Aghas closer. They approached with care, finally gathering in a tight knot around the battle plans. Bali Agha took over the briefing.

"Their most powerful battery is here," he said pointing to the charts, "at what they call the Tower of St. Nicholas. The knights' cannons are deadly accurate, and can reach in any direction. I have moved twelve of our best cannons to the shore across the Galley Port from the tower, and have been bombarding day and night. We have had no success, Majesty. The massive reinforcements to the fortress have swallowed our cannonballs as if they were pebbles hurled from a sling. In the daytime, our cannons can only fire for an hour before the counterfire makes it impossible to remain at the site. We have to move our batteries and reestablish our firing patterns. We've tried night attacks, but with no more success. They see our muzzle flashes and our fuse fires and are able to silence us."

"And?"

"So, we have given up on this tactic and moved the batteries back. Our greatest strength is the fighting skills of the Janissaries. We absolutely must make a hole large enough to use our overwhelming numbers of men against their few knights."

"Where would this be?"

"We have reason to believe that there are weaknesses at the Posts of Auvergne, Aragon, and England. Here, Sire, opposite Achmed Pasha and Qasim Pasha's sectors." He pointed to the south and southwest corners of the fort. "We are moving fourteen of our heaviest cannons to this sector, for in a few days—a week at the most—our earthworks will overtop their battlements by at least ten or twenty feet. Once we have mounted our cannon atop the earthworks, we will be able to fire down directly into the city. A breach there or the weaker Post of England could be our way into the city, Sire."

"Very good. Keep at it, and tell me what progress is made. I want to be there when the bastion falls and our men enter the city."

The spirits of the Aghas lifted a bit, for it seemed that Mustapha had managed to give the Sultan some hope. Murmuring could now be heard around the table, as the Aghas pointed and discussed the plans. Suleiman turned to Bali Agha and said, "And what of the sorties? Have we captured or killed many of the knights?"

Bali Agha moved to the front of the group and looked directly at Suleiman. "No, my Lord. There are no captives, and no dead knights that I know of. Each day and night, they have sent out small raiding parties of five or ten knights. Occasionally, as many as twenty. These knights know the terrain, and have been able to move undetected into our lines. There are many houses and stone walls behind which to hide, and they are very successfully ambushing our working parties. I've had to send my Janissaries out with the work details building the ditches and the earthworks to provide protection. But, each time, these devils strike where the parties are unguarded. We have thousands of miners at work, Sire, and I cannot provide a Janissary for each of them."

"What losses, then?"

"Many, Sire. I would say at least two hundred killed in these sorties and night raids."

"Two hundred! And not a single knight slain?"

"No, my lord. And..."

"And?"

"And we have word that three of my Janissaries are missing."

"Deserters?"

"Oh, no, my Lord. These were fine young soldiers, and they would gladly have died in your service. No, if they are missing, I can only assume they were killed in ambush. They were off duty at the market and never returned."

"And their bodies?"

"Not yet found, my Lord."

"Then surely, they are dead. Or worse, they might be captured. May Allah have pity on them." Suleiman rubbed his eyes and squeezed the bridge of his hawk-like nose. Ibrahim moved to his side and whispered in his ear. Suleiman nodded. He walked to a *divan* and sat down. He appeared to the Aghas weary and depressed. The siege had barely begun.

The sea was roiled with white foam as the northwesterly winds of August played upon the surface of the Mediterranean. The winds were steady, the sky clear. July and August were the rainless months of sun and fair breezes. For the navy, it was the time of the *Bel Tempo,* the good weather. The winds scoured the air clean. The visibility was limited only by the height of the vantage point or eyesight.

Cortoglu stood by the helm of his galley and surveyed the sea. This famous pirate manned the Sultan's fleet, blockading the island to interdict any resupply the knights might try to achieve. Though generally despised by the Turks for his cruelty, his presence freed up other of the Sultan's officers for more vital duties.

Cortoglu's fleet rowed north and then turned and ran south before the wind, plying the waters just out of range of the guns at Fort St. Nicholas, blockading the two ports. His orders were to board and destroy any ships attempting to depart or land at

Rhodes. Suleiman wanted no reinforcements of either knights or provisions to reach the island.

Cortoglu was dressed in his own non-military uniform, baggy pants and high leather boots. He was a big man, and obese. His skin was dark and heavily wrinkled from years of exposure to the sun and the sea. He wore a long, black mustache and a beard. His shirt was open-necked, and he wore no hat. His sword was the curved scimitar of the Ottomans, and he carried a jeweled dirk in his belt; a gift of war from the Sultan.

From the raised afterdeck of his flagship, Cortoglu's eyes continuously scanned from the horizon to the shore. Hour after hour, he patrolled his beat. Heading north into the wind, he made use of his oars. Coming about and heading south, he hoisted his lateen sails while the oarsmen rested. He shouted the occasional order to his crew to correct their heading or to change the cadence of the oars; otherwise he spent his days in brooding silence, for the knights had given him little to do. He sorely wanted them to come out upon the sea and fight.

Below decks, the slaves were chained to their posts. They sat naked, six to a rough hewn wooden bench less than four feet wide. In the Muslim ships, nearly all the oarsmen were slaves, chained to their places by one ankle. They rowed with one foot on the ground board and the other pushing against the bench in front of them. Sometimes they had wool padding covered in burlap as seats. Most of the time the benches were bare. The wood was darkened with the deep penetration of the blood of the many oarsmen who had labored there over the years.

Cortoglu stood next to the helm at the afterdeck, his first officer at his side. As he turned back into the wind, he gave the command to row. The officer signaled the slave masters below with the silver whistle chained around his neck. Two officers below decks gave the commands to the oarsmen, and the cadence began again. Slowly the galley accelerated as the oars dipped in unison. The slaves strained at the massive oar-looms, pushing with one leg against the benches and pulling with both arms on the rough oars. The handles were dark with the sweat and blood of the slaves; the bilges stank from the excrement that sloshed about with each surge of the galley. The holds were never cleaned or washed while at sea, and the filth could accumulate for months. The slaves, too, never washed, nor were they ever allowed to leave their benches or their oars. The width of the rowing bench was their world until they died in the service of the Sultan.

The cadence increased as the galley picked up speed and the water resistance lessened. Soon they were cruising at an easy three knots. In battle, when rowing with the wind at their backs and the sails raised, Cortoglu's galleys could, for a time, make six knots.

As they approached the northernmost end of their patrol, word came up to the helm that two slaves had fallen unconscious over their oars. Cortoglu ordered them whipped back to work. The slave master uncoiled his long, leather whip and began to beat the two men across their backs. After ten or more lashes, there was still no movement. The second-in-command below decks put a hand on the slave master's arm and stopped the whipping. He pointed to the lash marks on the backs of the two men. There was no bleeding. The slave master bent down and pulled the oarsman's head backwards by he hair. He looked into the glazed eyes and saw no moisture. He unchained all the men at the bench, and shipped the large oar to get it out of the way of the others. Then he ordered the two living slaves to drag out the naked bodies of the dead men. They were hauled up on deck and, without any delay, thrown overboard into the sea. Two more slaves were released from a locked holding room and brought to replace the dead men at the oars.

As the day grew hotter, two reserve slaves were sent aft to fetch provisions. With the boat heading south under sail and the oars at rest, the two slaves walked among the oarsmen and placed wine-soaked bread into their mouths. The bread would provide just enough nourishment to keep them alive, while the wine would dull some of their pain.

Virtually all of the slaves in the Muslim galleys were captured Christians. Because the Muslim galleys were manned solely by captive slaves, there was the occasional revolt at sea. During close engagements with hand-to-hand fighting, slaves would seize the opportunity to disrupt the galley. They would refuse to row, despite the lashes of the whip. Though chained to the deck to prevent real uprisings, they could seriously hamper the mobility of the galley in critical moments. When the galleys were in port, and the ships undergoing refitting, it was necessary to keep the slaves in specially built prisons to prevent rebellions and escapes.

In contrast, though the Christian galleys had some slaves on board, most of their oarsmen were *buonavoglie*, inmates of debtor's prison who were working off their debts. These *buonavoglie* could be distinguished from the slaves by their haircuts, which were shaved on both sides, leaving only a ridge on top running from back to front. The men were working their way back to freedom, and so rowing crews of the knights were far more reliable in battle.

Having restocked his galley with oarsmen, Cortoglu resumed his patrol. Light was fading as he moved slowly closer to shore. The batteries at Fort St. Nicholas demarcated Cortoglu's patrol zone. If he strayed within range of the cannon, his galleys could be sunk with a single shot.

As his small fleet turned to run south before the wind again, unseen to Cortoglu, a shadow appeared on the northern horizon. The sky grew slowly darker as the shadow closed upon the island, hidden in the decreasing light. Cortoglu's galleys plied their way south, watching for ships trying to leave the ports. They paid little attention to the waters abaft their beam.

Antonio Bosio's galley continued to move south toward the Galley Port. His galley was the pride of the Order's fleet. Over one hundred twenty-five feet long, and only eighteen feet wide, it was sleek and low and fast. The prow overhung the bow by fifteen feet, and held a *rambade*, a boarding platform from which the knights could board the enemy after ramming and grappling. There was space for two small cannon to be mounted there as well. Three masts supported huge lateen sails to assist the boat when running before the wind. The ship was propelled by twenty-six oars on each side, four to six men to each oar.

In battle, the knights made use of Greek Fire: a mixture of salt peter, pulverized sulfur, resin, ammonium, turpentine, and pitch.

Paradoxically, the mixture was ignited by applying water, which set off a chemical chain reaction that set the Greek Fire ablaze and could be directed from the nozzles of copper tubes like flame throwers. Once ignited, the fires were exceedingly difficult to extinguish. The flames would spatter and stick to the bodies of those unfortunate enough to get in its path. But, the knights feared a backflash that might set their own ships afire. So, on the galleys, they devised small clay-pot hand grenades. They were made of the same chemicals as the Greek Fire, and were covered in paper with sulfur-dipped fuses. The knights could effectively throw them a distance of twenty yards.

Bosio saw the small Turkish guard fleet. He recognized Cortoglu's galley, for he had slipped past the *corsair* on his way out of Rhodes on his mission. The Grand Master had sent Bosio to Naples and Rome to appeal for men, supplies, and money. Now Bosio was on his way home. He watched intently as his galley closed upon the slower Turkish craft. He stood next to his helmsman, with twenty knights in full battle gear arrayed around him. They spoke in whispers, for they had the wind at their backs, and the sound could carry a long way over the water. The oars were shipped for the moment, but the men were ready at their benches.

"I cannot slip back into the port without letting that son-of-a-whore know we have broken his blockade," Bosio said to his helmsman. "Not only once, but twice! Listen, we will continue our advance to the port. If Cortoglu does not see us in this darkness, we'll creep up on his stern and attack. Then we'll wheel to the right and row into the port." He turned to his captain. "Be ready with the signal flares. I want the chain and boom across the harbor withdrawn in time for us to slip in, and closed immediately behind us. Be sure of your signals. I don't want the batteries at Fort St. Nicholas to mistake us for the Turks."

Bosio turned to one of his lieutenants. "You, Guy, take some knights to the *rambade*. We'll have a gift for Cortoglu." Bosio pointed to the equipment on the deck and whispered further orders.

The knights took their stations. Bosio stayed with the helmsman. Leaning on the long center-pole tiller, the helmsman bore down upon the Turkish galleys. The wind slowed as it usually did at night. The seas became calmer, and the swells decreased. Cortoglu's ships gradually settled into the sea. The *corsair* did not start his oars, for he was in no hurry to come about and make the northerly run just yet. He wanted to clear well beyond both ports now that the darkness might be hiding blockade runners. He longed for action, and had been frustrated by the knights' unwillingness to engage him.

"These knights are cowards and pigs. They don't fight and they don't wash," he had complained to the *Reis*, Pilaq Mustapha Pasha. "But, their time will come!"

As Bosio's galley passed the northern tip of the Galley Port, he gave the command. The oars dropped into the water, and the cadence began. He ordered his sails splayed to both sides, and goose-winged his galley before the wind. With both oars and sails at full power he closed rapidly upon the Turkish galleys. He ignored the other ships, and closed upon Cortoglu alone, whose silhouette he could now see standing in the stern. When the noise of his oars alerted the Turks, there was a scramble to assemble. But, communication between galleys was primitive and it took some time for the rest of Cortoglu's little fleet to get organized. Before the Turkish galleys realized they were under attack—for who would think that a single ship with a handful of knights would attack such a superior force—Bosio closed on Cortoglu and caught him. The old *corsair* had no time to bring his ship around into ramming position.

Bosio's galley aimed itself perpendicularly toward the stern post, from which Cortoglu commanded. Cortoglu ordered his men to brace for the coming impact. Just as the knights were about to ram, the Turks saw dozens of flaming orange streaks arcing through the air toward their ship.

"Shields!" shouted Cortoglu to his men, for he thought they were under attack by a barrage of flaming arrows. Only too late did he discover that he had been hit with the awful Greek Fire. The clay pots burst all over his deck. A few of his men had caught the pots against their small leather shields and were covered in liquid flame. The fires burned in small circles all over the Turkish galley. Men ran about trying to extinguish the flames. Sails caught fire, and many of the sailors ran about the decks, their clothes burning. The night wind carried the screams of the burning men to the other galleys. The smell of charred flesh followed quickly behind.

Cortoglu called for his armed soldiers to assemble to repel the boarders. But, as the ships closed, the sky became filled with hundreds of arrows. They rained down upon the Turks who were trying to put out the fires. Fifty of his men fell to the deck with arrow wounds. A handful died on the spot, a chance arrow piercing the heart or the throat. Cortoglu drew this sword and again prepared his men to repel boarding.

Just as they braced for the inevitable ramming, Bosio's galley jibed its starboard sail and turned sharply away toward land. The starboard oars paused for five strokes while the port oars dug in with extra power at the command of the officer below decks. In one minute, the galley was on a broad reach and under full oar power heading for the Galley Port. Cortoglu's galley was dead in the water, its slaves waiting at their oars, hoping to be liberated by the knights.

By the time the Turkish galley was cleared again for action and the slaves whipped into submission, Bosio had slipped into the Galley Port and the chain booms were being drawn closed once more. Bosio and his men cheered at their small success, and the battery at Fort St. Nicholas sent a cannon salvo in the direction of Cortoglu's ships to bid them goodnight.

When the galley pulled alongside the stone wharf, Bosio commended his knights and seamen, then quickly hurried ashore to bring the news to the Grand Master. *If only*, he thought, *my news from Rome were as good as our little skirmish here tonight.*

He shook his head and hurried up to the city and into the Street of the Knights.

The Grand Master sat at his long oak table and listened quietly to the report of his inquisitors. "The older of the Janissaries gave us nothing, my Lord. Nothing but a good deal of spittle in our faces at the beginning. It seemed for a while that he would have much to tell us, for at first he took the rack with a great deal of screaming and crying out. I thought, surely he will break down. But, after a little while, he became completely calm. His screams and cries stropped, and he only stared at the ceiling. Then he was dead. He never uttered a word."

"Nothing?" Philippe said. "Nothing?"

"No, my Lord. Nothing. *Pas un mot.*" Not a word.

"And the other?"

"That was a different story. It took very little to have him babbling away. He listened to the screams of his colleague, and I think he assumed that we already knew the whole battle plan anyway. So, when he saw us carry out the dead body of his friend, he just gave up and began talking. It was hard to get him to stop. Of course, he had only limited knowledge. He is but a foot soldier with no rank. But, we learned some important things."

"Such as?"

"To begin with, you were quite correct in your assessment. They plan to hammer at the walls and bastions with cannon fire. But, the mortars and incendiaries hurled into the city are only for demoralization of the people. They will concentrate the attack on the walls by mining. They plan to attack the weakest appearing of the bastions first, and then blast holes big enough to send in large forces of foot soldiers. They will try to overpower us with sheer numbers."

"Where will they concentrate the first of the mining?"

"Of that he said nothing we didn't already know. They consider the walls of Aragon, England, and Provence to be the weakest points in our defense. Mainly Aragon. As we have seen, they are erecting a great earthworks opposite the Tower of Aragon, and will try to mount their cannon on top. From there, they could fire down into the city if the earthworks are tall enough."

"Indeed they could. And will, if we let them."

"And, they hope to silence our guns by bombarding the main towers. This will give some relief to their men digging the trenches and advancing to mine the walls."

"This is what we suspected. Now that it is verified, instruct my officers there to intensify their fire and the harassment of the workers. We will use all our strength to stop—or at least, delay—this work."

"Yes, my Lord. That is all the information I could get. What shall we do with the body, and the prisoner who is still alive? We don't have much space for corpses within these walls."

"No, indeed. We do not. Nor food and water. Give the dead body a day or two to become putrescent. Then load it into a catapult and fire it back into the camp of Bali Agha whence it came."

"And the young one, my lord?"

"Mmm. My instinct is to kill him as well. We have little space or time for prisoners. But, he *is* just a boy." Philippe mused for another moment. "Find someplace to lock him up. Have a guard bring him food and water once a day, but do not place him where we will need anyone to watch over him. We can't spare the manpower. That will be all for now. I hope we will have more use for your services in the future. *Au revoir.*"

———

Philippe stood on the ramparts of the fortress overlooking the harbors, as he did from time to time. He watched as the galley hove to and was secured to the wharf by the waiting knights on guard. Even by the dim light of the torches he could recognize the form of Antonio Bosio clambering over the side and down the ramp, followed by several uniformed knights he did not recognize. Behind the knights came about a dozen men wearing swords and civilian dress. They soon all merged into the waiting crowd of knights.

"Looks as if we have a few more broadswords to stand with us," Philippe said to his lieutenant, John Buck, who had appeared at his side.

"Yes, my Lord. But," he said squinting into the darkness, "they look a little young to me." He pointed at the five knights following behind Bosio and added, "That last one there looks no more than a lad."

"Aye, John. But, so were you and I when we first dipped our swords in blood. There has to be a first time for everyone." Buck nodded silently.

Philippe and Buck continued to watch as the small procession moved off the stone wharf and began the ascent into the city. Several knights and Rhodians stayed behind to unload what Philippe hoped would be more powder and supplies for his city. Then, as the little band was lost to view, Philippe and Buck climbed down from the walls and returned to his desk at the palace. He was at his desk, looking over the endless lists of supplies and armaments, when there was a knock at the door.

"*Entrez,*" he said without looking up.

Antonio Bosio entered the room and removed his helmet and gloves. He tossed his cape over a chair, and rushed to the Grand Master. "Sire," he said.

Embracing Bosio, Philippe exclaimed, "I heard that you gave that damned Cortoglu a good stiff kick in the arse."

Bosio laughed. "Indeed, my Lord. Indeed, I did. I'm only sorry I do not have his head to mount on our battlements. But, as you said, his position as *Kapudan* is more to our good, lest the Sultan replace him with someone competent."

"Yes, yes. He serves us well. He's a fool, to say the least." Then in a serious voice, "And of your mission?"

"That, my Lord, did not go as well. In a word, I bring you very little of what you asked for. I managed to find four more knights and a handful of mercenaries. Also, I obtained what provisions my money could buy. Some food. Some gunpowder. Nothing more. Both Rome and Naples made long speeches; shed some tears for our plight; then sent me away with their prayers and good wishes. I'm sorry, my Lord. I could do nothing more."

"Don't worry, Antonio. I know if you were turned away, no man could have done better. We will do with what we have, and to hell with all the princes of Europe."

Philippe waited for Bosio to leave. But, Bosio stood there, moving from one foot to another like a small boy.

"What is it, Antonio?"

"My Lord...I may have exceeded my authority, but..." He continued to fidget.

"What is it man? Speak!"

"My Lord, I have brought more than I told you. Believe me when I say that I tried to refuse...but, it was just no use."

"What is this, Antonio? Get to the point."

Bosio stepped back toward the door and said something to one of his aides. Philippe couldn't hear the words. He strained forward and moved in front of his desk. Bosio stepped to the side as a young man entered the room, dressed in the battle cloak of the knights. A broadsword hung at his side, nearly touching the floor as he stepped tentatively into the room. He held his head low, and did not meet the Grand Master's eyes.

What's this...?" Philippe began, puzzled. But, he stopped as the knight looked up and swept his hat from his head. Hélène's wavy black hair fell to her shoulders as she looked into Philippe's eyes.

Philippe turned toward Bosio, who had already slipped out of the door. He looked back at Hélène, who had dropped her hat to the floor and was standing there unsure of what to do.

Philippe could find no words to say what he felt. He crossed the room in three great strides, grabbing Hélène in a fierce embrace, pressing her to him. He brushed her broadsword aside, bringing her body still closer to his. The lovers held each other tightly, Philippe's face buried in Hélène's hair; her face pressed into his chest. The scent of her hair and her skin...it had been so long.

At last he pulled back enough to look into her dark eyes, yet never releasing her from his strong grasp, as if in doing so she might disappear. He smiled, shaking his head in disbelief. "How? How did you do this?"

"The knights in Paris learned that you were sending a ship for more men. I heard it from one of the women. A knight's woman..." She lowered her eyes momentarily. "Then when I heard the ships would come no further than Rome, I made my way there by coach..."

"Hélène, you might have been killed. France is a shambles. It's too dangerous for you to travel like that."

"Everyone tried to stop me, but I knew that I might never see you again. This was the only way."

"But Antonio...He should never have let you board my ship. He knows the danger. He..."

She placed her fingers across Philippe's lips, and as he kissed them, she said, "My love, it wasn't his fault. I snuck aboard in the night. Actually it was easy. There was so much loading and preparation that no one noticed one more knight carrying supplies. I hid among the stores until we were well out to sea, and then I went to Antonio. He was furious, and he wanted to put me ashore at once. But, by then we had sailed beyond any safe landfall, and he could not spare the time to take me back. He just didn't know what to do with me."

"Where did you stay for the rest of the voyage?"

"In Antonio's cabin."

Philippe flinched, but Hélène continued, "No, my love. Antonio stayed above decks for the rest of the voyage, bless his heart. The weather was awful, poor man. He brought me my meals himself, and he dressed me in this disguise. I think few if any of the knights knew I was there. He gave me these clothes and brought me straight here. To you."

Philippe smiled. "You know how much I love you, but you've picked a bad time to come. The Turks are determined to slaughter every one of us. Though I love you for coming to me, I must find a way to get you safely back to Paris."

Hélène stepped back, releasing herself from Philippe's embrace. "I'm not leaving *you*, Philippe, so I'm not leaving Rhodes."

"But, we may not be able to hold out very much longer. I've got to get you away."

"Philippe. Hear me. I'm staying here with you. I may not be able to fight with that thing," she said pointing to the broadsword on the floor, "but I can help. I can feed the wounded, or better still, I can help care for them. Surely you need help at the hospital?"

Philippe looked at her and was silent. He took a deep breath, "Of course you can. And how could I stop you anyway? I'll introduce you to Renato, the doctor, and Melina, his nurse. There's a great deal for you to do."

Hélène stepped into Philippe's arms again and hugged him closely. She sighed into his chest. "I love you, Philippe."

Philippe just breathed her familiar scent again, and said nothing.

⸻

Philippe lay with his head on Hélène's lap. It was nearly dawn and the battlefields were mercifully quiet. Hélène ran her fingers through his hair, combing and caressing the long white strands with her nails. Both were still naked and happily exhausted. It seemed like years to them—another lifetime—since they had made love in her Paris apartment. In some ways, for the moment at least, it was quieter on Rhodes than it ever was in the noisy streets of Paris.

"It would be so nice," Hélène said, "never to leave this room again. I could stay here forever."

Philippe nodded, the back of his head pressing on her soft abdomen and thighs. "If only it were possible." There was sadness in his voice this time; a resignation that Hélène had never heard before. "Rhodes was once a paradise. This island has been our home for over two hundred years. You and I could have been happier here than even in Paris."

"You're speaking as if it's all past, Philippe. As if you have already lost."

Philippe didn't answer, but reached up, his eyes still closed, and gently caressed Hélène's breasts. She shivered slightly and smiled at his rough touch. His hands were coarse and hard from hours of holding his sword in training and battle. Still, he tried to be as gentle as he could. She took his hands in her own and pressed her lips to them. Then she placed them back on his abdomen where they had been.

Philippe smiled and said, "Sorry."

"Don't be. Those are the hands that may yet save these poor people."

"There are many out there who say these are the hands of the man who condemns this city to destruction."

"Why?" she asked with real disbelief. "You and your knights are the only ones standing between them and the Turks. Why should they blame you?"

"This is a Greek island. Though we've been here for over two hundred years, we are still the outsiders to them. *Les autres.*" The Others. "They will never see us as one of them. Rhodes has been occupied by different people for centuries. Only the Rhodian Greeks remain constant. When we go, they'll still be here, and a new conqueror will rule them."

"You said *when* we go, Philippe. Is it that inevitable?"

"No. Not yet. Perhaps not even in this siege. The Sultan, we hope, still leads a 'Summer Army.' We can only pray that if we can hold out until winter, he will pack up and go back to Istanbul as his great-grandfather did forty years ago. And then again, he may not. He seems very determined to destroy us."

"Oh, my love..." Hélène said. She slid down alongside Philippe, holding his muscular body against her cool skin. With her fingertips she traced the hardraised scars of his many years in battle

Philippe felt her tears on his neck. He knew why she was crying, but he could not talk. His mind was focused on the danger she would face in the coming months, and he was afraid that if he tried to speak, he, too, would begin to cry. Instead, he touched her hair and her back, and ran his fingers gently as he could over her body.

"Philippe," she said quietly after a long silence, "do you think it's time for you and your knights to leave...to give up Rhodes?"

Philippe didn't answer, but rolled onto his back and released her from his grip.

"I've heard there have been terrible losses," she went on. "On both sides. I could see the bodies from the walls when we came up to the fortress. And the smell. Oh, Philippe...so much death...so many wounded. Yours and the Turks. Can it be worth it?"

"You don't know what you're saying," he said quietly. "We cannot surrender to the Sultan. If we do there will be still more carnage, more death and dying. The Rhodians will become his slaves; their women—yes, you too—will be taken into his harem; and all my knights slain. Is that what I should do?" His voice had begun to rise, and Hélène was frightened by his tone.

She said, "But, if you were to surrender...to offer to leave in peace, without further battle? Surely he would want you to leave without more loss of his soldiers. He would want to return home before the winter sets in?"

Philippe raised his hand, his palm open, telling Hélène that this conversation was over. He sighed and closed his eyes. Then he moved still closer to her and took her in his arms again and held her tightly, not speaking another word.

In the early light they made love again and fell asleep uncovered on the damp rough sheets. Philippe woke first and slipped quietly from his bed. He covered Hélène's body with the rough blanket and dressed. As he was leaving, Helen's head rose from the pillow and in a voice still hoarse from sleep she called out, "Philippe?"

Philippe returned to the bed and knelt. "Good morning, my love. Stay here a while. I'll send you some clothes and breakfast. Then, when there's time, we'll go to the hospital. You were right. The hospital is just where I need you. And…it's probably the safest place in Rhodes right now." There was no more talk of surrender. Philippe kissed her and left.

Hélène put her head back on the pillow and fell quickly asleep, a smile still on her lips.

As the sun touched the horizon once more, the knights on the battlements waited and watched.

⇥ 11 ⇤

THE CARNAGE

Rhodes
September, 1522

Suleiman sat in the shade of the afterdeck. His royal galley plowed through the light seas under both oar and sail. Mustapha and Piri Pasha sat on either side, while Ibrahim paced the deck. The captain of the galley stood next to the helmsman and kept his eyes averted from the Sultan.

On the prior evening, word had reached Suleiman that at least one galley had broken the blockade. This, of course, meant that the ship had also been allowed to leave Rhodes sometime earlier as well. The Sultan shook his head wearily as he wondered what to do with this Cortoglu.

"I will not stand for such incompetence," he said. "This is the second time the knights have made fools of us! It was bad enough that they could run the blockade totally unknown when they left Rhodes the first time. But, to come back and attack the very galley of the naval Chief-of-Staff! This is too much!"

Ibrahim and Mustapha had not uttered a word, but stared at the ground hoping that the Sultan would not act in haste. In fact, he had already ordered his galley prepared and had sent for a small detachment of fifty Janissaries.

Both Ibrahim and Mustapha, at great risk to themselves, had pleaded with him.

"Please, Majesty, do not depart tonight. It is so much more

dangerous in the darkness," Ibrahim had reasoned.

"He's right, my Lord," said Mustapha. "Wait until morning. There will be less chance of a sortie by the knights, and you can still punish this pirate fool."

In the end, Suleiman relented. Ibrahim and Mustapha stayed with the Sultan until late into the night. They both felt that he needed the comfort of close friends more than he needed consultation from his Aghas.

The Sultan ordered a midnight meal, and the three men sat on cushions on the carpeted floor. Suleiman was still seething over the ineffectiveness of his cannon against the knights' stronghold. The three men ate in silence. They took a short break from the constant conversation of war and strategy. Only after their dessert had been cleared did they return to the subject.

Mustapha was the first to speak. "My Lord, we will need to shift the emphasis of our attack. Clearly, cannon alone will not win this battle. We know that it is not for lack of skill that we have failed to break into the stronghold. Our master gunner, Mehmet, has great experience in these matters. He has never failed us before, and if he cannot penetrate the walls with his guns—and these are the finest cannons in the world—then it will be more because of the strength of the walls, not the weakness of the attack."

Suleiman nodded wearily. "Yes, brother-in-law. You're quite right. Mehmet is a great artilleryman, as was his father, Topgi Pasha. They are a family of talented fighters."

Suleiman turned to Mustapha. "But, surely our miners will make it possible for me to get my Janissaries into the city. They sit in their camps just waiting for the chance."

Ibrahim said, "I think that we need to keep up the barrage of cannonballs, my Lords. These may not break into the fortress, but they will distract the knights and keep them busy. That will take the pressure off the miners and sappers. For, they've only just started and have sustained terrible losses. They are totally exposed almost constantly to the arrows and gunfire from the towers."

"Indeed," Suleiman said. "I think we will keep up a heavy artillery attack no matter what happens." And then, almost visibly,

Ibrahim and Mustapha could see the shift in the Sultan's mind-set. They knew at once that he was back to the subject of Cortoglu. "Damned him, if I will not have his head for breakfast. And the *Kapudan* as well. The Admiral, Pilaq, should have been there to assure the blockade along with Cortoglu."

The Sultan's night was long. The three slept little, and as soon as the sun was up, the Sultan sent for his servants. Suleiman was bathed and dressed, then went to morning prayers. Ibrahim and Mustapha returned to their own tents for a change of clothes, a bath, and prayers as well. Then, after a light breakfast, the three rode with their guard to the temporary port at Kallitheas Bay and boarded the waiting galley.

The Sultan's ship hove to alongside Cortoglu's flagship. Though Suleiman had not sent word of his visit, Cortoglu seemed prepared for trouble. Ibrahim could see the pirate chief standing on the high afterdeck in the shade of a sail. Next to him was Pilaq Mustapha Pasha, *Kapudan* of the fleet.

When the ships were tied off, a ramp was secured between the galleys and twenty-five Janissaries immediately hurried aboard the flagship. Next, Ibrahim and Mustapha Pasha crossed to the other ship. Finally, the Sultan made his way aboard.

The remaining twenty-five Janissaries followed closely behind Suleiman and took up positions between the crew and their Sultan. When the soldiers were in place, there was a complete wall of armed men separating Suleiman's party from the sailors aboard Cortoglu's ship. Inside the protective ring were Suleiman, Mustapha Pasha, and Ibrahim facing Cortoglu and the *Kapudan*, Pilaq.

Cortoglu shifted uneasily. He liked neither the look on the Sultan's face nor the heavily armed bodyguard that accompanied him. Normally, the Sultan could take a small guard and depend upon the Azabs—the Sultan's marines—and the sailors on board the galley to ensure his safety. It was an insult to Cortoglu's security that the Sultan came so heavily protected with his own guard. As the *corsair* would soon find out, it was more than an insult.

Most of the damage from the night's battle had been cleared, though several burned areas still showed on the deck. Somehow, even in the fresh sea air, the smell of charred wood and burned flesh lingered.

Suleiman ignored the cushioned seat that had been hastily brought to the afterdeck when his galley was sighted. He stood facing the two naval leaders. His eyes bore into Cortoglu's, making the pirate look away. Cortoglu sensed what was coming next.

"Cortoglu! You are worse than a fool! You are completely incompetent, and I must wonder why I did not listen to my Aghas when they protested your appointment as *Reis* of my naval fleet. You have these two men to thank," and he gestured to Ibrahim and Mustapha, "that I did not come last night. For had I arrived here then, your head would be adorning the bowsprit of this ship even now." Cortoglu winced. "Instead, you will be bastinadoed in full sight of your crew."

Cortoglu stepped suddenly forward, and was about to protest, when he caught the eye of Pilaq, the Admiral. Pilaq frowned but held his place. Cortoglu said nothing, but sagged and stepped back. Suleiman nodded his head, and four Janissaries stepped into the small open space. Two of them grabbed Cortoglu by the elbows, while the other two bound his wrists tightly behind his back with leather thongs. The sailors and Azabs held their positions facing the detachment of Janissaries in the bright sunlight. Nobody moved aboard the galley. All eyes were on Cortoglu and the scene being played out on the afterdeck.

Cortoglu started to struggle against the tight leather thongs. Then he caught sight of Pilaq again, standing impassively next to the Janissaries. Cortoglu realized that no matter how painful and degrading this punishment might be, it would be better than death at the hands of Suleiman's executioners.

Suleiman stared at Pilaq for a moment and then turned back to Cortoglu. He nodded to the Janissaries. Suddenly, Cortoglu dropped directly to the deck. His feet had been kicked out from under him by his guards. He gave out a great exhalation of breath as he landed on his buttocks, sitting with his legs straight out in front of him. Next the guards pulled off his leather boots and tied each of his ankles over a wooden bar set up between two posts. His feet dangled over the end of the bar. The crew could see their *Reis* begin to tremble. Sweat broke out on his forehead as he struggled to keep from falling over onto his back. He stretched his hands down as far as he could and pressed upon the wooden deck to keep himself upright, to maintain what was left of his dignity.

The crew and the Janissaries were absolutely silent. The great galley rocked gently in the light chop and swell. Small waves lapped against the wooden hull. In the oppressive heat below decks, the slaves slept bent over their oar-looms. Their world did not include what was happening above decks. Had they known, they might have cheered.

The only sound heard on the ship was the light breeze moving through the rigging. Cortoglu looked into Suleiman's eyes. The *corsair* did not plead, he only stared. As his fear was replaced by anger, his face began to redden. His breathing quickened. Then, as if he had some inner revelation regarding his fate, he sagged and lowered his eyes to the deck. He stared at the white skin on his feet. He focused on the hairs of his toes. Anything was preferable to looking into the eyes of the Sultan.

The Janissaries stood stiffly at attention. Their plumed hats moved on the breeze. Ibrahim looked at the faces of the sailors. He thought he could see pleasure in their eyes. He knew that these men had suffered terribly under the command of this fearful pirate. It was time for Suleiman to replace Cortoglu with a more competent and respected *Reis*.

Again, Suleiman nodded to the captain of the Janissaries. The captain spoke softly to the Janissary at his right. The young soldier carefully took off his hat and handed it to one of his mates. Next, he removed his belt and scimitar, and, with a bow, handed over those as well. He stepped forward and faced the Janissary captain. The captain took a six-foot bamboo stick and flexed it in his two hands. It was about one inch in diameter, and had a leather handle at one end. The leather of the bastinado was darkened from the sweat of the many hands that had used it.

The soldier bowed to the captain, who held the bastinado in front of him with two hands palms up. The captain nodded his head. The soldier took the weapon and turned to face Cortoglu. He slashed the weapon twice through the air. Several of the sailors winced as they heard the terrible swish of the bamboo slicing through the breeze.

The young man stepped up to the bar, measuring his distance from Cortoglu's feet. He turned so that the bamboo would strike both soles of the *Reis's* feet simultaneously, parallel to the deck. He held the bastinado against the soles for a moment. Cortoglu tensed at the light touch of the stick. The soldier looked to his captain, who, in his turn, looked to Suleiman.

Suleiman nodded to the captain; the captain to the soldier. The stick was brought back to shoulder height, and the first stroke of Cortoglu's punishment was delivered. The stick whistled through the air, and the smack against the soft soles of the pirate's feet was heard all over the ship. It was immediately drowned out by the scream that came from Cortoglu himself. Not a single person watching the punishment could help but recoil at the terrible stroke. As the soldier brought the stick back to his shoulder, all eyes were on the bright red welt across both feet. Cortoglu shook with the pain and he squeezed his eyes shut in preparation for the next stroke.

Again, the stick whistled through the air, and again Cortoglu screamed in synchrony with the sound of the bamboo against his tender flesh. Now the crew and the Janissaries were transfixed. They saw that there was still only a single welt across both feet. The soldier, trained so well in the accurate use of his deadly scimitar, had struck the pirate in exactly the same spot as the first stroke. This time, Cortoglu's body shook with the impact, but he uttered no sound. His lips were pressed tightly together and the sweat poured down his face. He dared not look into the eyes of his Sultan. Though he knew that the extent of his suffering was in Suleiman's hands, he was afraid to challenge the Sultan with any eye contact. He knew that this punishment could end at any moment, depending upon a whim. It could also be the prelude to a beheading if the Sultan so chose.

Cortoglu squeezed his eyes tightly again and waited for the pain. And it came. Again and again, the bamboo whistled through the air and landed in precisely the same spot on Cortoglu's feet. The callused skin separated after only three strokes, and blood began to trickle from the crease. On the next stroke, the blood spattered across the deck, and Cortoglu bit down upon his lower lip to stifle his screams. Blood trickled from his lower lip.

The beating continued. Even the Janissaries began to look away from the ordeal. The sailors forgot their grievances against their captain. The obvious pain and brutality of the punishment affected everyone watching.

Pilaq Mustapha Pasha could barely contain his terror. He knew that he was next. He squeezed his buttock and bladder muscles, trying to keep himself from losing control in front of the entire command.

Ibrahim had long since looked away from the spectacle, and was gazing out over the blue-green waters of the Mediterranean Sea. He forced himself to see the green hills in the distance, and imagined his beloved falcons swooping down upon the hares and wild birds of Rhodes.

Mustapha Pasha looked straight ahead, but he, too, had taken his mind elsewhere. He thought of his wife, Suleiman's eldest sister, Ayse, and focused on her face and those of his children. Soon, he didn't even hear the sound of the stick.

Only Suleiman and the young soldier who wielded the stick focused directly upon the bleeding feet of Cortoglu. Suleiman showed no emotion at all. Cortoglu had failed in his duties, and for that he was being given the usual punishment. *He should be grateful that his head is not already adorning the bowsprit*, Suleiman thought again.

After fifty strokes, Cortoglu slumped backward onto the deck. His body had mercifully shut him off from the pain. His brain had protected him from any more of his Sultan's wrath.

As soon as the pirate's body relaxed, the captain looked to Suleiman. The Sultan nodded, and the captain ordered the soldier to step back. The soldier handed the bastinado to the Janissary captain and bowed. He wiped the sweat from his own forehead, and took his hat and scimitar from his mate. Though nobody had moved, all eyes were now on Pilaq Mustapha Pasha. The *Reis* was trembling, but stood at rigid attention. He, too, looked out over the sea, avoiding the gaze of his Sultan.

Suleiman gestured to Cortoglu and said, "This man has paid for his incompetence. Cut him loose and take him away. I want him on the next galley out of here, and if ever I lay eyes upon his miserable face again, he will die on the very spot. Make that known to him."

Then he turned to Pilaq. "Pilaq Mustapha Pasha, I think you have suffered much of the pain inflicted upon Cortoglu. The day grows hot and I must return to the battlefield. I will not, therefore, have you bastinadoed, as was this miserable wretch here before you. You are relieved of command of this fleet. Take yourself back to Istanbul if you so wish. You may live there unmolested. But, be sure that I do not see you again."

Pilaq bowed his head and kept it lowered for the remainder of the time that Suleiman was on the ship. The Sultan signaled to his men and turned from the afterdeck. He boarded the waiting galley and, as he took his seat, he could just see the still unconscious body of Cortoglu being dragged from the deck by four sailors.

Just south of the Palace of the Grand Master, behind the walls of the Post of Germany, was the Tower of the Church of St. John. From here the knights had an invaluable observation post, from which they could relay information throughout the city. The church bells were used in code to provide rapid dispersal of information to the knights at the other stations. Enemy troop movements and the disposition of the Turkish cannon could be known in minutes after being observed. Since knights were stationed inside the church tower twenty-four hours a day, this command post was at the very center of the defenders' intelligence.

Suleiman was resting after his morning on board the flagship. The punishment of Cortoglu and the firing of Pilaq had sapped his energy. He did not enjoy the terrible physical punishment that was traditional in his empire. But he could not think of a suitable way to replace it.

He lay upon the cushions in his tent and finished a small lunch. Ibrahim was with him, but had said little since the terrible spectacle on the ship. Most of his life with Suleiman had been spent in play or in learning together. Now that his boyhood friend was Sultan of the Ottoman Empire, the realities of a life of command were being thrust daily in Ibrahim's face. It was one thing to see the results of war. It was quite another to watch it as it happened. He had heard many stories of the punishments meted out by the Sultans. But, this was the first time he had witnessed it in person.

"Majesty," he said, breaking a long-standing rule that Suleiman must begin all conversations, "this ordeal has taken much energy from you. If you will allow me, perhaps you should rest here the remainder of the day. I will ride to the camps of the Aghas and report the day's progress to you later."

"Thank you. It's good to have somebody at my side who understands the burden of command. But, I must be seen by the troops to be in command and in control. It is hard enough to get them to fight at all sometimes. Not the Janissaries. But, the Azabs and the slaves. They must fear *me* more than they fear the knights. It must seem to them preferable to die in battle than to die in the wake of my wrath. No, I will rest awhile, and then we will review the battle together."

A messenger appeared at the door. Suleiman beckoned him in. The servant handed over the message, bowed, and backed out of the tent. Suleiman motioned Ibrahim closer and unrolled the paper. He read it in silence, and then smiled.

"What does it say, my Lord?"

"It is from one of our spies inside the fort. Apparently it was tied to an arrow and shot into the camp of Ayas Pasha before dawn. It seems that the knights have an observation post in a church behind the walls opposite the camp of Ayas Pasha. Our guns have done little if anything to damage the walls guarded by the Germans. But, perhaps we can use them to destroy the tower."

"Shall we make that our first stop?"

"Yes. Send word to Ayas Pasha to keep up the bombardment there. Then move more of Achmed Pasha's cannons in support. We'll ride out and see what we can see."

"Yes, Majesty." Ibrahim put on his turban and left the tent. Suleiman finished his lunch, now energized with the thought that he could issue commands that would, finally, advance the progress of his war against the Infidel.

———

Ayas Pasha and Achmed Pasha stood together behind a high stone wall in Ayas Pasha's camp. Together they watched as twelve of their most powerful cannons failed to destroy the fortifications in front of them.

"My captains tell me the Sultan is on his way here to see what progress we have made," Ayas said.

Achmed slowly shook his head and said, "I fear that we may be next on our Sultan's punishment list. He does not tolerate failure, no matter what the reason."

"What can he expect from us? These are the best cannons in the world. Our gunners are doing all they can. But, the knights' batteries have us spotted. We are being fired upon round for round. As soon as my batteries open fire, the Germans return fire and either destroy my guns or kill the gunner. Truly, I am running out of good men. And we have done nothing to breach the integrity of that wall. The Janissaries will not make their way into the city from here."

Both men watched the exchange of fire. The Turkish gunners shot huge stone balls directly at the Post of Germany. The blast was deafening, and the impact could be felt even as far away as Ayas and Achmed were stationed. When the smoke and dust was cleared by the afternoon breeze, all they could see was a hole in the stones, and more stone behind it. Their cannonball had only added to the mass of the wall, and had damaged nothing. The very same Florentine engineers who had made Fort St. Nicholas all but indestructible had done the same to most of the walls of the city.

As the Pashas watched the bombardment, Ayas Pasha saw several of his personal guard jump to their feet and stand at attention. He turned casually and saw twenty Janissaries on each side of Suleiman and Ibrahim, who were riding their horses into his camp. He placed his hand on Achmed's shoulder and said, "The Sultan. He's here."

Achmed turned and looked behind him. "Allah have mercy upon us now. He'll not like what he sees here today."

Suleiman and Ibrahim rode up to the two waiting Pashas. Neither dismounted, but remained in the saddles, their horses facing the city. Neither spoke. After several more rounds were fired from the most distant battery, Suleiman saw that there had been no effect at all. Then the German guns opened fire and, in a blast that shook the ground and made the horses stamp and turn, the Turkish cannon disappeared in a storm of smoke and dirt. Rocks fell from the sky and men screamed. The bodies of the dead gunners lay draped around the crater where their mangled cannon was lying on its side, the metal smoking in the sun. Two wounded soldiers crawled from the crater as fellow artillerymen ran to drag them out of harm's way.

Achmed and Ayas Pasha looked up at Suleiman, who could only shake his head. He turned to Achmed Pasha and said, "May Allah have mercy upon them." Then, in a voice of command, he said to Achmed Pasha, "Move all of yours and Ayas Pasha's cannon to one good firing position and direct your men to fire over the walls. Take Qasim Pasha with you. He is the finest artillery man we have now. Target the Tower of the Church of St. John. Look on the map. You will see it near the Palace. Destroy it! Send word to my camp when it is done."

Suleiman wheeled his horse and returned to his tour of the camps. Ibrahim waited for a moment and then turned to the two Pashas, who were standing there bewildered. "If you wish to keep your heads, or at very least, the soles of your feet, do exactly as the Sultan commands."

Then he, too, spurred his horse and caught up with Suleiman.

Philippe stood on the balcony of his Palace with Thomas Docwra and John Buck. The three faced south, discussing the disposition of their troops. Docwra said, "Right now, I think we need to support the weaker *langues*, my Lord. The Turks have not broken through any of the ramparts yet, but I fear that they are getting ready to make a major assault on the Post of England."

John Buck nodded in agreement. "He's right, my Lord. The Post of England is sorely undermanned, and the Muslims are concentrating still more fire power there. We should set up a mobile reserve of knights from several of the larger *langues*. They can be sent to any post that needs reinforcement at the moment. Also, I fear there may be spies in our city, for the Turk seems to be well aware of the disposition of our troops and the construction of our walls. They are concentrating their fire and assaults on our weakest posts."

Before the Grand Master could address the issue, and as if Buck's words needed affirmation, the three men watch in horror as the Tower of the Church of St. John disappeared in a cloud of smoke and dust. The stone walls collapsed, and the roof fell into the ruined structure. The first shot had weakened the walls, and three more cannonballs had impacted nearly simultaneously to finish off the weakened structure. The sound reached the three men a second after their eyes recorded the devastation of the cannonade.

"Sweet Jesus!" said Docwra.

"*Mon Dieu!*" said Philippe.

"*Merde!*" said John Buck.

Philippe turned to Docwra and said, "How many knights did we have stationed in the Church tower?"

"Three, my Lord."

"Get there, Thomas. See to them, if they survived. We can't afford such losses so early on. John, set up another observation post in another tower. But, see that it is kept completely secret. Use no bell or light signals. Have a runner deliver all messages to me directly. That was too determined an attack for such an innocent structure. The spies here must have informed the Turkish swine that we were using the church tower for an observation post. By God, I will make them suffer when I find out who has betrayed us! Get some of the knights on the job. We must find out who and how they are getting messages to the Turk."

Apella Renato had not slept in three days. The casualties were increasing daily, overwhelming him with his duties. Melina had been a godsend. She moved through the hospital ward as if she were possessed. She was able to tend to her babies, and then return to work the minute they were fed and asleep again. Renato insisted that she eat regularly, even though nobody else had time for meals. "You must keep nourished, Melina. The babies need your milk, and if you should go dry, they'll surely die. Keep eating. Take the time. I do not want their deaths on my conscience for working you too hard."

Melina did as she was told. She fed the babies, and rested when Renato ordered her to. But, she kept attending the wounded and the sick long after others had fallen asleep from exhaustion. It was as if every knight were the embodiment of Jean. Each knight she could help would help Jean. Somewhere, she was certain, there was a log, an accounting. Every soul she helped the doctor save was an entry in the book that might protect her beloved from harm.

When the Sultan stepped up the magnitude of his assault, the casualties rose proportionately. There were fewer civilians coming to the hospital now, for, over time, they had discovered suitable hiding places from the cannon salvos. But, more of the knights were exposed to danger. Not only were they injured as they stood their guard on the battlements, but knights were now being killed or wounded in the small sorties that were sent out to harass the Turkish troops.

Melina had just put the babies back to sleep in the little nest she had made of blankets and cloth in the protected little room in the hospital. She was returning to the ward when she nearly ran right into the Grand Master.

"*Pardon, Monsieur,*" she said.

"Melina," Philippe said, more ill at ease than Melina had ever seen him. "I was coming to see you and Doctor Renato."

Melina saw now that the Grand Master was accompanied by a young woman, nearly Melina's age she supposed. Thirty, thirty-five, perhaps, wearing a long, blue dress far too elegant to have been made in Rhodes. Both women were immediately struck by the extraordinary resemblance they had to each other. Philippe interrupted their thoughts.

"*Permettez-moi de vous presenter Hélène.* Hélène, this is Melina."

The two women nodded their heads, but did not speak. Philippe went on, now formally as if giving orders to his troops.

"Hélène will stay here in the hospital with you, Melina. Please show her what needs to be done. I haven't time to talk with the good doctor now, so please introduce Hélène to him. God bless you both for what you are doing for us."

The women curtsied formally to the Grand Master and waited silently until he left. Melina took both of Hélène's hands in hers and said, "I can't tell you how happy I am to see you. We need every bit of help we can get. Most of the women in the city are afraid to come out. We're very shorthanded. Come, let's find the doctor."

Hélène followed behind Melina as they hurried down the stairs and into the huge main ward. As they descended the stone stairs, Hélène said, "I have no experience at this. I hope I don't do something terribly wrong and hurt somebody."

"Don't worry. I knew nothing at first. But, you learn fast here. I'll help you, and so will Doctor Renato."

They made their way among the gathering crowd of wounded and searched the great hall for the doctor.

They found Renato bent over the operating table talking to a young knight Melina recognized as Michael. He was from the *langue* of England, and had been recovering from a severe infection in his arm. The knights had been preparing their swords when this young man's hand had slipped while sharpening his own. He had sustained a nasty gash in his left hand. Renato had instructed all the knights in the cleansing of wounds. But in his haste, the young knight had merely wrapped his hand in a piece of fabric and continued his work. The hand became infected, and he sought help from the doctor a few days later when he noticed red lines streaking from his hand up the outer aspect of his arm. That night his whole arm became painful and he could feel tender knots bulging from his armpit. By morning, his hand was so swollen that he could not close his fist, and he became feverish.

Renato had gently berated the young knight for his foolishness. "How many Muslims will you kill if I have to cut off your arm? How many can you fight if you lie dead of gangrene?"

Michael had merely shaken his head and said, "Forgive me, Doctor. I should have listened to you. But, there is so little time. The ships of the Turks were within sight of our islands, and ..."

"It's all right. I will do what I can, but you're a very sick young man."

Renato had worked day and night on the infected hand. He had given the knight as much wine and opium as he thought safe, and then began to cut away the infected flesh. Each day there was more dead tissue, and each day the doctor debrided what was clearly infected, trying to save the function of the hand. On the third day, a green, foul-smelling pus began to seep from the hand. Renato washed the pus away, and for a time it seemed as if he were gaining on the infection.

But, on the fourth day, Michael's condition worsened as the infection became generalized. He became delirious and went in and out of coma. His fever was high and he was no longer able to take anything by mouth. In his delirium, he began to flail about and had to be restrained with leather straps. Renato sent word to the Grand Master that an amputation was necessary. Philippe was desolate. "The Muslims have just set foot on our shore," he told Docwra, "and we might lose one of our brave young men already."

Now Renato was gently talking to the young knight, explaining that the only way to save his life was to sacrifice the gangrenous arm.

Melina stepped next to Renato and tapped him gently on the shoulder. Renato turned, giving her a wan and empty smile. Then he noticed Hélène standing just behind Melina. He raised his eyebrows and said, "Yes?"

"This is Hélène, Doctor. The Grand Master has brought her here to help us. Where is she needed?"

If Renato were puzzled, he did not show it. There was no time in his life now for anything but business. He said, "Well, she's just in time to help here. If you can stand it, my dear, we need someone to wash the wound as we proceed. Can you do it?"

Hélène felt a wave of revulsion wash over her at the sickly sweet smell of the gangrene. Then she looked into the eyes of the young knight, aware that her squeamishness was nothing compared to his suffering.

"*Oui, monsieur. Je suis prêt.*" I'm ready.

The knights placed Michael on a wooden table and bound him tightly with wide leather straps. Renato laid out the instruments.

Jean de Morelle was there assisting the doctor. The knights took regular turns at duty in the hospital, and Jean had been working for most of the day. He helped Renato arrange the last of the instruments, then waited at Michael's side.

Hélène could not help but fix her eyes on the brown stains dried deep into the wood of the table. Unlike the dark finish on the furniture, this finish was the color of death. The many lives that had lain in the balance had leaked their blood onto this table, creating a deep patina that would never be erased. Hélène had never witnessed any surgery before, but she knew what was in store for this brave young knight, and the thought made her chest tighten and her stomach heave.

Renato rolled up his sleeves and donned a long leather apron to protect his clothes. Jean tied the apron strings for the doctor, then grasped Michael's infected arm in his strong hands. He held on tightly high above the elbow almost to the shoulder. The young knight was nearly unconscious. They all hoped that he would stay that way until the worst of the operation was over. But, just in case, Jean placed a leather-covered stick between the young man's teeth.

Finally, after briefly looking over his table of instruments, Renato picked up a steel blade, twelve inches long, attached to a polished wooden handle. With a circular motion that lasted less than four seconds, Renato sliced through the uninfected skin and muscle that surrounded the upper arm of the young man. His knife just grazed the bone, and the doctor stopped immediately to keep from dulling his blade.

Hélène stared wide-eyed as more of the knight's blood was spilled among the dark stains on the table and the floor. *My God, this slaughter,* she thought. *These tables will soon be filled with the bodies of more knights. The floors will run red with their blood. And only this man,* she thought, looking up at Renato, *can save them.*

Renato dropped the knife onto his instrument table as gouts of blood spurted from the bleeding vessels. Bright-red fountains erupted from the large artery near the bone, while deep purple tides flowed steadily from the boy's severed veins. Hélène felt a lump rise in her throat. She tried not to look at the boy's arm, but could not take her eyes off the terrible spectacle. She swallowed hard to keep the contents of her stomach from spilling out.

Renato reached for the pile of clean rags that were stacked next to his knives and wadded a mass of them together. He used the rags to staunch the flow of blood and pushed the cut margins further above and below his incisions, exposing the white bone. Morelle held tightly to Michael's arm as the young man began to squirm around in his delirium and pain.

Renato took Hélène's hands and placed them against the wads of cloth that were now changing from white to bright red with the continued bleeding. In a nearly trance-like state, Hélène did as the doctor bid her. She held on hard to the tamponade of cloth as she willed herself to stay erect and awake. Her ears ringing, she fought not to faint at this crucial moment in the operation.

Within a minute, the young knight's blood was flowing through the wadding, seeping between Hélène's fingers and onto the floor. The color of the blood changed from red to crimson to maroon; then congealed into shining shivering lumps at Hélène's feet. One large clot had fallen on her shoe, and she could not make herself flick it off. It was almost as if casting that knight's blood aside would be an insult. Instead, she stared fixedly at it, unable to bring her eyes back to the now mercifully unconscious boy.

Renato reached up and twisted the leather tourniquet tighter about the knight's upper arm. The bleeding slowed, but did not stop.

"Oil! Oil!" Renato shouted to Jean. The knight reached out and took the copper pot of boiling oil off the metal stand over the flames. He held the copper container by its wooden handle and carried it carefully to the table.

Renato turned to Hélène. "Remove the cloths, my dear."

Hélène pulled the sodden rags away and dropped them into a wooden bucket on the floor.

Then to Jean, Renato said, "Go ahead, quickly! Pour it!"

Jean hesitated. He swallowed hard to keep the contents of his stomach from rising in his chest. He began to breath rapidly, and sweat appeared on his forehead and around his lips.

"Pour, damn it!"

He tipped the small pot and poured a stream of bubbling, steaming oil onto the bleeding surfaces of the amputation wound.

The young knight let out such a scream that everyone in the room stopped what they were doing and turned to see the poor boy's face. He was barely alive, his eyes closed. But, his handsome face was contorted with the pain. The cutting had been almost bearable. But, the oil...

The oil steamed and spattered as it touched the cooler, moist flesh of the partially severed arm. There was a hissing noise as it coagulated the blood seeping from the vessels. The crimson muscle turned brown, contracting like a separate living thing, shriveling away from the heat.

As the odor of the oil-seared muscle reached her nose, Hélène had to swallow forcibly again to keep from throwing up. This time she was only partially successful. She would never get used to the smell.

The bleeding slowed to a mere trickle. Renato reached down and picked up a steel saw with fine, off-set teeth. The blade was about twelve inches long and two inches wide, it tapered slightly toward the tip to allow access to tighter spaces.

Without hesitation, Renato sawed through the bone with less than ten forward strokes. Hélène closed her eyes, grimacing at the gritty sound of the blade cutting through the bone. Her teeth ached, and she found herself squeezing the boy's hand so tightly that she realized she might hurt the hand she was trying to comfort. Then she saw the utter stupidity of that idea, that she could do anything worse than was being done already. But still she eased her grip while keeping her eyes shut tight against the noise.

When the noise stopped, she relaxed the muscles in her face, which now ached with the force of her contraction. She opened her eyes and heard the saw drop to the table top. She saw Renato holding the boy's left hand in his own. His right hand cradled the elbow of the now amputated limb. It was as if the doctor were shaking the hand of the young man whose arm he had just cut off.

Renato dropped the arm into the wooden bucket, on top of the bloodied rags. He turned his attention to the cut end of the bone. From the large hollow marrow cavity, a steady stream of dark blood and velvety purple marrow issued forth. Renato took a wad of bee's wax from the table and rolled it between his palms. He held it briefly over the flame of the oil lamp and shaped it into an oblong sphere. Then he inserted it into the marrow cavity and wedged it home. The bleeding stopped.

In that brief interval of inactivity, Hélène once more became aware of the *variety* of smells in the room. The mingling of distinguishable odors drew her complete attention. The aroma of the hot oil overwhelmed almost everything. But, as she concentrated, she could detect the smell of the coagulated blood, then the disinfectant and the wine. Then, to her dismay, she smelled the faint odor of her own vomit.

Hélène shook her head and tried to focus. She looked at Michael, who seemed now to be asleep. Renato had pulled something out of a clean dish that was sitting on the table next to his instruments. He held what looked like a shining cap, the kind worn by Catholic clergy. Though she didn't recognize it, it was the recently removed bladder of a sheep. Renato applied it to the end of the stump as a dressing. He tied the bladder in place over the stump with sheep's sinews and wrapped the whole arm in cloth bandages. Then he made a sling and secured it to Michael's chest.

The doctor let out a great sigh and looked to Hélène. "Thank you, my dear, for all your help. You have now seen the worst, and are still standing. You're a brave woman, indeed. You should be proud. Now, go pray for him. Michael's life is in God's hands."

"Thank you, Doctor." And with that, she slipped quietly to the floor in a dead faint.

———

At the beginning of the second week in August, after more than a month of fighting, the knights were beginning to suffer heavy losses. The Turkish artillery massed its attacks against the Bastions of England and Aragon. The earthworks outside the ditch had finally overtopped the walls there, and the Turks were able to move heavy cannon in place on top of their newly built earthen mound. They could fire down into the city from the new vantage point. There were fourteen batteries—virtually all of Suleiman's remaining heavy cannons—concentrated in this sector. By the end of the week, there was significant damage to the Post of England and a large hole in the neighboring wall of Aragon.

Each night, the citizens and knights would repair and block up the breaches. Each dawn, the Turks would open fire again and reopen the breaches. Both sides sustained terrible losses, but the English suffered out of proportion to their numbers. The mobile reserves were sent wherever aid was needed, but it was not enough to secure their position if an all-out assault were made by the Turks.

While Hélène had virtually become Renato's first assistant, Melina was performing triage at the time of the cannon offensive against Aragon and England. Her job was to see if she could determine who needed the attention of the doctor first. This grisly aspect of her job meant she had to determine who were so badly hurt that they could not reasonably be expected to survive. Doctor Renato and his helpers had to give priority to those who could be healed enough to get quickly back into battle. Then he tended those who might live, even if they could not fight. Medical attention and supplies would be wasted on the rest. They would await their deaths alone.

Melina found herself overwhelmed with the responsibility. What if she were wrong? What if a knight might have lived after all, with just a little attention from the doctor?

"Triage is the hardest job, Melina," Renato had told her. "Not even the doctors can be sure at such a time. But, we do the best we can. If there were another doctor here I could spare, he would be doing what you are doing. I cannot be spared for such a job, so it falls to you. Do the best you can, and trust in God to guide your decision."

Melina did as she was told. But, she found herself crying almost continually. The dying young men made her weep. The pain of the wounded made her weep. The brave knights who were sent back into battle with their wounds still fresh, their bandages stained with blood, made her weep all the more. She dreaded every footstep in the corridor, for fear that the very next victim might be Jean.

No one could be spared to tend to the wounded on the battlements. So, all of the injured were carried to the hospital by fellow knights or citizens. Some of the knights were brought in still wearing their cloaks and helmets. She held her breath as the visors were removed, fearing the moment when she might see Jean's face. Day and night she waited for the terrible moment when she might have to decide to withhold treatment from the man she loved more than her own life. And she knew that every time another wounded knight was brought into the hospital, by wishing he were not Jean, she was wishing it on some other poor soul.

"I could *never* turn away Jean, *Docteur*," she had told Renato. "*Jamais!*"

"God will guide you, *Chèrie*. Trust in God."

On the night of the heaviest assault, the Commander of the Post of Aragon, Juan de Barbaran, was carried into the ward. Two knights had struggled with the heavy body, for he still wore his armor and sword. They placed him on the floor at the entrance to the ward. "*Ayudame, Señora.*" Help me, the wounded knight said in Spanish. Melina looked at the amount of blood on the man's cape and the blood puddling on the floor. De Barbaran had been struck with a flying shard of stone. It had severed two large vessels in his neck, and he was bleeding to death before her eyes. She put a hand against the flowing blood, as Renato had shown her to do. She wadded up some cloth from a basket and pressed it into the wound. But still the blood soaked through, seeping between her fingers. She began to cry again as the man's voice weakened. "*Ayudame, Señora. Por favore. Ayudame,*" his voice now no more than a gasp.

Soon the bleeding slowed, and the blood turned more purple than red. Finally, after a few minutes, the bleeding stopped altogether. Melina sat holding the Commander across her lap, still pressing the cloth into the wound. Renato had come to see what was happening, and gently took the cloth from her hand. He placed his fingers gently on de Baraban's neck. Then he signaled the two knights to take the body away. He had no room for the dead in his hospital.

He led Melina away by the hand. She tried to resist him, but he pulled her toward the small room where her babies were now asleep. "*Basta, Cara. Basta.* You have had enough for now. Sleep with your babies. Hélène will help me, and we'll carry on without you for a while. God bless you."

Then, Renato returned to the ward. As he passed the front door, another knight was being led into the hospital. The knight held a handkerchief to his right eye and was shrugging off the assistance of two comrades. But, it was clear he could not see, for each time the other knights let him go, he staggered in a crooked path. Renato took the man by the elbow and sat him down on the stone floor. He pushed the knight's shoulders until the man was resting against the wall. Then he removed the cloth from the knight's eye. There was a ragged wound to the eyeball, which was clearly destroyed. Renato knew instantly that the man would not see from that eye again. He replaced the cloth and placed the man's hand over it. "Hold this firmly, my Lord. I need to see if that other eye of yours will see again."

He examined the good eye and could find no injury. Then he placed a clean cloth over both eyes and wrapped the man's head in a bulky bandage. He took the man by the hand and led him to a corner where some blankets were stacked against the wall. "Sit here, my Lord. I'm afraid I have no bed for someone with a wound such as yours. Keep both eyes covered for the night. Then, in the morning, I will unbandage your good eye so that you can see your way back to your *Auberge*. I'm sorry for your wounds and your pain."

The knight nodded. "*Gracias, Doctor. Muchas gracias,*" was all the man said. Then, Juan d'Homedes y Cascón of the *langue* of Aragon put his head against the wall and tried to sleep.

Hélène walked unsteadily down the center of the huge main ward, stepping between the rows of bodies that now virtually filled the hall. Her hands were shaking from fatigue as she headed for the sanctuary of Melina's little room.

In the three weeks since she started working with Melina and Doctor Renato, Hélène had not left the hospital at all. Each time she thought of going to see Philippe, waves of wounded descended upon them and she was forced back to work. Philippe, for his part, came to inspect the wounded at least once a day, but his visits were brief and his moments alone with Hélène were few. At first she thought he was purposely ignoring her, perhaps punishing her for coming to Rhodes. Then she realized that he, too, was overwhelmed with the responsibility of command; that he carried the burden of the dead and the dying.

On her way to Melina's room, Hélène stopped briefly to help a young knight who was getting ready to return to the battlements. His wounds were fresh, his dressings saturated with old blood. But, still he struggled into his armor and fled the protection of the hospital walls. Hélène shook her head sadly, wondering if she would ever see this young man alive again. Would he come back with still more terrible wounds? Or would he never make it to the hospital at all, killed outright in battle and taken to the few remaining buildings where the bodies were stored for burial?

She hesitated outside Melina's door and listened. Through the constant low-level noise of the hospital ward—the groans and the cries; the noises of pain and of despair—Hélène could just hear the soft voice of Melina singing to her babies. She pushed the door open slowly, stepping carefully and quietly into the little room. A single candle burned on the floor in the corner, casting shadows of Melina and the twins onto the walls and ceiling. The flickering orange light made Hélène a little lightheaded, so she lowered herself quickly to the floor, taking up all that was left of the space in the small room.

The two women had grown very close over the past weeks. They shared more than the common bond of nursing the wounded back to health. It was that each of them was committed to a love that their society and religion had forbidden, had forged a friendship dearer and stronger than either had ever known before. Hélène envied without jealousy the small family that God had given to Jean and Melina. Barely an hour could go by without her wondering whether such a treasure would ever be hers and Philippe's. Indeed, she thought, would their love survive even this siege?

Melina's song grew lower and softer as the girls fell asleep against her breasts. Though their lips still sucked languidly at her nipples, their eyes were closed and their little hands hung limply against their chests. In another minute the sucking stopped, and they were sound asleep.

Melina wiped the milk off their lips and her nipples, and then closed her bodice. She continued to hold Maria and Ekaterina in her arms, as if she could protect them from the chaos that reigned around her own small fortress inside the hospital. She rocked slowly back and forth, willing the twins into a deeper and deeper sleep. She was smiling the whole time; one of the few moments in the day when life allowed her that luxury.

In a whisper, Hélène said, "Looking at the three of you makes me believe that there will be an end to all of this someday. That there is hope..."

"I know," Melina said. "Without these two I would have given up long ago. I cannot think that God would allow such an evil to harm such innocence."

The two women sat quietly, both thinking that what Melina had said was true, and equally true was that it violated every tenant of Hélène's religious teaching. They both struggled with the absurdity that these two little angels could be tainted with Original Sin. For Hélène, all her strict Catholic convictions had been turned upside down since she came to live with Melina. And for Melina, the beliefs of her Judaism had long ago swept away the Christian teachings of her youth. Neither woman believed the dogma under which the knights lived and fought. Yet, both loved men who lived by those rules, and were prepared to die for them.

In the silence, the noises of the ward intruded into the room, making both women more aware of the reality of their situation. Melina said, "Has the Grand Master said what he will do after the siege?" She could still not bring herself to call him Philippe.

"You mean about us?"

"Yes."

"No. He hasn't discussed it since I arrived here. And before that, it was never an issue. There was no way that we could be seen together in Paris, so near the seat of his power, or of his family." She wiped at a tear, and shivered though the room was overly warm from body heat. "And you and Jean?"

"Right now, Jean is focused completely on defending the city—and us. We talked once about what he would do if the Grand Master forbade us to be together. But we never resolved it. I think now that he's a father, he might very well leave the Order if it became an issue. But he would never do it until we have driven the Turks away. He'd never shirk his duty while the Order is still at war."

A shadow seemed to fall over the room, as both women thought the unthinkable.

Hélène was the one who finally said it. "And if the Turks cannot be driven away? What then?"

Melina looked down at the girls in her arms and drew them closer to her. "Then we shall see. I cannot even think of such a thing at the moment. That my two little girls could become the slaves of the Sultan. To live in a despicable harem. To be..." She shook her head and squeezed her eyes shut as if the vision in her mind could be blotted out. "Never!" she said sharply. The girls startled in their sleep, arching their backs, arms outstretched, fists clenched. "Never..." she whispered. "And if Philippe should offer to surrender the city to the Sultan?" Melina went on softly.

"Oh, I don't think that would ever happen. He is not a man who surrenders. He sees the world in very distinct terms; of good and evil; of them and us. I think he is committed in his heart to fight to the last knight; to the last Rhodian as well. No, I don't see him ever surrendering the city as long as there is a man left to fight alongside him on the battlements."

Hélène hugged herself tighter, then moved closer to Melina. She put her arm around Melina's shoulders and took the girls into her embrace with her free arm. The women let their heads fall together, and in a few moments all four of them were soundly asleep.

All through the first weeks of August, the Turkish slaves labored day and night to construct the earthworks that would bring the Sultan's cannon in position to fire down into the city. Thousands upon thousands of pounds of earth and rock were brought in from around the fortress. Turkish engineers coordinated the efforts, and Janissaries guarded the workers from the harassing sorties of the knights.

The huge ramp was sited just opposite the Post of Aragon. The mound of earth sloped gently up from the Turkish lines and topped the walls opposite the tower by more than fifteen feet. On top of the earthwork were mounted the Sultan's finest cannons. Enormous parties of men and draft animals had been required to drag the heavy cannons up the ramp and into position. Every hour of the day and night was spent bringing in powder and shot. The huge stone cannonballs were hauled to the top on wooden sledges, until the Turkish artillerymen were ready to begin firing down upon the knights' gunners manning the walls. By late August, after nearly a month of siege, everything had been set in place.

Once the earthwork was completed and armed, both sides fought completely exposed. The Turkish gunners and artillerymen were in clear sight of the defenders' guns, and the knights were exposed in their positions on the walls.

As the battle raged high in the air over Aragon, the knights from the *langue* of England, who had been helping defend the position, took a terrible beating. Most were killed, as was the Commander of Aragon, along with the Master Gunner.

The Turkish cannon pounded the walls and the tower from sunup to sunset. Huge piles of stone and earth rubble fell from the fortress and began to fill the protective ditch at the base of the wall. Slowly and inevitably, the Turkish troops moved closer to the city walls, covered by the firing from the earthwork.

At night, when the Turkish gunners could not see their targets, the knights sent slaves to the walls to repair the breaches that had been made during the day. Each day, as the sun rose over the Mediterranean Sea, the Turkish gunners would open fire and drive the workers back. Then, the cannons would begin their ceaseless pounding of the walls and more openings would appear.

Gabriele Tadini stood before the Grand Master. It was nearly midnight, and neither had slept very much in the past several days. "My Lord, we are sustaining terrible casualties. Up until now they had not been doing very much damage. But, as of today, they have become extremely dangerous."

"Haven't we been able to fire upon the workers on the earthworks?"

"We have, my Lord. And the Infidels have been slaughtered by the hundreds. But, the Sultan cares nothing for the lives of his men. He has tens of thousands to send in behind them. Why, he is filling our ditches with their bodies! But we cannot trade even twenty of them for one of our knights. They have too many waiting in the rear to replace those we kill."

"What can we do?"

"I know that you are against our making any further sorties. But, I think we need to silence their guns. I proposed to take a large contingent of mounted knights to attack the Turkish artillery. I think if we made a lightning strike, driving right up the earthwork, and returned quickly to the fortress, our casualties would be light and we could silence the guns on top."

"Very well. How many men will you need?"

"I would take the mobile force, and knights from the largest *langues*. Perhaps two hundred mounted men."

Philippe let out a long breath. "That's a third of my men, Gabriele."

"I know, *Seigneur*. But, this is a major battle and could be decisive in our defense of the city. And, I want to take one of your own knights as my second in command, Jean de Morelle?"

"*Oui. D'accord*," Philippe said, weary and resigned. "Jean will be perfect. Send for him. He is probably at the hospital."

"No doubt," replied Tadini, smiling to himself.

On the night of August 19th, Gabriele Tadini gathered the mobile force of knights, as well as the contingent from the *langues* of France, Germany, and Provence. Riding out from the Post of Italy, he led his men toward the no-man's-land between the fortress walls and the Turkish cannon. Jean de Morelle rode alongside Tadini.

"Keep our men close to the walls. I want to give our muskets and *arquebuses* a clear shot at the Turkish gunners should they try to attack us before we reach the cannon. Somehow, I don't think they'll leave the ditches."

"*Oui*." Jean wheeled his horse and rode back to pass the word to the knights, who were riding along the walls in columns of two. As the knights rode out, they crossed the ground toward the Turkish cannon. The earth was broken up by the trenches that the Turkish soldiers used for cover.

Tadini was mounted upon a huge white charger, a *grand cheval de bataille*. He approached the giant earthwork and urged his horse into a slow canter. The knights followed as the columns snaked along the base of the fortress. When the columns turned the corner between England and Aragon, Tadini increased his pace. The knights tightened their columns and joined the chase. Jean galloped his horse to the head of the column and joined Tadini. There, in the ditches, were more than a thousand Turkish Azabs guarding the ramp to the earthworks.

When the two hundred men were poised at the walls, they wheeled the columns and rode straight for the waiting Turkish troops. With his lance pointed to the sky, Tadini turned to his men and shouted, *"Andiamo!"* As a single body, the knights galloped forward and down upon the terrified soldiers waiting in the ditches.

Immediately the ground began to seethe with men scrambling across each other to get out of the way of the oncoming knights. Dirt and stones flew from the hooves of the onrushing horses. The terrified Turkish soldiers clawed their way out of the trenches and began running toward their own lines. They slipped and fell across their comrades, and bodies began to pile up in small heaps, impeding the troops trying to escape. Their commanders screamed and beat at them with their swords, but the troops continued to run.

Tadini and his knights increased their speed, trampling the fallen bodies of the enemy. The ground became muddy with the blood of the Azabs. As the knights came down upon the running soldiers, they lowered their lances and speared the men as they ran. When the Turks had been driven beyond their cannons, the knights wheeled the columns once more and rode up the incline to the waiting batteries. The heavy guns were pointed toward the fortress and could not be turned to fire upon the knights. Some of the Turks guarding the cannon scattered and scrambled down the steep embankment at the sides of the earthworks.

When the knights reached the cannon, they set fire to the wooden carriages supporting the heavy guns. The carriages crumbled as they burned and the cannon toppled over, rolling into the earth or down the sides into the ditches. Several of the fleeing Azabs were crushed to death beneath the massive tumbling cannons.

Turkish artillerymen who remained at their posts were cut to pieces by the swords and lances of the charging knights. Some rose to fight and died. The rest ran and were trampled or beheaded by the swords of the knights' cavalry.

With the guns destroyed and the Turkish soldiers fleeing in panic, Tadini set fire to the stores of powder, regretting as he did so that he could not carry the precious gunpowder back into the fortress. He wheeled his horse and led his small army back down the slopes toward the walls. As they neared the bottom of the incline, a small force of Turkish Azabs suddenly appeared in front of Tadini. His horse reared at the abrupt appearance of this wall of men. Tadini tried to regain control. As he struggled with his reins, his lance fell to the ground. Tadini reached for the falling weapon and lost his seat on the horse. The horse, unbalanced by the sudden shift in weight, staggered to the right. Tadini lurched in his saddle, his boot slipping from the stirrup. He realized that he had no chance of staying with the horse, and leaped from the saddle, landing on his side in the hard rubble of the earthworks. As he struck the ground, his chest armor prevented a serious injury to his ribs. But he landed on his right arm, and the combined weight of his body and the unyielding surface of the armor smashed into his elbow and upper arm.

He struggled to free himself as the Azabs closed in on him. He rolled to his left, but the pain and numbness in his right arm and hand prevented him from getting to the saber dangling from his left hip. In an awkward movement, he rotated his left wrist inward and tore the saber from its scabbard. He steadied himself and faced his attackers.

There were six Azabs, lined up abreast in front of him. His horse had gotten to its feet and was stamping back and forth behind Tadini. As it had been trained to do, it kicked its hind legs out at the approach of Azabs from the rear. Slowly the line of men formed into a crescent and closed in on the Italian engineer. Tadini assessed his position. There was no way he could fight his way through all six, and he knew he had to prevent an encirclement. He backed into the side of his nervous horse and felt for the saddle leather without taking his eyes from the enemy. He knew he had no chance to regain his mount. With only his left hand still working, they would cut him down as soon as he had one foot in the stirrup.

Tadini stood erect, looking directly into the eyes of the Azab officer. He smiled and lifted his chin in the officer's direction. He raised the saber, now held in his left hand, its point aimed between the eyes of the man in front of him, and said in perfect Turkish, "So, who will be the first to die?"

The Azab officer stared at Tadini in utter disbelief. Tadini lunged forward without warning. His saber made a soft swish as it moved through the air. A crimson streak stretched from the officer's left ear down across his neck and into the collar of his tunic. Blood poured from the wound, and bubbles of air mixed with the blood. The man looked surprised, but as he started to speak, no sound came from his lips. Only a red froth and ever-enlarging crimson bubbles issued from the front of his neck. He staggered back and forth for a moment, and then vacantly stared at his men. As he fell forward, he looked back at Tadini, but the knight was no longer there. At the very moment the Azab's face smashed into the dirt, Tadini had slashed the neck of another Turk and was about to run his saber through the chest of a third. But his time was running out.

The remaining Azabs had regrouped. Their fury exploded in one burst of energy. The three rushed Tadini, who had fallen back to the flanks of his horse. He knew it was over. Still, he smiled again at the onrushing men. He had killed two of them, and could surely take one more with him as he died on the swords of the remaining three.

He crouched low and picked his target. He would feint for the chest, and then decapitate a Turk with a backhanded slash. He raised his point and aimed at the middle of the three men. If he missed his target, he would take another. He would die in the company of his enemy.

As he looked into the eyes of the target, his saber was knocked from his hand. A terrible pain shot through his arm, and the weapon dropped into the earth. Tadini looked up. He wanted to look into the eyes of the man who was to kill him. But, instead, his visual field was filled with a blur of brown. The men rushing at him dropped back, as a gloved hand grabbed him under his left armpit. There was more pain from his armor digging into his chest as he was lifted from the ground. Only then did he realize that the arms holding him were those of a knight on a horse. He flew through the air, borne aloft at the side of the battle stallion, and after a few feet was suddenly released.

Tadini fell to the ground on his face. He looked up, wiping the blood and dirt from his eyes to see what was happening. There were the men who had attacked him. In the dust and the screaming, he could see his own horse skittering wildly about, and Jean de Morelle sitting upon his rearing charger. Jean's saber was slashing the air, making for the back of a running Azab. The two others lay in the dirt, trampled to death by Jean's horse. After a third slash missed the back of the fleeing soldier, now well away, Jean returned to Tadini.

Jean jumped from his horse and ran over to where Tadini was sitting in the dirt cleaning the debris from his face. "Gabriele. Are you all right?"

Tadini shook his head and tried to rise, but his right hand was still numb and weak from his fall. Jean took him by the left arm and pulled him up. Without a word, the two rushed to their horses. Jean helped Tadini into the saddle, handed him the reins, and then swung himself up onto his own mount. The horses circled for a moment before calming down. Then, the two men raced off after their retiring army of knights.

Tadini raced ahead of Jean, trying to regain command of his troops. Jean pulled alongside, spurring his horse as hard as he could. As they approached the main body of the knights, the pace slowed. Tadini shouted to Jean. But Jean could not hear him because of the musket fire now scouring the terrain behind them, the knights on the walls covering their retreat.

When they reached the bottom of the earthwork, they turned to the right and headed for the St. John's Gate at the Post of Provence.

Some of the Turks, thinking that the knights were in retreat, suddenly took heart and rallied to their positions. A counterattack began.

Tadini watched over his shoulder as the Turks pressed onward toward the city walls. His men wanted to return to the battle and engage the Turkish soldiers approaching the walls.

"Jean, ride the column and move the men back into the fortress. Do not engage the enemy further." Tadini raised his painful right arm and signaled his men to retreat. He wanted no unnecessary loss of life. His objective had been accomplished; the cannons were silenced, and he had miraculously lost none of his knights.

As the Turks chased after Tadini's men, musket fire rained down from the walls. The knights rode back toward the St. John's Gate, leading the Turkish army past Aragon and England. Knights on top of each of the battlements found easy targets as they fired down upon the Turks. A withering crossfire was set up between the Bastions of England and Aragon. Even the archers on the walls joined the attack, filling the sky with their arrows. As the knights reentered the fortress, hundreds of Turks lay dying and wounded in the rubble and the ditches.

When they entered the safety of the gates, Jean pulled up alongside Tadini.

"What did you say?"

"What?"

Jean repeated himself. "What did you say to me? Out there. I couldn't hear you."

"Oh, out there! I asked you why you knocked me down. You ruined my aim."

"Your aim?"

"Yes, my aim. I was about to behead three Turks with one stroke of the saber. I had them all lined up. They thought they were going to kill me, but I was really getting ready to do all three of them at once."

Jean's humor had not yet returned to him. His heart was racing and his face was flushed from the chase and the danger. Tadini seemed cool and unconcerned.

"I thought I saved your life," Jean said as they slowed their horses to a walk.

"*Grazie amico,* but I was never in danger. Never." With that, Tadini waved to Jean and trotted his horse to the head of the column. He patted his horse's flank and waved to the cheering crowd.

Tadini's men walked through the city to the cheers of the citizens and their fellow knights who had witnessed the splendid show from the protection of the ramparts. It was as if the people had gone to the theater and now applauded the players. Swords and pikes were held aloft by the returning knights, displaying the severed heads of the enemy, some still wearing their turbaned helmets. The once-proud egret's plumes that adorned the Turkish caps now sagged with drying blood and fell into the dirt as the knights cast the terrible souvenirs from their lances and sabers. The horses trampled several of the heads, skittering sideways in an effort to find firmer footing. Some of the Rhodians picked the heads from the dirt and hurled them over the walls at the Turkish troops below.

In the next few days, the knights sent more sorties out against Piri Pasha's sector at the Post of Italy; against Achmed Pasha at Aragon; against Ayas Pasha at Germany. The knights suffered very few wounded or killed, while the Turks continued to sustain terrible losses. After each sortie, the knights would return to the fortress carrying the heads of their victims, or dragging the bodies of their prisoners behind them. The heads were displayed upon the battlements for the Turkish armies to see. The prisoners were placed upon the rack and tortured until no more information could be obtained. Then they were killed, and their bodies thrown over the ramparts to rot in the stifling summer sun.

❧ 12 ❧

THE ENEMY BELOW

Rhodes
September, 1522

By early September, now more than six weeks into the siege, five-sixths of the perimeter walls of the fortress had been undermined. The Turkish sappers and miners had created fifty separate tunnels dug at different angles to the walls. They radiated from the walls of the city like the legs of a spider. Inside each of them, men were at work twenty-four hours a day. Light and dark were meaningless, for the workers never saw the sun.

On the knights' side of the walls, Tadini's men had dug a subway that extended around the entire perimeter of the fortress. His tunnels would intersect the Turkish tunnels at every point of contact with the city walls.

In a tunnel opposite the Bastion of Provence, several of the Turkish sappers stopped their forward movement. The small space made it impossible for anyone to move ahead. The tunnel now extended from the safety of the covered ditches to the earth directly under the wall itself. The miners had been digging for weeks. At first, when they were still out in the open ditches, they had come under continuous fire from the knights. But, soon they had managed to build a cover to their own ditches, made of wooden beams, animal hides, and earth. As they dug closer to the fortress itself, the heavy weapons fire had lessened because the cannons of the knights could not be aimed to fire downwards at such a steep angle. Immediately below the walls, the miners were under fire only from occasional arrows and a steady enfilade from the muskets. When they were deep inside the tunnels, they could work without the fear of being shot.

But, of fear, there was still plenty. The men sweated in the narrow confines of the tunnels. They were unable to stand up, and barely had room to turn around. They dug small amounts of dirt and rock, putting the rubble into bags, which they passed to the man behind them. Sometimes they worked in total darkness. The air quickly became fetid and rank. The men choked on the dust they created as they dug. Without warning, sections of the supporting walls would collapse, causing panic among the miners. Wooden boards were passed from man to man to shore up the fallen walls. The men lived with the constant fear of being buried alive, either from a cave-in or from a counter-mine set off by the enemy.

The miners crawled like worms in the darkness. Sometimes they had a candle or an oil lantern to light their way. Most often it was easier to dig in the darkness, feeling their way as they went. The engineers calculated distances and directions. At times they were dead on in positioning their tunnels. But, some tunnels were way off, the mines exploding harmlessly outside the walls rather than bringing down large sections of the fortress. At the entry to the tunnels, the officers stood guard and beat the men back into the shafts with the sides of their scimitars when they tried to leave. The miners were almost all slaves, sent to do the hardest and most dangerous work. As they extended the tunnels under the walls, they knew that on the other side knights were listening to detect their movement. At any moment they might feel the terrible impact of a counter-mine detonation collapsing the earth around them. The lucky ones would be killed outright by the blast. But other poor souls would be buried alive, suffering a prolonged and agonizing death by slow suffocation. For them, the only solace would be having the time necessary to pray to Allah for the salvation of their souls.

Slowly, in the cramped confines of his tunnel, eighteen-year-old Ismail, a Bosnian slave, tapped away with his pick. The miner directly behind him did not know Ismail's name. Ismail did not know his. There was no time for friendship; no time for histories. Each man hoped to live through the next few minutes; the next few hours; the next shift, which would get him out into the air again, to breathe and see the light.

Ismail scraped away a few large rocks, hardly bigger than his fist. He placed the rocks into the bag that he dragged behind him, then scooped up some more of the wet, cold earth. He pushed the earth into the bag with his hands. He had no shovel, only the small hand pick. After the bag was full, he tied it in a loose knot and shoved it behind him. Another bag was handed forward, and the full one was passed down the line to his waiting workers. His mind teemed with thoughts of the terrible death that might await him. With every handful of earth, he knew he might be blown to bits or buried alive.

He tried to take himself away by thinking of his family, of his life before the Sultan's army had made him a slave. He remembered working in the hot sunshine of Bosnia, sweating over his crops. Now the cold sweat of fear covered his body. He had not felt the sun shine upon his body for weeks. At times he could recall the smell of the freshly cut wheat and taste the cool water that his sister would bring in a wooden bucket. Then, like the collapse of earth around him, his mind would snap back to this place of darkness and dirt. He would never see his family again, of that he was sure. With that thought, he began to cry quietly as he dug beneath the fortress walls.

Sometimes there could be two hundred men in the human chain that moved the earth and rock. Each man had a story; a past; just like Ismail.

Measurements were taken and calculations made to see how far the tunnel extended, to locate its position under the fortress. The Turkish engineers waited outside the tunnels for more figures to arrive to add to their drawings. More measurements were made, and the calculations tallied. Soon they could send the sappers in to set the charges.

But, would soon be soon enough? Would there be enough gunpowder in the charge? Were the fuses properly timed? Would the miners and the sappers get out alive?

Ismail crept slowly forward, measuring his progress in inches. He shored up the tunnel with more wooden boards harvested from the countryside. He would press up a wide roof beam to keep the soil from pouring down upon him, and wedge the supporting side posts against the wall. Then he pounded the wooden supports into place with the handle of his pick. This he did very carefully. Ismail was a mole in the darkness, and chances were he would never live to see his work completed. Still, he scraped and tapped his pick into the soil and rock and removed yet another handful of debris. As long as he continued to dig just one more handful of earth, there was hope. He moved forward another inch, and tapped and tapped and tapped.

Only yards away, on the fortress side of Ismail's tunnel, in a small opening dug in the earth, another group of men gathered in the dimness. The space was big enough for several men crouching low. Candles burned on the floor, while the men listened in silence. In this space was Tadini's secret weapon. It was a drum covered with tightly stretched parchment. Glued to the drum's parchment were tiny silver bells. The drum was set firmly against the outermost wall of the enclosure.

Gabriele Tadini breathed slowly. He whispered into the ear of Jean de Morelle. "Listen, Jean. Do you hear anything?"

Jean shook his head. He heard nothing but his own breathing, and perhaps his own heart racing with the fear being buried alive. *How does Tadini do this every day and every night? He must be mad. And yet he enjoys it. Look, he is smiling. Waiting for his prey.* Tadini was, indeed, smiling in anticipation. He was waiting for his little bells to tell him when it was time to blow up the charges set in the wall of the tunnel.

The knights were dug in under the walls near the Bastion of Provence. On Tadini's instructions, there were tunnels such as this one all over the fortress. Rhodes was a honeycomb of tunnels and listening posts. The slaves on the side of the knights fared little better than those of the Sultan. They worked long hours in dark, dangerous holes. Only in their case, they often had the company of

Tadini, himself, setting up his sound detectors and checking on their progress.

"That's right," whispered Tadini. His voice was so low that Jean could feel Tadini's lips touch his ear as he spoke. "You hear nothing! Long before we can hear the digging with our ears, the little bells with hear them for us. The bells react to the slightest vibrations from their digging, which we cannot feel. And that, *mon ami*, is the few seconds advantage that will allow us to blow the dogs to hell before they can do it to us."

Tadini moved back a few feet and dragged a charge of gunpowder closer to the wall. Then he checked the vents. Jean turned to watch, fascinated with the skill of this Italian, now a brother Knight Grand Cross. He even had forgotten for a moment how hard it was to breathe. But, the dust and debris floating in the air made him want to cough and clear his throat. He suppressed the urge, fearful of giving away their position.

"What will keep us from blowing down our own walls? Doing the job for the Turks?"

Tadini smiled at his pupil. "You see these vertical shafts in the ceiling? They're spirals that vent to the outside. They will disperse much of any blast set off down here. Theirs or ours. I have dug these ventilating shafts all over the city. When the Turks set off their blasts, the charge just goes up, following the path of least resistance, like water. Right out the shaft. It dissipates the energy. Saves the wall. Also, I use a directional charge. We blow this wall *horizontally*, into the enemy tunnel. It will kill the men on the other side and bury their tunnel at the same time. It's a smaller charge than the one they use to blow up our walls. Doesn't take a big charge to kill men in a tunnel— not as much as they need to bring down a wall. So it's important that I set off my charge before they get theirs in place. Otherwise, I might set off their charge for them and destroy my own walls."

At the thought of burying the Turkish miners, Jean found himself breathing hard again. He was feeling their pain, their suffocation. "Is this new? Did you always do it this way?"

"It's very new," Tadini whispered. He was alive now with the excitement of training a new student, and the energy of his real passion. "The enemy miners used to dig tunnels under the walls and support them with heavy wooden beams. Eventually they had excavated the whole foundation of the city. Huge tunnels. Massive! Then they would set fire to the timber and get out before the fire suffocated them, or buried them alive. If all went right, the timbers would burn down and the walls would collapse. But, that gave us much more time to find them and to counter-mine them." Jean looked puzzled. Tadini explained, "The old mines and their support structures were much more extensive. They had to be. They held up the whole weight of the walls. So, we had more time to find them and set off our counter-mines. Now we have less time, because they use the gunpowder charges to blow up the walls instead of burning the supports to make them collapse. That's why I developed my little noise detector. It gives me the edge. A tiny margin in my favor, but crucial."

Jean nodded, still staring at Tadini's invention. He kept thinking of the poor souls of the other side of the wall. Could they guess what death awaited them a few yards from where he and Tadini were now sitting?

"*Eh bien*, Jean. Now we wait while my drums listen for us." Tadini was whispering. None of his men spoke. All were staring at the bells. Waiting.

Tadini shifted his position until he was sitting against the wall, shoulder to shoulder with Jean. Without taking his eyes off the little bells, he said, "This is not your style, is it?"

"No, Gabriele. Not all. I'd much preferred to be up on the walls looking the Muslims straight in the eye. I like to face my enemy. See whom I slay."

"Quite so. I've fought on the walls too, Jean, and I will again. I've cleaned my sword with gallons of Muslim blood. But, this job is critical. So I will dig these tunnels, and destroy the vermin before they make breaches in the walls too big to be plugged by the swords of the knights."

"And for that we are all grateful, Gabriele."

Tadini sat quietly nodding. He kept his eyes fixed on the tiny bells. He willed them to move; to vibrate from a minuscule tremor in the earth. But, there was nothing but silence. The bells would not move for him.

"How are Melina and the little angels, John?" Tadini whispered, breaking the tense silence in the cave.

"As well as I can hope. Melina is strong, but she works too hard. Too long. Ekaterina and Marie are fine. They are the only ones in the city getting absolutely *fat*." Jean laughed. "Only *they* sleep through the noise and the blasts. It's amazing. When this is over, I'm sure nothing will awaken them. But, I'm worried about Melina. It's nice for her to have a new friend in Hélène. They've become very close in just a short time. Hélène looks after the babies from time to time when Melina is busy." He paused, thinking for a moment of the right words. "She is in awe of the doctor, Renato. *Á la folie!* She tells me he does miracles in there. He seems never to sleep or rest as long as there are patients who need his care. And, there is a never-ending supply of casualties. Apparently, he's very well educated. Seems to know all the latest from the doctors of the East and the West. Makes no distinction, I'm told, between Christians and Muslims; Jews, Greeks, and Turks. They're all the same to him, people who need his help. Wouldn't do for a knight to behave that way. But, I suppose it's appropriate for a doctor."

Tadini listened to Jean, but did not take his eyes from the bells.

Jean looked at the Italian engineer. He realized that he knew almost nothing about Tadini, except that he seemed brave beyond reason. Apparently, Tadini had wanted to be a doctor. But, the fortunes of war had intervened and his career took another path. Nothing seemed to frighten the man. On the walls, he carried out his duties in the face of terrible danger. Always skillfully, always calmly. In the tunnels he showed no fear either. His breathing never accelerated. With a sword in his hand, he waded into the enemy with a fury and disdain that had become a legend among the other knights. His behavior after the attack on the earthworks was already a legend.

But, who is he? He never speaks of his family. Never talks of the past. Only the siege. The tunnels. The battles.

They sat in silence for a few more minutes. Jean strained to hear digging. But, there was nothing. Then, after a few minutes, a little bell began to ring. It was a tiny ring, but Jean jumped at the sound of it, banging his head on the ceiling of the tunnel. More little bells began to chime.

"Quick! Out! Out!" Tadini whispered as he lit a phosphorous match. He reached out and touched the flame to the long fuse coming from the directional charge set against the far wall. Then he pushed Jean ahead as they scrambled from the tunnel. *"Vite! Vite! Va-t-en! Va-t-en!* It's going to blow soon, Jean. You don't want to be here. *Ni moi, non plus!"* Me neither!

The men scrambled from the tunnel. Just as they emerged from the opening a tremendous blast rang in their ears. Tadini jumped up and down and slapped Jean on the back. *"Eh bien!* Now you are, *vraiment*, a counter-miner! Truly."

Ismail heard the little bells. He had been backing out of the shaft to make way for the sappers who would set the charge. After crawling back about ten feet, the ringing registered in his ears. He stopped. He had no idea what the tinkling sound meant. None of the Turks had seen Tadini's invention. Those who were close enough to hear the tolling of the little bells never survived long enough to tell anyone about it. Ismail thought it might be something wrong with his ears, too many blasts, too near. He hesitated for a moment, and then tried to turn in the tight space so he could crawl out faster. He didn't know what it was, but something was wrong.

He scrambled along on his knees, shouting ahead of him. Within only a few yards, his way was blocked by another miner facing him in the tunnel. The men became entangled in the darkness as they struggled in the small space. Panicked shouts filled the air. What candles remained were accidentally snuffed out in the confusion.

As the tunnel became darker, the confusion increased. Miners further down the line did not know what was happening ahead of them. An oil lamp was overturned and began a small blaze. In the tight space, the little fire turned into a major catastrophe. The oil burned poorly in the oxygen-deprived atmosphere, and black smoke replaced the dusty air. Ismail and his fellow miners began to cough and choke on the fumes. Those men on Ismail's side of the fire began to scramble for the fortress walls, trying to escape the fire and the fumes. The miners fleeing from the interior crawled head-long into the others. A pile-up ensued, and miners were fighting each other for space. The quality of the air plummeted and a panic of suffocation overwhelmed the men. Soon the tunnel was completely clogged with a writhing mass of humans, moving nowhere at all.

The blast tore through the mineshaft. On the knights' side of the tunnel, the explosion vented through the vertical shafts and blew harmlessly into the air. The main charge shot outward horizontally away from the walls and smashed the miners flat. Several men further down the line were caught by the full force of the blast and were killed as well. The remaining miners felt the shattering blow, and then realized to their horror that the worst had happened. As the flames seared their flesh, the roof fell in, crushing some to death beneath its immense weight. The remainder were buried alive, burned and slowly suffocating in the black grave that they, themselves, had dug.

Ismail felt the blast. Heat seared his face and sucked the breath from his chest. He tried to wipe the dirt from his eyes, but the earth poured down around him, binding his arms to his sides. The wet, thick soil wrapped his body and squeezed the air from his lungs. He opened his mouth to cry out, but the dirt rushed in before he could utter a sound. Involuntarily, he inhaled deeply to answer the call screaming for more air, but he only sucked the heavy, wet earth into his lungs.

Then Ismail saw the hot bright sun over his farm in the hills of Bosnia; he smelled the freshly cut hay and waited for his sister to bring him a cool drink of water.

Jean shook the dirt from his cape and wiped his hand across his face to clear the sweat. He left a streak of mud from his left cheek to his right. Tadini laughed and grabbed the hem of Jean's cape. "Here, *amico,* let me help you." He wiped the dirt from Jean's face and grabbed him by the shoulders and shook him. "Good work, eh? Now take a few minutes to see your wife and the babies. Then come back and we'll blow up some more Turks."

Jean nodded and smiled. "I think I'll do just that, Gabriele. But, I may stay at the hospital and help *Il Dottore*. I think he needs my help more than you." The two knights shook hands and turned in opposite directions. Jean began his walk from the walls of Provence through the Jewish Quarter to the Hospital within the *Collachio*. Tadini stayed to survey the negligible damage to his walls. Satisfied, he turned to see where else he might be needed.

Jean reached the hospital in a few minutes. The streets were emptier than they had been when he entered the tunnels with Gabriele, some hours before. He mounted the wide staircase and went directly to the ward. There were crowds of people waiting to be seen by the doctor and his assistants. Knights and citizens lined the corridors, crowding into every space. There were some groans and crying. But most of the people silently, resignedly, waited their turn. Nobody protested when Jean pushed his way to the front and walked into the ward. He saw Renato immersed in treating the wounded. A knight was on the table and the doctor was wrapping a dressing around the young man's head. Blood covered the floor, and several knights were moving back and forth in the wards bringing more supplies to the doctor.

Jean's chest tightened. He saw one of the knights from his own *Langue de France* lying on the table. It was a man he had known since he, himself, had joined the Order. Now, the knight lay there, his leg covered in bloody rags. Jean watched with a sad heart as another knight heated a cauldron of oil over the coal brazier. It could only mean that the doctor was preparing to take yet another limb from one of the brave knights. This time it would be from a close friend of Jean's.

Just as Jean was about to ask for Melina, Renato looked up from his work and saw him standing in the ward. He motioned toward Melina's room, then tilted his head sideways and closed his eyes. *"Elle se dors, Jean,"* She's sleeping.

Jean made his way through the bodies and the debris and gently pushed open the wooden door. He felt a great lump in his throat as he saw the peaceful scene. Melina was fast asleep in a makeshift bed on the floor, her back propped on a pillow against the stone wall. Ekaterina and Marie were in her arms, their faces flushed from the warmth of the small room. The three angels of his life were safe. He sat on the floor, and quietly removed his armor. He placed his broadsword against the wall and removed his gauntlets. Jean covered Melina with the woolen blanket. He rolled up his cape and made a pillow for his head. Then, he leaned back and quickly fell asleep.

The bombardment of the ramparts of Auvergne had been particularly brutal. Suleiman had concentrated his cannons there for most of the day. Achmed Pasha's guns roared throughout the morning and afternoon. By nightfall, the walls had taken a severe beating. Yet, no breach had been made in the massive stones.

"Their guns along the rampart are decimating our miners," Achmed said. "We have to silence them if we are to keep the men digging toward the wall."

Mustapha Pasha twisted his thick, black mustache. He looked grim in the failing light.

Achmed stared up at the wall. "My miners are suffering murderous fire," he continued. "The knights are using both *arquebuses* and matchlock rifles from what we can see. They are raining down shot upon the workers in the ditches without letup."

Mustapha merely nodded. Then he looked behind Achmed and immediately straightened up. He brushed off his uniform and straightened his hat. Achmed turned to see Suleiman approaching their position. He was with Ibrahim and Piri Pasha. All three were mounted and guarded with a large escort of Janissaries. The horses were jittery, reacting to the loud reports of the cannon and the small-arms fire. Though out of range and immediate danger, the position was close enough to appreciate the furor of the blasts.

"*Salaam Aleichum*, brother-in-law. *Salaam Aleichum*, Achmed Pasha."

Mustapha and Achmed bowed and said almost in unison, "*Aleichum salaam*, Majesty." They nodded to Piri Pasha and Ibrahim. The riders dismounted, and three pages appeared from the ranks to lead their horses away. Suleiman walked up to Mustapha and turned to view the scene.

From their vantage point, the leaders could look down into the ditches that were still being dug by the miners. Achmed waited for Mustapha, as Commander-in-Chief, to brief the Sultan. But, the *Seraskier* remained silent. Finally, Achmed offered, "Majesty, we are slowly extending the ditches and the tunnels. But, at a terrible cost in lives. Our men are suffering greatly. The losses have been worse here than anywhere. And much greater than we anticipated. There have been times when the bodies fill the ditches and hinder the escape of our own men. They slip on the blood of their brothers in their rush to find cover."

Suleiman listened in silence. There was a resignation in his face. He turned to Mustapha and said, "Have we any remedy for this?"

"Some, Majesty. We have made some cover for the workers. We constructed shields of animal hides stretched over frames to cover them from the view of the gunners. They offer no real protection from the shot, but at least they do not allow the gunners on the walls to actually see our diggers. But, the knights have found some way to discover where our men are digging. They have blown up several of our tunnels just before our sappers were placing the charges. The tunnels collapse and the men are buried. The walls still stand."

The five men stood side by side, shoulder to shoulder, and stared at the walls. For a while nobody spoke. They seemed to be waiting for word from the Sultan. Suleiman nodded toward the city. "We have no choice but to persist. We cannot leave this island until the walls fall and our soldiers can enter the city. As awful as it is, we will have to use all our manpower until we can make a breach."

Suleiman turned to Mustapha again and continued. "Keep the tunnels moving toward the bastion here and increase the bombardment and the tunneling against the Post of England. These are the best chances we have to make a breach. Our spies tell us that England is weak and poorly defended. So, increase the number of men and cannon working against that wall. There will be no letup. We will fire upon them day and night. They will have no rest. If nothing else, we might just spark a revolt by the citizens themselves. The people of Rhodes might stop this war from within the city. I cannot think that they love the knights. Perhaps they would rather have us as their rulers." He turned now to Ibrahim and said, "See what we can find out from inside the city."

Suleiman signaled to his pages, and the three horses were brought out. The men mounted and turned to continue the review of the battle positions. Mustapha slammed a fist into his left palm and glared at Achmed. Achmed met Mustapha's eyes, but did not utter a word. As he was about to leave, Mustapha saw several of the miners running from the ditches as the fire from the walls intensified. He drew his scimitar and went screaming after them. He raged and shouted, until the slaves' fear of him exceeded their fear of the gunfire from the knights. Mustapha barred the exit from the ditch with his massive frame, striking the slaves across the chest and back with the flat of his blade. He screamed obscenities at them and spit in their faces. Finally, there was order, and the slaves returned to the ditches and the tunnels. And the guns continued to fire.

—

Suleiman had stopped to walk among the troops dressed in his battle gear. Piri Pasha accompanied him. Ibrahim went ahead to prepare for the Sultan's arrival: to order a bath be heated and food set out for his dinner. Mustapha went with Ibrahim and the two sat in the main reception chamber waiting for the Sultan's return.

They sat on cushions against the wall, lounging in relative comfort for the first time since the siege had begun. It was September 30th, and Rhodes had been under attack for sixty-four days. The Sultan's armies were weary and depressed. By now nearly every man had lost a comrade, and the disposal of the bodies of the dead became a major task. Ibrahim drank from a jade goblet, while Mustapha removed his armor and sword.

"Come rest, Mustapha," Ibrahim said. "It is time to take leave of this war for a little while."

Mustapha's brows creased and his mouth turned down, accentuated by the curve of his great mustache. "My men are lying wounded and dead in the damnable trenches and tunnels; how am I to relax?"

"You are *here*, are you not? Why did you come, if not for a short rest?"

"I came to have a few words with my brother-in-law," he said, emphasizing the bond between him and the Sultan.

"And what do you hear from Ayse?" Ibrahim said, referring to Mustapha's wife, Suleiman's sister.

"She was well the last I heard. About two weeks ago I received a letter from her, and from my little boys."

"I am glad. I have just received this letter for the Sultan," Ibrahim said, holding a small packet in the air. "He should be glad to receive it. It bears the seal of his first lady, Gülbehar. Though she can't write, I am sure it is full of news transcribed by one of her slaves."

"Mnnnnhhh," Mustapha said, as he slid down onto a cushion.

The men sat a while in silence, eating and drinking the light snacks set out in the *serai*. Finally, Mustapha said, "You're close to our Sultan, Ibrahim. What plans does he have for this campaign? It is going so badly that there is little hope for a speedy and conclusive end to it. Does he plan to withdraw when the winter weather arrives?"

"I think he is determined to stay as long as it takes."

Mustapha did not answer this. He just stared at Ibrahim. Ibrahim sensed some measure of scorn from Mustapha for Ibrahim's own position in the royal household. Before Mustapha could speak, Ibrahim leaned forward and, in an almost menacing tone of voice, said, "Although I am the Sultan's slave, whatsoever I want done is done. On the spur of the moment I can make a stable boy into a Pasha. I can make men rich. I can make men poor. The Sultan is no better dressed than I am, and what is more, he pays all my expenses, so that *my* fortune never decreases. He trusts his power to me, with things both great and small, and I can do with it as I like. I am not a Pasha, nor even *Seraskier*. But do not trifle with me, Mustapha. We are on the same side now. Your scorn for my position will not serve you well."

Mustapha's remained completely immobile. He said nothing and his face betrayed no feeling. But, in his chest his heart raced, for there was no doubt of the threat implied in Ibrahim's message. Mustapha would have killed another man on the spot for such insolence. But the truth in Ibrahim's words could not be denied. Before another exchange could begin, a messenger entered the room and signed a message to Ibrahim. Ibrahim's ability to understand and reply to the Sultan's sign language only served to underscore the strong position held by the Captain of the Inner House.

"The Sultan is here," Ibrahim said after the page had left.

The two men stood and waited for Suleiman.

Within a few minutes, Suleiman appeared in the doorway, followed by three of his pages. The Janissaries stationed themselves outside the room, while the pages helped the Sultan out of his military dress. When Suleiman was comfortably dressed in a white silk robe, he motioned to Ibrahim and Mustapha to be seated. The three men took their places on the bounty of cushions. Fresh dishes and drinks were brought and served in silence.

When the servants were gone, Suleiman said, "Gentlemen, there is a line, once crossed, that can never be crossed again. History has told us this many times. We are at such a line now. We will not leave this island until all the knights are killed and the city is under my control." Neither Ibrahim or Mustapha responded to the Sultan's statement, for it was not a question to be answered, but a royal decree to be obeyed.

Suleiman was silent for another moment. Ibrahim and Mustapha too remained quiet. Then, the Sultan rose and gestured to the two men to follow him. "It is time for prayers, my friends. Tonight Allah and His Prophet will receive our obedience and our submission. Let us pray that He will smile upon us in what remains of this battle."

⁓ 13 ⁓

INTO THE BREACH

Rhodes
September, 1522

Philippe sat at the great oak table with his officers. They had finished a late lunch and were assessing the damage to the city. Tadini was speaking. "My Lord, I have reinforced the ramparts as best I can. The gunners on the walls have been deployed to fire on the approaches and the trenches that the Turks are using for cover."

"How, Gabriele?" Philippe asked in a tired monotone.

"I've placed my best marksmen on the towers and rooftops overlooking the approaches. They have been fitted with a new quick-aiming device for their muskets. When the miners appear from beneath the cover of the carcasses they have been using, my men can destroy them at will. The Turks are blinded by the sun as they emerge and it takes a moment to find their way. In that moment, we have them in our new sights. I have also mounted batteries of heavy and light cannon together. They cover the approaches as well. As long as our knights stay within the confines of the walls when they repel attacks, my gunners are free to fire an enfilade at will, without danger of hitting the knights. But, it is critical that we do not give chase in the heat of battle, for then the knights would fall under our own guns before we could cease fire."

Philippe turned to John Buck and said, "See that the order is given, John. Make sure it is sent to all the *langues.*"

"I will, my Lord."

Tadini went on. "The mining continues. They have poured thousands of men into the ground. I think that nearly every foot of our walls are undermined with their tunnels or mines. They have set off a number of mines without effect. The ventilating shafts that I've dug have allowed the blast to go harmlessly into the air in most cases. And, we have used the mine-detecting bells to good effect. We have been able to detonate our charges and kill them in the holes before they can plant their mines. But, this is terribly dangerous work. We have had one accident. I was not there, so I do not know exactly what happened. It seems there was a great explosion beneath the walls of Provence. My men were all killed along with the Turkish miners. I don't now if the Turks set off their blast too soon and killed themselves and my listeners, or whether my men set off our counter-mine, igniting the Turkish charge, killing everyone as well. But, these things are bound to happen."

"How long can we stop them from detonating their mines and destroying our walls, from creating a major breach?"

Tadini shrugged. *"Je ne sçay pas, Seigneur.* It could happen any time. With enough miners and enough tunnels, it's inevitable that they will succeed at some point. I can only impede their progress and hope that if a breach occurs, our knights will be able to repel them. If they open many breaches at once, we could never hold them off. But, if it is only one or two at a time, we can plug the hole with our men. Even though they have thousands of fighting men to throw at us, they cannot physically get through a small breach all at once. Their cavalry remains useless. If my gunners can pin them down from the walls and slaughter them *before* they enter the breach, then there's hope that we can stop them."

"Michel? Do you have any thoughts?"

Michel d'Argillemont was Captain of the Galleys. While his crews were stationed behind the booms of the blockaded harbor, Michel had little to do. He watched the battles from the city and kept his crews ready for any naval engagement that the Grand Master might order. "My Lord, I can only say that we are fortunate that

Gabriele has chosen to fight for us. God help us if he were born a Muslim."

The knights laughed, and Tadini nodded to d'Argillemont.

Gabriel de Pommerols, Philippe's lieutenant and close friend, raised a hand. "My Lord, have we any hope for reinforcement? This is getting to be a problem whose solution is clearly mathematical. We kill a hundred or a thousand Turks, and they kill twenty-five of us. We kill, they kill. In the long run, they will win. Our only hope is that our determination is made clear to them, and that they will tire of this slaughter of their people before they have taken the lives of all of us here."

"Quite right, Gabriel. To the point as usual," Philippe said. "No, I expect little if any help from Europe. They have shown their colors and will not step forward to aid us. And I don't expect any resupply. Perhaps our victory in the last siege has led them to believe that we are indestructible."

"It took us forty years to recover from our 'victory,'" Henry Mansell interjected.

"Yes," said Philippe, his voice weary and hoarse, "I was only a boy when I saw the results of that siege. I was not yet old enough to fight there, but it was difficult to look upon the rubble of Rhodes back then and decide who had won."

Mansell continued, "My Lord, I have carried your banner for these many years. Never has it fallen to the ground. Never will it fall if I have a single breath left to keep it aloft."

Mansell was Philippe's standard bearer. In every battle, he would be there at Philippe's side, holding the oak staff from which flew the silk banner of the crucifixion. The banner itself was presented to Grand Master Pierre d'Aubusson following his defeat of Suleiman's grandfather in 1480.

"Be there at my left side, Henry, and God will be on my right. Now, it is time for Vespers. All of you, come with me to the Church of Our Lady of Victories, and let us pray for a successful conclusion to our battles."

The knights left the Palace of the Grand Master and walked behind Philippe to join the mass at the church. The service was led by the Latin Bishop, Leonardo Balestrieri. The knights knelt in prayer, encumbered slightly by their armor and chain mail, which, with the battles still raging about their walls, they never took off. Swords were fastened to their hip belts, their helmets placed at their left knee. Other weapons, pikes and halberds, were set down upon the floor, where they could be reached with dispatch, should the occasion arise.

Together, they bowed their heads in prayer.

On their side of the walls, while the knights prayed, the Turks were waiting. They crouched in the ditches and hid beneath the carcasses. The Azabs and the Janissaries were poised in the vanguard, backed by mounted troops hidden from sight, hoping for the chance to follow the foot soldiers through a major breach in the walls. The Pashas stayed with their men. Mustapha was dressed in full battle gear, his forehead covered with sweat in the late summer heat. Silence was maintained throughout the ranks, as the men took shallow breaths of air. The minutes moved slowly by while the whole of the Turkish assault force waited for their chance.

Down in the tunnels, the charges were set. Tadini's men had not heard them this time, for the miners were wary now after so many terrible deaths in the tunnels. They had placed the mines with absolute stealth and silence, making no vibrations to set the alarm bells ringing. The sappers backed out of the tunnel in the darkness, and the last remaining man lit the fuse. He turned around with difficulty and crawled as fast as he could from the tunnel. He looked like a crab as he scampered away from danger. The fuse sizzled toward the massive charge of gunpowder.

It had taken almost three weeks to make this tunnel and plant the charge. Day and night the men waited as they worked, expecting at any moment to be blown to bits or buried alive by Tadini's counter-miners. Though they didn't know his name, they knew that behind the walls of the Sons of *Sheitan* worked a man who had taken thousands of their lives. Now their work was done, and in two more minutes there might be a hole in the great wall of the fortress; if the charge was big enough; if it didn't explode harmlessly up the venting shafts; if the counter-miners didn't blow it away first with their own charge. And, most uncertain of all, if they had measured correctly and placed it in exactly the right spot.

As Balestrieri intoned in Latin, few of the knights could concentrate upon the words. They could hear the battle outside and the cries of the wounded.

Philippe knelt in the very first row. Mansell had placed the holy standard in a holder nearby and was kneeling next to Philippe. The rest of the knights filled the rows to the rear. As Balestrieri was concluding his prayers and preparing the golden chalice for communion, the earth shook beneath the church. The mortar holding the massive stones together crumbled and dust filled the air. A powerful blast filled the church and rang in the ears of the knights. The foundations shook. Balestrieri fell to his knees, catching himself on the edge of the altar.

"A mine!" shouted several of the knights. Mansell grabbed the standard from its holder and rushed after Philippe, who was already up and pulling his helmet onto his head. His gray hair hung over his cape, and his great broadsword clanked against the pews as he rushed to see what had caused the blast. The rest of the knights followed quickly in his wake.

Tadini cursed, for he knew too well what had occurred. Once out of the church and into the piazza, the knights had a clear view of the city. From the south, they could see smoke and dust completely obliterating the horizon. Clearly, the explosion had occurred there, under the Bastion of England. In the confusion came the sounds of trumpets and drums, of flutes and cymbals, the inevitable overture to the Turkish attack.

The streets were filled with people rushing about in fear and panic. The knights fought their way across the city, pushing through the crowds. More knights joined them, emerging from the houses and the Inns. By the time they reached the walls near the bastions, some of the smoke had cleared. A giant, gaping hole stood in the middle of the Bastion. It was over thirty feet wide. For the first time since they landed on Rhodes, thousands of Turkish troops were preparing to force their way into the city.

———

Debris and dust hung in the air for several minutes. At first, the Turkish troops had no idea what damage the mine had done. They heard the blast and felt the earth rock beneath them. A few of those standing nearest the walls had fallen down from the impact. The front-line Janissaries and Azabs were momentarily deafened by the noise.

Mustapha Pasha waited with his troops, as did Bali Agha, Achmed Agha, and Qasim Agha. The dust and smoke slowly blew away in the breeze. When the air had cleared, the Aghas saw before them the enormous breach in the Bastion of England. Cheers filled the air, and the men waited for the order.

Mustapha rose from his crouching position. With his scimitar held high, he screamed into the air, *"Allahu akbar!"* God is great! At the sight of him and the sound of his voice, the Turkish forces rose as a unit and began running toward the breach. To the knights on the walls, the mass of bodies moving as a unit looked as if the earth itself had stood up and was rushing forward.

The Janissaries and the Azabs led the charge, scimitars waving in the air. There were long pikes and halberds. Some of the archers ran alongside the Azabs, and Arquebusiers joined the charge.

The Sultan watched the attack from a small hill just out of range of the knights' gunners. He sat upon his agitated horse and stared impassively at the erupting battle. Behind him waved the sacred green banner of the Prophet, carried, as always, into battle as the talisman for the Muslim armies.

Trumpets from the Sultan's band blasted the call; drums boomed as loud as the cannon fire that preceded the men's advance. Their famous cymbals crashed and nearly drowned out the sound of the martial music. With the music and the cannons and the screaming, nothing could be heard but the sounds of the attack. No orders given. No corrections made.

The Turkish soldiers crossed the first escarpment and dived down into the outer ditches. As they scrambled up the other side, they met a fusillade of small-arms fire. Some of the knights' smaller cannons could be lowered enough to cover the advance.

And the slaughter began.

On the knight's left flank, Frenchmen fired their muskets and *arquebuses* from the Post of Provence. The new quick-aiming muskets were deadlier than ever. Turks started falling as they ran. Men died on the spot as dozens at a time were blown to bits by light cannon and small-arms fire. From the right flank, Spaniards defending the Post of Aragon poured down musket fire. Hundreds of arrows filled the air, chasing the running Turks like a swarm of angry bees. Bodies began to litter the approaches, and within a few minutes the corpses completely covered the bottoms of the ditches. Musket holes ran with blood, and arrows stuck out from bodies like quills.

The attack upon the breach faltered slightly as the soldiers began to slip on the piled-up bodies of their fallen comrades. Blood congealed into slippery layers on top of the dead. The wounded could not be helped. There was no possibility of evacuation. The injured men lay in the bottom of the ditches alongside the dead, their bodies a walkway for their fellow warriors in the advance to the fortress wall. The Sipahis remained useless on their horses.

Cannon fire from the Turkish batteries raked the walls, distracting and disrupting some of the archers and musketeers. The Aghas urged the men onward, though the defenders were tearing the Turkish lines to pieces. The brave men of the Sultan's army never faltered in the face of the withering fire, but continued their advance up the sloping path to the walls.

As they neared the Post of England, they came under heavier fire. With each step forward, they became clearer targets for the gunners and bowmen above them. As the walls neared, a new plague erupted upon the frontline Turks. The dreaded Greek Fire poured down from copper hoses on the parapets, setting men afire, screaming in agony from the terrible burns they incurred.

But still the Turkish fighters advanced, scrambling over their dead and wounded, with only one thought: they would finally enter the citadel of the knights. They would face their enemy in hand-to-hand combat. After long weeks of waiting, the Sultan's army had been unleashed, and would finally get their first real taste of blood.

The first of the Janissaries and Azabs scrambled up the last of the approach and climbed through the rubble. The hole that appeared so wide from the trenches now would admit only fifteen or twenty men at a time. As the first Turks clawed their way up, with shot still raining from above, they rose to their feet and moved more cautiously through the opening. More and more of their comrades piled in through the opening, until there were two dozen men standing face-to-face with the enemy. There, in the dust and the smoke, they saw a sight that made their bowels turn to water.

And that was just what the knights had counted on.

For the first time since landing on the accursed island, the Janissaries stared into the face of the devil. Before them were fifty knights in full armor. All wore identical battle cloaks of deep scarlet, emblazoned over the left chest with a white, eight-pointed cross. Each wore a cylindrical iron helmet, visor in place, with only a horizontal slit through which the Turks could see the unblinking eyes of the knights. Broadswords were drawn, held almost carelessly, as if the knights feared nothing of the Janissaries' scimitars. Shoulder to shoulder they stood. A wall. Motionless. Immovable. Deadly.

For thirty seconds or more, the two enemy lines faced each other while the battle outside the walls continued. In the center of the line of knights, one man drew the attention of all the Turks. His white beard flowed out from his visor. Long, gray hair draped his shoulders. Next to him, another knight carried a long staff from which a banner waved in the afternoon air. The figure of Christ on the cross looked down upon them all. The old man raised his sword and shouted. A terrible cry filled the air as the knights rushed forward, swords in the air, lances leveled.

The Turks hesitated momentarily. Then another shout of *Allahu akbar!* was heard, and the two armies met for the first time in deadly hand-to-hand fighting.

The knights pressed forward, protecting each others' flanks with their bodies. Their body armor deflected the slashing sweep of the Turkish scimitar. Only their necks and limbs were open to attack. It took the Turks a few moments to know where to strike. Those few moments cost many Turkish lives. Men began to fall. The dead and wounded clogged the gap in the walls even more. The knights knew just how to use this human plug in the gap to their advantage, keeping the odds down to nearly one on one. They at all costs, had to prevent a massive breakthrough of Turkish soldiers.

Back in the ditches, the fire continued to decimate the Turks. The forward surge was wavering now, and the officers had to yell and push to keep the momentum toward the fortress. With every passing moment, the going became more difficult. Piles of bodies physically blocked the advance. Jellied blood sent the soldiers slipping down onto the bodies of the fallen. Some trampled their own men. The emotional horror of the slaughter took its toll as well, as the Turks began to lose heart. It had seemed so easy when the mine exploded. There was an open doorway to victory before them, and they had only to walk through it. Now, instead, they lay writhing in their own blood, burning and dying without even the chance to fight.

As the main body of the Turkish army tried to make its way across the no-man's land of the ditches under the fire from the wall, the knights engaged the first of the Janissaries to enter the city. The phalanx of armored knights moved forward in unison, swinging their heavy broadswords in front of them and clearing a swath of bloodied ground as they moved. The momentum of their advance was overpowering, and the Janissaries were forced back into the gap in the wall.

When the broadsword connected with the limbs or body of a Turkish soldier, there was little hope for survival. Great muscled arms, trained for years with the heavy swords, wielded a force behind the sharp steel edges that was unstoppable. Whole arms and legs fell to the ground, as the wounded man bled to death in minutes while the battle raged around him. The knights kept advancing against the enemy. Now, there was chaos as the Janissaries and the few Azabs who had joined them were pinned in the small space.

From his position in the front ranks, Mustapha Pasha saw the blockade at the breach and shouted his fury. He exhorted his men to press forward, even as they were sprayed with shot and arrows from the walls. Suddenly, the *Bunchuk* appeared on a rampart. There, in the early light, was the standard of the Sultan, himself; for from this standard waved the seven black horses' tails. The ringing of its little bells was drowned out by the melee, but the sight of the tails and the golden crescent of Islam gave heart to the attacking Turks. The rush forward began again.

Mustapha was carried onward by the crush of soldiers. So fierce was the attack that those who tried to retreat in the face of the guns had no choice but to move ahead.

Again and again, the Turks tried to force their huge army into the city, but the strategy of the knights was working too well. They pushed the advance soldiers back into the hole and effectively blocked the entry into their city with the living bodies of the enemy.

Gabriele Tadini fought viciously in the front line of knights, slashing away with abandon. He was furious that the Turks had blown a hole in *his* wall; that they dared to escape *his* countermeasures. It was personal, and Tadini would avenge it here on the forefront of the ramparts.

At Tadini's side stood Michel d'Argillemont, head of the knights' fleet, now caught up in the fighting with all the other knights. It was a welcome change from the inactivity on board his cloistered galleys. He pushed forward with his pike, swinging it in wide arcs and slashing away at the enemy. In one particularly forceful swing, he followed through too hard and lost his balance. As the point of his sword swung up, he nearly impaled Tadini, who was fighting shoulder to shoulder with him.

"Hiens!" Tadini shouted at Michel. "Over there! *They* are the enemy!" His smile lost beneath his steel visor, he moved forward another step, knocking a young Janissary to his knees and then splitting the man's skull directly down the middle with the sharp edge of his heavy sword. He looked to his right and was about to protest again in jest when he saw Michel fall to his knees. Tadini stepped forward, putting his own body in front of a Turk moving in for the kill. The scimitar slashed down and across Tadini's breastplate, tearing his cloak and scratching the metal. Before the Turk could strike

or thrust again, Tadini stepped forward, stomping his right foot as he drove his sword straight from the hip, skewering the soldier through the chest with a thrust more like a foil than a broadsword. As the Janissary fell, he grasped at the blade still protruding from his ribs. Tadini had to use his boot to push the man off and retrieve his weapon.

Another knight stepped up to the front line, blocking Tadini from further attack. Michel was still on his knees, struggling with something in his helmet. Tadini reached down and grabbed him by the cloak. When he had pulled Michel to his feet, he saw the wound. An arrow had pierced the inside corner of the left eye and had exited through the left temple, where it protruded though the knight's helmet.

"Dio mio!" Tadini said, as he dragged his wounded friend to the rear ranks. Once out of immediate danger from attack, he lowered Michel to the ground and knelt beside him. Michel was becoming rapidly incoherent.

"Can you walk?" Tadini shouted. Michel did not answer. "Do you hear me? Can you walk?" Again no response. Tadini sheathed his sword and lifted Michel's body by one arm. He pulled the man over his shoulder and slung the body over his back, grabbing the two thighs in his arms. He ran through the streets of the Merchant's Quarter, and made his way to the *Collachio*. Turing into the Street of the Knights, he moved as fast as the heavy weight would allow him and climbed the stairs to the hospital.

Renato was working on the wounded already brought in from the battle at the Bastion of England. He didn't look up when Tadini shouted to him. Tadini gently put Michel's body on an unused operating table and called to Melina. She was wrapping bandages about the head of a wounded knight who lay upon the floor. She finished and went over to Tadini. She knew him well, for Tadini had often visited the hospital in search of Jean, who had become his close friend. Tadini had stayed many a night to help out when he was needed there, and had grown very fond of Melina. He never missed the opportunity to make veiled comments about the poorly kept secret of Jean's and Melina's little family.

Melina reached the table and nodded to Tadini. "Who is it, Gabriele?" She looked down and said, "Oh, dear God! Not Michel." Then, when Michel in his pain and delirium turned his head in her direction, she saw the arrow feathers protruding from his eye. Her hands flew to her mouth, and she was unable to stifle the cry that rose in her throat. "Oh. Dear God!" she said again. She touched Tadini on the arm and said, "Go back to your post, Gabriele. I'll get Doctor Renato, and we'll take care of Michel."

Tadini touched her hand and walked quickly out of the hospital.

Philippe's eyes burned as he slashed his way into the enemy. At fifty-eight, he was the oldest man fighting in the field. But, his age belied the physical man. Years of battle and training had kept him as fit as any younger man. With his strong arms and chest, he slashed and drove the heavy weapon through dozens of unfortunate Turks that afternoon.

Henry Mansell stood behind Philippe, and to his left. He kept just enough distance to stay out of the way of the powerful sword strokes, but close enough to protect his master's back. Mansell held the banner of the Crucifixion high above the heads of the knights. At its tip, the wooden pole was sheathed in brass and sharpened to a point. If the need arose, Mansell could protect the Grand Master using the standard as a lance. He held the standard in his left hand, while in his right he carried his own unsheathed broadsword. The years he had spent as standard bearer had given him enormous strength in his shoulders and arms. It was nothing for him to spend hour after hour in battle or on parade holding both his heavy weapon and the Holy Banner of the Crucifixion.

Philippe moved a step forward as his brothers-in-arms advanced yet another foot against the incoming tide of Turks. One Janissary moved in under Philippe's upraised sword, hoping to gain safety by entering inside the killing perimeter of the sword's reach. He thrust his scimitar at Philippe's neck, trying for a skewer between the breastplate and the visor of the helmet. Philippe parried the thrust with his chain-mailed hand and, closing the distance, brought the shaft of his sword down upon the helmet of the Janissary. Though still conscious, the man was stunned enough to stagger for a second, dropping his guard long enough to regain his balance. Before he could recover for a second attack, Philippe raised his heavy sword from its place directly in front of his chest, up and over his left shoulder. With a downward, backhanded sweep of the blade—now notched from impacts with other blades, and running with blood and dirt—he cut through the right collarbone of the young soldier, through the chest, and out under the left armpit.

The man looked into the slit in Philippe's visor as he fell backwards from the impact. Before he could focus on the two cold eyes staring back at him, he collapsed in a pile of disconnected parts, like a child's doll ripped to pieces in a temper tantrum.

Philippe recovered his stance, and moved forward another six inches.

Mustapha Pasha felt the mass of his army slow, then waver. The crush of bodies impeded its own movement forward. Mustapha shouted again and again for his men to advance. He raised his scimitar and struck at his own troops with the side of the blade. He cursed and reviled them as cowards, but still the momentum stalled.

For two more hours the battle raged. Tears of frustration ran down the Pasha's cheeks as he tried to make his way to the breach in the wall. He saw the Sultan's *Bunchuk* waver on the rampart and suddenly disappear from sight. As he moved closer to the breach, pushing and raging at his men, he could see the tall knight with the gray beard and long, gray hair. Though he had never seen or met him, he knew this must be the infamous Grand Master, de L'Isle Adam. Then, he saw the great banner waving in the air, Christ on the cross, filling the space behind the Grand Master, and he knew he was right. How foolish, he thought, to expose the leader to injury or death on the front line of the fight. He would never take such a chance with the Sultan.

Mustapha charged ahead, knocking his own men to the ground, striking them with his fists to get to the fight. He would face this gray old man and cut him to pieces there on the bastion. Nothing would stop him. With their leader gone, the knights would crumble and surrender the fortress to the Sultan.

Philippe had fought for two hours without let-up. The strategy was working, the knights plugging the gap in the walls with their bodies and their swords. The Muslims were falling away, the attack losing its momentum. His muscles ached, and he felt weak from dehydration and constant exertion. But still he pressed on.

As he fought, Philippe kept an eye on the soldiers beyond the breach, trying to assess the strength and determination of the attack. He could see the ditches filling with the bodies of the men cut down by his marksmen on the parapets and the walls. For every knight he had lost this day, there must be hundreds of Turks lying dead or wounded. As he scanned the field, he saw a figure moving counter to the retreating mob. While the mass of the army was in a slow, disorganized retreat, one man was pressing forward, his scimitar waving in the air. The noise of the battle was so great that Philippe's ears could discern nothing, but he saw the huge mustached man screaming and raging as he pushed frantically forward. His turban had been lost and his uniform was covered in blood and dirt. As the man reached the bastion, Philippe stepped forward to face the charge. Their eyes locked, and the man stood facing Philippe for the briefest moment.

Suddenly, the knights surged forward, an unstoppable wall of armor bristling with swords. Even Philippe was surprised by the strength of the attack after so many hours of fighting. It was as if they wanted it over *now*. This very minute. They would not tolerate another Muslim within their city. The assault was so fierce that the Turks fell back at once. The force of the knights' thrust pushed the Turks from the breach, and a general panic spread through the Turkish line. While isolated Janissaries tried to continue their attack, the tide of men began to flow backwards from the walls. They slid down the sloping embankment, stumbling and falling over the bodies of their comrades, living and dead.

Mustapha found himself caught in the retreating crush and thrashed to break free. He pushed and swung his scimitar, trying for a chance to get to the Grand Master. But he was helpless. The throng pressed close about him, forcing him backwards down from the breach. At times he was lifted from his feet. He cursed and struck out at his men, but it was no use. He waved his sword in the air as he watched the figure of his enemy recede in the distance. Finally, he gave up his struggle.

For his part, Philippe did not have the luxury of watching the departure of the Agha. He faced still another attack, and cut another young Janissary from the fragile tether of life.

As the knights watched the armies of the Sultan retreat to their camps, they did not cheer. No swords were raised in victory. The wall of men stood facing the outer perimeters, swords at their sides. To the few Turks still able to see them, it was a chilling vision. The knights were a physical part of the stone walls. Seeing them there like that, the ordinary soldiers began to doubt that they could ever move them from their fortress.

The silent knights looked out over the ditches. As far as their vision could penetrate the coming darkness, they saw tens of thousands of soldiers waiting their turn to storm the city. There seemed no end of Turkish soldiers to replace the ones the knights had killed in this first assault.

Philippe moved back from the breach and turned to give orders to Mansell to oversee the repairs to the damaged wall. He could see his banner gently flowing in the breeze a few yards behind the knights. As a path cleared for him, he saw that it was not Henry holding the staff, but another knight of the French *langue*. At his feet lay Henry Mansell, an arrow protruding from the very center of his chest. A brother knight held Mansell in his arms, while another tried to remove the arrow. But, the armor plate held the wooden shaft tightly in its metal grasp. Philippe knelt down beside his lifelong friend and reached out to him. "Henry. Oh, Henry," he said in a low voice.

"I'm sorry, my Lord. He is dead," said the knight who held Mansell's body.

Philippe touched Mansell's forehead. Then his chest. Then his left and his right shoulders. *"Nominae Patria, Filia, Spiritus Sanctus. Amen. Au revoir, Henri, mon cher vieux ami."*

Philippe rose and began the long walk back to his palace. As his knights watched him go, he seemed suddenly older and smaller. His shoulders sagged and his head was slightly bowed. The spring in his step and the proud carriage by which they all knew him had somehow slipped away. And this, they thought, after a day of victory.

———

Suleiman watched the attack from the vantage point of his horse. Ibrahim was at his side. The small Janissary guard was deployed in a crescent around the Sultan, and all watched the battle in silence. The green banner of the Prophet sagged in the stillness of dusk, a backdrop to the Sultan's unfolding drama.

When the fighting was over, Suleiman stayed on his horse. He watched as his troops retreated over their hard-won terrain. They crossed the ditches and the escarpment, leaving the bodies of the wounded and the dead in their paths. Here and there, a soldier carried a comrade or helped a wounded man back to the lines. But, the overwhelming picture before the Sultan was that of an army, dead and dying, in a wretched grave dug to protect the walls of this hateful citadel.

Soon the troops reached the safety of their lines. The harassing musket fire slowed, and then stopped as the last of the Turks moved out of range. A silence permeated the air. After the hours of noise and chaos, the absence of sound was alarming. Not even the birds sang. In the silence, Suleiman was keenly aware of the movement of the fabric of his men's uniforms, the soft rattle of their weapons against armor as they walked and staggered back to their camps. The smell of gun smoke and burnt flesh drifted into his nose. He saw the looks on their faces. The fury and the hopefulness of the initial assault had been replaced by no expressions at all. Where he had expected to see pain and disappointment, he saw nothing.

The Sultan took a deep breath. He looked right past Ibrahim and turned his brown stallion west to his camp on Mount Saint Stephen. He thought of how bravely his army had fought; how many young lives were lost that day; how much pain his people had suffered at the hands of the knights. And he wondered what price he—his army—would pay for taking this wretched island.

Ibrahim followed behind, leaving his master alone with his thoughts.

Later, as darkness covered the no-man's land between the armies, the soldiers on both sides of the walls began the process of healing their wounds and burying their dead. The Turks lost more than two thousand brave soldiers in the field that day. The knights lost Henry Mansell and Commander Gabriel de Pommerols. Michel d'Argillemont died of his terrible wound without ever regaining consciousness. Nobody had counted the number of dead and wounded Rhodians and mercenaries.

For hours, in the ditches, the Turkish wounded lay crying and calling for help. Their voices reached out to the ears of both armies. Just after midnight, Philippe sent a party of knights to violate the most basic rule of warfare that had guided soldiers since war had begun. The knights went out into the fields, and with swords and pikes, moved among the wounded, executing them one by one. The knights wandered about in slow motion, stopping only long enough to pick out the wounded from among the dead. Here and there they poked and prodded with the sharp steel of their lances and swords. Then, with neither anger nor remorse, but with cold deliberation, they ran their swords straight in between the ribs nearest the breast bone. Withdrawing the swords from the chests of the Turks, the knights wandered on again to find another soldier who failed to die in the battle. Not a man was spared. Not a prisoner taken. For all the remaining hours of darkness, a savage war was waged in total silence.

At dawn, the knights walked back in through the St. John's Gate and across the city to the *Collachio*. They returned to their Inns, where they put away their bloodied weapons and changed into their clean scarlet capes with the white cross of St. John. Then they met at the chapel as the bells rang for Matins.

⇥ 14 ⇤

COUNCILS OF WAR

Rhodes
September, 1522

Suleiman sat in his tent in silence. His face was lined and pale, for in spite of the fierce summer heat, the Sultan had spent much of his time under the cover of his battle pavilion. Like Xerxes at Salamis, his own hero of two thousand years earlier, Suleiman ordered a raised platform built on the hillside west of the city. His throne was set in place, his Viziers and advisers surrounding him as he watched the progress of the battle from a safe distance. And, like Xerxes before him, the Sultan's heart ached at the carnage he saw unfolding in the field.

After more than eight weeks of siege, the bodies of his armies now nearly filled the ditches at the southern bastions of the fortress. In the summer heat, the stench was intolerable. Flies swarmed over the swollen corpses. The soothing sea breezes of the early fall were replaced by nauseating smells driven back into the faces of the Turks. Soon diseases spread among the men and the merchant camp followers.

And still, not a single Turkish soldier had set a foot inside the city of the knights.

Suleiman sighed deeply, staring into the closed space of his tent. The servants had been dismissed, and the Sultan waited for a few moments before beginning the *Divan*. All of the Sultan's commanding officers, Piri Pasha, Mustapha Pasha, Bali Agha, Achmed

Agha, Ayas Agha, and Qasim Pasha, sat in a crescent around him. All immobile, impassive. Ibrahim sat to the Sultan's right, facing the generals. Several of the Aghas wondered at Ibrahim's position at the right hand of the Sultan. None said anything aloud.

Suleiman wondered who among these men would serve him best. Piri Pasha was still his Grand Vizier, but clearly because of his lack of enthusiasm for the battle, his usefulness was waning. Ibrahim had been Suleiman's loyal friend and servant for nearly a decade, but there was much resistance in the court to any further elevation of his rank. And as for the rest of the Aghas, what of them? They fought among themselves like children. They sought power and riches. Though they served the Sultan today, what would they do if their position was suddenly threatened?

All eyes except Suleiman's and Ibrahim's were fixed upon the carpet at their feet. Ibrahim looked out over the faces of the Aghas. *What are they thinking?* he wondered. *Each of them wants my position close to the ear and heart of the Sultan. Each would kill me for it, if the chance arose. Well, perhaps not Piri. But, the others would.*

Two Janissaries stood at attention outside the entrance to the tent. Otherwise, the seven men and the Sultan were alone.

Suleiman began. "We have been on this accursed island for more than two months. Thousands of my soldiers lie dead and rotting in the ditches and fields. I cannot even bury these wretched souls, nor commend them properly to Allah. And, here we sit, no closer to evicting the Sons of *Sheitan* from our Empire. Piri Pasha, what do you say?"

Piri looked up, as if surprised to be called upon to speak. He was no longer the commanding presence that Suleiman remembered from Selim's reign. Here was a man pale and drawn, his face gaunt, his belly hanging over his sash. His mind often wandered; he spoke in stammering sentences and unfinished thoughts. Piri tried to pull himself together, and after a moment said, "Majesty, I pray that Allah will take the souls of all our dead, for they have died in a *jihad,* a struggle. We are, after all, in a holy war against..."

"Speak not of the dead, my Grand Vizier," Suleiman, interrupted gently. "I want to know your thoughts about the war we wage this day against the knights. You are the senior ranking official in my empire, and the right to speak goes to you first."

"Forgive me my Lord." Piri wrinkled his brows, and then said, "I fear that we have taken on an enemy who is willing to sacrifice every man, woman, and child on this island to defend it from us. I doubt they will surrender...ever. We will have to kill everyone inside and outside the walls. Everyone. At the cost we have sustained so far, I wonder if it is worth the price. At this rate we will return to Istanbul with the bare tatters of the army that left there."

Suleiman sighed and said kindly, "Thank you, Piri Pasha. As always, you see things in a clear and definitive light." He turned to his left, and said, "Bali Agha?"

Bali Agha, commander of the Janissaries, straightened in his seat and said, "Majesty, our tactics need to be reviewed in detail. If I may?" Suleiman nodded and Bali Agha continued. "The strategy of persisting in mining the walls seems to work only at great cost to us. It took us many weeks and hundreds—maybe thousands—of lives lost to make that breach in the Bastion of England. The knights plugged the gap with a disciplined force and drove our armies back with little loss to themselves. And, still we sit here after eight long weeks no further along the road to conquest.

"Since the battle at the Bastion of England, Majesty, we have tried the same thing again and again. Five days later, we made a breach in Provence, and we were beaten back again, with great losses and little damage to the knights. My Janissaries suffered greatly from the Greek Fire and the shot raining down from the walls. Two days later it was the same story at England, and again at Aragon. And Provence. Nothing changes. While I must say that Mustapha Pasha and his men have fought gallantly—no, *murderously* would be the word—it has not gained us anything of substance. A change in strategy is sorely overdue."

Achmed Agha rose and began to speak. But, Bali Agha could not contain his enthusiasm and jumped to his feet again, interrupting Achmed Agha and committing a serious breach of court protocol. But Suleiman let it pass. Bali Agha said, excitedly, "Majesty, it is not for nothing that the Janissaries are called the Sons of the Sultan.

They would do *anything* for you. Your great-grandfather said, 'The body of a Janissary is but a stepping stone for his brothers into the breach.' These men will fill the ditches to overflowing; and their bodies and the bodies of their brothers *will* be the stepping stones to allow our men to march into the city and destroy the cursed *Kuffar*. Just give us the chance, my Lord, and we will do the job."

Excitement was building in the tent, and Suleiman had lost his look of weariness. He turned back to Achmed Agha. "And, how can we make it possible for the Sons of the Sultan to enter the city, as your Sultan and Bali Agha wish?"

"By using our superior numbers to greatest advantage, Majesty. We must attack and enter the city in force. A general assault, not on one bastion, but on all fronts at once. We must not depend upon the entry into a single breach. We need to spread their defenders thin and capitalize on our strength in numbers. I propose a general assault, after a week of unceasing bombardment with all the artillery in our possession. We will keep them at it day and night; repairing, rearming, defending. They will have no sleep. No respite. Then we will attack the entire southern perimeter of the Fortress. Aragon! Italy! England! Provence! This way, they will not have enough defenders to plug all the gaps. We will enter the city and run wild through the streets. The Sons of the Sultan will command the fortress before nightfall."

The Aghas buzzed with excitement. Suleiman smiled, and for the first time in weeks seemed to swell with the prospect of victory. Even the passive Ibrahim caught the energy in the air and began to nod in agreement with the new plan.

Suleiman waved his hand, signaling the Aghas to return to their posts and plan the attack.

—

The constant bombardment had caused relatively little damage within the city walls. The people had grown used to the noises of war. But, living conditions were deteriorating.

There was no room within the walls of the city to bury the dead, and unburied, untended corpses were now beginning to rot. In spite of covering the bodies with quicklime, the smells of death and decay inside the walls permeated the air. Citizens walked about with cloths dipped in oil of camphor pressed to their noses to mask the odors. The nighttime breezes brought the added stench from the thousands of Turkish bodies rotting in the ditches.

Sewers were clogged with debris, and polluted waters overflowed into the houses. Drinking water was in short supply. In June, the knights had poisoned the wells outside the city to prevent the Turks from using them. Now, their own wells inside the fortress were running low, as the rainless summer gave way to autumn.

Fresh food ran out early in August, and tempers flared more easily after a long diet on dried foods and stale mealy breads. Many of the people grew ill. The hospital, always there to help them in the past, was now overflowing with the wounded. The people sick with fever and dehydration from diarrhea could only wait on the outside stairs and in the open courtyard, hoping for help and some medicine between breaks in the fighting.

Now as the casualties increased, there was virtually no break in the workload for the knights tending the sick. Renato, Melina, and Hélène had not had more than a few hours sleep at one time in several weeks. They had dark bags under their eyes, and their faces showed the strain. Renato's hands shook as he worked on the endless procession of bodies moving through the doors. At the other end of the ward, the knights removed those who had died silently in the night. But, once outside the hospital, they were hard pressed to find a place to put the corpses. No one wanted another heap of rotting flesh next to his house, yet nobody could offer a solution.

Pockets of discontentment were springing up all throughout the city of Rhodes. Citizens were sent by their neighbors to the Grand Master pleading for him to surrender. How could life under the Muslims be worse than the hell in which they now lived? No person was untouched. By mid-September, nearly everyone had lost a friend, a neighbor, a husband, a wife, a child. How could the Muslims hurt them any more? How could the mother who has lost her child suffer more than she suffers now?

Rumors spread of an insurrection being planned by the Rhodians, to overthrow the Order and surrender the city. As the end of the month approached, morale was at its lowest since the siege had begun. Though the Turkish losses exceeded those of the knights and the Rhodians by ten or twenty to one, their deaths were little consolation. Life inside the city was hell. The realization became clear to them all: if the knights surrendered and left Rhodes, there would be peace again, and plenty. Life on their island paradise would return to normal. The faces of the rulers would change, but that was a common occurrence in the history of these Greek islands, and especially on Rhodes.

Philippe Villiers de L'Isle Adam sat in an upper meeting room of the Palace of the Grand Master. The windows were shut against the heat and the constant bombardment by the Turkish guns. The room was stuffy. Nothing could keep out the odors that permeated the air, the wood, and even the clothing of the knights themselves.

Philippe was haggard. He had been at the front of virtually every battle and conflict that took place. He rushed to any breach to fight in the front lines with his men. Since the death of Henry Mansell, Philippe's banner flew constantly behind him, held by the new standard bearer, Joachim de Cluys, of the French *langue*. The huge flag with Christ upon the cross was now a familiar sight to the Muslims. It betrayed the presence of the leader of the knights and made a target of the man the Muslims wanted so fervently to kill. To the Turks, Philippe symbolized the determination and bravery of the knights. To the Muslim, he was the earthly representative of the Devil. Though it was a wonderment that he fought alongside his knights, not a man among the Turks wondered why the Sultan, Suleiman, remained in safety at the rear. Not one of them would think of placing the Shadow of God on Earth in harm's way.

But, as the banner of the Crucifixion betrayed Philippe's presence, so his survival after so many battles also supported the rumor among the Muslims that this banner provided some measure of protection from harm. The duel might now reduce itself to the strength of the belief in the power of Allah and His Prophet against that of the Christ.

As he waited for the last of his officers to assemble, Philippe again let his mind wander back to his beloved Hélène. He was torn between his happiness at having her near to him again, at her desire to be with him in this awful time, and the reality of the danger they were both in.

"My lord...?" It was Tadini. "We are all here..."

Philippe was momentarily startled. Fatigue had eroded his calm and even manner. He was on the edge almost constantly now, and rarely slept more than an hour or two in a night. He coughed, as if he had been caught in some embarrassing moment. Then he began. "Gentlemen," he said, "our time is short. We cannot waste a moment off the battlements. So let's get directly to the plans for the next several engagements, and be back at our stations as soon as we may. Gabriele, what news?"

"My Lord," Tadini said, "they have not slowed down the campaign to mine the walls. The more we kill them, the more they send after us. I think that every dead Turkish miner spawns ten more from his corpse. They are everywhere. More than five-sixths of the enceinte is undermined with tunnels, theirs and my own. Every day we blow up two or three of their tunnels, killing many men. Sometimes hundreds. And, the mines that they have detonated have, *grâce à Dieu*, detonated harmlessly up the air shafts without doing much damage.

"Yesterday, the Janissaries gathered for an attack on the *langue d'Italie*. They were, apparently, too close to the mine when it detonated, and more than two hundred were killed on the spot. Their artillery have increased in activity, ceaselessly firing at the whole southern sector. This could be a diversion for an attack from the west or the northern sectors; or it could be a preliminary to a general attack on the city." Philippe nodded, and Tadini continued. "I have no idea, and we have no intelligence from their lines." Tadini paused, then said, "My Lord, is there any hope of more knights arriving from Europe?"

"I think we should make all our plans as if there were not. We have received word now from every envoy I have sent but one. All requests were turned down. I have not yet heard from Thomas Newport. He is seeking help from the knights still in King Henry's domains. If he succeeds, we might expect a hundred knights or more. If not..." He shrugged and inclined his head.

"Thank you, my Lord," Tadini said, and sat down.

"John Buck?"

"My Lord, I have little to add. I agree with Gabriele. I think they have seen the failure of intense attacks at one breach, and may try to divide our strength among many breaches at once. We have had to stop chasing the Turks when they retreat. Mustapha Pasha has dug protective holes along the trenches and manned them with *arquebusiers* and musketeers to cover their retreats. It is too dangerous for us to follow."

Tadini interrupted. "My Lord, Jacques de Bourbon sends his apologies. He says that because he can no longer follow the enemy and change the retreat into a rout, he has captured no more Turkish standards since the attack on England. *Il est desolé.*"

Buck continued. "We continue to punish the Turks severely. I should think there are more than three thousand dead out there. But, we continue to take strategic losses we cannot sustain. Guyot de Marseille was the best of our artillerymen, and he is wounded so badly that he cannot return to action. Your standard bearer, Joachim de Cluys, has lost the eye that was injured at Provence yesterday. Though he rages to get back into battle, he will be too handicapped to guard your back. One miraculous occurrence was the survival of de Bidoux." Prejean de Bidoux was the Prior of the *langue* of Provence, who successfully defended the observation post on the island of Kos, though he had his horse shot out from under him in the battle. "He had his throat cut nearly from ear to ear with a scimitar yesterday. But, he is alive and demanding to be released from the hospital to fight again."

"As well as a miracle, there is also the skill of our surgeons," said Philippe.

Philippe waited to see if any of the other knights wished to speak. When none did, he stood, leaned forward, and placed his fists upon the table. "One thing more. I have heard much talk of an insurrection among the people. Be on your guard, gentlemen. Report any such activity to me, and I will deal with it immediately. Severely. Any traitors in our midst must be made an example to the others. They must fear *our* wrath more than they fear the Turks."

As the knights were reviewing their losses and their options, and unknown to Philippe, Thomas Newport had been immensely successful in his request. More than one hundred English knights set sail from England at the very time the knights on Rhodes were conferring with Philippe. But, there his luck ended. After a few days at sea, while off the coast of France in the Bay of Biscay, a terrible storm drove his ship upon the rocks. He and all his knights and crew were lost. No great force of knights was coming to relieve the besieged Order of St. John.

———

Long after dark, Jean strode into the hospital to find Melina busy changing dressings and washing wounds with salt water. She saw Jean and called his name. He turned and made his way through the overcrowded ward. Soldiers and citizens were everywhere. All the hundred beds were full, and barely a place was left on the floor. Blankets served as mattresses for the wounded. Patients leaned like spokes of a wheel against the huge stone columns that ran down the center of the ward and supported the high vaulted ceiling. The air was dense and reeked with the sickly sweet smell of infection and gangrene.

Jean walked through the aisle that had been cleared for the purpose, and knelt down beside Melina.

"How are you?" he said.

"I'm fine, Jean. And the girls are fine. They feed as if it were their last meal, and I think they're almost fat. Hélène is a godsend. She has become more brave than anyone, and never rests."

She handed Jean some clean dressings, and said, "Hold these for me. You can talk to me while I work."

Jean looked at the clean amputation stump and raised his eyebrows. "How long ago did that happen?"

"Three days ago." Melina looked at Jean, and waited for the question she knew would come next.

"But, how? It's too clean; no burns; it's too well healed."

"Amazing, isn't it? Three nights ago, we ran out of oil for cautery. Doctor Renato was beside himself with worry. But, there was nothing he could do. So he made an ointment with oil of willow and turpentine. He placed it on the wounds, with nothing else."

"But, how did he stop the bleeding. And what of the sheep-bladder dressings?"

"Compression. We packed the wounds and held the dressing tightly. It hurt them terribly, but much less than the boiling oil. We have no more sheep bladders anyway—there are no more sheep—so we wrapped them in clean rags. Renato could hardly sleep with worry. He was sure that without the cautery, the gunpowder and the dirt would cause infection and the poor men would be dead by morning. But, instead, when we changed the dressing, we found them to be clean and even healthier than the ones we burned with oil. He could hardly believe it. So now every wound is treated with willow and turpentine, and I wash the wounds every day with salt water. Nothing more. It is all we have to work with anyway. It's amazing. When I told him what a miracle his cure was, he quoted a French surgeon to me. Paré, I think he said. Ambroise Paré. *'Je le pansay; Dieu le guarit.'*"

"'I dress the wound; God heals the patient.'" Jean translated. "It's amazing." Jean looked about the ward, and said, "Where's the doctor? It's the first time I haven't seen him here. Is he off getting some sleep?"

"No. He told me to carry on while he went to visit some of the patients in the city. He's been gone for hours, now. He should be back any minute."

"Good." Jean shrugged and kissed Melina. He rose to go. "I'm needed at the Palace. The Grand Master summoned me a while ago. I sent word that I would be there in a moment. Here is my duty." He kissed Melina again, this time on the lips, and long. "I'll kiss the girls, too, and be back when I can."

Melina touched Jean's cheek and nodded. Jean turned and walked back down the ward, and out of the hospital.

⚊

Philippe stood behind his desk. His eyes blazed with a rage unknown to his knights. Never had they seen such fury exposed so openly by the Grand Master. His hand went instinctively to his sword, his knuckles turning white as he squeezed the hilt. He could not speak for a moment, so seized was he by his anger and his shock.

Three young knights stood before him. They were frightened by what they saw in the Grand Master's eyes. They had no idea what to expect. What would they do if he drew his sword? The three had seen him in battle, and marveled at the skill, strength, and speed of this gray-haired man, old enough to be their grandfather.

The knights suddenly released the man in the black cape. He fell to the ground, unable to stop his fall because his hands were tied behind his back with stout leather thongs. He had long since lost the feeling in either hand, so tightly was he bound. His face smashed into the cold stones and his nose cracked with the impact. A trickle of blood dribbled down from his left nostril and made its way around the corner of his mouth. His left lower eyelid began to swell from the small amount of bleeding that seeped under the skin at the site of a fracture. In a few minutes it would be purple, and his left eye would swell closed.

"It cannot be true! Not *you*. All these years? Tell me it's a lie. A mistake."

Philippe held the parchment in his right hand and the arrow in his left. "This is in Turkish. I do not read Turkish. What does it say?"

The man pulled himself painfully to his knees and struggled into an unsteady kneel. With his hands behind him, it was difficult to hold his position. The knights had not beaten him, nor had they abused him physically or verbally. After discovering the man as he tried to shoot a message on an arrow into the Turkish camps, they subdued him and brought him directly to the Grand Master. Their shock was as great as Philippe's.

"Speak to me. What does this say?"

The only sound was the obstructed breathing coming from the prisoner's right nostril. He held his mouth tightly shut, as if he were afraid that by opening it the words would pour forth.

Philippe looked at the knights. "Bring me a knight who can read Turkish. At once! There are several in the *langue de France*."

"No." It was the quiet voice of the prisoner. Devoid of feeling. No fear. No anger. No hatred. Just a simple statement.

"What?"

"I said, 'no,' there is no need. I speak Turkish. I'll tell you what it says."

Philippe handed the paper to a knight and said, "Here."

"There is no need," said the prisoner. "I wrote the letter. I know what it says."

"Very well, then. Tell me."

The prisoner looked into Philippe's eyes for the first time since he was thrown into the room. "Fear not, my Lord. The time for lies is over. It is well past that hour, and I am already dead."

Philippe sat down in his chair. He could barely define his feeling. There was sadness and fury; despair and betrayal; and a hopelessness if this man could turn on his brothers. He motioned to the knights. Two of them grabbed the prisoner by his elbows and pulled him to his feet. They dragged him backwards and dropped him into a wooden chair. He slumped awkwardly to his right, trying to make room for his bound hands. Philippe motioned the guards from the room. When he was alone with the prisoner he said, "Go on."

Jean walked from battlement to battlement, and inquired about Renato. He was beginning to worry about him. Now that it was completely dark, he was always alert to the possibility that Turkish fighters might slip into the city under the cover of night. He worried too that the doctor may have pushed himself too hard for too long, and might, himself, be lying sick among the many wounded who were dying in the streets.

After an hour, he became increasingly alarmed and returned to the hospital. He ran up the stairs and found Melina feeding the twins. She sat on the floor of her little room, one set of tiny pink lips at each breast. In spite of her fatigue, and the dark circles under her eyes, to Jean she was as beautiful to him as that first day he saw her in the market. The same Rhodian sun seemed to shine on her in the dank gloom of the hospital. She looked up and beamed at him. "This is why God has given us two breasts, *n'est-ce pas?*"

Jean laughed and pointed to the girls, "'It's best we stop with these two then."

Jean slipped down onto the mattress, pulling the rough blanket aside and taking his place alongside Melina. He had taken off all his armor and was dressed only in his shirt and trousers. Melina finished feeding the babies, who were sound asleep now. She turned to her left and settled them down into their nest. She covered them, and smiled at the one sight left that would still take her, if only for a moment, out of this hell she lived in.

She was about to place her breasts, still wet with milk, back into her bodice when she felt Jean's hand gently take her wrist and place it behind his neck. She pulled him down as he leaned into her body and began to suck on her breasts, gently at first and then with increasing hunger. Though the sensation of feeding her girls was always pleasurable for Melina, the pressure from Jean's lips and tongue made her nearly crazy. She felt herself becoming wet between her thighs for the first time since this terrible war had begun. And it had been so long since she and Jean had made love.

While he sucked at her breasts, Melina lifted her own skirts above her waist and then with some difficulty began to undo Jean's belt. She slipped her hands down into his trousers and smiled to find him hard and ready for her. She pulled his head gently from her breasts and kissed him long and deeply, tasting his familiar breath and the sweetness of her own milk. Then, she drew him toward her and guided him gently inside herself. All she could think of was the day they had made love in the river at Petaloudes, with her little angels already growing inside her womb. Now she held Jean so tightly to her that he could barely breath. As she came to her climax, he could feel the tears pouring from her and feel her sobbing against his chest.

Jean could find nothing to say to calm her, and he didn't try. He held her tight, and placed his face into her hair. They grew quiet, and fell asleep for a few moments while still locked together.

Then, they awoke together, and with great reluctance pulled apart. How they longed for those days when they could fall asleep in each other's embrace and never move again till the morning light interrupted their sleep.

Jean redid his trousers and began to assemble his armor and weapons. He grew serious again, and said, "I've searched all over for the Doctor. I'm worried, Melina, that something has happened to him. Has he returned while I was out?"

"No, he hasn't. I'll ask Hélène, but I've been in the ward all night, and only just came back to feed the girls. What could have happened?"

"I don't know, but I'm afraid he is ill and may be lying about the streets with the other bodies; perhaps, in need of help."

"What will you do, Jean?"

"I'll go to the Grand Master and ask for a party of knights to search for him. He may well need us, and by Jesus, we have need of him." Jean hurried from the room without another word. Melina finished dressing, and after tucking in the babies, returned to her work.

———

Philippe waited for the prisoner to begin. Finally, the man raised his head and stared again at Philippe. The blood had crusted now, and was no longer running from his nose. His left eye was completely swollen shut, the skin purple and tight. He was breathing through his mouth. He took a long breath and let out a longer sigh. And then he began to recite:

To Piri Pasha, Grand Vizier: conditions in the city are deteriorating. There is little food, and drinking water is scarce. The knights cannot hold on much longer. I have heard from your spies that there has been talk of your giving up the battle and returning to Istanbul. This would be a mistake. The garrison cannot be held much longer.

"And?"

"And nothing, my Lord. Nothing more."

Philippe exploded. He jumped to his feet and hurled his pewter water flask at the prisoner's head. It glanced off the side of his temple, opening another wound, so that the blood now flowed down into the prisoner's ear. The two men glared at each other in strained silence, when suddenly the door burst open and the knights rushed in at the sound of the flask crashing to the stone floor. Immediately behind them came Jean de Morelle, short of breath and sweating. "What has happened...*Mon Dieu!* What are *you* doing here? I have been searching everywhere for you."

Doctor Renato turned and looked at Jean through his one functioning eye. Only then did Jean see the thongs binding the prisoner's hands and the injuries to his face. He started forward, but stopped at once. Turning to Philippe, he said, "What...what's happened? Why is the Doctor...what is it?"

"Look at him well, Jean. This man you trusted—*we* trusted—has betrayed us to the Muslims."

John Buck and Thomas Docwra rushed into the room together, almost immediately followed by Gabriele Tadini. Then came Andrea d'Amaral and his servant, Blasco Diaz. Finally, Thomas Scheffield entered the room. All the knights stared in disbelief at the scene. Renato turned his head toward the knights, and then lowered his gaze to the floor. He could not look into the eyes of the men he had betrayed. These friends of so many years would now decide his fate, and there was little doubt as to what their decision would be.

Philippe motioned the knights to the table. Slowly the men moved to their seats, never taking their eyes off Renato. When everyone was seated, Philippe held up the paper and the arrow, and said, "Our guards found Doctor Renato on the walls near the Tower of Italy. He was about to shoot this letter into the camp of Piri Pasha with his crossbow."

The knights murmured to one another, but their eyes never left Renato. Philippe continued. "Though I have not had time to authenticate it's meaning, the doctor tells me that he has written to the Sultan of our condition. He told the Sultan that we are failing, and that he should intensify his war against us. That we cannot hold out much longer."

Thomas Docwra broke in, "My Lord, I read a bit of Turkish. Let me see the paper. Perhaps I can verify what he says."

Philippe handed the paper to Docwra who read it silently. Then, Docwra said, "Yes, my Lord. That is the essence of the letter."

Philippe said, "I don't doubt that he is telling the truth now. He has nothing to gain by lying at this point. However, I want to know,

THE SHADOW OF GOD

as I am sure do all of you, why this man, once our friend and ally, our dedicated doctor, at times our savior, has betrayed us. He will tell us now, here. Or, he will tell us on the rack. One way or another, he will talk."

The room was silent. Renato's head hung down, his chin almost touching his chest. Minutes went by, but Philippe said nothing. Then, barely raising his head and without looking at his captors, Renato began to speak. His voice was low, trembling, his words barely audible.

"Speak up, damn you!" Philippe shouted. He was furious and heartbroken.

Renato jumped in his seat. So did the knights at Philippe's table. Then he straightened up and looked directly into the eyes of the Grand Master. He cleared his throat and began again. All eyes were on his. Renato told his story in simple, unemotional words. His voice was even and clear. Once he began, he went on uninterrupted until he was finished. He answered all their unasked questions.

"I was born the son of a Jewish doctor in Spain. We were driven out during your Inquisition. All my family and friends were killed except for me. I escaped to Portugal. Then, your church forced the Portuguese king to expel us as well. We went to North Africa, and then to Istanbul. The Christians of Europe drove us all from our homes. Nobody there wanted any Jews left to soil their land. Only the Ottoman Sultans would take us in. The Muslim laws protected us as *dhimmis*, People of the Book, those who have received the scriptures from God. The same book that God gave to the Christians. The same words given to Islam. I lived with other Jews in the city. I had been trained by my father, and I continued my study in the Jewish Quarter in Istanbul. I became a doctor, and practiced my profession in Istanbul for several years."

Renato looked around at the silent knights, and then Philippe. There was no reaction. He continued, "One day I was summoned to the Palace, the residence of the Sultan, Selim. There were many Jewish physicians in attendance at the palace. I thought I was needed to minister to someone in the Sultan's household. Instead, I was taken to the Sultan, himself. No one else. Except for the guards at the door, we were alone. I was told that this meeting was a secret, and that if I betrayed my secret, I would be put to death. I believed him. Selim told me that he was preparing to take back Rhodes. That he wished to drive the Christian Knights of St. John from his Empire. He said you were pirates, and that you had, for centuries, slaughtered innocent Muslims all over his Empire; that until you were gone from the face of the Earth, there would be no safety for the Muslims. He told me how he had given the Christians and Jews a safe place to worship and to live in peace, as prescribed by the *Qur'an*. That you Christians abused your privileges and killed the Muslims at every opportunity. That you took Muslim slaves and slaughtered his people. I already knew what you had done to *my* people."

Renato's voice was failing. His throat was dry, and the words began to come with more difficulty. Philippe and his knights sat and listened impassively.

"He told me that he wanted me to perform a service to the Empire. That I was to convert to Christianity and make my way to Rhodes. That I was to apply for a position in the hospital, and serve the knights and the people of Rhodes as a doctor, and be a loyal citizen. But, all the while, I was to send information on a regular basis about the conditions and the repairs to the fortress. This I did. Each month, a messenger would come to the hospital and seek medical help. It was usually a different person, but the medical complaint was always the same. This is how I knew the man was from the Sultan. I would tell him my news, never putting anything in writing. Selim warned me of the danger, and he said I could minimize it as long as I identified the messenger carefully and never committed anything to paper.

"And this I did for eight years. Until June, when I could no longer send information out of the Fortress. Instead, I would fire the messages into the Turkish camp with my crossbow. It was I who told the Turks to stop their mortar fire into the city—that it was ineffectual. Many times, our guards...*your* guards...nearly caught me. Tonight they did. That is all there is to tell you."

Silence. Finally, Philippe asked quietly and slowly, "And did your treachery extend to my wounded knights as well? Did they die in your care, when they might have lived?"

Renato jumped to his feet, knocking over his chair. *"Jamais! Jamais!"* Never! He staggered and fell to his knees. "I treated every human being the same way. Muslim, Jew, Christian. It means nothing to me. I pray to 'Yahweh.' You call Him, 'God.' The Muslim calls Him 'Allah.' We all pray to the same God. We share some of the same prophets. We follow the same rules of conduct. You and I follow the Ten Commandments. The very *same* Commandments of the very *same* God! The Muslim follows the precepts of the *Qur'an*, and they are much the same as the Commandments. Yet, we kill each other. Over what? A few words. A nuance?"

Tadini stepped forward and replaced the toppled chair. He placed a hand gently on Renato's shoulder and helped him to his feet. Renato slumped back into his chair and continued. "No, my Lord. A traitor I may be. Sometimes I am a spy. But, I am *always* a doctor, and my oath in that regard has never been violated. Never!"

The knights continued to stare at Renato. His words stung them and chastised them. Jean, in particular, had been agonizing over the role of the knights on Rhodes. He had talked for long hours with Melina over the awful subject of the slaves and the piracy. Still, no one spoke.

Finally, Renato finished by saying, "You have known me these eight years. I have been as true to my post as any knight to his. But, just as Selim and his son, Suleiman, I was convinced that the interest of peace in this empire would be best served by your departure from these waters. I have no regrets for what I have done. In the long run, I think that more lives could be saved by your early surrender than by my loyalty to the Order." Renato looked directly into Philippe's eyes. "I have nothing more to say."

Philippe turned to his knights and said, "Gentlemen, we do not have time for a formal tribunal, nor would it serve any purpose. I will make this decision as Grand Master of the Order. If there are any objections, let them be known before we leave this room." He stood and faced Renato. "The prisoner will stand." Helped by Jean, Renato struggled to his feet once more, and looked directly into Philippe's eyes.

"You have admitted to the crime of treason. There is no mitigation in this regard. You have betrayed your brothers-at-arms. For that crime, you will suffer the usual consequences. Tomorrow at dawn, you will be hanged, drawn, and quartered. Your body will not be buried in consecrated ground. Instead, your remains will be placed into the catapult and thrown into the camp of the Muslims. They will see what is the fate of traitors and spies. And they can do with you what they will. Have you anything to say?"

Renato stared at Philippe, but never acknowledged the question.

"Nobody is to speak to the prisoner. He is to have no comfort. No food. No water. John Buck, see to his execution. Before he is locked away, turn him over to the Inquisitor. Let us see if the rack will yield information that he has secreted." Philippe turned his eyes away from Renato's. He seemed to sag very slightly. Then, he said, "Send in a priest and allow him to divest himself of his sins. He has converted to Christianity and lived these eight years as a Christian. We will allow him the small comfort of confessing his sins, though I doubt he will escape eternal damnation." With that, Philippe stormed from the room as if to free himself from the weight of this awful night.

He walked down the long stone corridor and entered his suite of rooms. As he closed the door and bolted it, he felt he was not alone. Placing his hand on the hilt of his sword, he turned slowly toward the inner bedroom. There was no candle lit, so he could not make out anything. He walked quietly to his room and slipped into the darkness. Something stirred.

"Philippe? *Chèrie?*" It was Hélène's sleepy voice coming from the bed. She struck a match and lit the bedside lamp as Philippe relaxed his grip on the sword. He sat at the side of the bed and placed his big hands on her cheeks. She reached up to kiss him, but he guided her to his side and hugged her instead.

"What is it, Philippe?" she asked.

"Who could ever have thought such a thing as this were possible?"

"Tell me."

"It's Renato..."

"Is he hurt? Dead?" she said with alarm.

"Far worse than that. A spy. He has betrayed us to the Muslims..."

Hélène gasped and held him tighter. Then he told her all of it. He knew that what Renato had said about the treatment of the Jews was true enough. But loyalty to the Order had overridden everything in Philippe's life since he was inducted as a teenager. It was almost as if he could not allow himself to hear anything Renato had said after he had admitted his treachery. Nothing could justify betraying his brothers on Rhodes.

But the worst part, Philippe knew, was not the treachery itself, but the part that the Order of St. John had played in its genesis.

Just before dawn, Jean entered the hospital once more. He was completely drained from the events of the evening. As he walked down the aisle of the ward, Melina turned from the patient she was tending and saw the terrible look on Jean's face. She stopped what she was doing and rushed to his side. "Jean. What is it? What's happened?"

Jean took Melina in his arms and hugged her close. Then, without a word, he led her to their private little room at the end of the ward. He closed the door, shutting out the commotion from the hospital. The twins were asleep in their nest. Jean held Melina close and told her about Renato.

"It can't be. Impossible!" she said, pushing Jean away.

Jean held on tightly and pulled Melina back to him. "I am so sorry. But, it's true. I was there, Melina. I heard him confess every word."

"But they tortured him! Of course he would confess!"

"No, no. He confessed of his own free will. All the knights heard him. Only after sentence was passed was he taken to the rack."

"Oh dear God. What will we do without him?"

Melina buried her face into Jean's chest. Jean stroked her hair and held her even tighter. "You and I seem to be the only ones asking that question. Everyone else is so horrified at his treachery that they've forgotten what Renato means to us. They only want revenge. They want to see him hanged and be damned."

"It will go badly for the knights now. Anyway, Jean, is it true?"

"What?"

"*Are* we nearly finished? Are we about to lose this war?"

Jean thought for a moment. Then, he said, "We still have a strong fighting force. Our supplies are going faster than we had thought. But, there is still hope that some reinforcements might arrive."

"And, if they don't?"

"Then, the Sultan might decide to leave when winter sets in. The rain and the cold may drive him away"

"And if he doesn't leave? What then?"

"Melina, there is always the possibility that we'll be overrun by the Turks. They nearly broke through last week, and they might again. They outnumber us by hundreds to one. I cannot promise that we will win. But, I'll fight to the death to defend you."

"I know that, Jean. I never doubted *you*. But, you are only one man. What happens if the Muslims overrun the city? What will happen to the twins?"

"Melina, look at me. I've never lied to you. I won't lie to you now. In the past, they've slaughtered the armies and made slaves of the women and children. Our girls could be taken back to Turkey and turned into Muslims. They could be slaves, or even girls of the harem. Anything is possible. Is death worse? I don't know. *My* duty is to die if I must, defending this city. Yours is to live, so that you can protect the girls. Whatever you have to do, you must protect them from the Turks. Do you understand?"

"Yes. But, couldn't we leave before the end? We could slip away in the night. I know this island. We could hide in the forest. Make our way to Lindos. We could be safe until this is over..."

Jean did not answer, nor did Melina expect one. She knew he would never leave his post, never desert his brothers-in-arms. She sagged against him and closed her eyes. Against her own wishes, she fell asleep in his arms. When she woke, the first light was streaming into the ward. The door to her little room was cracked open, and Jean was gone.

Apella Renato lay sprawled on the bare stone floor. The moisture had soaked through his clothes. He was shivering when the priest entered his cell. The priest knelt on the cold, wet stone and spoke gently to the prisoner.

"Would you like to confess your sins now, Doctor?"

"I have confessed before the knights, Father, and I am certain that God heard me."

"Have you nothing you wish for me to say to God for you?"

Renato had great difficulty talking. His throat was parched, and his body continually shook with spasms of pain and fever. "Forgive me, Father, but I speak directly to God. God understands what I have done. I know you cannot. But, I regret nothing. Not one thing that I have done. I have faithfully served God's children as a physician. All of them. Christians. Muslims. Jews. Hindus. The Godless, too. Slaves. Knights. Greeks. Turks." His voice faltered as the dryness in his throat further impeded his speech. "All of God's children who came to me for help, I helped...as God has taught me. I regret only that God did not see fit to give me a son, so that I could teach him to heal." He shivered again and closed his eyes.

"But, God requires repentance from you. Think carefully on your words, for God hears everything, and there is little time left."

Renato whispered, "Father, I thank you for your wishes. Perhaps you would kneel with me in prayer, while I speak to God silently."

The priest shrugged his shoulders, and faced Renato. He took the doctor's hands in his and lowered his head. With his right hand, he traced the sign of the cross on Renato and then on himself. Then the two men prayed to the same God in silence.

As the sun reached out from the edge of the frothy sea, Doctor Apella Renato was dragged from his cell into the streets of the *Collachio*. He was escorted by an armed guard of eight knights. His injuries sustained on the rack made walking impossible, so his guards supported him as they took him to the gallows. His legs wobbled and lurched with every painful yard. Though the defenders could scarcely afford the absence of even a single man on the walls that day, the Grand Master had ordered this escort to prevent the mobs in the city from killing the doctor before he was lawfully executed.

But, the Grand Master had little to fear. Word of Renato's treachery had spread throughout the population. By dawn there was barely a person within the walls who had not heard the story.

Oddly, there seemed little emotion in the streets other than sorrow. There was hardly a citizen alive who had not known Apella Renato as a doctor or as a friend. Crowds lined the path to the place of execution, but there was no trouble. A few citizens turned their backs as the doctor walked past, but most looked with pity and puzzlement upon this man they had come to trust and to love. Had they learned to honor his surrender to the Muslims? Could life get any worse than it was now? Was one foreign ruler any worse than another?

Renato was dragged the last few yards to the gallows. By now his legs stretched straight out behind him. His head sagged, and he did not speak. The executioner took him under the arms and dragged him up the gallows steps. A hood was placed over his head and tied lightly around his neck.

In the heat of the rising sun, the hood admitted very little air, and it rapidly became difficult for him to breathe. In his darkened world, Apella Renato, Doctor of Rhodes, quietly said his last words. Neither the crowd nor the executioner could hear him. With tears slowly falling from his cheeks and disappearing into the cloth of his hood, Renato whispered, "*Shema Yisrael, Adonoi Eloheynu, Adonoi Echod.*" Hear, oh Israel, the Lord our God, the Lord is one. Then, without pause, he said in Arabic, "There is no God but God, and Mohammed is his Prophet."

He felt the noose tighten as he was lifted from the ground. When the weight of his body was fully suspended in the air, he began to choke as the thick rope tightened fractionally. He could no longer even whisper, but in his mind he still heard the words. He could hear them in his ears, and see them written before his eyes. "Forgive me, Father, for I have sinned...Hear, oh Israel, the Lord our God...There is no God but God...There is no God but God...Forgive...Forgive."

As his world clouded, Renato's body fell to the ground. The rope had been cut. His body struck the wooden platform, crumpling into a shapeless form, his humanity hidden by the hood.

The executioner turned the body on its back and splayed Renato's limbs. Air slowly entered the doctor's lungs, and his heart circulated the refreshed blood to the brain. He began to recover consciousness, and the words formed on his lips again. "Hear, oh Israel, the Lord our God..."

Leather straps were attached to his wrists and ankles. Thongs were affixed to chains. The chains were securely lashed to the wooden traces of the four waiting horses. As the hooded man lay murmuring his prayers, whips cracked, and the horses galloped away in four directions. They were slowed down fractionally as the thongs grew suddenly tight. Renato's body snapped into the air between the horses, and he screamed as his recently tortured limbs were suddenly torn apart by the enormous strength of the four powerful animals. He screamed again and again as the horses, whipped by their masters, struggled against the leather and chain.

And then he was silent.

The horses were backed down a few feet, and Renato's body returned to the paving stones. The thongs were cut and the horses led away. The executioner drew his newly sharpened sword, and in less than a minute had cut the body into four quarters as prescribed by the Grand Master. Eight slaves carried the pieces to the walls, where a catapult was waiting, its long wooden arm drawn back and held in place against its powerful mechanism by a single rope.

The body parts were placed in the declivity of the throwing arm. When the slaves were clear, the executioner slashed the restraining rope with his sword, still wet with Apella Renato's blood. The huge wooden arm swung up in an arc, and slammed against the rope-wound crossbar. The remains of Apella Renato flew from the fortress where he had lived for almost a decade, to return home at last among his Turkish friends.

❧ 15 ❧

THE SWORD OF ISLAM

Rhodes
September 22nd, 1522

Suleiman walked his horse slowly in the early morning light. The sun had just broken over the ocean, and light shimmered on a frothy sea. The winds were stronger now that autumn was approaching, and the hint of worsening weather was unmistakable. At his right side rode Ibrahim, quiet and relaxed upon his stallion. On the Sultan's left rode a newcomer to these morning outings, Doctor Moses Hamon, the Royal Physician. In the Empire of the Ottomans, Jews were forbidden the privilege of riding a horse. Mules and donkeys could be used for transport, but horses were the sole province of the Muslims, a privilege of rank in the social hierarchy. However, the Sultan had waved this prohibition for his physician. Hamon had been busy during the first months of the siege. With the Sultan in perfect health, he had been bored at first. Then, he made his way into the hospital tents, and at once had found himself immersed in the care of the wounded and the tutoring of the young doctors and their assistants. Except for his daily rounds in the hospital, he had not left the security of the Sultan's camp. Suleiman treated the doctor as a precious resource, and kept him nearly as heavily guarded as he, himself.

"You'll enjoy this inspection, Doctor. You need some diversion, I think."

"Yes, Majesty. I'm anxious to see the disposition of the army, and to get a closer look at the city."

As they rode east toward the sea, the pounding of the cannons became more insistent. They had to raise their voices to be heard. By the time they reached the outskirts of Piri Pasha's encampment, Hamon could feel the earth rumble beneath his horse's feet as the massive cannonballs burst out of their huge bronze barrels and struck the towering walls. Two days earlier, Piri Pasha's troops made a furious assault at the Post of Italy, preceded and followed by unceasing bombardment. There had been serious damage to the walls. Simultaneously, Mustapha Pasha attacked Provence, England, and Aragon, reinforced with Bali Agha's Janissaries. The knights had been driven back, and several of their standards captured by the Turkish soldiers.

But, the knights rallied, and poured every piece of murderous equipment in their possession into the fight. Greek Fire spewed from copper tubing and incinerated large numbers of Azabs. Boiling pitch and oil were poured from the overhanging parapets, inflicting terrible burns and agony; musketeers and arquebusiers filled the ditches with bodies killed by their ceaseless volleys of well-aimed shot.

Even the archers, with their leather-fledged, metal-tipped arrows, slaughtered hundreds of Turks that day. Though slow to reload, the crossbow was powerful and accurate, and—unlike the longbow—required little skill to use. The slight twist to the leather feather caused the arrow to spin in flight, increasing its accuracy and penetration. It was an arrow exactly such as these that fatally wounded King Richard, the Lion Heart, some three hundred years before. Now, the Rhodian skies were filled with intermittent flights of longbow arrows as well, which looked like masses of migrating birds, flying in perfect formation, finally diving to the earth; down into the center of the attacking Turkish forces.

By the end of the day, again, the Turks were forced to retreat, leaving more than two thousand more dead in the ditches, after they had killed some two hundred mercenaries and a dozen knights.

Piri Pasha's sentries received word that the Sultan's party was approaching the camp, and Piri rode out to greet them. Suleiman's personal guard stopped at the entrance to the encampment and took up perimeter positions. Suleiman's groom took his horse, and another groom brought the Sultan's sword. The servant girded the Sultan with his fabled sword of the House of Osman, and Piri led them into the camp.

"*Salaam Aleichum*, Doctor Hamon," Piri said after formerly greeting Suleiman.

"*Aleichum salaam*, Piri Pasha."

"How good to see you here. Are you going to inspect the camps with our Sultan?"

"With your permission, Grand Vizier," Hamon replied with a bow.

Piri smiled at his friend, who had seen him through the long illnesses of Selim. "You have had all the permission you need," he added, looking at Suleiman, who was now walking ahead toward the front of the camp.

"Well?" Suleiman asked Piri, who had scurried to catch up to the Sultan.

"Difficult, my Lord. Difficult. The battles two days ago were very costly of both lives and morale. The men are grumbling, and I've had to be extremely harsh with anyone caught speaking treasonous words. And, this morning, something bizarre happened."

"Yes?"

"At first light, the knights fired a catapult at my camp. I expected flaming oil or pitch. Or at very least, a mass of dead rotting animals. They have done that many times before, hoping, I think, to spread disease among my troops. Of course we set fire to any of the carcasses that land within the camp. But, today, they sent us the body of a man. It was not rotting, and, in fact, the body was still warm. He had been quartered before they sent him to us. I don't know what to make of it. There," he said, pointing to a small crowd of soldiers. "There it is."

Suleiman turned toward the crowd, with Ibrahim and Hamon close behind. As the Sultan approached the men, the sentries cleared a path. A corridor opened, and all heads bowed low as Suleiman passed before them. Only the sounds of the cannon persisted, unchanged by the presence of the Sultan.

Suleiman and Piri walked to the center of the circle. There on the ground were the battered remains of Apella Renato. Ibrahim came and stood beside Suleiman. Finally, Hamon made his way to the body.

Renato's remains had been arranged by the soldiers into a semblance of normalcy. Though the clothes were in tatters, someone had lined up the legs with the torso. The head remained attached to the right side of the chest. Many had seen this grisly site before, a common form of execution then.

There were a few minutes of silence, when suddenly, there was a stifled gasp from Hamon. Suleiman and Piri turned to face him, and saw Hamon standing there with his hand over his mouth and the blood drained from his face. He looked up at Suleiman and said, "I know this man. I'm sure I know this man."

"Who is he?" said Suleiman.

"Well...he is...was...a doctor. I knew him in Istanbul, many years ago. Perhaps ten or fifteen years ago. His name is Apella Renato."

"And?"

"He practiced medicine in the Jewish Quarter. My father knew him, too. I think they worked together from time to time, in the royal court. About ten years or so ago, he disappeared. He had no family, so it was a while before anybody knew he was gone. Word spread about the community, as it will when one of us—a Jew—goes missing. But, we never heard. There were rumors. But, we never knew for sure. Why do you think he was up there?" Hamon asked pointing to the ramparts of the city.

Suleiman turned to Piri Pasha and raised his eyebrows in question. "Majesty, do you think...?"

"It's possible. Who else could this be? Who else would merit being drawn and quartered and thrown into our camp?"

Hamon looked back and forth between Suleiman and Piri. "My Lords?"

Suleiman hesitated, and then said to Hamon, "My father sent a spy to live among the knights about the time you said this man disappeared. We've received information from him regularly all these years, and several pieces of information during this siege. It makes sense that this is he. What else but treason would merit such an execution?"

Hamon knelt down in the sand and moved Renato's chin up a bit. "He was definitely hanged first. Look here, at these rope burns on the neck. And he lived long enough to sustain these purple bruises there, too," he added, pointing to the discoloration in Renato's neck. "From the rest of the bruising," he pointed to the body parts, "I would say he was alive until the time he was quartered, poor man. Dear God, what an awful thing to do."

Suleiman turned to walk away. Piri and Ibrahim followed without another word. Hamon stood in his place and said, "Majesty."

Suleiman stopped, and turned to see what the doctor wanted. Hamon looked at his Sultan with a hint of pleading in his eyes. "Majesty, this man worked for us. For the Muslim armies of the Sultan. He was a doctor and a Jew. I feel a commitment to what he did on our behalf; a proper service and burial for him. Surely he deserves more for his suffering than to lie here in this strange place to be eaten by the crows?"

Suleiman sighed, and said, "Doctor, I can understand how you feel. But, we do not have the time or the facilities to bury every soldier who dies in our cause," and he pointed in the direction of the ditches now overflowing with Turkish corpses. "But in deference to the services you and your family perform for the Sultan, I will allow you a little time to say the appropriate prayers and arrange for his body to be properly wrapped and buried in a small grave. You may see to it now. Some of my guards will escort you back to the *serai* when you are done." Hamon bowed his head, and remained in that position until the Sultan had left.

Suleiman said a few words to Piri Pasha, who gave the orders to five of the Janissaries. Then, Suleiman, Piri Pasha, and Ibrahim walked back along the corridor of soldiers to their horses.

Suleiman rode back to the tent on Mount Saint Stephen wondering about the siege he had started; weighing the cost in the lives of his loyal young army against the gain to the Empire. It troubled him deeply to sacrifice so many young men for this little island fortress. *This is the burden of command,* he thought, *that will bear down on my soul for the rest of my life.*

When the Sultan was gone, Hamon supervised the wrapping of the body in a plain white shroud. After the soldiers dug a shallow grave, he stood by the body and looked out over the sea south and east, in the direction of Jerusalem. Among the noises of the cannons and the shaking of the earth, he began to recite the *Kaddish*—the Sanctification—a prayer recited for the dead.

"Yis-gadal v'yis-kadash sh'mey raba, b'alma di v'ra hirutey…" Magnified and sanctified be God's great name in the world which He has created according to his will…

Hamon supervised the lowering of the body into the small grave, and threw a symbolic handful of dirt onto the white shrouded body. He stood over the hole in the ground as the soldiers shoveled the dirt back into the grave. When they were done, the soldiers picked up their shovels and returned to their duties.

Hamon stood there for a moment, and said quietly, "Goodbye, Apella. God's peace be with you." Then, he looked to the horizon again, and said, *"Shema Yisrael, Adonoi eloheynu, Adnoi echod."*

⌒

September 23rd, 1522. Philippe called the meeting to order. The Piliers, ranking officers from each of the *langues*, were seated at the long oak table. Even Andrea d'Amaral was on time for this critical strategy session. The Servants-at-Arms formed a second circle around the table, standing behind their masters.

Philippe looked weary as he began the session. Dark bags of loose skin hung beneath his eyes. His gray hair and beard served only to make him look old now, not distinguished and vibrant as they once did. He sat in a tall backed chair with leather padding, and leaned forward on his elbows. "Gentlemen, we have reason to believe that the Turks are preparing a major assault. The tactic has now changed, and we might be in for a general assault on several fronts at once." He looked to Thomas Scheffield, his *Seneschal*, and said, "Thomas?" Then Philippe reclined in his seat.

Thomas Sheffield, Commander of the Palace of the Grand Master, stood. "My Lords, there has been unprecedented activity in the Turkish lines. Troop movements and changes in the disposition of the artillery. Our sentries have reported a general shift of manpower away from the northern and western ramparts to the south and the southeast of the city. Though they have tried to conceal it, we can see that troops have massed in front of Aragon, England, Provence, and Italy. We have seen men moving in the night through the gardens outside the ditches, and concentrating to the south. There seems little question that the Sultan plans a general assault, so we must change our strategy in response. We don't have enough manpower to plug gaps in all the locations at once, should their cannon and mines break through on several fronts."

Scheffield sat down, and John Buck stood up. "Our only hope of repelling a general assault is to be mobile. We must have our system of sentries and runners in place so that we can know where and when more knights are needed. If the Turks make a breakthrough in *any* point in the walls, they will pour into the city like a tide, and we will then have them at our backs as well as our front. We cannot possibly confront so many men with the numbers of knights and mercenaries we have left. So, it's imperative that we continue to block each opening as it occurs, and repel each assault as it occurs." Buck looked to Philippe for any additional comments. Philippe said nothing.

Buck continued. "Gentlemen, this could be the decisive battle of the siege. I've heard that there is a great discontentment growing in the lines of the Sultan. His soldiers are unhappy and demoralized at the sight of the thousands of dead comrades lying in the ditches around our castle. And so they should be. If we can hold off this general assault, and continue to slaughter them with minimal loss on our side, it may turn the tide against them. Suleiman may find his men unwilling to fight. The great-grandfather retreated just before the bad weather in his assault forty years ago, and I expect Suleiman may do the same. The weather is just starting to deteriorate now, and will get worse in very short order. So, we must demoralize them with a resounding victory when the general assault comes. We will count upon Tadini's men, and their newfound accuracy from the parapets, to send death down upon the Turks from the sky. The enfilade must not stop until the Turk is in full retreat, and then we must harry them in their rout. Any questions?"

There were none. The somber faces spoke to the fact that the knights were all well aware of the critical nature of their condition. The coming battle could be the last of the siege.

The knights rose at a signal of dismissal from Philippe and left the Palace of the Grand Master. They returned to their *langues* and briefed the men under their commands.

Philippe remained alone, staring at the plans and the disposition of his men. As night approached, everyone in the city could hear the movement of the Sultan's troops and his machines of war. There was no doubt that the dawn would bring another day in hell.

—

September 24th, 1522. Nearly nine weeks of siege. The *muezzin's* voice broke the still morning air before first light. Even as the soldiers of Islam spread their prayer mats on the grass and turned their bodies to face the southeast—to the holy city of Mecca—the Sultan's artillery shattered the stillness. The sounds of the prayers mingled with voices of the cannon; the Faithful felt the earth shake beneath their knees as they asked Allah for his guidance and protection in the coming assault on the Infidel. There was the might of the cannons and the rumble of the earth as they spoke directly to God. Their song of faith and trust was backed by the accumulated might of their religion and their Sultan, Suleiman, the Shadow of God on Earth.

The Sultan sat upon his raised platform, flanked by Ibrahim and Hamon. Hamon had waited quietly while Suleiman and his friend concluded their prayers. All the Aghas were already in the field, commanding their men and ordering the sequence of the attack. The target for the artillery that morning was the entire southern perimeter. Just as the knights had guessed, the cannons were massed to strike simultaneously at the ramparts and bastions of Aragon, England, Provence, and Italy. The walls and towers at Italy were already a shambles. The rubble and debris were piled high, affording little protection.

In the first hours of the day, the smoke and the noise literally deafened and blinded both the attackers and the defenders at once. Smoke choked both sides of the conflict; dust and smoke obscured any view of the battlefield. The knights behind their wall could scarcely determine from where the attack was coming. There were no intervals in the barrage of stone and iron missiles. A continuous stream of fire poured into the city and against the walls. The knights answered with their batteries. Their pre-aimed cannons still fired with maximum effect. But, powder and cannonballs were in short supply, so the artillerymen were very stingy in their response to the Turkish barrage.

In spite of the massive reinforcements of the fortress, the Sultan's cannons were finally overpowering the defenses of the city. While the knights could make temporary repairs with existing materials from the walls, the Turks had an almost endless chain of ships bringing ever more cannons and powder and shot. There was no limit to the reserves of Suleiman's batteries.

Suleiman watched with satisfaction as the walls of the city started to crumble under the combined effects of his mines and his artillery. Time had finally caught up with the defenders of Rhodes, and the neverending mining and artillery barrages overpowered the stone walls of the fortress. As the morning wind picked up and blew away some of the dust, Suleiman could see whole sections of the bastions and the walls come down. While the Post of Italy was already in ruins, the Sultan did not take his eyes off the Bastion of Aragon. For, there, he knew, was where the first wave of his Janissaries would mass. Led by their *Seraskier*, Bali Agha, his elite troops would pour into the city and decimate the small defending force of knights. That was the plan of the Sultan, and Allah would make it so.

"Keep your eye on the walls there," Suleiman said, pointing to his left at the walls of Aragon. "Though you cannot tell yet, as I hope the knights cannot tell either, the heaviest cannonade is directed just there, and that will be the first breach. When the cannons stop and the smoke clears, you will see a wave of blue uniforms pour into that breach, and return only when they are red with the blood of the knights."

Ibrahim and Hamon strained to see where Suleiman was pointing, but there was still too much smoke. Then, the wind increased and the cannons stopped, and the charging forces of Bali Agha filled what had been emptiness. Even from so far away, the observers could see the Raging Lion at the head of his troops, waving his scimitar and shouting for the advance. To the accompaniment of the drums and cymbals and trumpets, a thousand cries of *"Allahu akbar"* drifted across the fields of fire to the ears of the Sultan sitting on his throne.

It took several minutes for the knights to respond. As the Janissaries scrambled over the rubble and the bodies of their brothers in the ditches, the knights sent word to their mobile troops. The few defenders were soon joined by hundreds more mercenaries and knights, who rallied at the Post of Aragon. The Rhodian men took up arms as well, grabbing at anything that could be used for a weapon. They, too, felt the rush of energy as the knights assembled in their battle capes. To the citizens of the city, the knights had begun to seem invincible as they drove back wave after wave of Turkish soldiers in the previous attacks. The stink of the rotting corpses in the ditches served only to verify their faith in the knights.

Women rushed along the battlements carrying powder and shot. They brought water to the knights and helped move the wounded. While the explosions of the Turkish artillery rained down into the city, the revitalized citizens ignored the danger and supported the defenders.

Opposite the walls of Aragon, Bali Agha surged forward at the head of his beloved Janissaries. As legend had decreed, his men did use the bodies of their brothers as stepping stones into the breach. Just before their advance, the Turkish artillery had finally opened a large hole in the Bastion of Aragon. "Forward!" screamed Bali Agha as the men slipped and scrambled up the sloping terrain. As they neared the walls, they encountered retrenchments that Tadini had constructed to slow their advance. A steep palisade confronted the Janissaries and further slowed them down.

The knights rallied to Aragon, gunners and archers on the nearby rooftops and battlements opening fire on the Janissaries who were now entering their range. Again, as before, a murderous crossfire tore into Bali Agha's men, and the Janissaries started to suffer terrible losses. But, none could stop to help their fallen comrades.

Bali Agha had made it clear that every man's sole duty was to reach the city and slay as many Christians as possible.

Four Janissaries in the vanguard reached the walls and planted their standards. Among them was the four-tailed standard of Bali Agha. But, the *Bunchuks* with their black horses' tails flew only briefly in the wind, and were soon cut down and trampled by the advancing knights.

Hand-to-hand battle began along the walls of Aragon as the knights assembled. Quickly, they formed their wall of iron men: as always, immovable. Implacable. Their reputation was not lost on the Janissaries, who, brave as they were, had never before encountered a foe so determined, so skillful at close-in fighting. The Janissaries' battle experience had often been against troops who broke and ran at the very sight of the Sultan's army. They were not used to such an unflappable foe.

The advance slowed, and Bali Agha began to rage at his men. He called them names. He swore, he sweated. He swung his scimitar wildly in the air to drive them forward. But, it was to little avail, for the fire pouring down upon them from the city was killing more soldiers than were reaching the walls.

Once there, the Janissaries could not get or maintain a foothold. The knights formed their phalanx and beat back every advance with broadsword, ax and pike. Then, to add to the slaughter, from the left, the guns on the walls of Auvergne opened up upon Bali Agha's forces.

Suleiman watched the massive movement. From his perspective, when the conditions allowed, he could view whole sections of his army move forward, and then retreat before the withering fire and the hand-to-hand fighting with the knights. After two hours of back-and-forth movement, Suleiman could see his Janissaries make one last determined effort, surging forward onto the battlements of Aragon. The fighting was wild, and the knights rushed more reinforcements to the scene.

The Grand Master was in every breach, in every parapet. To the Turks, it seemed that there must be a dozen gray-haired men upon the battlements that day, and a dozen banners of the Crucifixion.

THE SHADOW OF GOD

But, all were Philippe, rushing to where the battle raged against the knights, supporting his brave men with his presence and his sword. Toward the end of the morning, with no chance to rest, he arrived on the ramparts of Aragon, where the massive assault by Bali Agha was still contested.

He called to Jean de Morelle, who was fighting fiercely to protect the Bastion. "Jean?" he called as the battle went on around them.

"We have gained and lost this post today more times than I can count," Jean shouted over the din. "They plant their standards, and we push them back. But, they're moving more men into the breach, and I don't know if we can hold them much longer."

"Hold them, Jean. Whatever the cost, hold them! I'll help you all I can. I'll send for Jacques de Bourbon, and have him make a surprise attack from the Turkish rear. He'll split their forces."

"But, how....?" Jean never finished his question. He was suddenly attacked by two Janissaries at once. He turned back to his battle and lashed out with his heavy weapon. His sword slashed through the sword-arm of the man to his right, and in the follow-through, he backslashed the haft into the face of the other young man who had entered the space. As the man fell, Jean stabbed him in the neck, killing him on the spot. Then, he turned to where the Grand Master had been, but Philippe was gone. Jean took two deep breaths and rushed into the growing mass of Janissaries, slashing his way forward to wedge his shoulders against those of his brother knights.

—◆—

Jacques de Bourbon crawled through the tunnel directly beneath the Tower of Aragon, at the edge of the Post of Auvergne. The tower had fallen to the Turks less than an hour ago, and the Grand Master had ordered Jacques to retake it. "Take a small band of your best men, whomever you need, and slip out of the city through one of Tadini's tunnels. Attack them from the rear and fight your way back in."

For an hour, Jacques and his band of ten men crawled and choked and coughed in the darkness and the dust. They could feel the walls rumble as the Turkish cannon fire continued, trying to open still more breaches in the walls. The returning fire from the knights had silenced many of the Turkish positions, but now Jacques wished that they would stop, just for a while, before the damned tunnel collapsed in upon him. About halfway down the tunnel, Jacques felt a tremendous shudder beneath his feet as a Turkish cannon sent its massive stone ball into the walls. The earth shook harder than ever, and the walls began to collapse around his band of knights. "Forward!" he shouted to the men behind him. *"Vite! Vite!"*

The earth and rocks began to rain down upon their backs as they rushed in a crouch from the blackness of the tunnel. Several of his men stumbled to their knees as they tripped over fallen rocks. They felt their way through the blackness, their torches extinguished by the debris. One hand on the sword hilt, the other in front of their heads, they moved like blind subterranean dwellers through the unstable hell of the tunnel. After another thirty minutes of choking and stumbling, they saw ahead of them the gray, smoke-filled battlefield outlined in the concealed opening to the tunnel. Jacques and his men emerged into the air to fight their way back up onto the ramparts.

In a near frenzy now, Melina rushed through the choked ward, trying to be everywhere at once. The babies cried behind the closed door of her room, but she barely had time to tend to them. The ward was chaos. Since Doctor Renato had been executed, there was nobody left who worked with the speed and constancy that he could. They needed his direction and his energy. They needed his leadership. Morale in the hospital was at its lowest just when the doctors and their helpers were needed most. The other doctors and assistants were overwhelmed with the workload. Many of the wounded died from unintentional neglect. Most of the dead lay where they fell on the battlements, and some of the wounded were never carried to the hospital. Still, scores of soldiers and civilians arrived in the ward needing immediate care. Some did not receive it. Many lay on the broad staircase that led to the ward, placed there by others too harried and tired to bring them all the way into the ward. Several died on the staircase, neglected and alone.

Melina worked as best she could, but she was terrified for Jean. She knew that the Grand Master used him to plug every dangerous hole in the battle line, and that Jean had not rested since the battle had begun so many hours before. She kept glancing from her work toward the entryway, hoping that he would rush in to see her; dreading that he might be carried in wounded or....She could not finish the thought. Her mind closed itself to the possibility that her great knight could die.

In the afternoon, she had still not seen him. She questioned the wounded who could speak, and several had told her that Jean was fighting near Aragon, where the battle was at its fiercest. She worried all the more, but at least he had been seen alive, still fighting.

Finally, Melina could stand it no longer. She finished the dressing she was applying to the severed hand of a mercenary. When the dressing was tight and it seemed the bleeding had slowed sufficiently, she grabbed some stale bread and a skin of water. She ran down the steps of the hospital, hurried through the Street of the Knights, and out of the *Collachio*. Running through the rubble and between the ruined houses, she made her way to the Post of Aragon. When she turned the corner and mounted the wooden ladder, she could scarcely believe her eyes. The once-strong bastion was now barely a ruin. The walls had crumbled, and the knights were locked in a sea of entangled bodies struggling to force back the invading tide of Turks and secure the breach.

Melina climbed up on the flat stones of the walls, now littered with the debris of battle as well as the debris of death. Bodies and limbs were strewn about so that there was hardly a place to stand in safety. Knights continued to fight off the last remaining Janissaries, struggling for possession of the breach. The last of the Sultan's ferocious troops would not yield their ground, even as their brothers retreated before the oncoming darkness. The sun had already set behind the western walls of the fortress, and the Janissaries, locked in combat, were back-lit by evening glow. The ferocity of the fighting was hardly believable after so many long hours. But, neither side could find it in themselves to yield the hard-contested ground.

Melina protected herself as best she could as she searched for Jean. Now, she was determined to find him alive and fighting, or find his wounded body on the ground. She moved up and down the walls until, after many minutes of danger and frustration, she saw the silhouette of the banner of the Grand Master flowing in the fading light. She knew Jean would be close by.

She pressed on, and there he was. His unmistakable figure, so familiar in every aspect, was engaged in a terrible fight. The Grand Master was to his right, preparing for another threat from the foreground. Jean was about to parry a sword stoke, protecting Philippe, who never saw the attack on his flank. But, though Melina could not discern in her conscious what was wrong, she knew in her soul that Jean was in danger. She could not comprehend that he held his sword in the wrong hand. She could see that his right hand was badly injured. She saw only the awkwardness of his defense as the two blue-uniformed Janissaries plunged forward. One drove his sword directly into Jean's exposed neck, while the other slashed across his outstretched left arm. The only protection Jean could offer, a left-handed parry, had failed. Melina watched as Jean slipped slowly to the ground.

That he was dead was clear. The Janissaries immediately ignored the fallen knight and moved on to other targets.

Melina did not rush to Jean's side. She did not cry out. She did not scream. She only stood there, staring at the fallen body of her lover, the father of her twins. After several minutes, ignoring the knights fighting all around her, she walked slowly to Jean's side. She knelt down in the blood that spilled from his neck and his partially severed left arm, and looked into his eyes through the raised visor. There was recognition in his eyes, and a trace of a smile that curled the corners of his mouth. He opened his lips to speak, but there emerged only a red-frothed foam, and no sound. She looked again at his eyes, but no light shone back at her. She squeezed her own eyes shut for a second, then placed her thumb and forefinger on his lids and closed them.

Melina bent to Jean's face and kissed him on his lips, which were still warm and wet from the exertion of moments before. When she rose, her eyes were dry and her face impassive. She uncurled the fingers of his clenched fist and removed the sword from his hand. When she stood, at last, her long gray dress was covered with Jean's blood.

She turned from the battle and again, ignoring the knights, walked slowly from the parapet. She descended the wooden ladder, dragging the heavy broadsword at her side. She walked past the ruined streets without noticing anything, thinking only of her lover lying dead on the wall. As she turned into the *Collachio*, she increased her pace, so that by the time she reached the hospital she was running. Her long black hair flowed behind her. She raced up the wide outside stairs, and went directly into the huge hospital ward. She nodded to Hélène, who was busy in the ward, and without a word to anyone, opened the door to the room where her twins were waking up. She put the sword aside and picked the babies up in her arms. Now her tears began to flow, and the babies began to cry with her. She opened the top of her bodice, and removed her milk-swollen breasts one at a time. Then she curled the little girls into the crook of each arm and let them nurse.

She leaned back against the hard cold stone, closed her eyes, and let the tears flow as her milk flowed into the babies' lips. She felt the hardness against her back, and thought of Jean lying against the hard cold stone of the battlement that rumbled with the barrage. As the babies nursed, she remembered every day of her life with Jean. Their meeting in the market. His coming past her house each day, hoping to see her. Their trip to Petaloudes. She tried to remember every moment. Every single day of their short lives together. She recalled the last time they had made love in this very room, and now wondered whether another angel was growing inside her womb.

When she finally looked down, she saw that the girls were fast asleep. Time was lost to her, and she had no idea how long she had been dreaming. She wiped the milk from her babies' lips and placed them gently down into their bed. Then she tucked the babies snuggly in to their bed and tied the cords that closed her bodice. She leaned down and kissed them each again.

She closed the door and threw the latch shut, the first time she could recall locking the small room from the inside. Then she sat on the floor next to the sleeping twins. She took the pillow from her own bed, placed it lightly over the faces of her two baby girls, and pressed down.

After some time, she didn't know how long, she removed the pillow and placed it under their heads. Then she took the clean white cape that Jean kept on a peg behind the oak door and covered their bodies.

Melina unlatched the door, and picked up Jean's sword. She closed the door behind her to keep the sounds of pain and death out of the room of her little girls. Unseen by Hélène or the other busy workers, she left the hospital and walked slowly down the Street of the Knights, and out of the *Collachio*.

Melina climbed the stairs once more and stepped on to the battlefield atop the walls. She walked among knights even as they fought with the Janissaries, ignoring them all. She knelt again beside Jean's body, and carefully undid the leather straps that held his armored breastplate. She strapped it onto her own body, and then removed his helmet as well. Though the helmet was far too big for her, her full head of hair filled the space and held it snuggly in place. She lowered the steel visor, still pungent with her dead lover's breath. Then she stood again, holding the sword in front of her by its hilt, the blade pointing to the earth. With the cross of war in front of her, she murmured words of prayer in Latin and Hebrew for her fallen lover. Then, she turned the sword around and raised the blade high over her head. With the power of fury and little if any skill or grace, she waded into the Janissaries who stared at her with disbelief. Her small body smashed into the enemy, and in the first seconds of her vengeful attack, she slew three of the Turkish soldiers before they could react.

Covered now in the blood of both her lover and his killers, she turned her wrath on the next in line. Before her sword could fall again, a scimitar appeared before her eyes, like a specter, hanging free in the air. A second later, the blade transected her neck. She dropped her heavy sword and, as she fell, her helmet tumbled from her head, bouncing across the stones. The Janissaries watched her shiny black curls float free and encircle her face as she fell. She toppled backwards from the blow and, slumped across the body of her lover, now growing cold in the late afternoon air.

The Janissaries backed away, terrified of an enemy whose women would fight to the death alongside their men. As these Janissaries followed the last of Bali Agha's troops backing down from the walls, the light left the field and darkness closed over the dead bodies scattered all about the walls of Rhodes.

⊰ 16 ⊱

THE BREATH OF KINGS

Rhodes
September 25th, 1522

The Aghas gathered in the Sultan's tent. Mustapha Pasha had not had time to change into clean clothes. He stood before the Sultan with his head bowed, his face smeared with a brown dried crust, a mélange of blood and the dirt of Rhodes. A servant brought him a wet towel, with which he quickly wiped his face and hands. There was little he could do to improve the condition of his uniform without keeping the Sultan waiting longer than he dared.

The summons had come just as the Aghas returned to their camps from the battle. Couriers rushed to the *serais* of Bali Agha, Mustapha Pasha, Piri Pasha, Achmed Agha, Ayas Agha, and Qasim Pasha. All the generals stopped what they were doing, mounted their horses, and galloped to the tent of the Sultan. Ayas Agha, too, had been caught short, and showed up in his dirty battle gear, fresh with the blood of his enemy as well as that of his own men.

Suleiman sat upon his raised throne at the head of the tent. Ibrahim was standing at his side. The Aghas were bid by the household guard to stand before the Sultan. This, too, was a bad sign, because most of the meetings with the Sultan in the battle-field lately had been less formal. Usually, Suleiman reclined on a *divan,* and his generals and advisers were allowed to sit on their own *divans.*

The Aghas kept their eyes fixed upon the woven gilt carpet, fearing to attract Suleiman's attention. It was a child's ruse that would not work.

With slow and measured speech, Suleiman, his voice low, his eyes fixed on Mustapha Pasha, began, "You have deceived me, brother-in-law. No, rather, you have miscalculated badly, and that error has cost the lives of thousands of my soldiers. You promised me an early and easy victory over the Sons of *Sheitan*." His voice rose, and his speech quickened. "You promised me the heads of the knights to decorate the walls of their fortress, but *my* men are rotting in the ditches; *filling* the ditches with their bodies and their blood!" Signs of rage appeared on Suleiman's face, and Ibrahim squeezed his eyes against what he knew was coming next. "You are a *traitor* to your Sultan. You are a *coward* and a *liar!* You are..." he sputtered momentarily, "you are forthwith condemned to die for your treachery!" He turned to the Janissaries at the door and said, "Take him away. Hold him in chains until dawn, when I will arrange for his execution."

Ibrahim looked at Suleiman out of the corner of his eye. He dared not show his horror at this terrible injustice. Mustapha Pasha was an absolutely fearless soldier who had served his Sultan without a thought for his own safety. Not only was he married to the Sultan's eldest sister, he had been a lifelong close and loyal friend. Ibrahim could not believe his ears, nor could any of the Aghas.

The Janissaries rushed to surround Mustapha. Their haste was unnecessary. Mustapha never moved, nor did he protest. He removed his sword from his waistband and handed it to the Janissaries. With his head still bowed, he submitted to his master, and walked silently away with his jailers.

The only sound in the tent was the labored breathing of the Sultan, himself. He wiped a few flecks of spittle from his lips with a silk handkerchief and stuffed it back in the sleeve of his caftan. The Aghas remained silent, each wondering whose neck would become the next target for the executioner's axe.

The blood of Selim courses through the veins of our Sultan, Bali Agha thought. *May Allah have mercy upon us.*

In the silence, Suleiman continued to brood. His anger was not yet cooled by the sentence he had so cruelly inflicted upon Mustapha. He was about to turn on Ayas Pasha, whose losses in the attack against Auvergne and Germany had been the greatest of the day.

Before the Sultan could speak, Piri Pasha stepped forward. The Janissaries braced. One of the young troops closest to Suleiman placed his hand on the hilt of his scimitar as Piri stepped closer to the Sultan. Piri looked directly into the eyes of the young soldier and scowled. He put his hand out, and wagged a chastising finger, as if scolding a presumptuous child.

The Janissary took his hand off the scimitar and returned to attention, eyes staring off into the unfocused distance. Piri took another step, so that he was now only six feet from the Sultan's throne, and well in front of the other Aghas.

His voice was soft, the words slow and measured. There was unmistakable resolve in his tone and words. It was the voice Piri used when talking to his horse in the fury of battle, calming, reassuring, deliberate.

"Majesty, I beg you allow me these few words." Piri knelt and pressed his head to the carpet. He did not move until Suleiman spoke.

"Very well." The words were terse. Begrudgingly given.

Piri rose slowly, with dignity. He looked directly into the Sultan's eyes, and began to plead the case for his old friend, Mustapha. "Majesty, all the people of the Ottoman Empire know Suleiman as *Kanuni*. The Lawgiver. You have made justice part of your empire. The people know that they can come to the Imperial *Divan* and expect a fair hearing. Always law and justice."

Piri spoke evenly and without emotion. "Your *Seraskier*, your brother-in-law, your old friend, Mustapha Pasha, fought with all the valor and might that he possessed. If he erred, it was in the measurement of the knights' determination and bravery. But that does not in any way diminish the bravery of Mustapha and his men. For two months now, they have fought and died for you. Mustapha has been there at the vanguard of every attack, every battle. He is always the first into the breach, and the last to leave the field. He stood here in his bloodied battle dress because he was still fighting when your summons called him to your tent. He continued to fight, even though the battle was lost, and all the rest of us had left the field."

Suleiman stared at his Grand Vizier, but revealed nothing. Piri went on, his tone and pace unchanged. "To condemn this brave and valiant man to death because he lost the battle is a grave injustice. It does not befit *Kanuni*, the most just of the Sultans of the Osmanlis."

In that one second, that moment it took to utter the words, Piri knew he had gone too far. Before he could regret the indiscretion, Suleiman screamed back at him. "Injustice! You dare speak to *me* of injustice? Guard! Take this man away. Let him join Mustapha Pasha in his cell, and they can die together on the morrow!"

Now the Aghas gasped aloud. They all looked up to see the Sultan's face. Even Ibrahim could not take his eyes from Suleiman's. *Piri Pasha? He would execute Piri Pasha?* Ibrahim wondered. *And if Piri Pasha, then anyone can perish today!*

Piri remained absolutely calm. Piri had survived eight years with Selim. There was little that frightened him now. *I have lived a decade longer than I thought I would. I have spoken my truth. If I must die now, I have, at least, served two Sultans well,* he thought. *Who else on God's earth can say that?*

Suleiman turned back to the Aghas, as Piri was led quietly away by the Janissaries. "Achmed Agha!"

Achmed stepped forward, awaiting his sentence of death.

"You are now the *Seraskier* of all my armies. You will be Commander-in-Chief. Do not fail me." Suleiman's black eyes stared at his new commander, and the threat was audible in his words.

"Yes, Majesty. Thank you," was all that Achmed could say. Already, his mind swam with the prospect of how to reverse the defeats the knights had inflicted upon the Sultan's armies. How could he prevail, and preserve his own life? It was clear that the penalty for failure was death, either on the battlefield or at the hands of the Sultan. *Could* the knights be defeated? Was it possible that the Sultan's tens of thousands could not overcome the knights' hundreds? Achmed bowed and moved back to his place. Silence again filled the room.

Then, "Ayas Pasha!"

Ayas stepped forward, his eyes cast down. He knew, without doubt, his fate. His army suffered the greatest losses of the day in the battle for Auvergne and Germany. He would pay the penalty with his life.

"I have not yet determined the punishment for your inadequacy as a general. You will be placed in chains and held until I make up my mind. Take him away!"

Only Ibrahim, Bali Agha, Qasim, and Achmed remained in the room. But, the four men had each noticed the slightest change in the Sultan's mien. The very act of condemning the Grand Vizier and Mustapha to death seemed to have taken some of the fire from his rage. He appeared slightly calmer now, and the redness no longer suffused his face. The Sultan breathed easier, the tension in the room lessened. It seemed that, at last, the executions would end, and the remaining Aghas could get back to their war.

But, with what? Suleiman had removed his most experienced and bravest generals from the field. What would their dismissal do to the morale of the already demoralized troops?

Bali Agha, Suleiman's "Raging Lion," stepped forward. His eyes begged to be recognized. Suleiman nodded, and the Agha knelt in front of the throne. He slowly drew his scimitar, catching the attention of the Janissaries on guard on either side of the Sultan. They drew their weapons and placed themselves between Bali Agha and the Sultan, their blades just inches from Bali Agha's throat.

Bali Agha ignored them entirely. He balanced his scimitar across the open upturned palms of his two hands. He held it out before him, and placed it on the carpet at Suleiman's feet. At a hand signal from the Sultan, the Janissaries withdrew. Bali Agha knelt, pressing his head to the floor, exposing the back of his neck. "Majesty, take my head here and now, with my own sword, if you must. But, as your loyal servant all these years, as the leader of your own Janissaries, the Sons of the Sultan, I must speak my truth. My body may one day lie with my brothers in the ditches around the fortress of Rhodes. So be it. Or I may die at the hands of your executioner. So be it, too. But,

Majesty, do not do this terrible thing. Be *Kanuni*. Mustapha Pasha, Piri Pasha, Ayas Pasha; these men are the best we have. They are loyal. They are courageous. And they will die willingly to advance your Majesty's cause.

"Their deaths can only give comfort to the knights—may Allah curse them. The Grand Master will rejoice and celebrate at the news, when he hears of the deaths of these three generals. And, he will have good cause to celebrate, for we will have killed our most able leadership, and your most loyal servants. We will have done what the knights with their broadswords could not do."

Suleiman did not speak. Ibrahim stared at Bali Agha, marveling at the bravery of this man, still kneeling before the Sultan, his white neck exposed to the sword. Qasim Pasha, another trusted officer, took a step forward and asked permission to speak. Suleiman nodded.

"Majesty, Bali Agha has spoken from his heart, and indeed he has risked his head in doing so. I feel ashamed that it has taken me so long to speak my own heart's truth. But, I must agree. If for no other reason, I beg your Majesty spare the lives of your generals, only to prevent our helping the knights. Rhodes will fall to us one day, my Lord. But, we will need all the help that Allah and His Prophet—may sunshine warm his grave—can give us. With the Aghas now in chains, even Allah may not wish to help us in our *jihad*."

Qasim lowered his head and walked backwards to his place.

Bali Agha rose and resheathed his sword. Then, he, too, backed into his place next to Qasim.

Suleiman looked at Achmed Agha, who was standing in front of the others. "And you, my *Seraskier*?"

"Majesty, I cannot say it better than Bali Agha and Qasim have already said. I am a wretched coward who remained silent while my brother Aghas were marched off to their deaths. I beg of you, please, be merciful as Allah is merciful. Be just as Allah is just. Do not give aid to the *Kuffar*. All your Aghas serve you well. No Sultan ever lived who had more loyal servants than they. Restore them to their posts. I have no need to be the Commander-in-Chief. I will gladly return to my troops and resume my normal duties."

Suleiman did not respond to the pleas of the remaining Aghas. He commanded, "Return to your posts, and prepare a plan for the next assault."

The Aghas were taken by surprise. They had expected, perhaps, to join the others in the death cells, but not to be ignored. They bowed and backed through the doorway of the tent. When they were gone, Suleiman dismissed his guard. He motioned to Ibrahim, and the two left the *serai*, walking into the cool air together.

They found an open place above the sea, facing the north, away from the walls of Rhodes. The grass was just turning brown, and the seas were in a constant state of white froth and spume. Autumn was surely giving way to the coming of winter. The two men sat nearly shoulder to shoulder, out of the wind in the shelter of a large tree, looking out over the water. Ibrahim realized how long it had been since the fortress and the war were not in his view. They sat together there, the two old friends, and smelled the fresh air. The onshore winds blew the stink of the rotting corpses back toward Rhodes, away from the promontory. The Sultan and his friend took long deep breaths of the clean air. Neither spoke for what seemed like hours. Finally, the Sultan, now rid of the anger and frustration of the morning, said, "So, what am I to do now?"

⸺

Suleiman and Ibrahim left their quiet vigil by the water and walked back to join the Faithful for prayers. They knelt together on the prayer mats, side by side, and faced toward Mecca far across the water. When they had finished, Suleiman led the way back to his tent, and reclined on his *divan*. "So? Now we have some decisions to make. First of all, there is Mustapha."

Ibrahim had no doubt as to what he must tell the Sultan. He could not hide behind his friendship. If he were ever to rise to higher power than that of the Sultan's boyhood friend, he would have to speak truthfully. "My Lord, I think you *know* the truth. Mustapha is, if nothing else, the most courageous of your Aghas. He would slay the enemy by himself if he had to. His error was in his zeal and his confidence that he could win the battle. But, to die for this...?" Ibrahim held his palms upward with the question.

"You're right, of course," Suleiman replied. "This is not a capital offense. But, having been sentenced to death by me, I think he will have lost the energy and some of the loyalty that he once had. We will demote him." Then, he added with a little laugh, "I'm going to hear more of this, mark my word. He is, after all, still my brother-in-law, and my sister will not take this lightly. So, what shall become of him?"

"Perhaps you can make him governor of some far-off place? Promote him out of your sight. Far enough to be away from your Majesty for extended periods of time?"

"Mmmmm...Egypt? There's always trouble there to keep him busy. And he would be only slightly disgraced. Yes, let him stew a bit longer in his cell. Then have him quietly disappear to his new post. I want no demonstrations of loyalty by his troops. He will disappear, and a new Agha will appear."

"I will see to it. And, Piri Pasha?"

"Of course I will not kill Piri Pasha. Free him at once. Let him return to his old post. He will bear me no grudge for my anger. He survived Selim, his skin must be very tough by now."

"Yes, Majesty. I will see to that as well. And Ayas Pasha?"

"Yes, yes," Suleiman said, wearily waiving his hand in dismissal, "Ayas, too. He shall lead the troops as before."

Ibrahim bowed his head in response and waited. Suleiman had much more on his mind.

"I think that the knights underestimate my determination to stay and fight until I have attained my goal. Well, if that is the case, they have erred."

Suleiman paced the floor for several minutes. He sat down again, and said, "Have my architects make the necessary preparations to build a grand stone pavilion. Let it be in sight of the fortress. I want the knights and my own troops to see that I have made a permanent dwelling place. Send to Syria and Anatolia for more soldiers to fight here, in this place, for this battle. Let it be known by everyone that I am here to stay until all the knights are dead and the island is mine."

"I will, my Lord."

When Ibrahim returned from his mission, Suleiman motioned him to the *divan*. He sent his servants for more food. Clean dishes were brought and set out. The informality of the setting indicated to Ibrahim that Suleiman was ready to seek advice.

"In one moment," Suleiman said, "my Aghas are preparing for the Day of Reckoning. The next, they are back to their stations as if nothing has happened."

Ibrahim was quiet for a moment. Then he said, "Well, not quite, Majesty. Your words can undo what you have done. It is but a whisper that can separate a man from his life. And, a second whisper can restore it. Three lives were condemned last night. This morning three lives were restored. Bali Agha and Qasim Pasha also risked their lives last night. So much hangs on the words of the Sultan, Majesty; so much power in the breath of kings."

❧ 17 ❧

THE LAST TRAITOR

Rhodes
October, 1522

October 11th. At Italy, Provence, Aragon, and England, the breaches were now so great that the knights had been forced to withdraw to a position of safety *inside* the walls. In effect, the city was open. Where breaches had not yet been made, the Turkish miners had advanced completely under walls and emerged inside the city.

The only thing keeping the Janissaries and the rest of the Sultan's army from pouring into the great gaps was the fact that the towers and the high bastions were still standing. From their position, the knights could maintain a withering fire that created a curtain of death for any troops trying to enter.

As the battle resumed, Achmed Agha forced his men forward into the breaches and the tunnels. The guns from Auvergne only slowed his men down, never completely stopping them. Gunners atop the St. John's Gate fired into the trenches. The miners were partially shielded by the leather hides stretched over wooden frames to protect them. Still, the slaughter went on. The bodies of the Turkish dead filled the trenches as fast as their brothers could move them back, or cast them over the sides.

Achmed Agha drove his Azab troops forward. As the men died by the hundreds, the Agha merely sent for more. It was like a giant army of ants pressing forward to gain an important prize.

Unlike the knights, the Sultan, it seemed, would never run out of bodies.

———

Tadini rarely left the field now. He seemed to be everywhere at once. He ordered his knights and the remaining slaves back again and again to rebuild the damaged walls. Some of the rubble could be moved to fill in other breaches. He even ordered the less-used towers to be torn down, and the stones used to fill critical holes in the defenses.

But, as the major breaches widened, Tadini had to construct a strong, deep retrenchment—a wall inside a wall—enabling his men to control the breach, and requiring the Turks to build their own parapets in order to get into the city.

At the Bastion of England, the battle was fierce. Tadini had not left the site for many hours. He fought with his knights to stem the in-rushing tide of Turkish soldiers, and moved from wall to impoverished wall to command the battle.

Late in the morning, the Turkish line faltered. Masses of soldiers seemed to be retreating. The knights gathered at the inner retrenchment and peered through the small openings to assess the next move. Tadini pressed his forehead to the rock and searched the field. Most of the Turks were disappearing into the breach, forced back by the increasing fire from his towers.

Suddenly, Tadini's head snapped backwards, propelling him hard into the body of one of the knights. The two fell to the ground. As the knight rolled to free himself, he saw Tadini's limp body slip to the ground. Blood was flowing from his right eye and a growing stain of red was spreading down from his right temple.

A Turkish musketeer standing on the earthworks had propped his long-range weapon on a shooting stick and fired. The metal ball had scored a direct hit, entering Tadini's right eye near the top of the nose, exiting through the right temple at the top of his ear. As though guided by God's hand, the bullet had missed the brain, but took the sight of Gabriele's right eye and knocked him unconscious. In this age, when an infected finger could escalate to death within a few days, there was little hope among his brothers that

Tadini would survive his terrible wound. His bravery and expertise would be sorely missed by his brothers-at-arms.

The knights carried Tadini from the field, through the Street of the Knights to the hospital. There, he lay, attended by Hélène and the few remaining doctors, unable to serve the Grand Master, while the battle for Rhodes raged on about him.

October 27th. The Post of Auvergne.

The man vaulted up the wooden ladder, rushing in a crouch to the wall. He could see the fires of the camp, and even make out figures in front of the tents. It was remarkable how orderly this encampment was; how clean and precise its arrangement after so many months of war and weather and death. He rushed to the wall, crossbow in his left hand, and the arrow already nocked and set. The trigger mechanism was cocked. He took a long breath, let it slowly out, and prepared for his shot. As the last of the air left his lungs, he would complete the increasing pressure on the trigger, and the shaft would fly into Ayas Pasha's camp.

The impact knocked the wind out of the man's chest. He felt pain tear across his left shoulder as he crashed into the stones of the wall. Lights flashed before his eyes as his head struck the rock walk. Two gloved hands held the weapon tight against him.

He stopped his struggling, and as he heard the knight call for help, he knew that it was over. This huge knight, who happened to be on the wall for God knows what reason, would keep him pinned there like a butterfly until more knights arrived.

As the lantern's light washed over the fallen man's face, all three knights froze. The man in black slumped back to the ground in total surrender. The knight with the lantern let out his breath and gasped, *"Mon Dieu!"*

By the time the knights entered the courtyard of the Palace of the Grand Master, the prisoner's robe was torn and muddied. His hands were completely numb from the tight leather thong, and his face was abraded from stumbling into a wall. As he ascended the great staircase, he tripped so many times that he was finally lifted off the ground for the last six steps.

When the knights entered the room without knocking, the Grand Master leaped to his feet. The prisoner was hurled into the room and fell to the floor. He landed on the stones, striking his forehead and his right shoulder.

Philippe stared in utter disbelief as the spectacle before him. He bent slightly at the waist to make sure that he had not mistaken the face. Then, as he returned to his place behind the table, he spoke not a single word, merely shaking his head from side to side

The knights held their positions while the guards remained at attention. The crumpled parchment was placed before the Grand Master, and the guard returned to his place. The room was silent except for the rasping breath of the prisoner. Philippe took up the parchment and held it in front of a candle. His eyes moved across the single page. As he read on, his eyes widened in disbelief. After each sentence he looked at the prisoner's bowed head, then back to the parchment. When he finished reading, he threw the paper onto the table and stared.

Finally, his words measured, his voice cold and hard, Philippe addressed the prisoner. "Explain this. Who wrote this message?"

The prisoner moved his head, slowly raising his eyes to determine whether the Grand Master's words were directed at him. Still, he did not answer.

"Well?" Philippe asked shaking the parchment in the air.

Silence.

"Very well. Take him below. The rack will help him speak to us."

Philippe picked up the parchment and handed it to Antonio Bosio. Bosio read silently. When he finished, he reached out to return the parchment to Philippe. Philippe waved Bosio away. "Tell the Council its content, and then join me below." Philippe strode from the room, leaving Bosio and the knights alone.

As soon as the Grand Master strode from the room, Bosio sat down and read the paper once again. He addressed the knights, who remained standing at their places.

"It is addressed to Ayas Pasha. The handwriting is unmistakable." He turned the paper around and allowed each of the knights to see it. There were gasps of disbelief.

Bosio continued. "The message is to be delivered to the Sultan. It tells him not to abandon the siege, but to press his attack with greater vigor. It says that our morale is low, and that there is dissent among our forces. That our people are at the edge of rebellion. He tells the Sultan it is unlikely we have the will to repulse one more general attack. That our powder and shot are almost exhausted. It says that if the Sultan were to present the Grand Master with almost any reasonable proposal for surrender, it would be accepted."

The knights waited in silence for Bosio to continue. There was no more. Bosio placed the parchment carefully down on the table at the seat of the Grand Master. He motioned toward the door with his head, and the knights moved en masse to the lower chamber, to the prisoner waiting on the rack.

The senior knights stood in a line against the damp stone walls of the torture chamber. There were no windows, the only light coming from the candles placed along the walls. The orange flickering threw a pattern of light across the room, mixing the shadows cast by the structure of the room's only piece of furniture: the rack.

The rough-hewn wood was stained and dark with the sweat and blood of its prior tenants. At one end, a huge cogged wheel stood attached to the main frame. Its spokes radiated from the circumference, and its axle was ratcheted with a metal hinge.

The prisoner was stripped to the waist, shivering in the cold wet air. His wrists were separated now, each bound with a tight leather thong and stretched overhead to a wooden bar at the top end of the rack. His ankles were similarly bound, and fastened to a bar below his feet. In the middle of his body, an angle in the rack pressed upward into the small of his back, so that he lay like an inverted V on the instrument of torture.

In spite of the cold and the shivering, sweat trickled down his body onto the floor. He strained to look up over his head and scan the upside-down faces of the knights. As his eyes moved around the room, he regained his orientation and identified each man, name by name. Finally, his gaze stopped at the foot of the rack, where he found himself staring into the eyes of the Grand Master.

Philippe never took his gaze off the prisoner. "Who wrote the letter?" he asked in the same slow monotone.

Silence.

Philippe nodded to the man tending the wheel, all the while fixing his eyes on the prisoner. The man leaned on the long arm of the turning mechanism, and the wheel moved clockwise a few degrees. The thongs cut deeply into the prisoner's ankles and wrists, and his arms and legs straightened under the strain. The force of the torque pulled the man's back down into the angle of the bench, his spine pressed against the wood. The pressure was unrelenting, but the pain continued to escalate long after the ratchet had caught and the wheel ceased to turn.

The prisoner screamed on the very first turn, and spittle accumulated at the corner of his mouth. Still he did not speak the required words.

"Who wrote the letter?" Philippe repeated, nearly in a whisper now. When he received no reply, he nodded to the torturer again.

Again the lever was moved, the wheel turned, the thongs tightened, the body stretched, and the ratchet set.

Several of the younger knights looked down at their feet. This was the first time they had seen the rack in actual use, and the reality was far more fierce than the lighthearted banter of the stories told around the dinner tables of the *Auberges*.

Again, a scream filled the small room and resounded off the walls. But, this time, there were words in the screams, though no one could understand their meaning. Philippe raised his head a fraction, and again met the eyes of the prisoner, who was gagging from the intense pain.

Philippe nodded to the torturer, and the ratchet was released. The wheel moved back, and the thongs relaxed an inch. Now the prisoner was able to speak.

"Who wrote the letter?" Philippe asked.

The prisoner muttered three words. His voice was thin and his words garbled by his gasping. Philippe leaned forward, as did all the knights. Only the torturer kept his place at attention near the wheel.

The prisoner licked his lips, for now his tongue was dry and his mouth the consistency of sand. It was all he could do to utter the words.

Softly. Falteringly. The prisoner spoke the name again.

The thongs were cut and blood seeped from beneath the leather still tied to his ankles and his wrists. Three guards pulled Blasco Diaz, Servant-at-Arms to Chancellor Andrea d'Amaral, from the rack and dragged him to his cell.

Philippe and his knights returned to the Palace of Grand Master. They convened around the great oak table, awaiting in silence the arrival of d'Amaral.

Four knights raced to the Inn of Castile where d'Amaral was known to be sleeping. Though most of the knights lived in their own homes outside the *Auberges*, d'Amaral's house had been destroyed in the bombardment. Throughout the siege, he stayed in one of the small rooms in the Inn of Castile.

The knights burst through the front door and ran up the one flight of stairs to the Chancellor's room. The door was unlocked, and the four knights pounced upon the sleeping man. D'Amaral struggled at the attack, but in a few seconds he was pinioned beneath the strong arms of the knights. His sword and knife were kicked out of reach, and leather thongs tied his wrists.

To their surprise, the Chancellor did not struggle once he saw who the men were. The knights released his feet, and d'Amaral was helped into his boots. Since the start of the siege, all the knights had slept in their clothes, so d'Amaral was spared the indignity of being dragged through the streets in his nightshirt. He was helped into his boots, his hands rebound, and was marched directly to the Palace of the Grand Master.

Philippe and his knights sat without moving as d'Amaral was thrust into the room. A wooden chair had been placed between the table and the door. D'Amaral was roughly led to the chair and released. He stood facing the Grand Master. After a minute of silence, during which time the two men kept their eyes locked,

Philippe said, "Unbind the Chancellor."

The guards hesitated and looked at the Grand Master for affirmation of what they thought was a mistake. "I said, unbind the Chancellor!"

The guards stepped quickly to d'Amaral's side and cut the leather thongs. D'Amaral removed the leather wristlets and dropped them to the floor without taking his eyes from the Grand Master's. Slowly, he rubbed each wrist, and then sat down on the chair behind him. He sat straight in the chair, feet squarely on the floor. His head was erect, and never once did he take his eyes from Philippe.

Philippe began without preamble. He spoke slowly in the same monotone that he had with the prisoner, Diaz. "Your Servant-at-Arms, Blasco Diaz, was caught tonight attempting to send this message into the camp of the Turks." Philippe shoved the letter across the table, turning it around so that d'Amaral could read it. D'Amaral did not look down, but continued to stare at Philippe. Philippe went on, "Diaz confessed that he has sent many of these letters to the Turk, and that he was acting on your orders; that you wrote the letters in your own hand." Still, there was no reaction by d'Amaral. The other knights were beginning to stir in their places, looking from Philippe to d'Amaral.

"You are charged with treason. We shall gather the witnesses against you and convene a Military Tribunal at the earliest moment." D'Amaral remained mute.

"You will be taken under guard and confined in the Tower of St. Nicholas. Prepare your defense well, Chancellor, for if you are found guilty, you will, I assure you, hang."

Philippe waited two full minutes for d'Amaral to respond. During that time their eyes were locked, the hate between the two old colleagues palpable. When d'Amaral did not respond, Philippe waved his hand toward the door. The guards stepped forward, each holding fresh leather restraints in his hand. Philippe shook his head and nodded toward the door again.

The guards moved to take d'Amaral by the elbows, but the Chancellor stood quickly and turned to go before they could grasp him. The guards hurried alongside as d'Amaral strode out the door and down the stairs of the Palace.

———

Philippe was alone in the planning room for the first time in many weeks. It was late, and life had been an unending round of battle and battleplans. The treachery of d'Amaral had completely absorbed him. So much remained unexplained, incomprehensible. He had known Andrea for decades, had fought together, had lived life as brothers-at-arms. No matter the jealousy. No matter the enmity. It was beyond Philippe's imagination that a hatred could run so deep as to betray the entire Order.

But, of d'Amaral's guilt, Philippe had no doubt. In the mind of the Grand Master, the witnesses and the evidence at the trial were overwhelming. D'Amaral was a traitor, and for this he would die.

Philippe was excruciatingly weary, but sleep would not come. He sat down at his desk and thought he might compose a letter home to his family in Paris, though God alone knew when a ship might be able to leave Rhodes to deliver it. There was a light tapping at his door. He looked up to see Hélène move into the room, wringing her hands and shaking her head.

"The news is all over the city, Philippe. It's not to be believed," she said. "That d'Amaral could have done this..."

"Yes, it's true enough. Andrea was—is—a traitor. He's been spying for the Turks, or at least sending messages for some time. And he has been hiding stores from us. It's unbelievable. But it's true." Philippe motioned to Hélène to come to him.

Hélène nearly tripped on the torn hem of her now-ragged dress. She hugged him tightly to her, her small arms barely able to reach around his large chest. She breathed in the smells of war and death that still clung to his hastily cleaned cloak. As the two stood in the room in silence, her eyes went to his sword and scabbard; his helmet; his armor. All lying in a neat pile, ready for the next attack. How far they were from Paris now, she thought. And she wondered whether they would ever see her city again.

Philippe took her arms and moved her away from him so he could see her. He looked at her in her disheveled state and smiled for a few seconds, when a sadness came over him that he could not control. She, too, had been working unthinkable hours. He also found himself overwhelmed at the thought of all the young knights who had died under his command; of Jean and Melina and their twin babies; of his loyal friend, Henry Mansell; and all the families who would never see their young men again.

Hélène saw the tears forming in Philippe's eyes and pulled him back to her. She felt his body start to shake and heard the beginnings of his sobs. She drew him away from his desk and the room filled with battleplans and weapons. Finally, she took him by his hand and led him to his bed. She gently pushed him down and helped him off with his boots. Then she lay down beside him and held him.

An hour passed in silence. Philippe had dozed briefly, but Hélène remained awake, her mind teeming with questions for Philippe. Finally their eyes met in the dim light.

"Philippe," she said softly, "you must consider surrendering this island to the Sultan."

She could feel Philippe stiffen next to her, but he did not move, did not take his eyes from her. Then, after a long exhalation of breath, he began to speak to her in a voice she had never heard from him. There was no authority, no command. It was as if he were exploring an internal conversation, and she were eavesdropping.

"We still control the city. We hold the walls, and all their military machinery is limited to their cannons and their Janissaries; a few sappers. Their cavalry sits idly by, useless in the face of our walls and our ditches.

"My men are tired; exhausted; but, so it is in every siege. The whole object of siege warfare is to wear us down, and our only chance is to hold off for one more day. Each day, we must live to see still one *more* day. The weather is going to deteriorate soon. His men will be wet and sick and dispirited even more than they are now. You've only to look into the ditches and see the bodies rotting there to know how his armies are suffering..."

"But, Philippe," she said, interrupting him, "our people suffer, too. The hospital is full; we have no real doctors anymore; the people are frightened and they, too, are exhausted. The dead are piling up around us as well. It is not only the Turks whose bodies lie outside to rot. Could we not leave this place and find another home? Your knights have moved so many times. Is it not better to flee with most of your men and pick a better place to defend?"

Philippe did not react, but seemed to stare past her. Hélène fell back upon the pillow, her fire gone. She had pleaded her case for all the people on the island. And still she had no idea what Philippe would do. His knights, she was sure, would do whatever he said. They would never betray their oaths.

When Philippe woke, it was still dark. Hélène was gone, a bedside candle guttering. He rose and pulled on his boots. Then he went to his dresser and washed his face with a few drops of precious fresh water. There had been no bathing for anyone for several weeks now, and Philippe felt as if he wanted to take off his filthy skin.

He lit a new candle and walked into his main room. He still had to have a final word with the man he had condemned to death, and witness the execution. He rubbed his eyes and ran his fingers through the tangles of his white hair. Overwhelmed by his exhaustion, he finally laid his head upon the hard oak table, and again fell into a deep sleep.

Philippe sat quietly in d'Amaral's cell in the basement of the Tower of St. Nicholas. This fortress was set off on the northernmost spur of land between the Galley Port and the Mandraccio. Its cannons covered both harbors, and could reach out to the west nearly into the camps of the Janissaries.

Philippe pulled his robes tighter about him in a vain effort to keep out the dampness and the cold. The room was barely big enough for the wooden bed and a chair. It smelled of urine and sweat. Dried food was left uneaten on a pewter plate on the floor by the bed. The jailers had placed a lighted candle on the floor, so that Philippe would not stumble in the darkness.

Philippe had been sitting in the cell for almost an hour. Word had been sent to the Palace that d'Amaral was now conscious. But, by the time Philippe arrived, the Chancellor was asleep again. Philippe waited.

Finally, d'Amaral stirred and reached for his drink. But his arm would not obey his commands, and he sent the drink spilling across the floor. His moments on the rack had assured that none of his limbs would ever function effectively again. This was the price of his silence.

Philippe ordered more water. When the jailer returned, he took the flagon from him. He knelt down at the side of d'Amaral's cot and held the water to Andrea's cracked lips. D'Amaral drank too fast, and coughed most of the water up onto Philippe's cloak. Philippe wiped himself with his handkerchief and held the flagon to d'Amaral's lips once more. *"Doucement, Andrea. Doucement.* Do not hurry. You will choke."

D'Amaral opened his eyes and stared at Philippe as he drank. "Yes," he rasped, "I will choke soon enough."

Philippe finished feeding d'Amaral the water, and then moved back to his seat. "Andrea," he said, "we have known each other for more than forty years. You have served the Order in battle; at my side; on land; at sea. What happened? What's made you betray your brothers? Surely, it is not that I was elected Grand Master and not you? There is always a loser in an election, yet none before you have gone to such extremes as to betray the Order; to betray the oath you swore before God Almighty."

D'Amaral stared at Philippe, but said nothing.

"Andrea. We are alone now. Diaz is dead. He was hanged this morning, and even as we speak, his quartered parts hang from the battlements. Speak to me, for this might be our last chance. Tell me why you have done this."

D'Amaral licked his lips. He looked up at the ceiling. Then in a calm but hoarse voice, he began. "We quarreled at the Battle of Laiazzo. And, yes, I thought it was my destiny to be the Grand Master of Rhodes. You French have dominated the post for far too long. I was angry, yes. I was hurt. But, I'm a grown man, and know that such defeats are not grounds for treasonous acts. When I was heard to say that you will be the last Grand Master of Rhodes, I was not speaking of treason. I was speaking my truth, as I saw it. The Ottomans have grown too strong for us. We are a small island manned by a small force that cannot expect to remain here forever. The Sultan is determined that we will be destroyed. And, so we shall. We cannot succeed. The Sultan grows stronger and richer every day."

D'Amaral paused, and motioned for the flagon of water. Philippe reached down and helped him to another drink. Then Philippe sat back again and let his comrade continue. "Suleiman now holds Egypt as well as parts of Europe. It is only a matter of time. And, we have lost all our support from Europe. The Pope ignores us; Spain and France are too busy slaughtering each other to send us help; Italy cannot even govern itself, and is crushed by its civil wars. And as for our old friend, Venice...."

Philippe waited for d'Amaral to continue. He knew what Andrea said was true. But, he would not let the knights capitulate to the Muslims. The Order had been on Rhodes for more than two hundred years. They had stopped Mehmet the Conqueror in 1480, and they would stop his great-grandson now.

"What would you have us do, Andrea? The Muslims will slaughter every living person on this island. Not just the knights, but the mercenaries, the citizens. Those they spare will be slaves; the men to row their lives away in some stinking Ottoman galley, the women to be whores in the harem. Is this what we have sworn to Jesus to do? Is this how we are to keep our oaths to protect and to heal?"

D'Amaral closed his eyes. He squeezed his lids shut tight as spasms of pain lancinated through his legs. When the spasms had passed, he said, "Philippe, you have failed to learn about our enemy. So great is your contempt for the Muslims that you refused to know them. Your stubbornness has caused unthinkable suffering for the knights and the Rhodians as well." Philippe began to protest, but d'Amaral continued without pause. "What is driving you, Philippe? Is it your duty to God and Jesus? To the Order? Or are you making up for your sins in Paris? Your broken vows?"

Philippe stiffened in his seat. His fist tightened around the hilt of his sword until his hand hurt. But, he said nothing. D'Amaral went on. "Hasn't the Sultan offered us the opportunity to surrender with honor? With the choice to remain Christians? Have we not been given the chance to stop the slaughter and live beside the Muslims in peace?"

"And you believe this from the Infidel? You've seen our brothers slaughtered. You know what happened at Jerusalem. At Krak de Chevaliers. At Acre. Every remaining person was killed when the Muslims entered the cities. Their promises were lies. Damned lies. It is only by the grace of God that a few knights survived those massacres for the Order to survive with them."

"That was centuries ago, Philippe. Look to Istanbul. Now. The Jews and the Christians live in peace with Muslims there. What will you accomplish by sacrificing all those who still remain alive on Rhodes? For what? The end is already ordained." D'Amaral began coughing and stopped talking while Philippe helped him to some more water.

Philippe slammed his right fist into his left palm. "It is *not* ordained. It is *not* over. Jesus will carry our banner, and we *will* drive the Infidels out of our home." D'Amaral closed his eyes against the verbal onslaught. Philippe stood and said, "Andrea, your treachery is greater than that of Judas; at least *his* resulted in the ultimate greatest good to mankind. But, *yours,* yours might yet cost us Rhodes!"

D'Amaral tore open the remains of his tunic, exposing the red raised scars on his chest. "See my wounds, Philippe. See them? These are my gifts from forty years of service to my Order."

Philippe looked down at the old battle scars spread out across the naked body. D'Amaral licked his lips and caught his breath. His voice was now just a croak and a whisper. "Am I then, now, to tell a lie and sell my honor to save my old limbs from the mere pain of the rack?"

Without another word, Philippe turned his back on d'Amaral and stormed from the cell.

———

Judge Fontanus stood in the doorway to d'Amaral's cell. D'Amaral was dressed in simple prison attire. His robes and his badges of honor had been ripped from him. He was helped to a chair by two guards, for he was unable to stand on his own. His arms hung limply by his sides. D'Amaral looked directly at the judge.

"You have been found guilty of treason by a Military Tribunal of the Order of the Knights Hospitaller of St. John. You have failed to make any defense or statements of mitigation. You have refused the solace of a priest of the Holy Roman Church. If you have no further statement to make, it is my duty to order that your execution proceed at once."

D'Amaral stared at Fontanus, but said nothing. Fontanus said, "Very well. You will be hanged by the neck until dead. Your remains will be displayed upon the walls of the city. May God Almighty have mercy upon your soul." With that, Fontanus led the way to the gallows. Two knights carried the broken body of the once powerful Grand Chancellor Andrea d'Amaral from his cell.

In front of a gathering of two hundred knights, Rhodians, and mercenaries, Andrea d'Amaral was hanged. When he was dead, his body was quartered and his head removed. The pieces were taken each to a separate battlement and set upon a spike, where they were left until nearly completely devoured by hungry ravens. After several days, what little remained of Grand Chancellor Andrea d'Amaral was placed in a catapult and hurled from the battlements into the camps of the Turks.

✄ 18 ✄

SHOULDER TO SHOULDER

Rhodes
November, 1522

The weather on Rhodes had been deteriorating since the middle of October. By November, the prevailing easterly winds brought bitterly cold wet gales across the water from the direction of the Turkish mainland. The rain rarely let up long enough for the Sultan's troops to dry out before being soaked again. It was difficult to keep the fires going, for there was little dry wood to be found.

The ditches around the city had filled with water, and the resulting mix of mud and blood made movement within them all but impossible. The bodies of the dead lay unburied, swollen and stinking in the rain. Attempts at digging graves were hopelessly inadequate, for the water and mud filled the graves before the bodies could be set down and covered.

Disease spread through the camps. The doctors were kept busy trying to fight illnesses whose causes were unknown, and for which they had no effective medicines anyway. From time to time, in their frustration, each side resorted to catapulting the most odorous and decayed corpses into the camp of their enemy, hoping to somehow spread crippling and fatal diseases among the troops.

The rain would stop for a few hours—sometimes for a day—and just as the spirit of the Sultan's army would lift with the change in the weather, they would be pummeled again by a sudden storm and monster hail, knocking down their tents and putting out their cooking fires. The Sultan's quarters, alone, remained dry and warm, for his *serai* had been transferred to a stone pavilion left undestroyed when the knights retreated into the city.

The Sultan left his camp before dawn. The morning was cold and damp, but the easterly gales of winter had subsided for the past two days. The air was still, and as the sun moved up over the horizon, there was the promise of a break in the weather.

Ibrahim had been asking Suleiman to take a break from the war. After more than three months of constant fighting, the Sultan had grown increasingly morose and distant. The emotional strain was evident on his now haggard face. Heavy dark bags hung down under his eyes. His skin looked pale and wan. After Suleiman relented, lifting the orders of execution on his Grand Vizier and Aghas, he had found it difficult to communicate directly with them. His night of rage had placed a barrier between him and his most trusted leaders, and he did not know if their relationship could ever be the same. So, he retreated into the solitude and isolation of so many of history's sovereigns. He closeted himself in his *serai* with Ibrahim, and rarely saw anyone else but his mute servants. Only Ibrahim remained his stolid self, apparently unchanged by the ordeal.

The two friends left the encampment and rode to the northwest. They picked up the coast road and continued through the morning at a slow walk. When the sea was in sight, they stopped and gazed out to the north, watching the waves crash upon the shore. With the passage of the hours, the sun burned off the mist, and for the first time in weeks, they could feel its slight warmth on their skin. Suleiman put his hand on the brown neck of his stallion, feeling the animal's energy. Muscles rippled beneath the skin, and the brown hair warmed in the morning light.

After about ten miles, they turned their horses inland to the south, and began the steep winding climb that would take them to the summit of Mt. Fileremos. From Phoenician times, the nine hundred-foot hill was used as a strategic observation point for almost every army that had occupied the island.

The Janissary guard and the Sipahis rode ahead and behind the Sultan. As they approached the summit, the remains of the ancient

Temple of Athena Ialysia became visible through the mountain mist. Some of the stone foundations were intact, and a few columns were recognizable by their sculpted bases.

"We've come on a good day, haven't we, Majesty?" Ibrahim said as they rode into the ruined city.

"Mmmm. Look there, that is the monastery that the knights built, I think."

"Yes, Majesty."

The two rode slowly around the old city, and then returned to the northern slopes of the hillside overlooking the sea. There, they dismounted. Two grooms rushed to take the horses, and several servants set up a small breakfast and chairs. Hot drinks were brought, and plates set out before the Sultan. Soon, the servants withdrew, and Ibrahim was alone with Suleiman.

"Majesty, I've been worried these last weeks. You have been overly quiet and withdrawn. I'm afraid the strain of command has taken a greater toll on you than any of the previous campaigns we have been on together. Even Belgrade did not present your Majesty with such difficult conditions and decisions."

Suleiman nodded, still looking off toward the sea. "Yes, it is so. The hardest part has been with the Aghas. I'm not sure what will come of it. I had no choice but to send Mustapha Pasha away. He has not recovered from the incident, and though I have no doubt of his bravery, he cannot be regarded in the same way as before. Sending Mustapha to govern in Egypt and transferring his sector to Qasim Pasha has saved face all around." He paused, and then turned to Ibrahim and added, "And, may save me fighting another battle when we return to Istanbul." They both laughed, Ibrahim a bit nervously.

"What have we heard from our spies within the city? Is the end any nearer?" Ibrahim asked.

"Actually, we are getting less and less news from our highly placed informants. But, it seems that every day more arrows fly into our camps. The sentries pick them up like so much debris on the ground. Though our spies are silent, the ordinary citizens are betraying the knights now. They tell us of shortages, of disease. They plead for us to enter the city and rescue them from this hell;

the city is a shambles. There is little food, shot, or powder left, and the citizens are at the edge of revolt. Apparently, there have been several hangings. I suspect these may have been some of our spies who were discovered. Ayas Pasha has had no news from his source for some days now. But, we *will* stay here until it is over, and if it means that we will kill every knight in that wretched city, so be it. The knights will receive no help from their friends. If the winter weather makes my men miserable, it will also make hazardous any travel to and from Europe. No, Ibrahim, I am not leaving until my *Bunchuk* flies over the battlements of the city. *Inch' Allah.*"

"I don't know why the Grand Master is so stubborn," Ibrahim said. "It almost seems as if he thinks it is better for his subjects to die in battle than to surrender to you. The message we sent to him has offered him mercy if he surrenders. You have been most generous, but he treats you with contempt."

"And so will his blood answer for his arrogance. Pity his people."

As the Sultan and Ibrahim planned to maintain the siege, the Turkish sappers continued to move in under the walls of the city. Though the trenches were filled with bodies and blood, still they dug and crept like worms to undermine the structure protecting the city.

Gabriele Tadini lay in his hospital bed, slowly recovering from his terrible wound. The knights swore that only the hand of God could have saved a man from such an injury. Even with the sight of his right eye gone and part of his skull blown away, Tadini directed his men from his bed. Several times a day, his officers would come to him and plan strategy. It was all the doctors could do to keep the great engineer in bed. Each day he tried to return to the tunnels and lead his men in the dangerous work of counter-mining. It was only the orders of Philippe, himself, that kept Tadini in the hospital. "I shall send you back to Crete on the next galley if you disobey me, Gabriele," Philippe had shouted. "You'll have more to fear from the Venetian governor there than from the Turks, mark my words. For the sake of Jesus, we *need* your skill. But you are no good to us dead. Listen to the doctors. *They* have saved you thus far. *They* will tell you when it is safe to leave the hospital."

Tadini slumped back in his bed and pouted. He did not try to leave the hospital again for several more weeks.

Towards the middle of the month of November, Philippe sent for Fra Nicholas Fairfax of the *langue* of England. "I have a mission for you, Nicholas. We've begun to see the fruits of our search for reinforcements, and I need still more men and supplies if we are to continue to hold off the Turks. Sit down."

Fairfax took a seat opposite Philippe. Philippe continued, "Last week, two brigantines arrived from Anatolia—from the Castle of St. Peter on Bodrum—with twelve knights and a hundred mercenaries. They brought food, powder, and shot. Not enough, but we can still use it. Also, two barques arrived from Lindos with twelve knights and provisions." Fairfax nodded, and listened in silence.

"I want you to take a small force of men—only enough to defend your ship—and break the blockade. It should be easy enough in this terrible weather. You will sail to Crete, and rendezvous at Candia. There is a barque and a carrack waiting for you, laden with supplies. Bring them back and go ashore anywhere you can. Preferably into our harbors, but at all costs bring us those provisions. Find Fra Emeric Depreaulx and dispatch him to Naples, to plead our cause one last time. I'm sending a small galley to Kos, and ordering the garrison there to abandon their post and to gather here to help defend the city."

Philippe looked carefully at Fairfax. "Nicholas, this is our last chance. If I cannot get more men and supplies, we shall all die at the hands of the Turk. They have endless food and weapons, and they will sacrifice any number of men to this siege. They must not see us falter. We have been terribly hurt by the treachery within our ranks; this is the only chance I have left."

"My Lord, I shall see to all of this. If there are men and arms to be had, I shall return with them."

"God be with you, Nicholas."

"And with you, my Lord."

During the last week of November, Suleiman unleashed two general attacks on the city. Each Agha led his troops personally, and every able man was thrown into the attack. The first assault began against the Posts of England and Italy. Qasim and Piri Pasha drove their men through the trenches and up onto the walls. They were badly impeded by the mud and the bodies lying dead under their feet, but their huge numbers pressed forward, as always, accompanied by the beating of drums and cymbals and the blare of trumpets. Scimitars waving, the Aghas and their Azabs pushed through the breaches again and again throughout the next several days. Hundreds of Turkish soldiers made it into the city itself, and there was fighting in every alley and street. The knights rushed from one post to another, reinforcing their brothers wherever they were needed. Mercenaries and citizens fought off the onslaught, and backed up the knights when they could.

Each night as the darkness closed over the battlefield, the Turks were pushed back out into the trenches again. They slipped and fell and scrambled back as their retreat was followed by enfilades of shot and arrows from the remaining towers. When the blackness was complete, the city was secured again for one more night.

Suleiman met with the Aghas again, and again he was briefed on the happenings of the day. The Aghas told their tales honestly and without excuse. The knights had fought hard. The Turks had fought hard. And the city still belonged to the Order.

"Majesty," Bali Agha said. "Each battle brings us closer to victory. Though it's disappointing that we are driven back out of the city every night, with each day we fight our way further and further inside. They lose many in the battles, and they have very few left to lose. While we can replace our losses, they cannot. While we have shot and powder, they are running out. Their batteries still fire, but I have noticed that they fire less frequently than before. I think they're saving what little they have left. If we persevere, we will see the day when there is nothing left for them to fight us with; no knights to man the breaches."

Suleiman didn't answer. Piri bowed, and then spoke. "Majesty, Bali Agha is right. If we continue these assaults, and do not falter, we will, *Inch' Allah*, win the battle."

So, all the Aghas spoke to Suleiman, and all agreed that the pressure must be kept up if the siege were to end with a Turkish victory. There was no talk—at least among the leaders—of a return to Istanbul. The Sipahis, the Janissaries, and the Azabs would, if necessary, spend the winter on Rhodes.

"Very well. Prepare our quarters for the winter. Send word to my ships that they are to weigh anchor and move offshore to the Anatolian coast, there to await my further orders out of sight of this land. Let our armies see these preparations, so that there can be no doubt that their only transport home has already left for the winter. Let them know that we will stay until the city is ours, if I must slay every last one of their accursed souls. Let this be known!"

November 30th. Nicholas Roberts stood on the battlements at the side of the Grand Master. Philippe stared out at the spectacle before him. In the lowering gloom and drizzle, he could see tens of thousands of Turkish troops moving towards every wall and battlement in the city. Trumpets and drums preceded the advance. As usual, there was no surprise when the Turks attacked, as it was announced with martial music and fanfare. The citizens of Rhodes had learned to fear the coming of the music, for they knew it preceded still another day of death.

Philippe turned to Roberts and asked, "Are the knights in place, Nicholas?"

"They are, my Lord. What knights we have. I've ordered them to defend the breaches that are still open. The mercenaries will back them up. The few loyal Rhodian citizens we have left fighting are organized into small roaming bands to fight where they can. Many of the Turks will get into the city, I'm afraid, so our fighting force is now diluted. We cannot stand and plug every breach as we once could."

"I know, Nicholas, I know." There was a sadness and a resignation that Roberts had not seen in the Grand Master before. It seemed as if Philippe had given up all hope, and only his legendary bravery—some called it stubbornness—kept him going.

Soon, the music began to fade, overwhelmed by the shouts of the advancing armies. On all sides at once, the Turkish soldiers moved through the trenches and began to climb the earth embankments that led to the walls. Simultaneously, Azabs descended into the tunnels, digging and clawing their way inside the city. Fighting raged at every post, and none were spared a moment's rest.

The Turkish Aghas had learned from their earlier battles that they could not afford to allow the knights the luxury of defending a single point of attack. Only by capitalizing on their superior forces could they sweep into the city. And they did.

Philippe fought alongside his knights through much of the morning. He stood, as always, shoulder to shoulder with his brothers, and slashed his heavy sword through the onrushing bodies of the Turks. His strength was incredible, as he matched the younger knights stroke for stroke, paring down the advancing troops. Several times he was forced to retreat, but each time he and his knights rejoined the battle from a more defensible ground. Soon, they were fighting well within the walls, and the Turkish soldiers were both behind and in front of the pockets of resistance.

Towards afternoon, the furor of the battle abated slightly. Both sides were drained by fatigue, thirst, and hunger. Incredibly, as the early darkness drew near, the knights once again pressed the Turkish assault back. It was as if the coming night were the goal itself; if only they could survive until darkness, the knights might live to fight yet one more day. No one, it seemed, within the city walls, could manage to think beyond that.

Darkness came, and the last of the Sultan's army disappeared back into the trenches. When night had fallen, more than five thousand brave young Turkish soldiers joined their brothers lying dead in ditches. And hundreds of knights, mercenaries, and Rhodians lay dead as well.

Quiet descended upon both camps, as their leaders met yet again to decide the fate of the living.

⊰ 19 ⊱

THE BEGINNING
OF THE END

Rhodes
December, 1522

Gabriele Tadini awoke before dawn on the first day of December, more than four months into the endless siege. The wind drove freezing rain against the shuttered windows of the hospital, rattling the wood against the huge iron hinges. In an effort to conserve the fast-dwindling supplies, only a few lamps remained burning through the night. The yellow glow flickered weakly, barely lighting the massive hospital ward. The vaulted ceilings remained in darkness, like a huge indoor night sky.

Most of the patients were asleep. The doctors and their assistants had just retired for a moment's rest before the start of the new day. The air in the ward was rank, for the windows and doors had been closed for days against the constant cold and dampness, as well as the bombardment. The smells of infected wounds and disinfectants mixed in their nostrils, and few of the knights or inmates ever became fully tolerant of the odor.

Tadini sat up on the edge of his cot, pausing while he regained his balance. Seeing the world through his left eye had been disorienting for him. He constantly turned his head to the right to widen his field of vision.

He removed the cloth bandages that wrapped his temples. After six weeks, the skin was now completely closed, and the dressings served no purpose. He threw the soiled mass of cloth into the corner and took a brown leather patch from his pocket. Thin leather thongs had been fixed to the two edges, and the stiff leather worked into a gentle curve that would hug Tadini's cheek and forehead.

The tissues of the right eye were almost completely gone. Tadini's now-useless orbit filled first with fluid secretions, and finally a fibrous scar tissue that had, in the past two weeks, hardened into an exquisitely tender gray mass.

In the darkness, Tadini placed the patch over his right eye socket, padding the surface of the orbit with the clean remnants of a silk handkerchief. He held the silk in place and secured the leather patch by tying the ends behind his head. After testing the whole apparatus by shaking his head, he nodded to himself with satisfaction. The leather patch stayed in place.

Next, he grasped the side of the bed and raised himself carefully to a standing position. His balance was a bit precarious since his injury, though he couldn't tell if it were from the loss of half his visual field or from some damage inflicted upon his brain by the bullet. Satisfied that he would not fall, Tadini got dressed.

The young French knight Jean Parisot de la Valette had been assigned by the Grand Master to look after Tadini's needs while he was recuperating. Valette stayed with Tadini day and night, often shuttling back and forth between the hospital and the battlements bringing news of the battle to Tadini and conveying orders to the knights.

He had quietly brought Tadini's battle clothes into the hospital during the night. Knowing that the doctors would argue and create a row, Tadini had the clothes and his sword brought secretly and stored beneath his bed. Valette had balked, especially after the stern words from the Grand Master that Tadini was not to leave the hospital until the doctors released him. Now, in the darkness, with the quiet broken only by the background of snoring and coughing, Tadini dressed for battle. He girded himself with the broadsword, meticulously sharpened and polished by Valette. Then he placed his helmet carefully on his head and, beckoning impatiently for Valette, he strode from the ward. He hesitated at the top of the wide stone staircase to face the driving wind and icy rain. With the wetness fresh in his face, he took a deep breath of air and thought, *Beware, soldiers of the Sultan. Take care and beware of me. Tadini is back!*

———

Philippe sat crouched over the battle plans for the day. He rotated his neck slowly to relieve the pain that gathered between his shoulders and radiated into his back. Nothing seemed to ease the tension that had built there over the months of battle. He began to feel as if he were being pulled apart by the divisiveness around him. The citizens were now on the edge of open revolt. Nothing, they thought, could be worse than the lives they now led. How could rule by the Sultan be worse than the disease, starvation, and death that now gripped the city? Even Hélène had cast doubt upon Philippe's resolve to stay the course. But, Philippe also recognized that his own determination might be affected by his need to protect Hélène.

Most of the knights followed Philippe's orders without hesitation. But, each day he could see the brightness in their eyes diminish as they went off to their posts. They fought bravely, but the odds were overwhelming them. A few had broached the subject of an honorable surrender. Philippe had thundered at them and squelched their pleas with his rage at the idea of capitulation with the Muslims. Death with honor, he told them, was far preferable to the disgrace of surrender to the Infidels. "I would rather die in the service of Christ than surrender to live under the yoke of the Muslims," he said.

Philippe rubbed his red eyes and reached for a piece of stale bread. The oil lamps flickered, reminding him that he should have them refilled before his command post was plunged into darkness. His Palace had been divinely blessed, he thought; not a single shot had struck her walls. Amidst all the destruction of his beautiful city, no cannonball had found the Palace of the Grand Master.

As he dwelt upon the wonder of God's protection, he heard the door open. A knight took several steps into the room, and waited to be recognized. Philippe closed his eyes and wondered what more impossibly bad news would come to him now. "Yes?" he said wearily as he looked up. "Dear Jesus!" he said, and brought his hand to his chest.

Philippe hesitated for a second. Then, as if new blood had been injected into his body, he rose from his seat and rounded the edge of the table. He reached out and took Tadini's shoulders between his two large hands. The two men stared at each other, and then Philippe pulled Tadini to him, embracing him in a hug that nearly took Tadini's breath away. Valette remained in the hallway, out of range of Philippe's possible reprimand.

"Figlio mio," he murmured, still holding Tadini close. "My son, my son..." Barely stopping the tears that formed on his cheeks, Philippe stepped back and looked at his knight.

Tadini began to smile. Soon, he could contain his joy no more. His teeth showed through the edges of his mustache, and he began to laugh and nod. "Did you think a mere bullet through my head would stop me, my Lord?"

Philippe began to shake his head. He wiped the tears from his face and stepped back. He put his left hand out to touch the leather patch, then withdrew it, clasping his hand in front of him, as if to prevent himself from reaching out again. "No, my son. Not you. It will take more than that to keep you from the enemy's throat."

Philippe returned to his seat and motioned Tadini to the empty chair across the table. Tadini sat and, without waiting, began to tell Philippe his plans.

The guard on the Gate of St. John peered through the dim light, straining to see what was moving toward them. There had been no fanfare, no music. So, it was unlikely that a general assault was in the making. They could see no significant troop movements. As the minutes passed, the figure took on the shape of a man, walking upright through the trenches toward the gate.

The Master of the Guard moved his musketeers into position and ordered them to take aim, but to hold their fire. The man proceeded through the trench, stepping over the bodies of the dead. From time to time, he slipped, and twice fell completely down out of sight. At each of these sudden movements, the musketeers nearly opened fire. Only the shortage of powder and shot kept them from wasting any ammunition on this solitary figure.

Soon it was clear that the man was carrying a staff at the end of which the guards could clearly see a white flag. The man stepped out into clear sight, and the Master of the Guard waved his musketeers back. The guns were lowered, and the man stepped up to the gate.

The guard stood waiting. The man looked up. He planted his staff in the rubble and mud. He waited to be recognized, for the gate to be opened. But, nothing of the sort happened. Finally, he said, "I am Girolamo Monile of Genoa. I have come under this flag of truce as an emissary from the Sultan, Suleiman."

The guards kept their silence. A knight arrived and moved into position next to the Master of the Guard. "Who is this man?" he asked.

"He says he is Girolamo Monile. A Genoese. He says he is an emissary from the Sultan."

The knight leaned over the parapet and said, "What do you wish to tell us?"

"The Sultan has ordered me to bring you this offer: if you surrender the city now, all lives will be spared, knights, mercenaries, citizens. You will be free to stay here in peace, or to go in peace. The slaughter will end. The war will be over." Then he paused and leaned forward, clearly now speaking for himself, rather than the Sultan. He said, "I beg of you. Save your lives and the lives of the people."

The knight stood upon the parapet and stared down at the man, who was now holding on to his staff of truce for support.

The knight had heard Philippe's outbursts at the talk of surrender. He had seen the Grand Master's fury at the suggestion of capitulation. No. There was no way that the city would be turned over to the Muslims. They might all die on these cursed walls, but they would defend their home.

The knight raised his chin a fraction. Still looking directly down into the eyes of the emissary, he raised his gloved right hand and waved the man away.

Hélène finished dressing the wounds of the knight lying on the operating table. His infection was rising higher and higher along his arm, gangrene threatening his life. The doctors were barely keeping the infections at bay with daily removal of the dead tissue.

Hélène applied the last of the bandages—now fashioned from the washed bandages of the dead—and tied a knot to hold them together. She placed a hand on the knight's forehead, still wet with fever. *"C'est finis, mon cher. À tout à l'heure."* It's done, my dear. See you later.

She stretched her aching back and stifled a yawn. Then, she signaled to some helpers to take the knight to his bed to make room for the next patient.

Hélène rubbed her eyes, suddenly dizzy. She staggered a few steps before catching herself, leaning against one of the stone pillars that supported the massive vaulted roof. She waited there while her vision cleared, then walked to an alcove where she lowered herself carefully to the ground and rested her back against the wall. Almost all the available space in the huge hospital was now taken up by the wounded and the dying; knights, mercenaries, and citizens.

She sat thinking for a moment, trying to understand her lack of strength; she was afraid that she had caught something from one of the sick patients in the hospital. There were hundreds of patients with fevers from God-only-knew what diseases were ravaging the city now. But she had no fever herself. And there was no rash on her hands or feet like the patients with the dreaded typhus. No, she thought, I've just pushed myself too far. When she considered it further, she realized that she had been without sleep for more than three days and nights, and that her last real food of any kind had been at breakfast the day before. *No wonder I feel so dreadful,* she thought.

Hélène had not recovered from the loss of Melina, Jean, and their babies. But, most of all, it was Melina's companionship she missed. They had grown so close so quickly under the stress of the siege as well as the shared quandary about the future of their lives with their knights. Hardly a conversation would go by when the two of them would not pour out their dreams and their fears to each other. Hélène had found a sister in Melina, and now she missed her sorely.

Other than Philippe, she realized, there was literally not another soul on that island with whom she could share her story or seek advice. She was more alone in the crowded confines of the fortress than she had ever been in her life.

She pulled herself to her feet, and grabbed her cape from a peg on the wall near the small room she had shared with Melina and the babies. She never failed to become choked with tears as she passed that room or thought of Melina and Jean; of Ekaterina and Marie. They had grown to be like her own family in the short time she knew them, almost her own children. She had not entered the room since.

As she started to go, she again felt a wave of dizziness and once more steadied herself against the stone pillars. She knew now it was the combination of lack of food and exhaustion that was causing it, and headed downstairs to the field kitchen on the first floor.

She thought of Philippe as she made her way through the crowded rooms where the meals—meager as they were—were prepared for the patients and the hospital staff. He, too, must be suffering from the same deprivations as she. *He never takes the time he needs to eat or rest,* she thought. *He must be as weak as I am by now. His officers say he never leaves the field when there is fighting to be done, then he goes back to his rooms and pours over the battleplans all night.*

Hélène pushed past the workers who were waiting their turn in line. "Make me something to bring to the Grand Master," she shouted to one of the cooks. All the heads turned, the room plunged into near silence. Hélène ignored the awkward moment. Damn them if they thought she would hide who she was. "And something to drink," she added. "Quickly!"

The cooks wrapped some bread and dried meat in paper, and handed the small bundle to Hélène along with an open wine bottle filled with some liquid that she did not recognize.

Hélène tied her cloak around her shoulders and headed out into the street level. She made her way along the Street of the Knights in the direction of the Palace. She would find Philippe, put some hot soup into their stomachs from his kitchen, and force him to take some of this bread and meat. Then they would try to get a few hours sleep. She would be no good to anyone at the hospital if she collapsed from exhaustion or illness. And neither would he.

She reached the Palace short of breath and sweating. She climbed the stairs and shrugged her cloak off her shoulders as she went. Unannounced, she went into Philippe's quarters expecting to find him going through his maps, or in a planning meeting with his officers. But, the room was empty. She put her parcel on the great oak desk in the outer room and went into the bedroom. Philippe was sitting on the edge of the bed, his head buried in his hands. He was still in his battle clothes and boots. He had taken only the time to remove his sword from his waist and place it on the floor beside the bed.

He looked up as Hélène reached him, and started to rise to greet her. Hélène placed her hand on his shoulder and dropped to the bed beside him. "Dear God! You look awful, Philippe. Oh, look at your poor face!"

Philippe unconsciously rubbed his callused fingers over his beard and cheeks. "Well," he said smiling, "this is the face of a hundred days of war." Hélène was touched at his attempt at light-heartedness, but she knew it was a ruse. She could see the pallor in his face, the sallow color, the wrinkles that had not been there before.

"You must rest, Philippe, and get something into your stomach. I've brought you a meal," she said, pointing to his desk in the other room. "Let's just take a few minutes to eat together and then sleep for a few hours. Neither of us will be any good if we go on this way."

She waited for his inevitable protest; his bluster and bravado that she knew so well. But, instead, he nodded and rose from the bed. He took her by the hand and then embraced her tightly without kissing her. He let her go, and walked into the outer room. She watched him depart, more frightened by this uncharacteristic response than she would have been if he had refused the meal and the sleep and rushed off to his men on the battlements. Though she knew he was near the end of his strength, it frightened her more to see this frailness in him.

Hélène followed Philippe into the outer room and opened the bundle of bread and meat. He went to the door and called to his aide. "Some soup, if there's any," he said to the young man. "For the

395

two of us." Then he went to the sideboard and took down a half-full bottle of wine. He moved the bottle that Hélène had brought without examining it, and poured two golden goblets from his own. He handed Hélène one of them, and lifted his own in a toast. "To Paris. To Rhodes. To us."

Hélène relaxed for the first time since she had walked into the room. "To us," she said.

They both emptied their goblets and then sat adjacent to each other at the old battered oak desk. Philippe pushed aside the maps and the papers and broke the hard loaf of bread, giving a piece to Hélène and taking one for himself. He ignored the dried meat entirely, chewing slowly on his piece of bread as if it were a fresh-baked delight from the finest *boulangerie* in Paris.

"You're right," he admitted, "I'm so very tired."

"We must both rest, Philippe. The others can take our places for awhile. No one can go on indefinitely like this. If you are too tired....Oh, Philippe. I'm so worried for you out there on the walls. Every time another wounded knight is carried into the hospital, I'm afraid it will be you."

"Listen, my love. This fight...all our fights...there is always the possibility that I could die out there. One parry missed. One feint. The blade that comes out of nowhere and....You know what can happen."

Hélène finished her half of the bread and took another small drink of wine. Then she took Philippe by the hand and led him to the bedroom. "Come. We need to sleep, and I'll sleep better knowing you're within reach."

They took off their outer clothes and crawled under the blankets. The odor was stronger now than Hélène had remembered. The smell was different from those at the hospital; distinctly hers and Philippe's. It had been a long time since anyone or anything in Rhodes had been washed.

When they were settled under the covers, Hélène and Philippe lay on their sides, cradling each other. Hélène said, "Philippe, is this not the time to bargain with the Sultan to raise the siege? To end this war before many more are dead?"

"In good time, Hélène. We'll talk of it in good time."

Before she could speak, she heard the unmistakable snores of her lover's deepest sleep. *It can wait,* she told herself. *I'll talk to him before the sun comes up.* "I love you," she whispered.

—◆—

The morning light broke the darkness through a single chink in the shutters, falling across Hélène's face and waking her. She reached out for Philippe and was startled to find him gone, and the hour so clearly late. The bedclothes were tucked tightly about her, the pillow placed under her head.

"Philippe?" she called, hoping to find him in the outer room. There was no answer. In the light coming through the shutters, she could see that his armor and sword were gone as well. She would have to wait for still another chance to talk about the possibility of surrender.

She dressed quickly and grabbed the remains of the bread as she left the office, chewing as she ran down the steps of the Palace. She left the courtyard and turned down the familiar route along the Street of the Knights. As she passed each Inn, she looked around to see if any of the knights she knew were there. The street was filling with knights and mercenaries and citizens readying themselves for another day of fighting. There were enormous obstacles created by the rubble of the bombardment that went on day and night. The crowds moved in small groups, directed more by the rubble than their goal. There was still sporadic firing into the heart of the city, more to unnerve and demoralize the citizens of Rhodes than for strategic destruction. The majority of the artillery still concentrated on destroying the fortress walls.

Hélène continued her way toward the hospital when she came upon a small crowd of people hovering in a tight circle around the debris of a blasted building. There was a lot of agitated conversation, which was nearly drowned out by the sobbing and cries of a Greek woman. Hélène pushed her way into the circle to see what was going on. There, on the pile of stones, sat a woman of about thirty years of age, dressed in rags, holding the body of a small child, perhaps three or four years old. There was blood coming from the child's forehead and her right arm was twisted at an odd angle near the elbow. The woman clutched the child to her breast, rocking back and forth making the most awful keening noises. All of the others were talking at once.

Hélène reached for the child, telling the mother in French that she had to get the little girl to the hospital. *'Je vous en prie, madam; donnez-moi votre jeune fille.'* But the woman only cried louder and harder, crushing the child to her more tightly. Hélène tried again in Greek.

Just then a door slammed behind the group, and a knight from the Inn of Aragon stepped into the street, trying to push his way past the group of citizens. He appeared angry and flustered by the people preventing him from getting back to his post. He started to shove two of the men aside when Hélène grabbed his sleeve. *"Ayudame, Señor."* Help me, sir, she pleaded in Spanish. The knight at first tried to shake free, but then realized that this was the Grand Master's woman. He pulled up short and bowed slightly. *"Si, Señorita?"*

"I need your help. We must get this child to the hospital before it's too late. She could die any minute unless we do."

Without another word, the knight turned to the woman and placed a hand on her shoulder. He whispered something to her, and took the child from her arms. He cradled the child with his body, and to the mother said, *"Gracias, Señora. Vaya con Dios."*

Then, he hurried with Hélène back toward the hospital. They were walking quickly along the street dodging between the wildly strewn rocks and debris. "What did you say to her?" she asked as they went.

"I told her to give me her child, and that God would help us to heal her. I don't know if she thinks we're going to the hospital or to the church, but in any case, she gave me the child, didn't she?"

Hélène smiled. Then, just as she opened her mouth to speak, the cannonball struck. Neither she nor the knight had heard the blast from that particular cannon. It was just another beat in a background timpani of destruction.

The stone struck the knight and the child directly, crushing them to death in an instant. It shattered into fragments as it hit the wall of the nearest inn, creating a shower of sharp pieces of rock that flew out in a semicircle, taking down everyone who had been standing in the street at that moment. Among the dozens of wounded and dead, Hélène lay with her back against the remaining stone walls of the inn. A large piece of the cannonball—nearly half its mass—lay resting across her knees, pinning her to the ground like a butterfly. Oddly, she felt little pain in her crushed legs, only a chill spreading rapidly through her body.

Several shards of stone had cut their way into Hélène's chest, making her breath labored and shallow. Most of the blood stayed inside, leaving her dress free of any sign of her injuries.

She thought of her night with Philippe, glad she had taken him some food; had been able to spend the night in his arms. If only he would surrender the city and stop the dying. She recalled Paris, and the day she broke his nose at the fountain; and the nights secreted away in her room or his. She smiled at the thought at the same time as tears began to roll down her cheek.

Then a warmth suffused her, chasing away the cold that had permeated her body only a minute before.

She saw Philippe's face staring at her through his open visor. His scarlet cloak was spotless as it was the day she first saw him. His sword was shining in his hand, his eyes clear and rested. He blew her a kiss, then turned his back and strode quickly back down the Street of the Knights.

As soon as Philippe was gone from sight, Hélène closed her eyes and let him go.

———

Antonio Bosio stepped quietly into Philippe's office without knocking. The Grand Master was at his desk, his head folded in his crossed arms, asleep on a pile of maps and drawings of the fortress. He stirred as soon as Bosio approached, then sat up rubbing his already red eyes. A few crusts of dried tears of sleep had collected in the corner of each eye, which he wiped away without any thought.

"Antonio," he said, his voice still hoarse with sleep. "What time is it?"

"Grand Master..."

Philippe looked at Bosio and could see the pain etched in knight's weathered face. "What is it, Antonio? Not another of our officers killed...dear God, please not another."

Bosio rounded the corner of the desk as Philippe made to rise from his chair. Bosio placed a hand upon the old man's shoulder and forced him firmly but gently down into his seat, a gesture unheard of and almost unimaginable in the hierarchy of the Order.

In that momentary contact between their bodies and their eyes, Philippe knew. He slumped into his chair and buried his face in his hands. Bosio could hear only the rasping breath as it escaped Philippe's lips.

The Grand Master shuddered, his whole body shaking as he tried to hold himself together. Then, after some minutes, the spasms of grief gave way to a numb surrender. His body sank deeper into his chair, his once powerful chest sunken and frail.

"How, Antonio? When?"

Bosio kept a firm hand on Philippe's shoulders, now comforting more than restraining. "In the past hour, my Lord. A cannonball. She and a knight from Aragon were taking a wounded child to the hospital..."

"Who was the knight?"

Bosio hesitated, then said, "We're not sure, my Lord. The cannonball was...it was one of their largest. We...we cannot tell who he is, only that he is in the uniform of Aragon."

Philippe squeezed his eyes more tightly shut as if he could push away the image of his beautiful Hélène, his destroyed Hélène. He thought about their last hours together; how Hélène had been so concerned for his health; how she had fed him and caressed him and tried to convince him yet again to give up the battle. To surrender Rhodes. Had he kissed her goodbye? Had he told her he loved her? He couldn't remember, and it made his chest feel hollow.

He tried to rise again, but Bosio held him firmly in his seat.

"I need to go to her, Antonio. To see her." His voice was barely audible, little more than a breath.

But, Philippe was unable to push through Bosio's grip nor the weight of Bosio's body. At first, the Grand Master struggled weakly

THE SHADOW OF GOD

against the insubordination of his long-time Servant-at-Arms. Then he gave up his struggle.

Bosio said softly and kindly, "Please, my Lord. Remember her as she was when you last saw her. Let me attend to her personally. I will see her prepared for burial in the most Christian way. I will spare nothing for her. When she is ready, I will call you to the chapel where the Bishop will say prayers for her and the knight, and for the little girl. Please, as I am your servant and your friend."

———

Tadini stood atop the walls at the Gate of St. John. Wounded again in another skirmish in one of the tunnels, he supported his weight with a rough-hewn crutch made by one of his miners from a supporting beam of a collapsed tunnel. His knee was wrapped in several layers of cloth bandages. Blood had seeped through at several places. Instead of changing them, Tadini merely sought out more cloth, and tied yet another layer on top. He could not bend the limb anyway, so the bulky bandages did not impede his movement further.

At his side was his knight, Valette, and the guards assigned to the Gate. Word had come of the return of the emissary, and Tadini wanted to be there for the exchange.

Valette saw him first. Monile was making his way through the same trench with the same standard and the same large white flag of truce. Again, the musketeers took aim, and again they were told to hold their fire.

Tadini waited as Monile slipped and staggered through the bodies. When, at last, he planted his standard in the mud and looked up, Tadini greeted him in Italian. "*Buon giorno, Signore Monile.*" Monile was startled to be addressed in his own language. "What a fine day for a walk in the country. Eh?" Tadini said.

Monile could not figure out who this maniac was, standing there with his eye patched and blood staining the bulky bandages about his knee. Monile stood beneath the walls and stammered in Italian, "*Signore,* I have a letter from the Sultan Suleiman to the Grand Master Philippe Villiers de L'Isle Adam."

Tadini smiled at Monile. Without listening to another word, he said, "Take this back to the Sultan, Suleiman." He turned to the musketeer nearest him and said, "Send him on his way, but do not hurt him."

A shot rang out, the blast making Tadini wince. A thud came from the direction of Monile, as the bullet struck the mud next to his feet. Monile dropped the standard with the white flag, and began to scramble back through the trench far faster than he had come.

The knights and the guards watched until he disappeared into the Turkish lines.

Tadini turned and hobbled back along the walls in the direction of the Palace. As he passed the musketeer, he smiled and said, "*Grazie.*"

—

Suleiman sat in the newly constructed stone *serai*. All his Aghas and Ibrahim were with him. The fire had dried out the dampness in the air, and the room had a cozy, welcoming air about it. Piri Pasha was comfortable for the first time in several weeks. His arthritis was plaguing him in the damp cold weather, and every movement had been torture. Even Qasim Pasha and Bali Agha, the most fit of the Aghas, admitted to suffering from aches and pains more than usual.

Piri explained the events of the past few days. "Majesty, our envoys have not even been allowed into the gates of the city. The Genoese, Monile, delivered your offer, but he was not allowed in. The second time he went to the gates, they fired upon him. I'm sure they only meant to humiliate him, but I don't think he'll go back."

Suleiman tapped his fingers on the quilted arm of his chair. "When they humiliate my envoy, Piri, they humiliate me. It will not *do* to humiliate me."

"No, Majesty, it will not."

"And the Albanian? Was he received?"

"He has only just returned to the camp, Majesty. He, too, was rebuffed before he could deliver his message."

The Aghas sat in silence. They were all happy to have the Sultan focused on the failure of the diplomatic envoys and not the military missions.

Suleiman leaned forward and placed his elbow on his knee. He tucked his chin onto the palm of his hand and tapped his forefinger against his upper lip as he concentrated on his thoughts. "Must I slaughter every man, woman, and child on this accursed island in order to be free of these Christian knights? Must blood fill the ditches and fire burn their city to the ground? Have I not done as Allah directs me? Do I not conduct my war as the *Qur'an* instructs me? Do I not follow the words of the Prophet, may Allah bless his eternal soul? What more can I do?"

None of the Aghas so much as raised an eye toward the Sultan. None wanted the privilege of offering advice. Piri backed away from Suleiman and returned to his seat.

Suleiman stirred in his throne. He looked up and scanned the faces of his Aghas. "There will be no more general attacks. The loss of life is too wasteful now for the results we gain. Achmed Agha, keep your sappers and miners burrowing and undermining the walls. We can, at least, continue to make the city crumble beneath the enemy's feet. And the bombardment. I want our cannon to fire ceaselessly into the city and against the walls and towers. Never should the knights have a chance to rest. Never should they sleep without the constant fear of one of our balls smashing into their dreams. I want the people of Rhodes to rise up against the knights and demand their surrender. I want them to open the gates and welcome us into the city as their salvation, rather than their conquerors."

The Aghas bowed and acknowledged the will of the Sultan. All murmured assent, and backed out of the room.

—

The Grand Master sat in the Council Chamber of the Palace and prepared to receive the delegation. With him were the Piliers and the Conventual Bailiffs of all the *langues*. The Greek Bishop, Clement, and the Latin Bishop, Balestrieri, were in attendance as well. Tadini sat along the wall with several Knights Grand Cross.

When the entire Council was seated, Philippe gaveled the meeting to order. It was with great reluctance that he had agreed to convene his knights. On the surface, he declared that he could not spare so many of his officers from the battlefield. But, in reality, his heart had already told him what he was about to hear.

Bishop Balestrieri bowed to the Grand Master. Philippe nodded for him to speak. The Bishop rose from his place and walked to the center. He was used to talking to large groups of people, and made eye contact with every man in the room.

"My Lord," he said addressing Philippe, "brothers-in-arms. The time has come for me to speak to you for the people of Rhodes. We have asked much from them these nearly five months, and they have responded beyond all possible expectations. They have suffered grievously, and they have fought and died alongside the knights. They have lost fathers, mothers, and children. We are a small community, and so there is now no person on this island who has not been touched by the hand of Death."

Balestrieri paused, and let his words settle into the hearts of the knights. "Yesterday, a deputation of citizens came to see me and Bishop Clement. Though they were very afraid of what might befall them if they were perceived as entertaining treasonous thoughts— they have not failed to see the body parts displayed upon the battlements—they are more afraid of what will happen when the Sultan's armies force their way into the city in a massive assault. They have heard that there have been envoys sent by the Sultan to allow us to surrender with honor. They have told me that the knights care more about the honor of the Order than the lives of the citizens. Though they would not say it to me, my Lord, I fear that if the Order is not prepared to make peace with the Sultan, that the citizens are prepared to make a separate peace."

The room was completely silent at these words. Philippe's face reddened, and several of the knights began to shift in discomfort in their seats. Philippe held his temper in check. But Balestrieri was talking of overt rebellion. Dangerous talk.

Balestrieri continued. "My Lord, the Order has been on this island for over two centuries. Your bonds to these people run deep. Their destiny is yours. And, though you may not care to admit it, your destiny is theirs. You have a grave responsibility to these people. They have gone far beyond any bounds of devotion to you in this fight. Do not, my Lord, ask them all to perish in a battle that cannot be won. They are not knights. Do not ask *them* to perish for *your* honor."

Tadini moved from his place along the wall. He tried to walk without using the cane that he now carried in place of his makeshift crutch. But, his knee was too unstable, and his wounds too fresh. After only two steps, he staggered, prevented from falling only through a quick rescue by young Valette. He recovered his balance, pulling his elbow from the grip of the knight. He leaned on his cane and spoke from the side of the room. Philippe motioned toward an empty chair, but Tadini shook his head.

"My Lord, forgive me for what I must tell you. But, you would want only the truth from your loyal knights." He looked around the room, and then returned his eyes to Philippe. "The enemy is *already* inside the city. The numbers are few today, but growing every new day. They are above the ground. They are in the tunnels. They have crossed each new *enceinte*. They have crossed our inner retrenchments. I would fight next to you with my last breath if that is your wish. But, when you make your decision, know well that our city is beyond...*salvezza*..." Tadini snapped his fingers, struggling for the right French word. "Salvation. Yes, beyond salvation." He shrugged, and lowered his eyes. Then, he hobbled back to his place and leaned against the wall once again.

Philippe waited for Tadini to return to his place before he spoke. "*Mes Frères. Mes amis. Mes Chevalières. Mes citoyens.* I have heard what you say, and what you say is true. But, I have taken an oath to God, to Christ Almighty, that I would defend to death the honor and the position of our Order. And all of you here have taken that same oath. We, as knights, have lived our lives by that oath. We are all sworn to die in the service of Christ. The Holy Fathers here among us," he said inclining his head toward Balestrieri and Clement, "have taken their own oaths in a different form. But, it is all the same. I am prepared to fight on, here in our home of two hundred years, until every drop of blood has seeped from our veins. Better to die in battle with honor than to surrender to the Infidel and live as slaves."

Several of the knights rose from their places and cried, "Here, here!"

Philippe put up his hand, and continued. "If you will follow me to the battlements once more, I will lead you. If only we knights fight to the end, then so be it, and damned be the Rhodians who would become slaves of the Sultan. But, if you will deny your oaths to God, Jesus, and St. John, I don't know what to think." With those last words, the Grand Master sat back wearily on his seat and waited for a response. In his heart, he wanted overwhelming affirmation by the knights; he wanted to rush from the Palace and end it all with his brothers in one last glorious battle on the walls of Rhodes. And with Hélène dead, there was little more to lose.

Breathing and the rustling of battle capes were the only sounds now. The knights stirred in their places; whispered words were exchanged. But, if Philippe were waiting for the call to arms, it did not come. Finally, a silence prevailed, and Fra Lopes de Pas, from the *langue* of Aragon, rose to speak.

He moved to the center of the room and waited until he had Philippe's attention. De Pas began in Spanish, but after only a few words, he started again in French. "*Mon Seigneur, mes amis, Cheval-ières de St. Jean,*" he said formally. "Everything we have heard here this morning is true. No false words were spoken. Our chances for victory over the enemy are gone. But, if the end must come, if we must go down to defeat, then we should guard that we do not make the enemy's victory all the more splendid by our deaths. When all human hopes are gone, a wise man surrenders to necessity. There is no dishonor in that. The Spartan mother said to her son, 'Come back *with* your shield, or *on* it.' And Sparta is no more. No matter how praiseworthy our death might be, in the long run, it will be more damaging to the Holy Religion than our surrender. For, if we live to fight another day, then we have another chance to gain the field and to prevail. There will be no such chance if we all lie dead upon these ruined walls."

Philippe stared at de Pas. The glow was gone from Philippe's eyes. As the knights considered de Pas' words, there was a clamor at the door. The guards rushed to see what was happening. The Master of the Guard unlocked the big oak doors. Twelve men dressed in rags burst into the room. They scattered, off balance at the sudden opening of the big doors. Embarrassed by their own cries, they collected themselves into a knot at the center of the hall. One man, hat crumpled in his hands, stepped forward. He looked around until his eyes met Philippe's. He straightened up to speak. His voice was choked, and it was all he could do to hold back the tears.

"My Lord," he began, bowing his head, and looking now at the floor. "My Lord...we...we have been sent here by our neighbors. We...we have heard that you are meeting to discuss the fate of the city; that there have been deputations...emissaries...from the Sultan asking for our surrender. For *your* surrender. The people are afraid you will not accept them. My Lord, our supplies are gone. Some of the people are starving to death. The army is slain. The knights are slain. No help will come from outside. We have no shot, no powder, scant water. The dead litter our streets. There is disease....There is..."

The others moved in behind their spokesman and began to talk at once. They sobbed and wailed; tears flowed, hands were wringing. The same words echoed in Philippe's ears. "No food...no soldiers...all dead...it is over...over...over."

Philippe looked into the eyes of the deputation. Then he looked about his room full of knights.

Not a soul breathed, not an eye moved from the Grand Master. De Pas and Tadini looked away, for they could not bear to see this man, so fearsome in battle, diminished this way.

Philippe sat back in his chair. His hand swept across his face, he raised his body to its usual erect posture, and, in a voice barely audible, said, *"D'accord."* I agree.

⊰ 20 ⊱

THE ENVOYS

Rhodes
December, 1522

The Aghas gathered in Suleiman's *serai*, happy once again to be warm and sheltered from the weather. The mood was lighter now, as word from the spies had reached the Sultan that the Rhodians were on the verge of rebellion. The Grand Master, he heard, was under intense pressure to surrender.

"What other word do we have of the conditions within the city, Piri Pasha?"

Piri rose from his *divan*. "Majesty, the city is in ruins, and the population is starving. Even the knights have been reduced to so few in number that they cannot man the breaches sufficiently to repel our attacks. At each foray, more of our men enter the city. But," he said, spreading his two hands, palms up, "we have not yet made the massive decisive breakthrough in any one post. So, while I think our ultimate victory is assured by mere perseverance, the cost is going to be very high."

Suleiman nodded and turned to Achmed Agha, now the Sultan's *Seraskier*. "And what of our troops, how do they fare?"

"Majesty," Achmed Agha replied with a deep bow, "things are not so bad among our men as they are for the knights. At least *we* have sufficient food and water, and by now the encampments have been reinforced to provide better shelter and warmth for the troops. But, still, we are in a sorry state when compared to the army that disembarked at Kallitheas Bay over four months ago. They are battle weary and disappointed. Every man among them has lost many comrades dead, or wounded and dying. Sickness is spreading throughout the camp, and the doctors are unable to keep up with it. The Sons of *Sheitan* have thrown diseased and fly-blown corpses into our camp to spread contagion. The stench is terrible. We have done the same to the knights, but I don't know if they can tell the difference up there. Still, in our camp there is the mud, the cold, the bodies of the dead, the awful smells. Even homesickness—for most of them are just boys—is taking a serious toll. They will, however, fight for you for as long as it takes.

"The slaves are more difficult. They look for any opportunity to flee. It is only the steel of our scimitars against their backs that drives them forward. But, it is always thus with the slaves. Majesty, the quicker this is over, the better." Achmed Agha started to return to the *divan*, but hesitated.

"Yes, Achmed? Did you have something to add?"

"Majesty, it is not for me to say. But, I must speak my truth for the sake of the men I lead. These Janissaries—the Sons of the Sultan—are the world's most loyal soldiers, and each would die a thousand times for you. But, if we could get the knights to surrender without further loss of life among our *yeni cheri*, it would be a blessing from Allah." He bowed, and returned to his seat.

Suleiman seemed about to poll the Aghas, but then changed his mind. He called for no further comments. He sat forward in his high armchair, and said to all of them, "We will allow the knights one last chance. Achmed Agha, have your nephew brought here, along with our official interpreter. I want no mistakes made when the knights hear my ultimatum. Signal our intention by raising the white flag of truce from the tower of that church that lies within our lines. We will not send that Genoese fool again. Only *my* men will carry this message, delivered by mouth as well as in writing. Tell your nephew to bring these terms to the knights: they are to surrender *at once*. I will tolerate no delay. They are invited to stay on Rhodes and live in peace under Islam; they may retain their religion, or convert. They may stay or they may go unharmed. They may take personal property if they wish, and the citizens will have the same choice; they can accept Islam, or retain their own religion. They, too, may stay or go, taking all their possessions with them." Suleiman paused, wondering if there were other conditions that should be included. "But, tell them this: if these terms are not met with immediate and unequivocal acceptance, I shall massacre every man, woman, and child on this island. Now go."

At dawn on December 10th, the sentries on the Tower of St. John looked out over the Turkish lines. There, in the morning gloom, they saw something new in the landscape. Above the tower of the Church of Our Lady of Mercy, the only church outside the walls of the fortress, was a large white flag moving in the gentle breeze. Word was sent to the Grand Master, who immediately sent for Tadini and Prejean de Bidoux. The two knights entered the palace within minutes, and confirmed that the Sultan was flying a flag of truce from the church.

Tadini and de Bidoux were shocked at the appearance of the Grand Master. Though his uniform was presentable, his eyes were red and the skin below his eyelids was puffed and purple. When he spoke, his voice was frail. The power of command was gone. "Good morning, Gabriele. Prejean. What word?"

Tadini spoke first. "My Lord, there can be no mistake. The Sultan's cannons are not firing, and there is no movement in the lines. No trumpets, no drums. We have no reason to think there will be an attack today. I think he will be sending a message to us if we reply with a truce flag of our own."

Philippe nodded slowly without looking up. "By all means. Raise the white flag over the Tower of St. John. We'll see what the Sultan wishes of us."

Tadini and de Bidoux bowed and left. They walked to the walls, de Bidoux carrying the folded white flag under his arm. The two knights left the *Collachio* and crossed the entire inner city to the Jewish Quarter and the Tower of St. John. Every step they took brought them past the bodies of the dying and the dead. Animals lay blocking several streets, forcing the men to detour around the swollen, stinking bodies. Barely a house was left standing or undamaged. A few fires burned, fueled by the remaining sticks and scraps of their wrecked city. The excrement ran in rivulets through the streets and down the slopes to the walls, where it puddled and rose, until it found a crack to take it to the ditches. De Bidoux slowly shook his head at the awful scene, and said, *"Mon ami, c'est fini."*

Tadini didn't reply. He thought he might cry if he tried to speak. When they reached the southern walls, they went quickly to the Tower of St. John to raise their white flag. Then, the two men stood at the edge of battlement and waited.

The envoy, Achmed Agha's nephew, and his interpreter waited among the troops until the white flag appeared on the tower. They walked together through the lines and into the ditches. They, too, were horrified at the scene on the Turkish side of the walls. The could barely find a path that was not strewn with Turkish dead, soldiers and slaves. Neither man had ever experienced such carnage before. They had to support each other to keep from stumbling as they scrambled though the ditches now overflowing with bodies.

When they arrived at the gate, the interpreter called to the men standing at the parapet. Tadini waved them through, then he and de Bidoux met the emissaries at the door.

Achmed's nephew repeated the Sultan's ultimatum word for word, and the interpreter carefully translated each sentence into French. Then Tadini was given the parchment with the words written in both Turkish and French, and sealed with the Sultan's own emblem, the *tuğra*. The emissaries bowed, and left the gate to return to the Sultan's *serai*.

This time Tadini made no remarks or gestures of contempt. No gunfire hurried the Turks on their way.

December 11th, 1522: one hundred thirty-three days of siege. The two men were dressed in black robes as they made their way out of the city and into the Turkish lines. They walked to the walls at the Post of Aragon, then crossed the ditches to the pavilion of Achmed Agha.

Four Janissaries stopped the men and searched them for weapons. Then, with a guard on each flank, they were taken to Achmed's tent. He kept the two men waiting for two hours while he dressed in his formal uniform and high-feathered turban. He finished his breakfast, and then sent for the envoys.

The black-robed men were led into the room. The Janissaries took positions on either side of the room, near enough to protect the Agha in the unlikely event of treachery. When the interpreter was ready, Achmed Agha began. "Who are you who brings a message to Achmed Agha?"

The taller of the two men stepped forward. "I am Antoine de Grollée, Judge of the Court of Rhodes."

"Yes, I see you're not wearing the cape of the Knights," said Achmed. "And who is this with you?"

The second man stepped forward. "*Je m'appelle* Roberto Peruzzi, also a Judge of the Court of Rhodes," he said in French. The interpreter translated into Turkish for Achmed, and added that the second man was not speaking in his native language. Achmed smiled at his interpreter's skill, and went on. "What is your message?"

De Grollée answered. "I have a message from the Grand Master, Philippe Villiers de L'Isle Adam, to the Sultan, Suleiman Khan. Our message asks for a truce of three more days, to allow preparations for the surrender of the city, and to clarify the terms of the surrender."

"Very well. You shall be taken to the Sultan, himself, to deliver your message."

Achmed rose and motioned to the guards. The small group left the pavilion. They were escorted a short way to where horses were waiting. Achmed mounted his stallion, and the two envoys were led to theirs. The Janissaries and the interpreter walked behind the procession, with a small escort of mounted Sipahis leading the way out of the camp. The group wound its way through the troops, and then ascended the hillside to the west of the city to Suleiman's pavilion.

The envoys said nothing on the journey, but both men were astounded at the conditions of the Turkish camps they passed on the way. Though in no way comparable to the usual discipline and cleanliness of a Janissary army in the field, when compared to the conditions within the city, the differences were staggering. Not only was there the smell of real food cooking in the giant pots, but, after so much death and destruction, the sheer numbers of the Turkish soldiers seemed inconceivable to Grollée and Peruzzi. *We have made the right decision to surrender,* thought Peruzzi, *otherwise there is nothing ahead for us but death.*

The party entered the encampment of the Sultan on the slopes of Mount Saint Stephen, where they were taken directly to Suleiman's *serai* by his personal Janissary Guard.

The horses were led away, and Achmed led the envoys and the interpreter into the presence of the Sultan. Suleiman was seated on his throne. Piri Pasha and Ibrahim were seated on a *divan* to his right. Achmed bowed to the Sultan. Suleiman motioned him closer while the envoys were kept standing near the door. In a low voice, he asked, "Who are these men, and what word do they bring?" The Sultan wanted to know everything *before* the fact, to maintain the advantage over his adversaries.

"These are two Judges of the Court of Rhodes. Perhaps the Grand Master felt that they might be more believable than an envoy of knights. In any case, Majesty, the Grand Master requests a three-day truce to prepare for the surrender and a clarification of the terms."

Suleiman considered for a moment, and then waved Achmed Agha to the side. He nodded to the Janissaries, and the envoys were led toward the throne. The two men stood before the throne, hands folded in front of their robes. Suddenly, they felt their legs buckle as they were forced to their knees by the Janissaries. They held their positions with equanimity, but both men wondered if they were to be slain on the spot in a display of the Sultan's power over them. Finally, the interpreter told them to bow and then rise, maintaining their distance from the Sultan.

Both men complied, but both refused to touch their heads to the ground. The Sultan had made his point, and so had they. The men rose to their feet and waited for permission to speak.

In an unexpectedly pleasant voice, Suleiman said, "*Salaam Aleichum.* You are welcome to my camp. What word do you bring me from your Grand Master, Philippe Villiers de L'Isle Adam?"

Grollée stepped an inch forward and looked up into the eyes of the Sultan. He had heard about this man for so long that it shocked him when he finally saw Suleiman in person. The power of the Ottoman army and Empire had led Grollée to picture a man of massive physical proportions; a deep stentorian voice and bush-black beard. Instead, he found a slightly built man almost effeminately dressed in robes of white silk brocade with gold patterns stitched into the hem. He wore a high white turban with a gold crown. His slippers were embroidered, and as the envoy glanced about him, he was astonished by the opulence of what should have been an austere military camp. This was a different man than the envoy was expecting, and it unnerved him.

Suleiman's dark eyes never left Grollée's, as he waited for his reply.

"The Grand Master bids you good day and good health," Grollée said, clearing his throat.

Suleiman seemed pleased with the tone of the message. He had expected a preamble of extensive haggling, and was prepared to reply with an instant assault upon the city. Instead, he turned to his interpreter and asked if there was any problem in the translation.

"No, Majesty. There is none."

"Very well, tell the envoy this: I will accede to his request for three days of truce to prepare his city for surrender." Grollée and Peruzzi were surprised at the Sultan's immediate accession to the request. Suleiman continued, "There must be no work on any of the defenses of the city during the three days, nor any preparation of cannons or weapons. If there is any deviation from these conditions, it will be followed by a massive assault, which will not cease until every person within the walls is dead."

Both envoys bowed. Suleiman turned to Achmed and said in Turkish, "Send that man," pointing to Peruzzi, "back with my reply. The other you will keep with you as a hostage."

Achmed bowed to Suleiman, and then spoke to the interpreter. The interpreter walked up to the envoys. He turned to Peruzzi and said, "You will return to the city escorted by the Janissaries as far as the walls. You," he said to Grollée, "will remain as the guest of Achmed Agha until the surrender is agreed upon."

Grollée recoiled at the news that he was now a hostage, no matter how nicely it was worded. There was no doubt in his mind that should the surrender go awry, his head would be displayed upon a pike at the vanguard of Suleiman's assault wave.

Grollée nodded to Peruzzi, and was led, backing away, by the Janissaries.

Outside the *serai*, Achmed Agha ordered the Janissaries to escort Peruzzi back to the city. He smiled at Grollée and motioned him to the horses. The two men rode out behind the Sipahi guards, back to the Turkish lines and Achmed's pavilion.

Antoine de Grollée was shocked at his treatment by Achmed Agha. He was taken by horseback down to the Agha's pavilion. They spoke little along the way, and Grollée was nervous at the way the Sipahis kept such a close guard. *Why,* he thought, *should I be under such tight surveillance by these guards, unless I have something to fear at the hands of these Turks?*

When they arrived in the camps, he was led directly into Achmed Agha's personal tent. Achmed motioned him inside, and then apologized. "I must spend about an hour inspecting my troops and the lines. I will return as soon as I can." With that, he turned and left.

Grollée was alone for only a few minutes. He paced the tent, not knowing whether it was permitted for him to sit. Before he could make any decisions, a servant entered the tent. In his arms he carried clean undergarments and a brocade caftan. He placed them on a low table, and motioned for Grollée to undress and put on the clean clothes. Slippers were traded for Grollée's tattered boots, and a small tray of food and wine was set down near the *divan*.

Grollée washed his hands and face, and settled down on the *divan* in his new clothes. His diet of stale bread and water for the past weeks had begun to sap his strength. The aroma of the fresh food set him salivating.

He ate part of the meal and then waited, for he didn't know whether this food was to be shared with his host. The wait was torture.

After about an hour, Achmed returned to the tent. He ordered the interpreter to stay. "Ah," he said in Turkish, " I see my servants have taken good care of you," he said, as if it had been the servants' idea to clothe and feed the hostage. "Good. Good. Eat up. That's a small meal, all for you. We will have a proper dinner when it grows dark."

Grollée could hardly believe his good fortune. He immediately finished all the sweet meats and fruit on the table, and, a little guiltily, washed it down with some red wine. Achmed changed out of his uniform in a side room and dressed in a caftan and under-garments similar to those of his guest. "Well," he said finally, "with any luck, this siege will end before your Christmas, and by your New Year some of us might be on the way home as well. And, *Inch' Allah,* the death and the dying may be over."

Grollée listened with interest as Achmed spoke. The Agha cer-tainly seemed keenly aware of the Christian calendar and holy days. Was this some way to test the determination of the knights? Surely not, he thought, as the battle was already conceded.

"Our armies and the people have suffered terribly since it all began," Grollée volunteered in French. "It has been a trial for everyone"

"Indeed," said Achmed. "Both armies have suffered. We have spent lives prodigally these past months. My officers have estimated that we have nearly sixty-five thousand dead, and another fifty thousand wounded or dying. More than one hundred thousand casualties in only four months!"

"*Mon Dieu!*" Grollée replied. "More than one hundred thousand casualties! It's hard to believe. Not, that I doubt your word," he said carefully, "but so many lives. Then, one only has to look in the ditches to see that this is true."

Grollée shifted uneasily. "Why," he asked, "was the Sultan so determined to destroy us that he would sacrifice thousands of men to do so?"

"We are here," Achmed replied, "because the Sultan—as his father and his grandfather and his great-grandfather—sees the Knights of the Order of St. John as an island of trouble in an other-wise tranquil Ottoman Sea. Surely, you must realize that the

Ottoman Empire surrounds you on every side for thousands of miles. We control the law, trade, everything but this Island of Rhodes."

Achmed paused, and reached for a sweet. Then, when Grollée did not reply, he went on. "The knights have been pirates here for more than two hundred years on this island alone. The Ottoman Sultans have driven them from one fortress to another for five hundred years. The Sultan is determined to be the one who rids the Empire of this nuisance once and forever. I, for one, am surprised at his offer of honorable surrender. Up until yesterday, I would have sworn that he would not be content until every last one of you were dead. *Why* he has changed his mind, he has not shared with me. But, if your Grand Master is as wise as his knights think he is, he will capitulate quickly and decisively. The Sultan could just as easily change his mind again."

Grollée pulled his caftan closer around his body. Suddenly, even with the coal-fired warmth in the tent, he was beginning to shiver.

⊰ 21 ⊱

FACE TO FACE

Rhodes
Christmas, 1522

The weather was still wet and cold as Philippe rode through the Gate of St. John. He was wrapped in a fresh scarlet battle cloak, with the white, eight-pointed cross. He wore no helmet, but his broadsword hung on his belt at his left hip. His white horse was adorned in gold ceremonial armor. Eight Knights Grand Cross rode at escort before and after him.

The Grand Master and his small procession followed a path that had been cleared through the trenches, and then turned west toward Mount Saint Stephen. Janissaries and Sipahis lined the route, and assured Philippe's safe passage. Though the wind cut through his garments, Philippe kept his back straight and his head up. He resisted the temptation to tuck his chin down into his surcoat to keep the wind from his neck.

The Turkish soldiers along the wayside stared at the figure now ascending the slopes. This was the man who had led the slaughter of their comrades for one hundred forty-five days. Now, he rode through their lines to a meeting with their Sultan, Suleiman.

⸺

Suleiman and Ibrahim sat in the *serai* warming themselves in front of the coal brazier. The heat had permeated the rock structure of the house, and warmth radiated from the walls and the ceiling.

The men were alone in the room. Servants and guards waited just outside the doors.

"So, he is on his way?"

"Yes, Majesty," Ibrahim answered. "The messengers say he will be here within the half hour. His party is already climbing the slopes of the hillside."

Suleiman said, "I will admit to you, my friend, that I never anticipated such fierce resistance from these knights. I knew when we came here that my cavalry would be useless for most of the battle; that when winter came, the horses and the men might as well be at home for all the good they could do in a siege. But, just think of the numbers of Janissaries and Azabs that I threw at them. Just think of it!" He shook his head in disbelief. "Nobody could have predicted such a battle, even if they did have the world's best fortifications. I expected my artillery and the miners to reduce them to rubble within days. Amazing."

Ibrahim sat silently, allowing his Sultan to continue the monologue. Suleiman seemed to need the moment to reflect on the war. "I think," Suleiman went on, "that the Grand Master would have fought to the death of every last man. I can despise his beliefs and his piracy, but I cannot demean his bravery."

"Majesty, how shall we receive the Grand Master?"

"We shall receive him as we would any head of state. With courtesy and dignity. Of course...he might be made to wait upon me...perhaps only a few hours."

—

Philippe gave his horses to the Sultan's servants. He told his knights to wait outside the *serai*. "I'm quite safe here. The Sultan would never dishonor his word by violating my safe passage."

Philippe was led into the waiting room next to Suleiman's reception chamber. The coal brazier had been burning all night long, so the room was dry and warm. Philippe shivered, as if expelling the cold from his body. He opened his cloak and noticed that there was mud spattered on the hem from the long ride through the wet countryside

After an hour, Philippe was growing stiff from sitting in one place. His knees and thighs were sore from the unaccustomed ride.

He shifted uneasily in his seat, but he would not allow himself to show his impatience by pacing about the room. At length, a servant entered, carrying a long white robe in his arms. He motioned to Philippe, and spoke a few words of Turkish. Philippe could not understand the man, but it was clear that garment was a present from the Sultan.

He stood to take the garment, but the servant held it back. Another servant had entered the room, and helped Philippe remove his muddied surcoat. Only then did the first servant unfold the gift from the Sultan. Philippe was shocked at the opulence. The present was a floor-length robe and caftan of gold brocade, with a heavily quilted lining. The servant moved behind Philippe and helped him into it. As he shrugged the heavy robe onto his broad shoulders, he was amazed at the exactness of the fit. How could the Sultan's tailors have guessed his size so well? It was a frightening thought. There was something else. Something about the robe was different, and it took a minute for Philippe to discover what it was. The robe was as warm as if he had been sleeping in it. The servant had *heated* the garment so that the Grand Master would not have to slip on a cold silk robe. The Sultan, he realized, must *always* have his clothing heated for him.

Philippe made a cursory bow to the servants, and then again found himself alone in the room. Soon, slippers were brought to him, his dirty boots removed from his feet. At the end of another hour, a tray of food and drink were placed before him. He felt as if he had been imprisoned in luxury. His instinct was to show his contempt for this imperial rudeness and leave the *serai*. What galled him most at the moment was that Suleiman had placed him in such an *impossible* position. Philippe was being bribed with the trappings of opulence and comfort. Here he sat, before a warm fire, in a silk robe and slippers. His own boots and surcoat were gone, God knows where. This was comfort that he had not experienced since the siege had begun. And, he was enjoying it even though the overall effect was insult.

After the second hour had passed, a page entered the waiting room and motioned for Philippe to follow. The Grand Master rose, following the man to the inner chamber.

Ibrahim was standing, and bowed to the Grand Master. *"Bonjour, Seigneur. Bienvenue. Je vous en prie..."* and he pointed to the *divan* that had been placed opposite the Sultan. Philippe looked at Suleiman, who had said nothing, but had not taken his eyes from Philippe's. The Sultan was dressed in a golden brocade robe and slippers similar to those he had given to Philippe. But, Philippe saw immediately that the Sultan's slippers were just noticeably finer; the stitching more perfect, the quilting thicker. The throne upon which Suleiman sat was made of intricately carved dark wood, and upholstered with silk brocade. Even after so many months in the field, there was not a spot of dirt anywhere to be seen. He stared into the dark brown eyes. Those eyes, and Suleiman's famous hawk-like nose, drew his attention away from the rest of the Sultan's face. Philippe realized that in all these months, he had not seen so much as a picture of his enemy, the Sultan. He was confused, for now that he was staring into Suleiman's eyes, he lost whatever preconceived ideas he had carried in his mind for all these months.

The room was fully carpeted in a rich silk; there were cushions all along the walls. Philippe walked to the *divan*, and sat down. The placement of the throne had been carefully planned. What was immediately apparent was that this interview would be conducted with Philippe having to strain his neck to look up into the eyes of the Sultan.

After Philippe was settled, Ibrahim sat on a set of cushions next to Suleiman. He, too, was slightly higher than Philippe. Philippe looked around the room for the interpreter. No one was in sight. The three men were the only people in the room. Since he knew no Turkish, Philippe had no choice but to wait for the Sultan to begin.

Neither leader took his eyes away. Ibrahim, too, sat and stared at the Grand Master. But, Philippe never acknowledged Ibrahim's attention. He kept his eyes fixed upon Suleiman's.

Suleiman finally broke the silence. "Philippe Villiers de L'Isle Adam, welcome to my *serai*," he began in Turkish. Philippe cocked his head. He wanted to look around for the interpreter, but he would not take his eyes from Suleiman. It was Ibrahim who spoke. In barely accented French, he began to translate the words of the Sultan.

Philippe bowed and replied, "It is my honor to be here, Majesty. And, I thank you for your generous gifts and your hospitality."

"I am sorry that circumstances have forced us to meet under such conditions. In other times, we might have been allies; we might have fought together. But, it is not the will of Allah or his Prophet, Mohammed, blessings be upon Him."

Philippe nodded. There was, he realized, no appropriate reply. Suleiman continued, with Ibrahim just a few words behind. As he translated, Ibrahim maintained the same pace and inflection as the Sultan, the same nuances rendered into nearly perfect French. "I also must pay my condolences for the deaths of so many of your knights and your people. It has been a tragic siege, costing the lives of so many fine young men."

"*C'est vrai*, Majesty. I only hope that this will be the end of the killing, though I know that the dying will go on for some time to come."

Suleiman nodded. "But, such is the fate of all princes, of all leaders. Sooner or later, the realm is lost; cities are lost; lives are lost; nothing but Allah endures forever. Your men have made a gallant, if futile, defense of your city. In the end, it was inevitable that we should prevail. No one will ever doubt your valor or your commitment to your cause. When I raise the siege, your honor will remain intact."

"Thank you."

"But, we must move on to the realities of this 'peace.' We must spell out, in detail, the terms. They are these:

"You will send me twenty-five knights, including several of high rank—perhaps Knights Grand Cross—to be held as hostages until the surrender and the debarkation are complete. They will be treated with courtesy and respect, I assure you, as has your Fra Antoine de Grollée, who is at the moment in the company of Achmed Agha. Also, you will furnish twenty-five hostages from among the prominent leaders of the Rhodian citizens. They, too, will be protected by my word."

Philippe said nothing; he continued to stare at the Sultan, even as Ibrahim spoke the words.

"I will send a small force of four hundred Janissaries into the city to maintain order and assure the peaceful evacuation of the city." Philippe tried not to smile at the Sultan's suggestion that four hundred Janissaries was a small force.

Suleiman continued. "The rest of my armies will withdraw the enceinte to a distance of one mile from the walls, and wait there until the evacuation is complete.

"My personal word will safeguard the lives and well-being of the knights and the citizens. The Knights of the Order of St. John Hospitaller shall be free to depart in safety and with honor. If your fleet is not capable of the task, I shall furnish seaworthy ships to take you as far as Crete. You will have twelve days from now to leave."

Suleiman paused while Ibrahim caught up with him. He waited for Philippe to absorb the details. Then he went on. "My word will protect the lives and the property of the citizens in *every* regard: they may return and keep their own homes. For five years hence, there will be no taxation. This will allow the time necessary for rebuilding the city and restoration of commerce. The citizens will be free to leave or to stay; to adopt Islam, or to keep their religion, Greek or Latin. They may change their minds, and have up to three years to leave, taking their possessions and their wealth."

When he was finished outlining the terms, Suleiman leaned back on his throne and folded his hands. Philippe took this as the signal that the terms had been delivered. He leaned forward on the *divan* and said, "Majesty, your terms are more than fair. You have left me and my Order our honor, which above all else—even life, itself—we treasure. The citizens of Rhodes, I am sure, have nothing to fear from your armies. Your word is beyond question. I would like to celebrate the Christmas Midnight Mass tonight in our Church for the last time before our departure. It would be my pleasure to receive you in the Palace of the Grand Master two days after Christmas, on the Feast of St. John the Baptist." The irony was clear to both Suleiman and Ibrahim.

Suleiman looked at Ibrahim, as his friend translated the words of the Grand Master. When Ibrahim was finished, Suleiman turned back to Philippe and said, "The honor will be mine."

When Philippe returned to the outer room, his cloak had been returned, cleaned and pressed...and heated. His boots had been cleaned, and a small defect had been repaired. When he pulled them on, he smiled that they, too, had been warmed.

On the feast day of St. John the Baptist, Suleiman and Ibrahim mounted their stallions, and, in full ceremonial dress, rode out from the *serai* at Mount Saint Stephen and into the city. The two moved down the slopes with an escort of one hundred Janissaries and Sipahis. As they crossed the open fields and neared the city walls, the citizens appeared along the battlements to see the coming of the Sultan. The path through the trenches had been further cleared since Philippe's trip to see Suleiman. The smell of death still hung in the air, as it would for months afterward. But, Suleiman and Ibrahim passed the bodies of their soldiers without turning their heads.

As the large escort reached the Gate of St. John, Suleiman signaled his party to a halt. "Dismiss the guard."

Ibrahim looked at Suleiman and hesitated. He saw that the Sultan was determined, and turned to the officer in charge. "Dismiss the guard. Wait for us at our lines." He looked back to the Sultan.

Suleiman said, loud enough to be heard by everyone in earshot, "My safe conduct is guaranteed by the word of the Grand Master of the Knights of St. John, and that is better than all the world's armies."

The Sultan and his friend turned their horses and rode in through the gate. Once inside the walls, Suleiman dismounted and handed the reins to a waiting knight. The streets were lined with curious citizens, who had waited hours in the cold wet morning to catch sight of this almost mythical leader of the Ottomans. They were there to see the man whose will would determine the future of their lives. The knights might leave Rhodes to settle their Order elsewhere, but for most of the citizens, life under Muslim rule was only days away.

An escort of Knights Grand Cross was waiting just inside the gate. The Sultan seemed a mere youth to many of the older, war-hardened knights. Suleiman was dressed in a simple caftan of white and gold. His slender body and youthful face belied the immense power wielded by this twenty-six-year-old man. With Ibrahim as his interpreter, Suleiman moved among the waiting knights. He stopped along the way, and turned to one of the knights from the *langue* of France. "I have come to see your Grand Master," he said, "and inquire as to his health." The knight was so surprised at being addressed with such informality by the legendary Sultan that he merely stared, jaw open, saying nothing.

Tadini witnessed the exchange and smiled. He and Prejean de Bidoux led the way. The knights walked ahead, in full battle gear. They wore helmets and chain mail; their swords were sheathed, but they held their fists at the ready near the hilt. They were now protecting their own honor by guarding their conqueror. When they reached the Street of the Knights, the crowds had to be held back by the mercenaries and the surviving one hundred fifty knights. The procession entered the *Collachio*. When they arrived at the Palace of the Grand Master, two junior knights took the horses and led them into the courtyard, while Suleiman and Ibrahim were escorted to the grand staircase. They ascended together, with Tadini in the lead. No words were spoken.

Philippe waited for the Sultan in his great room. He quickly rose to greet Suleiman, who was led to a large oak chair. He sat next to Philippe while Ibrahim waited near the doorway with the knights. When Philippe began to speak, Ibrahim moved closer to translate. Philippe had his own interpreter present, but the conversation with Suleiman on Mount Saint Stephen was so successful that Ibrahim was allowed to continue.

"Sultan Suleiman Khan, it is an honor to receive you here in my palace. You do us a great honor by your presence."

Ibrahim translated this into Turkish, and Suleiman bowed his head in acknowledgment. Philippe continued. "Please allow me to present you with these poor gifts, as a token of our respect for you." He signaled to one of the knights, who brought out a carved wooden box. The knight knelt before the Sultan and opened the box. It was lined with crimson velvet, and contained four golden goblets. Suleiman reached into the box and removed one of them.

He held up and turned the goblet in his hands. Then he showed it to Ibrahim, and with a smile of appreciation said, "Your generosity is most greatly appreciated."

When Suleiman had replaced the goblet and the box was removed, Philippe said, "Preparations have been made for our departure. I and my knights will leave the island on the morning of January 1st. A few citizens and all the mercenaries will depart with us. We agree to all your terms, and I am assured that there will be no resistance to your occupation of the city after the Order has left. You have shown great mercy, Majesty, which is more the mark of a great man than that of conquest."

After an hour more of pleasantries and protocol, Suleiman and Ibrahim took their leave. When the Sultan rose, Philippe bowed. He knelt and took Suleiman's hand, touching his head to the sleeve of the Sultan's caftan, and kissing his hand.

Suleiman and Ibrahim walked down the great staircase to the courtyard and remounted their waiting horses. The procession continued back to the Gate of St. John, with Tadini and de Bidoux, once again, in command. The knights saluted the Sultan at the gate, forming two columns as Suleiman and Ibrahim rode back to the Turkish lines.

⊰ 22 ⊱

FROM THE ENDS
OF THE EARTH

Rhodes
Christmas Day to New Year's Day, 1523

As the knights prepared for their departure, the Turkish lines were withdrawn to a distance of a mile from the walls of the city. The Sultan's camps were restored to their usual clean, disciplined conditions. The soldiers rested, as the doctors continued to work on the backlog of wounded. The weather was still cold and wet, but the morale of Suleiman's army improved each day.

A corps of four hundred Janissaries was sent into the city under the leadership of Achmed Agha. The knights watched from their positions as the Janissaries entered the gates. They moved into the city as a unit, forming a block of silent armed warriors. Their uniforms were freshly washed, and their swords polished. Their helmets carried the traditional herons' feathers, and their blue vests glowed in the morning light. Not a word was spoken nor any orders given by the officers. The Sultan's elite corps moved to their positions and established their guard posts.

Bali Agha commanded the remaining Janissaries outside the walls. The young troops were deployed at strategic outposts throughout the inner city, but remained away from the Street of the Knights and the Palace of the Grand Master. Suleiman had given strict orders that none of the knights or the citizens were to be molested or insulted in any way. The usual wartime practice of free looting by the troops was forbidden.

But, the heady taste of victory was too much to bear for some of the troops. Oddly, it fell upon the youngest and freshest Janissaries to disobey their commanders. A group of Janissaries newly arrived from Syria had missed virtually all the fighting. They were disappointed that they had not been given their chance for glory against the invidious knights. They imagined themselves slashing through the vanguard, their scimitars dripping with Infidel blood. They could never have imagined the impenetrable wall of fierce warriors that had cut their comrades down in wave after wave for the past one hundred forty-five days. Only the ditches brimming with fallen corpses reminded them of the realities of the war.

When they entered the city, the wildest of the new arrivals went directly to the churches and began desecrating anything that spoke of Christianity. They destroyed icons and defaced images of Christ and the Virgin Mary. Townspeople were knocked aside when they tried to protect their holy places, and several were severely wounded with slashes from the as-yet-unbloodied scimitars. Several women were raped and beaten, and one old man was thrown from a wall into the rubble of the ditches. Private homes were entered, and food taken from the owners. Some of the people were stripped of their clothes, and made to walk naked in the streets in the freezing dampness.

A deputation of Christian citizens appeared before Achmed Agha and complained bitterly of the destruction and terror that the Janissaries were spreading through their town. They told the Agha that they had the protection of the Sultan, Suleiman. Could they not trust the word of the Emperor of the Ottomans?

Achmed was furious. He immediately sent a detail of officers and his more seasoned Janissaries to stop the looting and the violence. The guilty soldiers were brought before him and severely reprimanded. When confronted with their crimes, they tried to explain that they had acted as good Muslims. "Did not the Holy *Qur'an* forbid the presence of graven human images inside a mosque? Were not the churches soon to be converted to mosques? Therefore, was it not our duty to erase the images of Christ and any others that we might find?"

The young troops were ordered to return stolen goods, and then sent from the city back to their own lines to wait out the rest of the occupation.

~

Suleiman stood alone outside his pavilion on the slopes of Mount Saint Stephen, watching the knights prepare for their departure from Rhodes. It looked to him like a swarm of ants dismantling their nest.

A messenger appeared quietly at his side, bringing written news of the violence caused by the newly arrived Janissaries. Suleiman was furious. He said, "I have pledged my word and my honor, and woe be he who stains it." He quickly wrote out an order and handed it to the messenger, who was to deliver it to Achmed Agha. The penalty for any further disobedience would be death.

Suleiman stared into the waning light. As darkness settled over the island, the few remaining fires in the city grew brighter. In the flickering shadows, knights and citizens hurried to collect their belongings and gather their families together for their flight. In the darkness, the lights in the Palace of the Grand Master dominated the northwestern part of the city. Figures passed back and forth in front of the lighted windows, disappearing again as quickly as they had come. Suleiman knew that one of those shadows must be Philippe.

As he walked back alone into his *serai*, Suleiman felt a sense of sadness. The euphoria of victory over the knights was gone, replaced by a thread inexplicably connecting him with his former enemy. For the first time since he arrived on Rhodes, he felt he understood the passions that drove the Grand Master.

~

In the Palace of the Grand Master, the knights were busy gathering their possessions. Suleiman had agreed that they could take their swords, pikes, halberds, muskets, and the scant remaining supply of shot and powder. He forbade the removal of the cannons from the city, though the ships could retain their cannons for their own protection against piracy on the high seas.

Philippe ordered the Sacred Holy Relics to be brought to his quarters for packing and cataloging. "Gabriele, see to the protection of these treasures," he said to Tadini. "The Infidels will care nothing for them. They have already begun desecrating the churches; who knows what will happen to our churches after we leave?"

"Aye, my Lord, I'll see to it."

William Weston was cataloging the treasures. He stepped forward and showed the Grand Master his list. "We have already packed away the Sacred Relics of the True Cross, my Lord. Also the Holy Thorn and the Holy Body of St. Euphemia. We are just now wrapping the Right Hand of St. John, and a Holy Icon of Our Lady of Fileremos. The rest of the relics are all safely put away."

"Well done, William. Keep these near to us at all times. They will not be left unguarded until we are installed in our new home; only God and Jesus know where that will be."

January 1st, 1523. In the late afternoon, just before darkness overtook the island, the Gate of St. John was opened by the Grand Master's guard. Philippe sat astride his horse, dressed now in the black robes worn by the knights during peacetime, and walked at the head of the solemn procession. His broadsword hung from the wide leather belt at his left side. His head was bare, and his thin white hair blew in the chill January breeze. At his side was Gabriele Tadini da Martinengo. Tadini still wore the worn leather patch over his right eye. Following close behind was Antonio Bosio.

The other knights walked in lines of two, carrying only their personal weapons. William Weston was waiting at the ships with his guard of fifty knights. There were several more transports and four galleys. All the possessions and treasures were loaded and secured. The most valuable—the Holy Relics—were stored deep in the hold of the flagship, the carrack *Sancta Maria*; this very same ship that had, only sixteen months before, brought Philippe from Marseilles to his new home on Rhodes. The mercenaries and some of the citizen-soldiers of Rhodes followed the knights as the procession wound its way through the periphery of the city to the harbor.

Philippe tried with all his might to maintain his dignity as the Grand Master. But, as he descended to the harbor, he found it increasingly hard to breathe. A great weight pressed on his chest, as he fought to hold back the tears. His mind reeled with the real cost of the siege. After one hundred forty-five days of fighting and two hundred years of occupation by the Order, he was leaving his island home, deserting the remains of hundreds of his brothers-at-arms.

Later, on the afterdeck of the *Sancta Maria,* in a darkness that seemed to hang from the shrouds of the ship, Philippe looked back toward Rhodes. Squinting into the night, he could just make out the silhouette of the mountainous island blacking out the stars where they met the sea. The crisp winter air cut though his robes as the light wind propelled him and his knights away from their island home. The vastness of the black sea and the infinity of the stars made him wonder where on Earth he and his knights would ultimately land. And he thought again—as he had almost constantly since he admitted the inevitability of defeat—of Hélène.

He wrapped his black robes closer about him, and sighed deeply. Then he leaned over the rail and peered for the last time back toward Rhodes. Now the shadow of her mountains were gone, and the stars dipped down to touch the surface of the sea.

EPILOGUE
"NOTHING SO WELL LOST"

Shortly after the fall of Rhodes, word was brought to the newly installed Holy Roman Emperor, Charles V. When he heard the news of the knights' defeat, with tears in his eyes he said, "Nothing in the world was ever so well lost as Rhodes."

On January 2nd, 1523, Suleiman led a Muslim service in his new mosque in the city of Rhodes. Under the knights, the building had been the Conventual Church of St. John. With the graven Christian images removed, the Faithful joined their Sultan in prayer. When he watched the departure of the knights, he is said to have told Ibrahim, "It breaks my heart to see this old man evicted from his home of so many years."

Suleiman commanded over one thousand Janissaries and troops to remain on the island and assure order. On January 6th, he began the return trip to Marmarice; then across Asia Minor to a triumphal reception in Istanbul.

Flushed with the exultation of finally driving the Knights of St. John from Rhodes after two hundred years of occupation, Suleiman settled down to the task of consolidating his Empire and extending its massive reach. But despite his costly victory, Suleiman and the Knights of St. John were destined to meet in battle again.

Philippe and his defeated knights sailed from Rhodes to the island of Crete. There, at the port of Khaniá, the remnants of the Knights Hospitaller of St. John waited out the terrible storms of winter. The knights resupplied their ships and tended to the recovery of the remaining wounded. When the weather improved, the knights set out for Messina, at the eastern edge of Sicily. Upon their arrival, plague erupted among the ships, and the Order was quarantined for several weeks. Finally, Philippe was invited by the Pope to sail with his small fleet to Civitavecchia, near Rome.

In November, 1523, Giulio de Medici was elected Pope Clement VII. The new Pope had himself been a Knight Hospitaller, and was sympathetic to the plight of the Order. While turbulence and war erupted all around him, Philippe made it his sole task to secure a new home for his knights. The German Lutherans of Charles V were pillaging Rome, and slaughtering the Pope's monks and nuns. For the next several years, Philippe visited the monarchs of Europe, enlisting supplies and arms. The knights wandered from city to city, still seeking a place of their own. Antonio Bosio even made secret return visits to Rhodes to assess the possibility of recapturing the island paradise for the knights. But, it was not to be.

Finally, in 1530, Charles V was crowned Emperor. Philippe and the Order petitioned Charles for possession of the island of Malta as a new home for the knights. While Malta was little more than a rocky desert, it did have two excellent natural harbors. Philippe immediately appreciated Malta's strategic position in the Mediterranean Sea. From there, the knights could once again harass shipping between Africa and Asia Minor or Europe. Charles granted Philippe's request, with the proviso that he also garrison Tripoli, on the African coast directly south of Malta. With these two posts, the knights could control all the regional shipping, while protecting Charles from attacks against his territories in Sicily and Italy.

In 1530, the Order of the Knight of St. John Hospitaller became known as the Knights of Malta. It would be decades before the knights would give up their hopes for a return to Rhodes. Unknown to the Order, they still had another rendezvous with their sworn enemy, Suleiman.

For his part, Suleiman wished never to see or hear of Rhodes again. Many of the Christians remained on their island home and took up life under the Muslim's generous terms. Though there was some inevitable violence and rancor, peace finally settled on the island. Eventually, some three thousand Latin Christians left Rhodes to follow the knights to Malta.

Though Philippe de L'Isle Adam would die on Malta in 1534, the knights would continue to make life miserable for the Ottoman fleet plying the Mediterranean. Eventually, regretting his merciful and generous behavior towards the knights at Rhodes, Suleiman would lead his armies against the knights once more, this time against Grand Master Jean Parisot de la Valette.

In 1565, on the island of Malta, two strong men from the ends of the Earth would once again stand face to face.

◄ STORY AND HISTORY ►

As an avid reader of historical fiction, I often find myself anxious to know exactly where the author has drawn the line between history and fiction.

This is a work of fiction. I have drawn extensively upon both current and historical documents collected over twenty years to try to paint the most accurate picture of both the times and the personalities of the characters.

One cannot know the thoughts of people who have been dead for nearly five hundred years, but contemporaneous letters and descriptions can give us a fairly accurate peek into their thoughts and their lives.

As for the characters, all were drawn from real people except the following:

Hélène did not exist outside the imagination of the author. There is no evidence that Philippe Villiers de l'Isle Adam had ever strayed from his vows of celibacy from the day he entered the Order of the Knights of St. John until the day he died.

Melina, Jean, and their twin girls are *legendary* characters. There is a substantial folklore about a woman who did see her knight slain on the battlements of Rhodes, and then killed her children before entering the battle herself and being killed by the Janissaries. It is said that the Turks retreated after they saw she was a woman in knight's armor.

The fisherman, Basilios, is an historical figure, while his three associates are not.

All the remaining characters existed in real life. If there is any discrepancy between the lives and actions of the real characters and this story, the errors are entirely mine.

⇥ GLOSSARY ⇤

Word origins: a = Arabic; t = Turkish; f = French; mf = Middle French; e = English; me = Middle English; g = Greek; i = Italian; s = Spanish.

Agha. (t) Military: a general officer. Any high-ranking officer. Similar to **Pasha**.

aigrette. (f) Decorative tuft of long, white herons' plumes, generally used in a headdress.

Allah. (a) God.

arquebus. (mf) Small-caliber long gun, operated by matchlock mechanism.

asper. (t) Silver coin of low value.

Ayyüb. (a) Ayyüb al Ansari (also Eyyüb al Enseri). Companion and standard bearer to the Prophet. Also a section of Istanbul where his small tomb was built.

Azab. (t) Military soldier, equivalent to current-day Marine.

bastinado. (s) Corporal punishment by striking the soles of the feet with a stiff stick.

Beylerbey. (t) Provincial Governor and/or general of a feudal cavalry.

Bunchuk. (t) Military standard made of varying number of horses' tails mounted on a wooden bar. The Sultan's *Bunchuk*—the highest—held seven black horses' tails.

caravanserai. (t) Rural wayside inn. A stopping place for caravans.

Chorbaji. (t) Soup Kitchen. Title of Janissary officer.

Collachio. (i) Convent of the knights.

corsair. (f) Pirate.

dervish. (t) Muslim monk who has taken vows of celibacy, austerity, and poverty.

Devshirmé. (t) The levy of young non-Muslim (generally Christian) boys for conscription into the service of the Sultan. Usually admitted to military or government posts depending upon the results of rigorous testing.

dhimmi. (t) Protected People. Designation given to Jews and Christians, as People of the Book (Bible). The *Qur'an* prescribed protection of these people within Muslim society.

Divan. (t) Ottoman council of state. Taken from the Turkish word for a low couch—the seats upon which members of the council would be seated.

Eis teen polin. (g) Literally, "into the city." Origin of the word "Istanbul," the major city of Turkey and the Ottomans.

enceinte. (f) An enclosure; a fence; a girdling. Refers to the encircling battlelines.

firman. (t) A legal decree issued by the Sultan. Also, "ferman."

ferenghi. (t) Europeans or foreigners in general. Pejorative.

fetvà. (a) A judicial ruling made by the Sheik-ul-Islam, the chief Islamic scholar of the community.

Grand Vizier. (t) Chief advisor to the Sultan in both military and civil affairs. Highest rank attainable in the Devshirmé system.

Gülbehar. (t) Literally, "Flower of Spring." Name of Suleiman's First Lady.

harem. (a) Area of palace or Muslim house where the women live. Set apart from the remainder of the palace. Literally, "inviolable area."

Ixarette. Sign language used by the Palace mutes and by Suleiman to converse with servants.

Inch' Allah. (a) "God be willing."

Janissary. (t) Elite military guard or force. Corruption of the Turkish, *"yeni cheri,"* or "young soldiers."

jihad. (a) Literally, "a struggle." Often used by Muslims to describe a holy war.

Kadin. (t) Literally "first girl," or the woman most special to the Sultan at the time. Sultans rarely married the mothers of their children.

Kapudan. (t) Fleet admiral.

Khürrem. (t) Literally, "Smiling or laughing one." The name of the second wife of Suleiman.

kilim. (t) Woven rug or tapestry, without a pile.

kohl. (t) Eye shadow.

Kubbealti. (t) Another term for the Imperial Council. *See* **Divan**.

Kuffar. (a) Infidels. Foreigners.

langue. (f) Literally, "tongue." Refers to the divisions by language and country among the Knights Hospitaller of St. John.

Loggia. (l) An architectural arcade open to the outside on at least one side.

Mameluke. (Egyptian) Military order that seized control over Egypt from 1254–1811.

Mufti. (t) The definitive authority on Muslim law and the Muslim Institution.

odalisque. (f) Female slave or resident in a Turkish harem.

Osmanli. (t) Refers to the House of Osman, founder of the Ottoman Empire. "Ottoman" in Italian.

Ottoman. (t) Dynasty founded in the fourteenth century by Osman, and reaching its pinnacle under Suleiman the Magnificent in the sixteenth century.

Pasha. (t) Any high-ranking Turkish official, either military or civil. Agha.

Pilier. (f) High-ranking officer of a langue.

rambade. (f) A wooden platform at the bow of galleys. Used to ram, grapple, and board the enemy galley.

Reis. (t) Naval Commander-in-Chief.

quarrel. (me) Square-headed bolt or arrow used with the crossbow.

Qur'an. (a) The Koran. Muslim Holy Book.

sappers. (e) Soldiers employed in building trenches and fortifications.

Selim. Father of Suleiman. Known as *"Yavuz,"* (the Grim), as well as "Protector of the Faithful."

Seneschal. (me) Officer in charge of domestic arrangements, justice, and ceremony.

serai. (t) House or dwelling place (tent, pavilion, etc).

Seraskier. (t) A Commander-in-Chief.

Sheik-ul-Islam. (a) "Ancient of Islam." The Mufti of Istanbul and the leader and authority of the Muslim community.

Sheitan. (a) From "Ash-Shaytan." Satan, the devil.

Shiite. (a) Member of the Shiite movement of Islam, which considers Mohammed's true successor to be Ali, the Fourth Caliph, and cousin of the Prophet.

Sipahi. (or spahi) (t) Calvary soldier. Can be either permanent professional cavalry or feudal cavalry.

Sultan Valideh. (t) The current Queen Mother.

tuğra. (t) Official seal of the Sultan, affixed to any official decree, and confirming its authenticity.

Turcopilier. (t) Commander-in-Chief of the light cavalry.

Vizier. (a) High official in a Muslim country; minister of state. *See* **Grand Vizier**.

yarak. (t) In fine condition. Physically fit.

yeni cheri. (t) Literally, "young soldier." Later Anglicized to "Janissary."

⊰BIBLIOGRAPHY⊱

Abdalati, H. *Islam in Focus.* Islamic Teaching Center, 1975.

Angel, M.D. *The Jews of Rhodes.* New York: Sepher-Hermon Press, 1978.

Atil E., ed. *Turkish Art.* Washington, D.C.: Smithsonian Press, 1980.

Atil, E. *The Age of Süleyman the Magnificent.* New York: Abrams, 1987.

Bradford, Ernle. *The Shield and the Sword.* New York: Dutton, 1973.

Foster, C.T. and Daniell, FHB. *Life and Letters of Ogier Ghiselin de Busbecq.* Vol I. London: C. Kegan Paul & Co., 1881.

Foster, E.S. *The Turkish Letters of Oghier Ghiselin de Busbecq, Imperial Ambassador at Constantinople 1554-1562.* Oxford, 1968.

Friedenwald, H. *The Jews and Medicine.* 2 Volumes. Baltimore: Johns Hopkins Press, 1994.

Gordon, B.L. *Medieval and Renaissance Medicine.* New York: Philosophical Library, 1959.

Guilmartin, Jr., J.F. *Gunpowder and Galleys.* Cambridge: Cambridge University Press, 1974.

Halman, T.S. *Süleyman the Magnificent Poet.* Istanbul: Dost Publications, 1987.

Heyd, Uriel. *Moses Hamon, Chief Jewish Physician to Sultan Süleyman the Magnificent.* Oriens. Vol. 16. pp. 152-170. Dec. 31, 1963.

Irving, T.B. (translator) *The Qur'an.* Brattleboro: Amana Books, 1985.

Kunt, M. & Woodhead, C. *Süleyman the Magnificent and His Age.* London: Longman, 1995.

Mansel, P. *Constantinople.* New York: St. Martin's Press, 1996.

McCarthy, J. *The Ottoman Turks.* London: Longman, 1997.

Meijer, F. *A History of Seafaring in the Classical World.* New York: St. Martin's Press, 1986.

Merriman, Roger Bigelow, *Suleiman the Magnificent.* Harvard: Cambridge, 1944.

Pallis, A. *In the Days of the Janissaries.* Hutchenson & Co, 1951.

Phipps, W.E. *Muhammad and Jesus.* Continuum, New York: Phipps, 1995.

Porter, R. *The Greatest Benefit to Mankind.* New York: WW Norton & Co, 1997.

Riley-Smith, Jonathan, Ed. *Oxford Illustrated History of the Crusades.* Oxford: Oxford Press, 1995.

Shaw, Stanford J. *History of the Ottoman Empire and Modern Turkey.* Volume I. York: Cambridge University Press, 1976.

Shaw, Stanford J. *The Jews of the Ottoman Empire and the Turkish Republic.* New York: New York University Press, 1991.

Sherif, F. *A Guide to the Contents of the Qur'an.* London: Ithaca Press, 1985.

Sire, H.J.A. *The Knights of Malta.* New Haven: Yale University Press, 1994.

Wheatcroft, Andrew. *The Ottomans.* New York: Viking, 1993.

⊰ MAPS ⊱

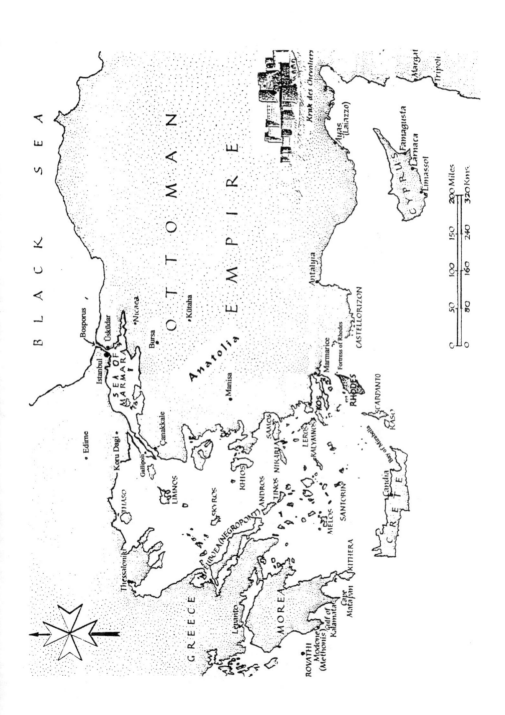

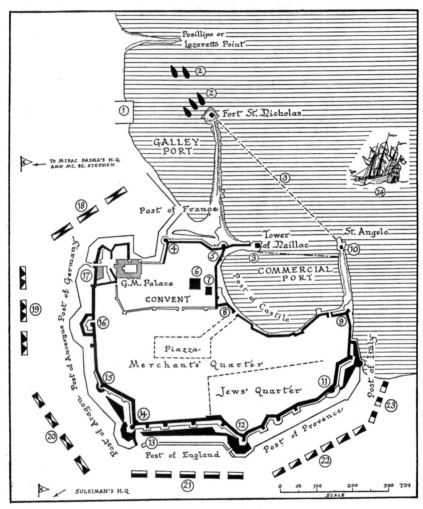

RHODES — 1480/1522

KEY
1. Turkish Batteries – 1480
2. Blockships – 1522
3. Boom Defence – 1522
4. St. Paul's Gate
5. St. Peter's Gate
6. Arsenal
7. 'Inn' of England
8. Sea Gate
9. St. Catherine's Gate
10. Tower of the Windmills
   (or St. Angelo)
11. Tower of Italy
12. St. John's
   (or Koskino) Gate

13. St. Anthony's Gate
14. St. Mary's Tower
15. Tower of Aragon (Spain)
16. Tower of St. George
17. D'Amboise Gate
18. Bali Agha and Janissaries – 1522
19. Ayas Pasha – 1522
20. Ahmed Pasha – 1522
21. Qasim Pasha – 1522
22. Mustafa Pasha – 1522
23. Pir Pasha – 1522
24. Cortoglu – 1522

(Defences relate to 1522)

✥ACKNOWLEDGMENTS✥

The idea for this book was conceived in August of 1982 as I stood on the battlements of Rhodes and watched the sound and light show with my daughter, Katie. My special thanks to her and my family for listening to me ramble through the ideas for a story as the next two decades slipped by, buried in research and musings.

I want to thank Jerry Gross, the Editor's Editor, for his invaluable help in shaping and refining my writing, as well as playing the roles of father and advisor.

And thank you to Hillel Black, Executive Editor at Sourcebooks, who also stood on the battlements of Rhodes with *his* son eighteen years later, and listened to the same story of Suleiman and the Knights of St. John; who read the original manuscript and was able to see a book in there somewhere. I am grateful for his editing and his private tutorial on writing.

To Peter Lynch at Sourcebooks for his editing skills and patience; and to Taylor Poole for allowing me to participate in the overall artistic design. Finally, to Judith Kelly, Maggy Tinucci, Sean Murray, Jeff Tegge, Todd Stocke, Jon Malysiak, and Jennifer Fusco.

⤛ABOUT THE AUTHOR⤜

Anthony A. Goodman is an adjunct Professor of Medicine at Montana State University. *The Shadow of God*, his first novel, was inspired by a visit to Rhodes, where he became fascinated by the conflict that engulfed the three great monotheisms five hundred years ago. He lives in Bozeman, Montana.